The Chicken Thief Soldier

A Death at Valley Forge

Michael Fields

To order additional copies of this book, contact:
Xlibris Corporation
1-888-795-4274
www.Xlibris.com
Orders@Xlibris.com
40388

Dedication

To Mon and Dad; To my favorite sisters, Jeannie, Bobbie, and Kathy.

To Don Sjustrom who was killed in 1967 working with Lao refugees in Laos; To Sergeant William Port, MIA-POW, 1970 Congressional Medal of Honor recipient.

To all the players, coaches, parents, school administrators, and fans of the 1996 Juniata Valley PIAA State Championship Team; To Doug Fouse who was undoubtedly "The Best of the Best".

Special thanks to the National Steinbeck Center (*info@steinbeck.org*) for their assistance.

Special acknowledgements to Tony Payne who supplied one hundred percent of the technical expertise for this book.

Final proofreading by Shelly Carolus.

"What is Serving God? 'Tis doing Good for Man."

Poor Richard's Almanac, 1747

PROLOGUE

VALLEY FORGE   1778

The sky was dark gray, and the temperature was in the low twenties. Throughout the morning, the wind had steadily gained intensity and made a shrill roaring sound as it pelted the deserted road with a mixture of snow and icy crystals of sleet. The snow stung the boy's unprotected face, and he held his hand over his eyes. Standing on the hill overlooking the army encampment at Valley Forge, Bruce Jenkins was freezing. He wore old shoes, no socks, ragged brown pants, and three layers of ripped shirts, the outer one white, then blue, and the inner one a dark red. He had pulled a tight-fitting spring jacket over the shirts. He tried to see the camp and the army of soldiers below, but the snow squall formed a white barrier that limited his vision to a few feet of the road.

Bruce was fifteen years old. He had a smooth angular face, a delicate nose, and big blue eyes. Thick black curls of hair fell from under the old farm hat he wore. Thin and tall at six feet one inch, he had developed a strong, muscular frame working on the small family farm bordering French Creek. Bruce lowered his hands and rubbed them together against the cold. His hands were large, calloused, and weather-beaten. Shoving them deep into his jacket, Bruce hesitated a moment. The icy snow and sleet burned deeper into his exposed face, and Bruce began to have second thoughts about joining the army. Turning sideways to get out of the direct blast of the wind, Bruce remembered the warmth of his last trip to Valley Forge.

That summer, Bruce and his uncle traveled by buckboard to buy some grain from a farmer at Valley Forge. They crossed French Creek into Phoenixville and drove the buckboard down Main Street, which consisted of a planked two-story hotel, a small Mennonite church with windows bordered shut, an inn with the front porch steps crowded with customers, a few shops, and an iron smith. At the inn, his uncle gave the reins to Bruce and stepped down from the buckboard and went inside. He drank a mug of ale and talked to a group of farmers.

After an hour, his uncle returned to the wagon, and he and Bruce continued down the dirt road that led to Valley Forge. At the edge of town, they approached a three-story brick house separated from the road by an ornate iron fence. The barn, half hidden in a cluster of pine trees, was twice the size of the house. Barking loudly and charging from the porch, two black dogs raced to the barrier of the fence.

"They make a good drink," his uncle said, holding the reins tightly and ignoring the dogs. "Good German whiskey, and cheap, too. We'll stop here on the way back."

As they went by the house, Bruce saw a group of men at the open door of the barn. There was a line of four wagons on the narrow road that circled around the house. Beyond the road was a wide pasture, and the horses grazing there were big and strong. Bruce looked at the brown horse pulling his uncle's buckboard. A swirling mix of black flies and smaller gnats circled its head, landing and feasting on the wetness and open sores.

The road led past log houses and farmlands. The fences on the side of the road were broken, and the pastures were covered with high weeds and brush. The level land gave way to a series of hills, and soon the buckboard entered dense forest. On one sharp incline, the horse shook his head, scattering the flies, and stopped. Bruce and his uncle stepped down from the buckboard. A hot wind blew swirls of dust in the air. Pulling on the reins, his uncle walked the horse to the crest of the hill. Bruce wiped the perspiration from his forehead and climbed back on the buckboard. At the bottom of the hill, the meandering waters of Valley Creek were silver in the afternoon light.

Bruce sat up on the plank board and shielded his eyes from the sun. Pointing to the stone structure and barn on the other side of the creek, his uncle said it was the Potts house. As they descended the hill, his uncle also told him that thirty years ago there used to be an iron forge on the creek.

"That's how Valley Forge got its name," he said. "The forge is gone now. A German man from Phoenixville built a saw mill on the same land, but the redcoats went through and burned it months ago."

His uncle turned the buckboard onto a narrow road that led into a thick forest of pine trees. After a short distance, the road ended in a clearing enclosed by a wooded fence. A house and a large barn were at the far edge of the clearing. Some geese and a flock of chickens scattered out of their way, and Bruce watched a man and a woman step onto the porch when his uncle stopped the buckboard. Much shorter than the man, the woman wore a pale blue dress. The man wore brown trousers and a brown sleeveless shirt, and he had a scarlet wool cap pulled down over his ears. His body was thin and sinewy, and Bruce noticed how the shirt hung loosely over his shoulders. His uncle shook hands with the man, and then he introduced Beatrice and Jacob Wood to Bruce.

His uncle and Jacob Wood talked for a while and then headed for the barn. Looking at the grime on Bruce's face, Beatrice said that Bruce had time to refresh himself at the creek. She pointed to a path beyond the fence. Bruce thanked her and went through the fence and onto the path. It led up a hill, and when Bruce reached the top, he could hear the rippling sound of the water below. He thought there was another sound, and as he descended the hill, he heard someone humming a tune. It was cool in the shade of the trees, and looking ahead, Bruce could see the glistening stream of water through the dark shadows.

Reaching the edge of the trees, Bruce stopped suddenly and quietly. He saw a girl at the edge of the creek. Her hair reached to her shoulders and was golden yellow in the light. She was on her knees and swinging a brown shirt into the moving current. The shirt splashed water high in the air, and the girl began humming again when she lifted the shirt. She twisted her hands and squeezed a stream of the water out of the wrinkles of the shirt. Some of the water splashed onto her white blouse.

Bruce noticed that the top buttons of the blouse were open, and he couldn't stop from looking. It was unbelievable to him. He could clearly see the exposed white skin and even the curved lines of her breasts. Her blouse was wet, and through the wetness, as she twisted the last drops of water from the brown shirt, Bruce saw the pointed outline of her nipples take shape.

It was too much. Bruce felt his face redden, and there was a warming sensation deep in his groin. He lowered his hands over his trousers and felt the growing stiffness there. The girl finished with the brown shirt and dropped it on the top of a pile of wet clothes. Then still humming in a clear voice, she stood up; and in one simple, magical moment, she unbuttoned her blouse and dropped it and her skirt to the ground.

Bruce had never seen total nakedness like this. Guilty and alarmed, aroused and excited, he tripped forward. She turned at the noise, and the clear sound of her humming stopped. At first she looked surprised, but when she saw he was a boy, she smiled. She walked into the creek, the rounded curves of her buttocks gleaming in the sunshine. Reaching the middle of the pool, standing glistening white and waist deep in the water, she turned and looked at Bruce. Then lifting her hand forward, she motioned to him to come into the water.

Bruce started to move immediately, but his feet were heavy and clumsy. Staring at the girl, the bright smile on her face, the smooth milky whiteness of her breasts, he found himself stumbling forward. It was awkward untying his shoes, but he flipped them to the ground. He pulled his shirt over his head and tossed it to the side. The trousers presented the biggest obstacle. He still felt the heat pulsating through his whole body. The hardness in his groin became heavier, and Bruce saw a smear of wetness on his trousers.

Bruce hesitated. He didn't know how he would be able to remove his trousers without falling down. But he resolutely pulled them off and found himself walking naked in the creek. The cool water had no effect on his body. As he waded deeper, the heat of the arousal only intensified. The movement of his body generated a series of waves that spread out across the pool and lapped gently against the girl's waist. She stood there in the shimmering water with her hand stretched forward and waited for him.

"What's your name?" she asked.

"Bruce," he said quietly.

"My name's Olivia," she said with a smile. He was closer now, within reaching distance. "You're only a boy. But you have those big blue eyes."

"You're beautiful," Bruce managed to say.

"And you're handsome."

Olivia reached out her hand and touched his shoulder. Then she slid her hand lower, and Bruce felt his face redden when she began to gently rub his chest, gently pinch the skin there. Her hand slid down to the ribbed muscles of his abdomen, and her fingers were soft and warm against his wet skin.

"And I can see you're a very strong boy."

Bruce wanted to say thank you, but he kept his lips squeezed together tightly, and he only managed to smile. His body was burning now, a great pressure building, quaking inside. His mind was racing out of control, and pleasurable sensations he had never experienced before rippled through his body. The softness of her touch became unbearable. He reached out for her breast, but she stopped him. Olivia took his hand and led him to the bank of Valley Creek.

Hours later, when he and his uncle left the Wood's farm, Bruce sat quietly on the buckboard, completely overwhelmed by his experience at the creek. All he knew was that the girl's name was Olivia, and he knew he must see her again. His uncle said something about how washed clean Bruce was and how he and Mr. Wood had to lift the heavy sacks of grain without any help, but Bruce didn't respond. Approaching the intersection, Bruce looked down at Valley Creek and the surrounding wilderness.

The one dirt road across the creek led through an area of rolling hills covered with heavy forests. The pine trees were dark green, and spaced between them, the dogwood trees blossomed thick umbrellas of white and pink flowers. Bright yellow butterflies fluttered across the road, and the bird sounds were everywhere.

It was quiet and peaceful, and Bruce didn't want to leave. As his uncle turned the buckboard north, Bruce looked back at the towering pine forest on the hills of Valley Forge, the sparkling waters of the creek, and the dirt road that led to the Wood's farm.

An icy wind blew across the hills, and Bruce was shocked back to the present. The heavy snow squall had passed, and staring at the military encampment in front of him, Bruce was startled to see the broken rows of stumps that covered the fields and hills. In the center of the ruined landscape, hundreds of log cabins had been squared into sections by gutted roads.

Rising from the cabins, spirals of black smoke lifted a dark cloud over Valley Forge. Under the cloud, the rows of cabins formed a large, desolate, snow-covered village that stretched as far as he could see. Shaking his head, Bruce looked at the one thing in Valley Forge that he recognized. Across Valley Creek, the three-story Potts house, now with a solitary flagpole in the front lawn, was intact. The house was the largest structure in the encampment.

There were loud shouts from the hill on his left, and then Bruce heard a musket shot. He saw two men running down the hill toward Valley Creek. One of the men was swinging a large feathered creature, and as the man got closer, Bruce saw the chicken in his hand. It made loud, squawking sounds, and the man stopped and slammed the body into the ground. Feathers flew in the air, and the chicken became suddenly quiet.

There was another musket shot, and the two men started running again. They splashed across Valley Creek, and the man holding the chicken slipped and fell clumsily in the snow. The other man helped him to his feet, and they both disappeared into the maze of log cabins and smoke on the other side. A farmer appeared on the top of the hill and pointed his musket toward the camp. Bruce recognized the brown shirt, scarlet cap, and thin figure of the farmer. Raising a fist in the air, Mr. Wood lowered his musket and stomped away.

After Mr. Wood was out of sight, Bruce walked down the road, and stepping carefully on stone piles and planks of wood, he crossed Valley Creek. As he approached the Potts house, he saw that it was separated from the soldiers' village by an empty field and a wooden fence. On the other side of the fence, there was a dirt road gutted by wagon tracks and holes filled with glistening pockets of ice.

Blowing fiercely across the barren landscape, the wind caught the Colonial flag in front of the Potts house. Thirteen alternating red-and-white bars of color unfurled into motion. Bruce looked closer and saw the circle of white stars in the blue square in the upper corner. As he walked under the flag, Bruce noticed a sentry step out from the corner of the building. Eyes peering out from under a heavy blanket, the sentry advised Bruce that he was standing in front of Washington's Headquarters and should be moving on before he got into trouble. Bruce looked at the Potts house again and saw the large number of officers congregated at the front entrance. Behind the house was a stable and beyond the stable, Bruce could see the waters of the Schuylkill River.

Bruce hesitated, and shielding his face from the wind, he asked the sentry where he should go to enlist. Lowering his blanket, the sentry had a surprised, almost amused look on his face. He studied the young face and worn clothing and muttered "farm boy" under his breath.

Bruce waited patiently, and finally the sentry pointed to the building next to the Potts house and gave him directions to the side door. Bruce walked down the path to the house, past some handsomely-tailored officers who spoke in a language he didn't understand, and knocked on the door.

Someone inside shouted orders to enter, and Bruce walked into a small room where an officer sat behind the only desk. Shocked by the burst of cold air, the officer looked up quickly and yelled at Bruce to shut the door. The officer was middle-aged, unshaven, and the heavy bulk of his body filled the chair. Still staring at Bruce, the chair creaking under his weight, he demanded to know why Bruce was standing in front of his desk.

Without hesitating, Bruce explained his intentions to join the fight against the redcoats. The officer shook his head and took the official contract from the desk drawer. With the officer prompting him in every word and action, Bruce pledged allegiance to the new government and signed the paper that enlisted him in the Continental Army for one year.

When Bruce asked about pay and the talk he heard about free land, the officer told him he would receive fifteen pounds at the end of the enlistment. He also said that after three years of service in the Continental Army, he could apply for one hundred acres. Bruce said that's what he planned to do. He wanted to farm his own land.

The officer slid the enlistment papers inside the side drawer. Without looking up from the desk, he explained to Bruce that the members of Congress were displaced from their fine residences in Philadelphia and were now hiding in York. Congress was not yet organized to fight a war, and consequently, the Continental Army was having trouble getting supplies. There were no uniforms, no weapons, and only sparse provisions available. But he did assign Bruce to a cabin and directed him to General Conway's Pennsylvania brigade. It was somewhere on the outer defense embankments. The officer told Bruce there were actually two empty bed spaces in the cabin due to the desertions the day before.

For no apparent reason, the officer's mood suddenly changed, and he became angry and began shouting at Bruce about the heavy desertions in the Pennsylvania companies. What made it worse was that the two deserters yesterday had taken their muskets with them, so Bruce would have to wait until the next supply wagons arrived before he would get a weapon. The junior officer wasn't sure when that would be.

Bruce thought the officer was finished, but he only became louder. He berated all Pennsylvanians as traitors, stating that the deputy mayor of Philadelphia and a host of prominent businessmen had welcomed General Howe and the British into the city. When Bruce didn't respond to the insult, the officer shook his head. Reaching to the floor, he picked up a small knapsack and canteen and threw them to Bruce. Bruce looked inside the knapsack and saw a tin cup, a fork, and a hard bar of soap.

It was early evening and just turning dark when Bruce left the headquarters. With the knapsack slung over his shoulder, he walked past a row of well-constructed log cabins and noticed the soldiers on duty were warmly dressed and armed with shiny new muskets. Later, he learned they were soldiers from Virginia, the elite guard unit for General George Washington.

Bruce walked by them slowly with his head bowed. The winter wind made a low roar as it sliced through the narrow passageways between the rows of cabins. The smoke billowing from the chimneys threw out hot embers that mixed with the snow. It was a fierce black wind that hit Bruce in the face, leaving dark red welts. His teeth began to chatter, and he wrapped his arms inside his coat. Bruce wandered around the camp for twenty minutes before he found the Pennsylvania block of cabins at the outer line of the Valley Forge military encampment.

Bruce went inside the first cabin and closed the door behind him. He immediately welcomed the heat but was sickened by the stale, smoky air. His eyes reddened and began to water, and the sitting forms in the cabin grew hazy and indistinct in the glow of the burning fire. Rubbing his eyes with his hand only made the condition worse. Through his blurry vision, he saw two rows of soldiers, ten men altogether, crouched in front of the fireplace at the end of the cabin. On some silent signal, they turned from the burning fire, and dark eyes studied him momentarily before looking back to the heat.

The squad leader, Hank Greene, a big bearded man in a heavy jacket, stood up, asked Bruce what he wanted, and listened to the boy's story. He gazed at the figure in the flimsy jacket and asked Bruce about his blanket. Bruce shrugged his shoulders and said he didn't have one. Telling Bruce it wasn't quite a real blanket but it might keep him from freezing to death the first night, Hank threw Bruce a light blue, woolen bathrobe left by one of the deserters. He told him he could also have the deserter's bunk and pointed to the top one by the door.

Bruce looked up and saw an uneven row of wooden planks covered with a thin layer of straw. Hank Greene mumbled something about kids should be at home and not fighting in a war, and then he sat down with the group of men around the fire. There was some noise and loud grumbling when one of them opened his hand and rolled dice on the smooth ground.

Bruce hesitated and then climbed up to the bunk. Attempting to sit down, he bumped his head on the slanted log of the ceiling. The wind howled across the roof, and icy drafts of air blew in from the cracks in the door. Bruce curled on his side away from the cold wind and covered his nose against the smoke and the strong smell of urine from the straw bedding. As he pulled the blue robe over his head, his whole body began to ache from the cold.

Minutes later, Bruce began to think about the warmth of the farm. His body shaking so hard, the planks rattling beneath him, he began to question his judgment about running away to join the Continental Army of General Washington. Sure, he and his neighbor and best friend had talked about it. Henry Wells was the same age, and he told Bruce he was leaving to fight the British, but Bruce didn't believe him.

Then standing there fixing a fence post the next day, Bruce watched a group of soldiers walk by; and at the end of the line, there was Henry, wearing a black military cap with a white feather sticking out the side. When he saw Bruce, he waved the cap, feather swinging wildly in the air, and then he disappeared down the road.

Two weeks later, without saying a word to his aunt or uncle, Bruce walked out the back door early in the morning. Climbing over the fence, he began his journey down the same road. Now, alone, his body shaking in the straw, his stomach cramped in pain, Bruce remembered the eggs and slab of bacon they usually had for breakfast, and he wished he had eaten something before he left the farm. He was helpless against the all-consuming hunger. There was some shouting and loud laughter from the men around the fire, and Bruce was distracted. Listening to the noise and half choking from the cloud of smoke, he realized that tomorrow would begin his first day as a soldier.

Bruce coughed loudly, and his body ached with the convulsions that followed. Thinking that he couldn't be a real soldier until he had a weapon, he hoped the army would find him a musket soon so he could be shooting at and killing the redcoats. He liked the idea because he remembered how much his dad hated the redcoats.

And just as he thought about his dad, his eyes opened wide. The curling smoke became darker and began to blur his vision. Rubbing the wetness out of his eyes, Bruce felt the old fears return. He tried hard to be brave and shake the fear, but the anguish of that night took hold of him again.

Five years ago, Bruce and his parents lived on a small plot of land on the outskirts of Morgantown. That day, his uncle and aunt had come over early in the morning, and both families began building a small addition to the cabin. It was a bedroom for Bruce, and Bruce worked harder than everyone in the expectation of having his own room.

Behind the cabin in the shade of a giant oak tree, its thick branches casting black shadows over the cabin's roof, was a small chicken coop. Throughout the morning, the flock of Dominique chickens foraged around the grove of apple trees and sometimes wandered to the underbrush at the edge of the forest. They were short, fat chickens that produced large brown eggs for the family. The rooster had a big, drooping red comb, and the black-and-white plumed hens clucked and followed obediently.

By late afternoon the chickens were digging close to the house and darting in and out of the new room. They became so annoying that Bruce had to waste time rounding them up and shutting them in the coop. As he latched the door to the coop with a section of rope, a sudden gust of wind rustled through the trees, and a line of dark clouds moved across the sky, blotting out the sun.

After the room was finished and his uncle and aunt had left, Bruce was exhausted and went to bed early. The room smelled of fresh pine, and breathing deeply, Bruce closed his eyes and soon had dreams that he was hidden somewhere deep in the middle of the forest. It was warm and quiet and comfortable. From behind the house there was noise in the chicken coop, and the rooster began to crow. Then there was the loudest crack of thunder he had ever heard, and Bruce jumped up in bed. The thunder seemed to shake the cabin, and heavy rain spattered against the roof.

Except for the sound of the rain, it became very still, and Bruce looked up at the ceiling. He thought he heard water splashing somewhere in the room, and straining to see, he was blinded by a tremendous flash of light. There was the instant roar of thunder, and as Bruce covered his ears, he heard the cracking and splintering of wood. Looking through the window, he saw a large dark shadow hover momentarily in the sky, quiver menacingly to the side, and then the great white oak came crashing downward.

Bruce felt a strange dryness envelop his face and body. As he cowered on the edge of the bed, he heard a terrifying explosion of noise and watched the roof of the main cabin collapse under the weight of the tree. The black sky opened up in front of him, and a cool, wet breeze blew across his face. In this mixture of rain and wind, he could smell the acrid aroma of burnt tar and wood. Bruce was too scared to move.

When lightning flashed across the sky again, Bruce saw the massive trunk of the oak tree slanting upward through the deluge into the night sky. The rain spattered off the trunk and the tumble of logs and jagged branches around it. There was some movement deep in the shadows of the debris, and Bruce saw the rooster, wet and shaking, clinging to a branch. After another sharp flash of lightning and crack of thunder, the rooster disappeared. Between the flashes of lightning and dark rolling thunder, Bruce could see his newly constructed bedroom was intact, untouched by the falling tree.

A gust of wind blew rain into his room, and wiping the water from his face, Bruce stared into the darkness of the log cabin. He called his parents' names and then began shouting into the wreckage of logs and branches. There was no answer.

Bruce stood up and made a wild charge into the room, but in the darkness, the branches cut into his body and threw him back. He swung at them with his fists, breaking branches and advancing a short distance into the room. Then he made a wild charge, ran into the side of the trunk, and fell exhausted to the ground. The heavy rain slanted down from the night sky. It soaked through his body and turned the earth to mud.

There was a light drizzle the next morning. Moisture mixed with the blood in the deep cuts across his face and arms. Bruce sat up slowly. He leaned back against the trunk and rubbed his eyes. Looking into the maze of logs and twisted branches, Bruce saw the outline of a hand. It was resting smooth and delicate on a large section of white bark, and rain water was dripping off the silver ring on the finger. Bruce fought to reach it but was knocked back by the tangle of wood. Becoming tired and confused, Bruce broke free of the suffocating, watery debris of the wrecked cabin, and in a daze, he began running down the path to the main road.

A dim glow of lightning and a resounding crack of thunder ripped through the dreary, morning stillness. Bruce ran wildly when he heard the noise. Twice, he lost his balance and fell hard in the mud. He got up quickly each time, and gasping for air and fighting the pain in his body, Bruce ran the four miles to his uncle's house.

When he reached the house, Bruce was too distraught to speak clearly. His uncle sat him down and gave him black coffee to drink. After a few minutes, the coffee burning his lips, Bruce steadied himself and explained about the storm and the large tree crushing the cabin. He explained how there was no movement inside the cabin, no sounds from his mom and dad. His uncle quickly got the buckboard ready. He threw two shovels in the buckboard, and he and Bruce started back to the cabin.

The rain had stopped, but drops of water fell from the trees onto the buckboard. They splashed off the black hide of the horse, and some hit Bruce in the face and chest. As the morning mist began to evaporate, a high, arching rainbow formed in the sky. The bottom blue, the yellow gold center, and red crest of the rainbow grew bright and distinct and filled the horizon. Bouncing with the slow movement of the wagon, Bruce pointed out the rainbow to his uncle. His finger followed the arched blue, yellow, and red lines as they dropped down to earth and disappeared into the dark hill of trees where the cabin was.

When his uncle turned the buckboard off the road, the rainbow was gone, and the sun was shining brightly. Approaching the cleared field in front of the cabin, Bruce sat dead still on the buckboard. Looking at the scene and seeing it clearly for the first time, he was shaken by how small his bedroom looked next to the gigantic tree. The white oak protruded at a sharp angle from the crushed foundation. Pointing to the heavens, the top end of the oak was caught firmly in the branches of a towering pine tree, and balanced there, it formed the shape of a large cross.

Bruce followed his uncle under the tree and into the cabin. Breaking away a wall of branches, some making loud cracking noises, his uncle cleared a narrow path. Rays of sunlight filtered through the web of drooping leaves and broken branches. Looking through the light and shadow, Bruce watched his uncle lean his body against a large branch and snap it in half. Then for a moment he stared into the dark fissure left by the branch. Motioning for Bruce to stay back, his uncle bent low to the ground and crawled into the darkness. He returned a few moments later, and talking softly to Bruce, he told him to go to the wagon and bring back the shovels.

Walking slowly, dragging his feet, and then dropping to his knees and crawling through the debris of logs and tree, Bruce carried the two shovels to the only open area in the middle of the wrecked cabin. He hacked off some overhead branches and cleared enough space so that he could stand. Directly under the dark shadow of the gigantic oak that angled upward and pierced the morning sky, Bruce began digging the first grave. His head hurt, and his shirt was soaked with perspiration. His mouth was dry, and after a few minutes, Bruce found he had difficulty swallowing.

There was a large mound of dirt next to the grave when his uncle returned. Nodding to Bruce, his uncle picked up the other shovel and went back into the collapsed end of the cabin. Soon, Bruce heard the cracking noise of the shovel against the larger branches. The noise sent vibrations the length of the tree and rustled some leaves that fell into the grave.

Bruce kept digging mechanically and was waist deep in the hole when his uncle returned. Looking over the top of the mound of dirt, he saw his uncle pull his dad's body out of the shadows and place it next to the open grave. Then his uncle went back inside.

Bruce finished the first grave and was about to drag himself out of the hole. Then he thought his mom and dad should be together, and he continued to widen the grave. The pain had long ago left his shoulders and back. Bruce didn't feel anything. He continued digging into the hard clay and only stopped when he saw lines of blood dripping down the handle of the shovel. He tried to free his grip from the wood, but his hand didn't move.

Bruce wiped the perspiration from his forehead and eyes and looked closely at his hand. Incredulous, he saw that the dried blood and intense pressure had glued his palm to the wooden surface of the shovel. Using his free hand to hold the shovel steady, Bruce pulled fiercely and ripped his hand free.

A sharp pain knifed up his arm to his shoulder and neck. Screaming out, Bruce looked at the thin layer of skin and bloody tissue left on the wooden handle. He lifted his hand to the light and saw the raw tissue and the streams of blood flowing down to his wrist. There was a fierce burning sensation the length of his arm, and Bruce collapsed against the side of the grave.

Bruce was motionless with the pain for what seemed a long time. When he heard the sound of his uncle returning, he grabbed onto the shovel with his bloodied hand and began digging again. Through the blinding red explosion of pain, he saw his uncle rest his mom's body next to his dad's. Then his uncle slid into the hole next to Bruce.

When they finished digging the grave, Bruce helped his uncle place the bodies next to each other. Bruce and his uncle stood silently for a moment, and then they began shoveling the dirt into the grave. Perspiration and salt washed into his eyes and blinded him, and although he looked, Bruce couldn't see how the dirt hit the bodies and rolled off to the side.

When they had filled the grave and flattened the loose dirt with the shovels, his uncle opened his clenched fist and gave Bruce a small silver ring. Then he took both shovels and returned to the buckboard. In the shadow of the oak tree, Bruce knelt down on the fresh dirt. He took a broken branch and slid the silver ring down until it was tight against the wood. Bruce stuck the branch deep into the loose earth, and bowing his head toward the grave, he said a silent prayer.

As Bruce tried to stand up, he felt the weakness in his legs and fell down on his face. Damp pieces of dirt stuck to his mouth and cheek. Everything was quiet. He noticed a cloud of movement against the side of the white oak. Bruce looked up and saw the yellow and black wings of monarch butterflies fluttering around the fresh sap of the tree. Then some doves alighted on the edge of the broken roof and made soft cooing sounds. On the road in front of the cabin, the horse trotted nervously and rattled the buckboard.

Watching the butterflies and doves, Bruce swayed back from the grave. Suddenly, he felt a heavy strain on his eyes, and there under the shadow of the oak, Bruce was blinded by the fiery burst of lightning again, and with the thunder exploding in his mind, he saw the bright glow of light flood over his mother's hand. He was frightened then and screamed her name into the wreckage of oak and cabin. The noise sent the doves flapping frantically into the blue sky. Clucking weakly, the rooster appeared from under a branch and strutted cautiously to the freshly-dug grave.

Bruce heard his name and looked up when his uncle burst hurriedly into the enclosure. He helped Bruce to his feet, and holding him around the shoulders, he walked him to the buckboard. His uncle turned and went back into the cabin. It was momentarily quiet, and then there was a loud commotion of crashing branches and thumping wings. It took a few frantic minutes for his uncle to catch the rooster. He tied its legs together with a piece of vine and tossed it in the back of the buckboard.

Picking up the reins, he looked at his nephew sitting there quietly and how the boy held his bloodied hand away from any contact with his body. His uncle shook the reins, and the buckboard jerked forward, rattling the shovels in the back. At the sudden motion, the rooster scratched wildly against the wood, and making deep clucking noises, it slid to the corner of the buckboard and was quiet.

Bruce turned at the noise from the fireplace. The soldiers were arguing loudly again. The wind grew fiercer and emitted a low roaring sound as it buffeted the cabin walls. A strong blast of wind swirled deep into the chimney and exploded a cloud of black smoke into the cabin. His eyes tearing up, Bruce turned his head away from the smoke. An icy spray of snow burst through the crack in the roof, cutting into his face. Bruce wiped at the tears and closed his eyes tightly. He hated crying and being weak like a boy. Bruce silently willed himself to become strong like a real soldier, a soldier that would make his dad proud.

In the morning, Bruce was too cold to go outside and look for the latrine. Sitting cross-legged in front of the blackened ashes of the night's fire, Bruce felt the frigid air sliding down the chimney. Smothered by a heavy wool blanket, an older man next to him coughed and spat on the ground. Before the man covered up, Bruce looked at his face and saw that oblong drops of yellow liquid had frozen on his beard.

Hank Greene pulled open the cabin door and closed it quickly behind him. He rousted the rest of the soldiers from their bunks and handed out salted meat and a loaf of bread. There was a rough bout of pushing and shoving, and Bruce managed to grab a small piece of crust. He ate the bread quickly and picked up a dry piece of meat from the ground. Shouting to get their attention, Hank Greene walked in front of the fireplace.

The squad leader told them that General Washington had ordered a morning assembly. They would meet in front of the cabins in thirty minutes and march to the parade ground at Mount Joy with the rest of the Pennsylvania troops. The bearded man argued that it was too cold to be standing at attention. Greene ignored him and left the cabin.

Listening to the men complain about the cold, the food, and the boredom, Bruce quickly learned that many of them were sick of Valley Forge. They seemed angry and determined to desert the army. Some talked openly about their plans to sneak out in the night and go home to their families.

Bruce went outside to a dark morning sky. Snow was falling, but there was only a light wind. He looked around for the latrine and saw a man walk around to the back of the cabin, pull down his trousers, and squat over what looked like a hole in the ground. When the man finished and walked back, he saw Bruce standing there. He told Bruce he could use the latrine, even though it was frozen full of shit and piss, or if that wasn't good enough for him, he could walk down to the river.

Not accustomed to the rough language, Bruce hesitated. Then feeling bloated and uncomfortable, he walked around the corner of the cabin. The sight of the latrine stopped him in his tracks. Now rising a foot out of the ground, the hole was a rounded pile of frozen brown and black globs of excrement. Bright yellow and red icicles streaked down the sides of the mound. Some of the icicles had broken off and lay in pieces on the ground.

Bruce was repulsed. He turned away quickly and began a fast walk to the river. On the bank behind some bushes, he relieved himself. Then going to the river's edge, he knelt down and washed his hands and rinsed icy water over his face. The stinging cold water cleared the smoke from his eyes.

Bruce heard a sharp snap from across the river, and shaking water from his hands, he stood up quickly. There, under the branches of a large tree, two soldiers in bright red uniforms were mounted on brown horses. They stared at Bruce, who began to back away from the river. One soldier lifted his musket slowly and pointed it straight at Bruce. When Bruce tripped and fell backward into the snow, both redcoats burst into laughter. Bruce got up quickly and ran through the tree stumps toward the encampment. When he returned, out of breath and dry mouthed, he saw the men were assembling in front of the cabin. Greene told him to stand at the end of the line.

It was a short walk to the parade ground. As the soldiers in the surrounding cabins joined the march, Bruce could see the ragtag condition of the men. Some of the men had neat, dark blue military uniforms, but many had old coats and worn trousers. A few soldiers were coatless and wore only shirts to protect themselves against the cold. Bruce noticed the coughing and sickly soldiers were helped along by their friends. It was a dismal scene, and Bruce felt lucky under the warmth of his own blue bathrobe.

During the walk, Bruce searched the faces for any sign of Henry, but he couldn't find him. When they reached the open space of the parade ground, the men stopped and formed ranks with the other soldiers from their state. Eleven states were represented, with the largest contingent of soldiers being from Pennsylvania. The men stood there with their officers at the base of Mount Joy. The smartly dressed officers sat stiffly on horses that snorted bursts of steam in the cold air.

Bruce noticed that there was a huge, solitary oak tree on the top of Mount Joy. The oak was actually the size of two trees since the trunk broke into a large V-shape. Both sides of the V shot high in the sky, but on the right side a long branch extended straight and parallel to the ground. Bruce saw there was something hanging from the branch.

Crammed in the middle of the line of soldiers, Bruce strained to see around the big body in front of him. Then he saw clearly what it was. There was a noose hanging from the branch. When the wind whistled through the dark branches of the tree, the noose moved back and forth in a slow, circular motion.

Holding their sticks in the air, a row of six drummers marched up the hill and stood at attention. Behind them a group of about thirty officers on horses strutted briskly up the hill and stopped. In front of them was General George Washington. The officer next to him got off his horse, gave the reins to an attendant, and walked to the base of the tree. The man was red-faced as he unfurled a white parchment and began shouting a lengthy proclamation to the soldiers and officers of the Continental Army.

Through the sudden gusts of wind that blew down from Mount Joy and the sullen comments of the soldier next to him, Bruce heard most of the proclamation. The officer stated that the Continental Army fought well and had stopped General Howe and the British at Brandywine Creek.

"Then why did the British march safely into Philadelphia, and we do nothing but retreat?" the soldier next to Bruce muttered.

The officer commented on the courage of the Continental soldiers and how the army endured the march to Valley Forge. The army had twelve thousand men that December, and in a few weeks, they turned the wilderness of Valley Forge into a village of two thousand cabins. But now, three months later, because of lack of discipline and desertions, the army has less than seven thousand men.

"And what about the ones that's frozen or starved to death or died from the disease?" the soldier mumbled to himself. "Did they desert, too?"

The officer paused and looked over the top of the parchment at the sparse units of men on the parade ground. The array of tattered clothing and different colors was bewildering. He began again and shouted more loudly into the wind.

"We must keep the army together and stay strong to fight the British in the spring. We must stand ready to die for our country. We must stand ready to die for our freedom."

As the officer finished speaking, the wind slackened, and everything became quiet on the parade ground. Even the old soldier next to Bruce stood head bowed and quiet. In the sky above the V-shaped oak tree, the dark clouds opened momentarily to show patches of sunlight.

The officer began again slowly, but his voice grew furious when he brought up the subject of King George and the British. He ranted about how the British used their power to steal everything from the colonies.

"The British take our food, our money, our land, and our women. We came to America to be rid of the British, and yet they still try to own us. We cannot be slaves to the British. We must remember we are fighting for our country's freedom. We must be strong together." The officer paused, breathed deeply, and collecting himself, he shouted at the ranks of soldiers.

"We must keep the spirit of liberty alive this winter!"

Then the officer turned his head and looked over at the commander in chief. Mounted regally on the majestic white horse, blue winter cape folded over his shoulder and stretching down to the stirrups, General Washington was motionless in front of his retinue of officers. On the horse next to him was an equally impressive officer, resplendent in a blue-and-gold military uniform. The light reflected brilliant colors off the array of medals on his uniform. A large gray dog sat erect and motionless at the side of his horse.

Behind the group of officers on Mount Joy, half hidden by the train of horses, Bruce saw the blurred outline of a ghostly figure. The hapless soldier, his hands tied by a heavy rope, was scantly clothed in a dirty white shirt and brown breeches.

Bruce shielded his eyes from the sunlight and studied the features of the soldier. Seeing the black hat and the white feather high in the air, seeing Henry's ashen face, Bruce felt a fear and anger worse than the freezing cold, and his body began to shake.

The officer looked back to the squads of soldiers in the Continental Army and shouted more loudly than before at the lines of men. "We must not lose this war. The British are waiting across the river for the cowards and deserters to join them. Sometimes hundreds of men cross the river every week. This must stop. From today, the punishment for desertion is death by hanging."

The six drummers picked up their sticks and began a steady drum roll. Bruce watched as an officer grabbed the rope and pulled the bound figure toward the tree. Henry stumbled and fell and was pulled to his feet. The officer led Henry to the tree, and grabbing him by the shoulders, he straightened him under the branch. With the absence of wind, the noose was now motionless over his head. The officer signaled to his attendant, and holding the reins, the man led the horse to the tree.

The officer ripped the hat from Henry's head and threw it on the ground. As he pulled down the rope and placed the noose over Henry's neck, the boy began to sway, and the officer had to hold Henry's arm firmly to keep him from falling. With his other arm, he signaled to the group of soldiers, and a buckboard moved from behind the line. The driver led the horse to the tree and stopped. Getting out and walking around the side, the driver pulled a wooden casket from the back and dropped it to the ground. Then he climbed back on the buckboard and circled it behind the oak tree.

Bruce was shaking violently now. Tears filled his eyes. He felt a surge of hatred for the officer, and knocking down the soldier next to him, he broke rank. With a wild yell, he began running down the lane separating the squads of soldiers. Bruce was almost at the bottom of the hill when he heard the sound of hoofs striking the frozen ground behind him. Then he felt the presence of the horse at his side, and strong hands lifted him off the ground. The horse slid to a stop, kicking up sparks of ice and stone, and the officer dismounted. He held Bruce by the arm, and when Bruce continued to struggle, another soldier appeared and held Bruce in a headlock.

Bruce was twisted forward in such a way that he could clearly see what was happening under the oak tree. With Henry now being supported by two other soldiers, the officer walked his horse under the tree branch, picked up the loose end of the swinging rope, and wrapped it around the saddle horn.

Staring at the struggling boy, the officer led the horse slowly away from Henry, taking the slack out of the rope, bending the branch slightly downward. The rope was pulled tighter, and Henry's body straightened rigidly from the pressure on his neck. There was a sudden bulge in Henry's face, and he gagged loudly and coughed a thick volume of liquid over his chin and shirt.

The drummer in the middle of the line, a thin boy in a ragged blue coat, his fingers frozen by the cold, lost his concentration and dropped one stick. The steady cadence was broken for a few seconds while he bent to retrieve it from the snow. Then the boy was straight in the line again, and the drum roll began louder than it was before.

Casually, the officer tightened his grip on the rope wrapped around the saddle horn. He kneed the horse forward, and the rope slid further over the branch. Lifted slowly off the ground, Henry struggled and tried to balance himself on his toes. His face reddened and then lost all color. The horse continued to prance forward slowly, and Henry was lifted completely off the ground. The two soldiers still held onto him, balanced him between them, and waited for the officer's orders.

Bruce kicked hard at the man holding his head and found the grip on his neck loosen. He managed to pull his arm free, and with a violent motion, he swung his fist into the soldier's stomach. The soldier released his headlock, and Bruce was free, scrambling on hands and knees up the hill toward Henry.

Halfway up the hill, Bruce saw the officer's horse step forward again. And then, inexplicably, the officer raised his hands in the air, turned the horse around, and staring into the faces of the soldiers, he loosened the rope from the saddle horn and threw it in the air. With the pressure around his neck gone, Henry fell forward, and with the rope trailing behind him, he hit the frozen ground. His body wobbled momentarily, but as both feet slid out from under him, he began to roll awkwardly down the hill. Gaining momentum, Henry crashed into Bruce, and together they bounced in a tangle of arms and feet and blue bathrobe to the bottom of Mount Joy.

Watching the two bodies tumble down the hill, the drummers stopped all motion and stood quietly at attention. The shock of the eminent execution, and then the unexpected release of the victim left the soldiers of the Continental Army in a confused silence. Bruce struggled to his feet, and removing the noose from Henry's neck and untying his hands, he lifted Henry by the shoulder. At the top of the hill, the officer straightened on his horse and looked down at the army.

"This demonstration is for your benefit," he shouted as loudly as he could. "Your commander in chief, General Washington, ordered that you have one warning. But after today, any soldier caught trying to desert will be hanged here." The officer looked at the lines of soldiers at attention. Except for some low grumbling, the men were quiet.

"And the local farmers are complaining that soldiers are stealing their chickens and pigs. From this day, all thieves will be treated as deserters. The farmers have permission to shoot anyone on their land. If a thief is captured, he will be hanged here. And you all will watch."

The officer pulled the reins and left in a trot to join the others. As he moved his horse into the line, the drummers became active again and began beating a slow marching cadence. With General Washington in front, the mounted officers began to leave the parade ground. One of the soldiers from the top of the hill slid down and took the rope from Bruce. He coiled it in his hand and scrambled back to the departing soldiers.

Still holding Henry by the arm, Bruce watched the mounted officers disappear over the side of Mount Joy. The soldiers on the parade ground broke ranks and began walking back to the cabins. Some of them stopped and looked closely at Henry, studying the dark bruise on his neck. A few came up to him and shook his hand.

"I'm all right," Henry said.

Bruce released his grip on Henry's arm and stepped back. His leg buckled slightly. He was exhausted. Bruce began to feel the cold again, and his stomach hurt. The soldiers still filed past the two boys. Many of them nodded their heads in a gesture of approval.

"My cap!" Henry shouted. He grabbed Bruce by the arm, and they raced to the top of the hill. Panting and trying to catch his breath, Henry picked up the cap. The feather was broken and bent forward at an angle. Straightening the feather, he pulled the hat over his head.

"I saw you charging up the hill," Henry said. "That was crazy, what you did. Thanks."

"I didn't believe it was you. Did you really try to desert?"

"No," Henry said. He laughed and shrugged his shoulders. "I was on my way to the river. I had to crap. Then my stomach really hurt bad, and right there on the hill, it exploded. The smell was terrible, and my pants were soiled. I went to the river and took off my pants and began washing the stains when these soldiers came at me. They said I was trying to cross the river and desert to the British. They grabbed me. They said they would hang me."

"And you told them what happened?"

"I tried to. I asked them how could I desert with my pants off. But they said I was a traitor. They took me to the Virginia cabins. The officer there said I would be an example for the whole army. But he gave me dry clothes. And later when he saw how terrified I was, he said not to worry about the hanging. He said I would only be an example."

"Then you knew it was a trick?"

"I was never sure of anything," Henry said. "They kept me in the officer's cabin and fed me real food. In the morning, they took me to Mount Joy for the assembly. And you saw what happened."

"I was scared," Bruce said.

"Not scared enough to stop you from charging the whole army."

"You're my best friend," Bruce said. "I couldn't watch you be hanged like that."

"I was scared, too," Henry said. "I threw up all that good food, and then I saw this blue form running up the hill. I had tears in my eyes, but I could still see it was you. What were you going to do?"

"I was going to kill them," Bruce said. "With my bare hands, I was going to kill them."

Henry laughed at this. Then he saw the wooden casket. He pushed Bruce to it and kicked the cover to the ground.

"Get in," he said.

"What?"

"Get in," he said again.

"It's for dead people!" Bruce shouted.

Henry laughed and half knocked Bruce over the side into the casket. Then he got behind it and began pushing the casket forward. It slid easily in the crushed snow. Reaching the top of the hill, Henry jumped inside, and the casket was propelled down the steep slope.

Bruce held onto the sides of the casket with both hands, but Henry was shouting and waving his hands in the air. His blue robe flying in the air, Bruce began shouting also. Through the sting of the cold air in his face, he looked ahead and saw the lines of soldiers moving quickly out of the way.

When the casket hit the bottom, it turned sideways and rolled over. Planks shattered and slid across the frozen parade ground. Bruce and Henry were tossed in the snow, and the rows of soldiers cheered. Some came over and picked up the planks of wood. With a large smile on his whiskered face, Hank Greene walked over and picked up the last plank.

Bruce was still dizzy from the ride when he heard barking. He looked up and saw a large gray dog racing down the hill. The uniformed officer who was next to General Washington and another rider were chasing it.

The dog was barking loudly, and as it raced closer, Bruce wasn't sure what was happening. Standing next to him, Henry wiped the snow from his face. Lifting the plank of wood in the air, Hank Greene stepped next to Bruce and looked at the charging animal.

"What's going on now?" he asked.

"Azor!" the officer shouted. "Azor!" he shouted again.

The dog was only yards from Bruce when it tried to stop, slid on the snow, and rolled on its back, before straightening itself. It crouched there in front of Bruce. Short-haired, elongated head, the dog barked once and was quiet. Bruce reached out his hand and petted the dog on the neck.

"Azor," Baron von Steuben, said, reining his horse to a stop next to the dog. The officer with him got off his horse and walked over to Mr. Greene.

"The baron can't speak much English," the officer said. He and Mr. Green talked quietly, and after a few minutes, he saluted and returned to his horse.

Bruce looked at the hard, stern face of the baron. A wide gold ribbon was around his neck, and hanging from it was a gold medal that glistened in the light. It was in the form of a cross or a star. Bruce wasn't sure. The baron studied Bruce carefully and then began conversing with the officer in a foreign language. When he was done, the officer saluted and walked stiffly over to Bruce.

"I am the translator for General von Steuben," he said. "The general is forming a select group of soldiers for special training. He wants you to join his group. I have explained everything about the program to Mr. Greene. He agrees that you are very brave and would be a good soldier, although maybe a little young. You will learn everything a soldier must know: how to march, how to position yourself, and how to quick fire a musket. You will learn discipline and how to obey orders. When the schedule is approved by General Washington, I will come for you."

The translator finished, and not waiting for any comments from Bruce, he returned to his horse. General von Steuben, his face dark and fierce, looked at Bruce for a moment. Then he called for Azor and turned his horse up the slope of Mount Joy. The dog was in full sprint and was barking loudly as they disappeared over the top of Mount Joy.

"I'll talk to you later about this," Hank Greene said. "The baron is from Germany. They say he's a volunteer to the army and working for nothing. This is unusual for these officers from Europe. Many of them are greedy and want paid for their service. But the baron is different. He is a good man to know. What do you think about working with him?"

"I don't know," Bruce said. He felt the convulsions of pain that shot through his stomach. "But I would like to eat the dog."

"Me too," Hank Greene laughed. He turned and walked toward the cabins.

"Let's see what's for lunch," Henry said.

Bruce and Henry walked to the half-finished mess hall and joined a line of soldiers by the door. Bruce felt the painful emptiness in his stomach and moved his feet impatiently. After ten minutes of sliding forward ever so slowly, they reached the front counter, a long plank of wood that held a row of empty tin cups.

A server behind the counter dropped a ladle into an enormous black pot of steaming liquid and filled two of the cups. Bruce and Henry each took a cup, and seeing the benches were filled, they walked to an empty space along the back wall. His fingers burning from the handle, Bruce lifted the cup carefully to his mouth and took a sip of the liquid.

"What the . . . ," he began but choked on the rest of his words. The thin, soupy liquid was hot, and a burning sensation filled the inside of his mouth. The liquid that reached his throat left a bitter taste of dirt. Standing next to him, Henry was blowing over the top of his cup. When the steam subsided, he took a drink. Closing his eyes, he gasped at the taste of the soup.

"It's terrible," he said, squinting at Bruce.

"What is it?"

"Burned leaves and bark," Henry said. "We haven't had real food for days. The officers keep saying the supply wagons will get here soon, but they never do. I was lucky to get soup with big chunks of chicken from the Virginia officers."

"You call being hanged lucky?" Bruce asked. He took another sip of the soup. Leaning back against the log wall, he tried to keep it in his throat and gagged, some liquid squeezing out between his lips. He wiped his chin with his hand.

"I have to get some real food, or I'll die."

"Maybe the wagons will come tomorrow," Henry said. They returned the cups to the table and left the mess hall. Outside, the soldiers were huddled together in small groups.

"Hey!" One of the soldiers, a thin older man in a ragged black coat, called out as Bruce and Henry walked past. He was the only man smoking tobacco, and ashes dropped from the short stub in the corner of his mouth. The man removed the brown-wrapped paper from his lips and pointed it at Bruce.

"That was a good thing you done today. You're a real Patriot."

"We need men like you," another soldier said.

"It was nothing," Bruce said.

"You keep doing nothing like that, and we'll whip the redcoats," the older man said. "You'll make Pennsylvania proud."

Bruce nodded at the compliment, and he followed Henry back across Mount Joy. As they passed under the large oak, Henry stopped and looked up at the branch. A large black crow was perched there. It cawed and flapped wings at them.

"I wish I had my gun," Bruce said. He looked over at Henry who wasn't paying any attention to him. Breathing softly, he seemed to be in some kind of trance.

"It would of pecked out my eyes," Henry whispered.

"What?"

"Nothing," Henry said. "I'm getting my stuff and moving to your cabin."

"Great," Bruce said. They walked across the deserted parade ground and in a few minutes approached the log cabins of the Pennsylvania brigades. Henry said something to the man at the door and went inside. When he returned, he was carrying his musket and knapsack.

That evening Bruce climbed up to his bunk, and Henry took the lower one. The other soldiers sat next to the fire. Five of them were in a circle and gambling with the dice. Bruce could barely see them through the thick smoke of the fire. Outside, the howling of the wind was incessant, and when it was the loudest, the fire flickered brightly and dark smoke drifted back into the cabin.

Bruce pulled his blue bathrobe over his head and tried to protect himself from the cold and the smoke. His stomach burned, and then his hands began to shake violently. Placing his arms across his chest, he buried his hands under his armpits and crouched his body into the fetal position.

Later that night, a hand jabbed into his shoulder, and Bruce was startled awake. Pulling the blue robe from his head, he turned to see Hank Greene next to the bunk. Bruce sat up and saw the men walking through the open door into the darkness. He jumped down from the bunk and joined Henry who was waiting for him at the door. Snow swirled around him, and the icy wind took his breath away. Fast moving clouds filled the dark sky and threw eerie shadows over the encampment.

Clearing his eyes, Bruce saw groups of Pennsylvania soldiers emerging from the line of cabins. The dark forms trudged silently against the force of the wind. Bruce and Henry joined them on the road, and they began walking toward Mount Joy. The soldiers in front of Bruce had something slung over their shoulders, and in the moonlight Bruce saw the sharp silver glint of axe metal.

The soldiers reached the parade ground and began climbing the steep grade of the hill. It was slippery, and at times Bruce felt himself falling backward. Hands grabbed him and steadied him. Soon he and Henry were at the top of Mount Joy.

The wind on the hill was strong and rattled through the branches of the V-shaped oak tree. The thick trunk was still and solid against the force of the wind, but some of the outer branches broke off and fell to the ground. Through the crowd of men, Bruce could see the circle of soldiers around the tree. He pulled Henry forward to the front of the line.

Hank Greene stood next to the tree with two other men. One of the men was a tall Negro. He had a long saw, at least five feet in length with deep, jagged teeth, bent over his shoulder. The men grabbed the round wooden handle at each end and lowered the saw across the trunk of the oak. In the darkness, Bruce could barely make out the outline of Greene's face, but he heard the words clearly.

"The damn officers can proclaim all they want, but no soldier from Pennsylvania will ever hang from this tree," Hank said.

The wind roared through the branches overhead as the two men positioned the saw against the trunk. They began a slow, steady motion, and the teeth sank a deep groove into the tree. Every ten minutes, other soldiers walked up to take their places. Bruce watched the old soldier, a thin piece of tobacco hanging from his lips, take his turn. Then he walked over to Bruce and offered him the remainder.

Bruce saw the eyes of the other men on him and took the piece of tobacco. The wind blew red ashes in the air as he lifted it to his face. Closing his lips around the stub of tobacco and taking a deep breath, Bruce felt an acrid taste and a thick, suffocating blockage in his throat. He spit out the tobacco and began to cough loudly. The old man laughed and began slapping Bruce on the back.

It took over an hour to cut the tree down. The soldiers on the steep side of Mount Joy moved out of the way, and with six men pushing on the trunk, the oak wavered back and forth, branches swaying in the wind. The men gave one concerted effort, and the tree came crashing to the ground. The spring in the branches made the tree bounce up in the air before it settled onto the frozen ground.

There was a hushed silence, and suddenly, a large black squirrel, and then two smaller ones, scampered from the wreckage of branches. The two smaller squirrels were stomped on immediately, but the larger one raced into the tight circle of soldiers. Bodies were jumping everywhere until one soldier threw himself onto the squirrel. When he got back on his feet, he had the squirrel by the tail and was cheering loudly.

The men with the squirrels ran back to the cabins, and the excitement of the unexpected hunt gradually died down. Groups of soldiers carrying axes and all sizes of saws descended on the fallen tree and began hacking away in a flurry of activity. The wind slackened, and heavy snowflakes fell from the night sky.

Bruce watched as the huge dark outline of the fallen tree began to diminish in size. The smaller branches were cut into kindling wood, the branches into logs, and the trunk itself was cut into sections. It took two, sometimes three, men to roll the larger sections away. Carrying armfuls of branches and logs, the soldiers moved in lines that led down Mount Joy and back to the cabins. There they stacked the wood inside where it would be safe from thieves.

Bruce and Henry picked up the last huge section of trunk. They rolled it down the hill and half carried and half slid it to the cabin. It could barely fit through the door. Inside the cabin, the fire was burning and hot from the fresh wood. Hank Greene bent down and helped the two boys roll the log to the corner of the fireplace. There, they slammed it flat on the dirt floor, and Bruce and Henry sat down, their legs swinging over the side, their faces flushed red and bright in the light of the fire.

His body suddenly became alert, and Bruce sensed a fine aroma of something in the cabin. It created an ache in his stomach, and he looked around. The wood was piled high in the corner, and the soldiers were beginning to settle around the fire. The aroma became stronger.

Bruce looked at Henry who was holding his hands out to the fire. The red glow of light reflected off his face. Bruce could think of nothing but the aroma. Feeling a strange dizziness, he closed his eyes and steadied himself.

"This is yours," the voice said. It seemed to come from a great distance. Bruce opened his eyes.

Hank Greene stood next to him and held out two legs of blackened squirrel. Bruce took his leg gratefully and began chewing the meat off the bone. His mouth filled with saliva, and a wonderful sweet taste began to send shock waves into his stomach. He tried to chew slowly, but the meat disappeared in seconds. Then Bruce put the bone in his mouth and ground it into small pieces. Next to him, Henry was still chewing on his piece of squirrel. Bruce envied him.

On the top of Mount Joy, the massive, circular stump of the oak protruded black and solitary from the frozen ground. A six-inch blanket of snow covered the mountain and the flat field of the parade ground below it. The piles of sawdust left by the cutters were buried deep under the snow. Smooth and glistening in the light, they formed rounded mounds that stretched out from the base of the tree. A large black bird swooped down from the sky and began to caw loudly. Eyes wide and searching, it circled the empty space and then disappeared in the night.

The next morning the snowstorm had passed, but dark clouds moved across the sky. It was bitter cold, and there was no movement or activity in the encampment of soldiers. The only traffic was back and forth from the Potts house. Lieutenant Jones, aide-de-camp to General Washington, threw the leather knapsack over his shoulder and left headquarters.

Lieutenant Jones was from Williamsburg, Virginia, and had been with General Washington since the beginning of the war. He was twenty-five years old, a good horseman and rifleman, and he looked very aristocratic in the blue-and-white military uniform. His father was a rich merchant and had expressed alarm when his son left to join the new army. His father thought General Howe would put down the revolt in a few months, and it would be back to business with the British as usual.

At the stables Lieutenant Jones met Lieutenant Stevens and Sergeant Wilson, and they got on their horses and left the encampment. Forty soldiers from the elite Virginia Brigade followed them down the road to the supply depot. The fifteen wagons and drivers were lined up, and with half the brigade in front and the other half in the back, the wagon train forded Valley Creek.

There were a dozen soldiers constructing a small guard station on the other side of the creek. Some of them were positioning a long pole across the road that could be raised and lowered by a rope connected in the wooden station. The lone officer saluted the lieutenants when they passed, but the rest of the men kept working.

"What are they building?" Lieutenant Stevens asked. "That won't stop the British."

"It's not for the British," Lieutenant Jones said. "General Washington ordered the guard stations built to keep all visitors out of the camp."

"Why?"

"He's embarrassed by the way the army looks," Lieutenant Jones said. "He doesn't want anyone seeing them so ragged and poorly dressed. If reports got out, it would hurt recruitment. It would hurt the morale of the people."

Sergeant Wilson joined the lieutenants in the front of the column of wagons and marching soldiers. He wore a nonmilitary buckskin hat and a heavy brown coat. A beard and bushy eyebrows covered most of his face. Born and raised in Phoenixville, he knew the area well.

"We're going into town?" he asked.

"The local brewery," Lieutenant Jones said.

"Then the rumor's true," Sergeant Wilson said. "The army will have whiskey."

"The general didn't want to give the order, but we officers argued we needed something to help the soldier's spirit. There are too many desertions. We thought good German whiskey would keep the soldiers in camp."

"It will do that," Sergeant Wilson said. "It's just what the army needs, or this winter will be the death of us. The work is boring. And there's no food. It gets worse every day. Those words that the captain proclaimed on Mount Joy yesterday were true."

"What words?"

"He said we needed the spirit of liberty to beat the redcoats," Sergeant Wilson quoted the captain. "The brewery in Phoenixville will give us all the spirit we need."

The sergeant laughed loudly at his joke and joined the column of soldiers. Looking at the intersection ahead, Lieutenant Jones saw a farmer and a boy. The boy was pulling a rope tied to a cow's neck. Two other cows were strung behind the lead one. The cows were thin and haggard, the skin hanging on their bones. Lieutenant Jones stopped the column in front of the farmer.

"You planning to sell those cows?" he asked.

The farmer looked around. He walked over to the boy and took the rope from his hand. The boy stepped back. Pulling the rope tighter, the farmer shook his head.

"You going to Philadelphia?" Lieutenant Jones asked.

The farmer looked up. His face was dark, and deep grooves crossed his forehead. The snow began to settle white crystals on his hat. The soldiers in the frontline stepped forward, some motioning to the cows and the farmer.

The boy had a frightened look on his face and moved closer to the lead cow. He tried to push it across the road. Looking at the line of soldiers, his eyes barely visible under the brow of the hat, the farmer was silent.

"You going to sell them to the British?" Lieutenant Jones asked loudly.

His question was met with silence. The farmer pulled on the rope, and the boy was able to push the lead cow forward a few steps. Frozen dribble stuck to the cow's nose and mouth.

"Our soldiers are starving," Lieutenant Jones said. "And you take food to the British?"

The boy stopped pushing on the cow. His hand resting on the skin of flab on the cow's belly, he looked at his dad. The farmer hesitated a moment and then pulled on the rope. Without lifting his head, he muttered at the lieutenant.

"You give us worthless paper receipts," he said. "The British pay gold." He pulled harder on the rope, and the lead cow was jerked into motion. The boy followed his father. Soon the last cow was across the road. The soldiers were cold and angry and shouted profanities. Lieutenant Jones looked at the farmer with disgust. Reaching into his saddlebag, he pulled out some paper receipts and gave them to Lieutenant Stevens.

"Take two men and go after the farmer. Give him these receipts for the cows and then take the cows back to Valley Forge."

"What if he complains?"

"Tell him the Continental Army has new orders," Lieutenant Jones said. "Any one caught selling provisions to the British is to be arrested and tried for treason." Lieutenant Stevens saluted and galloped off quickly after the farmer.

It took another hour for Lieutenant Jones and the column of wagons to reach Phoenixville. Sergeant Wilson immediately got into a heated conversation with the owner of the brewery, and when he returned to the lieutenant, he had a smile on his face. Lieutenant Jones paid the German distiller in real gold coins, and after the crates of whiskey were loaded on the wagons, Lieutenant Jones opened up some bottles and began passing them around. He laughed at the mounting excitement and shouts of anticipation from the soldiers. When they all had whiskey in their cups, he watched Sergeant Wilson raise a half-empty bottle high in the air.

"To the spirit of liberty!" Sergeant Wilson shouted. Even though tired and cold and with no food to eat on the march, the men cheered and roared their approval. They gulped the whiskey down and cheered even louder. The two dogs from the house ran to the gate and began howling at the noise.

Lieutenant Jones finished the rest of his bottle, and with the waves of heat soothing his body, he slowly mounted his horse. It took some time for the wagons to be turned around. Then the column was straightened, and they began the trip back to Valley Forge.

The column was a few kilometers from the encampment when Lieutenant Jones saw two riders on the road. As they got closer, he recognized the French officers. They both wore elegant uniforms, cocked hats, and heavy blue capes. Their horses were strong and healthy. Major Beaumont pulled his black horse next to Lieutenant Jones and saluted. His companion, Major Legard, fell in behind them.

"You are bringing supplies?" Major Beaumont asked.

"German whiskey," Lieutenant Jones said.

"That's good news," Beaumont said. "Since the British have commandeered the ships from the East Indies, we have had no rum to drink. Maybe you could spare a few bottles for the officers?"

"Of course," Lieutenant Jones said.

"The last good rum I had was in Philadelphia," Beaumont said. "The British are living very well there."

"You saw the army there?"

"My ship disembarked in Philadelphia, and I stayed there for a week," Beaumont said. "I met some officers. As a French gentleman of considerable rank, I was treated as an equal. The British are living a life of luxury compared to us. But some of the officers seemed bitter."

"Why?"

"They want to return home to England. They want to attack Valley Forge and end the war quickly," Beaumont said. "They have their informants. They know about the desertions and how few men we have left."

"They're right," Lieutenant Jones said. "We couldn't resist very long. Why don't they attack?"

"General Howe and his staff are very comfortable in Philadelphia. They have all the provisions and housing they need, and they delight in the social gatherings. And that's not all. The general is distracted in another way. He has taken a mistress."

"How do you know?"

"She was pointed out to me," Beaumont said. "She is healthy and very plump. They go everywhere together."

"Then that's good for us," Lieutenant Jones said. "Let them have their parties and stuff themselves with food. We will stay lean and hungry and angry. Then we will defeat them in the spring."

"If we have an army left," Beaumont said. "Valley Forge is nothing but a death camp."

"What do you mean?"

"The men have no proper uniforms, no boots, no food. The camp is filthy and disgusting. The men purge themselves at the nearest tree. The camp is nothing but a big American latrine. A shithouse, if you ask me." Major Beaumont was speaking quickly, and his face reddened with the effort.

"The soldiers are pitiful, you know, the worst I've seen. And there's no discipline. The men wander about anywhere. And because they complain about being hungry, they shoot their guns at any animal they see. Tell them about yesterday, Legard." Beaumont turned and pointed his finger at Legard. "Tell them what you saw."

"I was with Major Beaumont when we stopped to check the outer defenses near Lafayette's quarters. We walked to the first sunken entrenchment. It was deserted. Then I turned, and there were two men. They came out of nowhere. While one was looking around, the other approached the horses. I alerted the major, and he quickly took his pistol and shot at them. They disappeared. But I know they planned to take our horses and eat them."

"No civilized people eat horse meat," Major Beaumont said. "Now, I have to worry more about my horse than I do about killing the British. These Valley Forge men are not soldiers. They lie and steal anything. That deserter yesterday, he should have been hung. It's the only thing the rabble understands. Stay and obey orders or be executed for treason."

"The men here are mostly farmers and not experienced in warfare like you Europeans," Lieutenant Jones said. "General Washington believes they should have ample warning before there is any punishment."

"We had farmers in France, too," Major Beaumont said. He was emphatic and confident and spoke with authority. "Of course, we also conscripted thieves and prisoners if we needed them. We taught this rabble how to fight. We taught them discipline. Obey orders or be punished, even executed. It's what we do in France. As anyone in Europe will tell you, the French way is best."

Lieutenant Jones sat straight in the saddle. He face hardened as he listened to his superior officer. His horse lifted its head and snorted steam in the cold air, and Jones held the reins tightly. Major Beaumont was silent for a moment. His hand rested on the hilt of his sword. It was gold, and a gold border went the length of the silver scabbard. There was an intricate emblem in the middle of the scabbard, and it too was engrained in gold. As his hands moved lightly over the hilt, the sword rattled slightly, and the scabbard swayed back and forth, glistening in the light.

"Yes, I would have hung that deserter," Major Beaumont said. "When the captain released the noose, it was a bad sign of weakness. But there are other ways than hanging to make examples of deserters and thieves." He turned and looked at the major. "Legard, show them."

Legard reached into his saddlebag and took out a steel spike. It was about two feet long, and when Legard lifted it in the air, the sharpened end reflected silver in the sunlight.

"I don't understand," Lieutenant Jones said as Legard slid the spike inside his saddlebag.

"It's something I used in Prussia," Major Beaumont said. "It works well." Relaxed now, he began speaking in a quieter tone of voice. "Can you explain something to me? Why did your General Washington ever pick Valley Forge to winter in? There are cities he could have taken his army, and we wouldn't have to suffer like this."

"It was not his choice," Lieutenant Jones said. "The Congress wanted the Continental Army between them and the British."

"So they could be safe!" Beaumont said in disgust. "The politicians always think about themselves first. They don't consider how the soldiers suffer."

"And the officers," Lieutenant Jones said.

"Yes, of course," Beaumont said. "The officers suffer, too." He looked at Lieutenant Jones and then turned his attention to the road. The snow had stopped, and the sky was clearing. In the distance, the myriad of burning fires lifted hazy lines of smoke that formed a heavy black mushroom cloud over the Valley Forge encampment.

Lieutenant Jones turned to Sergeant Wilson and told him to get some bottles from the wagon. Wilson went back to the first wagon and returned with two bottles of whiskey. He gave them to Lieutenant Jones who then gave them to Major Beaumont. The major thanked him profusely, slid the bottles inside his cape, and saluted. He and Major Legard turned their horses out of the column. When they were down the road, Sergeant Wilson brought his horse next to Lieutenant Jones.

"He stayed in Philadelphia?" Sergeant Wilson asked. "Why would he be friendly with the British?"

"French officers," Lieutenant Jones said. "They have no wars now. They're out of work. They need money to pay their expenses like the Germans and the Prussians."

"He would fight for the British?"

"Of course," Lieutenant Jones said. "When they didn't offer him enough, he came to us. Who knows what we pay him?"

"Did you see that sword? The gold and silver on it? That must have cost some money."

"All for show," Lieutenant Jones said. "The metal scabbard is useless. It rattles around and dulls the edge of the sword." He pointed to his scabbard. "That's why I use good American leather. It's quiet and doesn't alert anyone. Sure, it's not fancy like Mr. Beaumont's, but the blade stays sharp as a razor."

"The foreign officers are all show and talk." Sergeant Wilson had an angry look on his face. "Those things he said about us. The French are real bastards."

"Aristocratic bastards," Lieutenant Jones said. "But some of them are sincere. Some of them hate the British as much as we do and want to help."

"Maybe," Sergeant Wilson said. "But they think they know everything."

"They are born that way."

"Born stupid if you ask me," Sergeant Wilson said. "Do you remember that lieutenant general, the one who drowned at the river crossing?"

"Lieutenant General LeBlanc," Lieutenant Jones said. "He was on his way to headquarters. I never knew what happened."

"He was too stupid or too proud to get off his horse at the ferry," Sergeant Wilson said. "The Schuylkill River was flooded and a wild torrent. He jumped his horse onto the ferry, and the horse slid and kept going and broke through the railing at the other end. The current swamped the horse, and they both disappeared downriver."

"LeBlanc was commissioned to help with training," Lieutenant Jones said. "He was highly recommended by the French counsel."

"Horsemanship," Sergeant Wilson laughed. "He was probably commissioned to teach us horsemanship."

"Probably," Lieutenant Jones said. They laughed together and laughed even louder when Sergeant Wilson took a bottle from under his coat. They passed the bottle between them until it was empty.

"LeBlanc's replacement is already here," Lieutenant Jones said. "It's General Steuben, who comes highly recommended by our own Ben Franklin. He seems to be superior to the foreign officers we've been getting. He's serving in the army without pay, so we know he's not here for personal profit. But he can't speak any English. He only knows some profanities. Goddamn this. And goddamn that."

"The men will understand him then," Sergeant Wilson said. He laughed again. "I don't know, Lieutenant. Maybe it's the spirit of liberty talking, but this has been a most enjoyable ride."

When the column approached Valley Creek, the lieutenant saw that the sentry post was completed, and a heavy log was blocking the road. He shouted to the soldier inside the wooden shack, and immediately, the window opened. A hand began pulling at the rope connected to the system of pulleys. The log was lifted high in the air, and the column of men and wagons passed under it.

That evening officers from the Virginia Guard distributed bottles of German rye whiskey to all the log cabins. Sitting in front of the fire, Hank Greene was loud and boisterous and in a good humor. He balanced five bottles in his lap, and as one emptied, he opened another one. He filled the tin cups thrust at him with careful precision.

Bruce sat with Henry on the bottom bunk. He swirled the clear liquid in his cup. Then he took a drink. He was shocked when it burned his mouth and throat. Worst of all, it caused a fire in his empty stomach.

"Here," he said, giving the cup to Henry. Henry had finished his cup and accepted the second without hesitation.

"It's great," Henry said and gulped it down. His face reddened, and there was a gleam of perspiration on his forehead.

"I don't know how you do it," Bruce said. He tried to rub the pain from his stomach. "I'm starving."

"There are no more squirrels," Henry said. He laughed and took another drink from the cup. "This will have to do. It will knock me out, and I won't think about eating until tomorrow morning."

"I can't do that. I've got to eat something. When I first came to camp, I saw a farm on the other side of the creek," Bruce said. "I'm going there tonight."

"Jacob Wood's farm," Henry said. He smiled and swayed back and forth. "You can't go there. Farmer Wood shoots at everyone."

"I think I know his daughter," Bruce said.

"He doesn't have a daughter," Henry said. "He has a niece, a beautiful niece. Her name is Olivia. But she's very selective now. She only meets with officers. But you say you know her? Maybe I should go with you." Henry smiled again and tried to sit up. He hovered for a moment, and then his head settled back in the straw. The empty cup dropped to the ground and rolled under the bunk.

"Henry," Bruce said and watched Henry close his eyes. Feeling a little dizzy, Bruce stood up and lifted Henry's legs onto the bunk. At the fireplace, another bottle of whiskey was passed around. The men began shouting toasts at each other, the boisterous noise echoing off the wooden logs of the cabin.

Backing away, watching their shadows dance across the walls, Bruce reached the door and opened it. He stepped outside and pushed the door shut. The sky was clear, and the air was frigid cold. The moon was a white, perfectly rounded sphere, and it shone a ghostly light over Valley Forge. Bruce pulled the blue robe over his head and began walking toward Valley Creek. His footsteps made a crunching sound in the frozen layer of snow. A dark cloud moved slowly across the sky, casting Valley Forge under a gray landscape of shifting smoke and shadow.

Major Beaumont was impeccably dressed in his uniform and blue flowing cape. As he walked to his horse, the cold air burned his nostrils, but he could still smell the heavy, sweet fragrance of perfume he had poured over his chest and shirt. He held the silver flask of whiskey carefully in his hand and mounted his horse, the sword clinking lightly against the saddle. Major Beaumont pulled the reins, and the horse turned toward the road. He met Legard at the officer's quarters, and they trotted the horses through the network of log cabins.

Beaumont was in high spirits as he thought about the girl worker on the farm. The reports from the other officers said she was beautiful and firm fleshed, and that she worked for the farmer during the day, and she worked for herself during the night. Beaumont hit the horse with impatience, and it broke into a gallop down the deserted road.

As he approached Valley Creek, Bruce could hear the loud singing and bouts of laughter from the sentry post. The guards were drunk and rowdy. Keeping his eyes on the glow of the fire from the newly constructed hut, he crossed a shallow section of Valley Creek and began walking quickly, sometimes slipping in the snow, toward the far hill. Ten minutes later, he stopped and looked down at the darkened farmhouse and barn.

Bruce was about to move out of the trees when he heard something scraping, brushing against the low hanging branches. He turned quickly to look when a buck with a massive rack of antlers emerged from the trees. Numerous deer shapes appeared from the shadows. Directly behind the buck was another animal, but it was difficult for Bruce to see what it was. Then the slight outline of the body stepped forward, moved even with the buck's brown body. In amazement, Bruce saw clearly that the doe was perfectly white.

"An albino," Bruce whispered. Gasping loudly, a strange noise escaping from his lungs, Bruce was startled and stumbled forward. The buck bolted at the noise, and leaping in the air, it raced across the clearing. Snorting clouds of steam in the bitter, cold air and kicking up thick patches of snow, the doe trampled after it. Bruce grabbed onto a tree for support, and slowly catching his breath, he watched the herd of deer disappear in the shadows behind the barn.

After Bruce regained his strength, the pain in his stomach growing more intense, he made his way quietly to the barn and pushed the door open. He could hear hoofs rustling in the straw and saw a horse in a stall. Then he heard the deep clucking sound and saw the wooden enclosure along the wall. Feeling the retching pain in his stomach, Bruce dropped to the ground.

All he could think about was food. Bruce squinted his eyes, and getting used to the darkness in the barn, he saw the shadowy figures strut around behind the planks of wood. Trying to control the convulsions in his stomach, Bruce began a slow crawl toward the chickens. He didn't know why, but his breathing became heavy and perspiration formed and began to drip down his face.

Major Beaumont and Legard stopped their horses at Valley Creek. The noise and laughter from the sentry shack drifted across the water. Beaumont took a drink from his flask and handed it to Legard.

"Against the cold," Beaumont said.

"Thank you very much," Legard said. He took a long, slow drink and smiled. "You'll be warm enough soon," he said, handing the flask back to Beaumont. The laughter inside the sentry post stopped, and a lone soldier began singing in a deep, sonorous voice.

> Father and I went down to camp
> Along with Captain Gooding
> And there we saw the men and boys
> As thick as hasty pudding.

At the sound of the last word, the rest of the soldiers broke out into a loud, tumultuous chorus that reverberated against the sides of the sentry post.

> Yankee doodle, keep it up
> Yankee doodle dandy
> Mind the music and the step
> And with the girls be handy.

"The lazy bastards!" Listening to the lyrics, Beaumont felt a surge of anger. "We should go in there and arrest them for their drunkenness. It would be a hundred lashes on the parade ground tomorrow."

"It's late," Legard said. "And she's waiting. Take another drink and relax. Don't let the drunken Americans spoil the moment."

"You're right as always, Legard," Beaumont said. He took a drink and slipped the flask inside his coat. Coaxing the horse across the creek, he gave it free rein on the other side, and he and Legard trotted up the hill at a fast pace.

There was no light anywhere in the barn. It took several long minutes before Bruce became accustomed to the darkness. He lifted the rope over the post, opened the rickety door of the makeshift chicken coup, and slid inside. He was breathing heavily, and he could feel his heart beating wildly inside his chest cavity. Bruce willed himself to be quiet as he crawled slowly over the droppings and dry stalks of hay. Stooping lower to the ground, he rested and waited. His eyes focused on the movement directly in front of him. Two chickens were up and strutting around the nesting ones. One moved away from the other.

"This way," Bruce whispered to himself. His hands were limp at his side as he watched the chicken step closer. It paused, stretched its neck high in the air, and seemed to study Bruce. A low clucking sound came from deep in the chicken's neck, and it took a step forward.

"Please, closer," Bruce prayed. He strained hard to see, and things in the barn began to blur slightly. His body was rigid, and the muscles ached in his legs and back. When the chicken lifted its front leg, Bruce couldn't wait any longer and lunged forward. His right hand closed around the chicken's neck, and there was a great outburst of noise as the resting chickens flew into motion. Ignoring the commotion, Bruce tightened his grip, and with the wings flogging against his hand, he pulled the chicken closer and crushed it against his chest.

Bruce stood up quickly. The noise in the barn was overwhelming. Swinging the chicken at his side, Bruce raced for the door, and within seconds, he burst into the front yard. Alarmed by the noise and moving too fast, he lost his balance and tripped forward. Trying to catch himself with his hands, he lost his grip on the chicken. Bruce hit the ground hard, and the sudden impact knocked the air from his chest.

Major Beaumont had just crested the hill with Legard when he heard the noise from the farm. He reined in his horse and looked at the buildings in the clearing below. He heard the loud chicken squawking from the barn, and then he saw the shadowy figure run from the barn door. Beaumont focused on the swinging, noisy object at the man's side, and when the object opened wings and its feathers flew wildly in the air, he knew exactly what was happening.

"Chicken thief!" Beaumont shouted. He drew his sword out of the scabbard and kicked the horse into motion. Legard hurriedly followed him at a gallop down the hill.

A sudden burst of wind swirled snow around Bruce and blasted cold into his face. The wind cleared an opening in the clouds, and bright moonlight flooded the farm. Wiping his eyes, Bruce saw the stunned chicken off to his side; and arms outstretched, he dove for the bird. His right hand found feathers, and Bruce grabbed onto the wing. He pulled the chicken closer, the loose wing flapping against his wrist and forearm. Reaching for the other wing, Bruce heard a shout from the house. The front door flew open, and a man ran onto the porch. He was holding a musket.

Bruce froze as he watched the man level the musket in his direction. A lantern appeared behind the man. The bright light illuminated the scarlet cap on his head and the black outline of the musket. A woman in a nightgown held the lantern and raised it toward the clearing. She saw the flapping chicken and Bruce in the bright circle of moonlight, and she put her hand to her mouth.

"No!" she half shouted to the man.

The farmer studied Bruce for a second. He saw the young face, blue nightgown, torn pants, and then he began to lower his musket. Bruce wasn't sure what to do. He smiled and released his grip on the chicken. It dropped to the ground and made a flapping run to the barn. Then Bruce lifted his hands in the air.

It was then that Bruce heard the sound of galloping horses behind him. The noise thundered closer, and Bruce turned slowly. For a second, he saw a silver blade of light swing through the air. It flashed downward, and Bruce felt a burning sensation in his throat, and then, a red flash exploded around him. Watching the rearing figure and horse in the red light, Bruce fell to the ground. He gagged at the liquid filling his throat and mouth. Bruce closed his hand around his neck and felt the bloody flow of liquid gushing between his fingers.

Major Beaumont dismounted and looked at the gash in Bruce's neck. The boy tried to raise his hand, but Beaumont kicked it away. He reached down and tore the boy's other hand away from his neck. Blood spurted in the air. Taking a step backward, Beaumont raised his sword and brought it down savagely into the exposed neck. The gash in the neck widened slightly, and the boy's head fell sideways on the ground. Major Beaumont hacked at the neck with four powerful swings before the head was severed and rolled away from the body.

A girl appeared at the side of the house. She saw the body and the large, dark spattering of blood on the white snow. Recognizing the face of the farm boy, she placed both hands over her mouth and shrieked into the night air. Then she collapsed on the ground.

"Get it," Major Beaumont ordered, and Legard dismounted. He ripped the blue robe from the boy's body and laid it flat on the ground. Grabbing a handful of hair, Legard picked up the head and placed it the middle of the robe. He twisted the corners of the robe into a knot and tied it to his saddle.

The farmer and his wife walked slowly from the porch. The lantern swung nervously in the lady's hand, and her steps were cautious and uncertain. The farmer grabbed her free hand and held it tightly. When they reached the body, Beaumont and Legard were both mounted on their horses.

"Bury the bastard!" Beaumont shouted. "Bury the chicken thief!"

The major turned the horse, and he and Legard galloped away from the farm. He was furious that his night had been ruined. But he also experienced excitement at the unexpected kill, his first in this new country of America. Whipping the reins against the horse's neck, he splashed across Valley Creek toward the empty parade ground at Mount Joy.

There was a light snow at Valley Forge the next morning. Hung over from the large quantity of whiskey, the soldiers woke up with headaches and dry mouths. Henry lay in his bunk and listened to the loud grumbling and complaining voices. He stood up, feeling the ache in his body, and brushed the straw off his coat and trousers. Stretching his arms forward, increasing the ache in his back and shoulders, Henry saw the top bunk was empty. He was the only one left in the cabin.

Henry walked outside and watched the movement of men marching slowly toward Mount Joy. No one had said anything about an assembly, and he half turned to go back inside the cabin. But Hank Greene was at the door and pointed Henry toward the line of men. Putting on his hat with its broken feather, Henry joined the group. As they walked toward Mount Joy, the clouds on the horizon opened, and slanted lines of sunlight filtered through the lightly falling snow.

When Henry reached the hill, he stepped into line with the Pennsylvania soldiers. With the falling snow and periods of bright sunlight, the morning was tranquil and extremely quiet. The soldiers around him whispered in hushed tones. Henry looked up and saw there was no movement on the hill.

When Henry looked again, he saw that something had been placed on top of the stump. It was covered by a light dusting of snow, and when the wind blew over the hill, some of the snow rolled away. At that instance, briefly but explosively clear, Henry saw a slight hint of blue color.

"One of the Frenchies killed him last night," a voice whispered next to him.

Hank Greene walked away from the company of soldiers. At the foot of Mount Joy, he turned momentarily and looked back at Henry. Then he slowly began making his way up the hill to the stump. Henry watched him closely, and an ache, a dull sensation of pain, began to form in the back of his neck. Hank Greene paused on the slope of the hill, his feet sliding sideways in the snow. Then he straightened himself and started forward again.

At first, the noise from the Schuylkill River was vague and indistinct. Then it intensified and spread in stages throughout the encampment. It became a loud clamor of noise that drifted through the falling snow and rolled across Mount Joy. Hank Greene stopped in his tracks, and Henry, looking back toward the river, was confused, and afraid.

"Is it the redcoats?" he shouted to Hank Greene.

"No," Hank said. "There's some kind of celebration."

The echo of noise became louder, and there was a mass stampede of men from the cabins. Watching the activity on Mount Joy and the wild charge of soldiers, two French officers sat stiffly on their horses a short distance away. Major Beaumont took another drink, put his flask of whiskey inside his coat, and he and Legard lashed their horses into a fast trot toward Washington's Headquarters.

Shouting at each other, the Pennsylvania soldiers waiting at the foot of Mount Joy became animated and restless. Suddenly, a man, and then another broke from the group, and then they all began running toward the Schuylkill. Within seconds, Henry found himself standing alone at the foot of Mount Joy.

Cheering and laughing and some singing songs, the men coming from the bank of the river carried baskets and heavy, drooping blankets that dragged along the ground. One man tripped and fell, and when his blanket spilled open, Henry saw silver bodies of fish flopping in the snow. His friends waited while he quickly picked them up. Laughing and joking, they looked at Henry across the field.

"In the river!" one shouted. "They're trapped in the shallows."

"There are thousands!" another man said.

"The shad run," the first man shouted to Henry. "It's early this year."

Henry watched them gather up the fish and walk quickly toward the cabins. Only he and the squad leader were left on Mount Joy. It took Hank Greene a few seconds to make up his mind. Turning his back to the stump, he started running and sliding down the hill. When he reached Henry, he had a look of excitement and hope on his face.

"Come on, Henry," he shouted. "Real food! We finally have real food!" Hank began running faster to catch up to the others. In his haste, he slipped and fell in the snow. He rolled over once, and for a man his bulk, he jumped up running faster than before.

Henry was left bewildered and alone on the parade ground. The roar of noise and shouting from the river became deafening, and already Henry could see the wispy lines of smoke from the hastily built fires. A light breeze from the river blew across the parade ground, and it carried with it the strong, unbearable aroma of hot, cooked food.

Henry felt a tremendous ache of hunger in his stomach. The sweet smell from the fires became stronger with the thickening clouds of smoke. Tears blurred his vision, and Henry hesitated. Then, shutting out the noise of celebration, he moved upward into the slanting rays of sunlight and falling crystals of snow.

Henry was exhausted when he reached the top of Mount Joy. He fell to his knees in front of the stump and was still for a moment. The celebrations from the Schuylkill River grew louder, and the sporadic cheers and shouting echoed across the valley. Muskets were fired, and a lone cannon went off from headquarters, the discharge rolling like thunder across Mount Joy.

Confused and shaken by the pain and heartache that now gripped his body, Henry reached a trembling hand toward the stump. His fingers grasped the familiar blue fabric, now shrouded under a layer of glistening snow, and he lifted it in the air. Lowering the robe to the ground, Henry saw the pale, frozen image of Bruce Jenkins. The eyes, blue pupils cracked into sections by thin, jagged red lines, seemed to be staring directly at him.

Brushing the snow and ice crystals from the face of his friend, Henry was immediately transfixed by the expression of peaceful serenity. As he moved closer, Henry saw with extreme clarity the true spirit of the colonial soldier. There, in a visage sculptured for all time, for all generations, Henry saw the youth, strength, and nobility of the chicken thief soldier.

Chicken Thief Monument
Valley Forge National Park 2007

Baron von Steuben Statue facing Parade Ground
Valley Forge National Park 2007

CHAPTER 1

VALLEY FORGE   1959

There was a light drizzle on Thanksgiving Day. The Benson family, Tim and Nancy and their ten-year-old son Drew, celebrated the holiday with a lavish Thanksgiving dinner at the Sheraton Hotel on the outskirts of Valley Forge. Drew had never seen so much food. Smothered under lumps of blue cheese, the salad was on a huge crystal plate that was cold to the touch. With butter dripping over the sides, the Italian rolls were warm and sweet tasting. Then in the main course, Drew had a dish heaped with slices of turkey, stuffing and gravy, and sweet potatoes. Although completely full, Drew refused the pumpkin pie but tried hard and managed to eat two large pieces of lemon meringue pie that he topped with extra whipped cream.

After dinner, the family drove to the theatre complex at the King of Prussia Mall and watched *The Old Man and the Sea*. The sky had clouded, and there was a light drizzle when Drew and his parents exited the movie. In a hurry to get to their cars, some people bumped past Drew. Thinking about the old man in the movie, Drew ignored the haste and rudeness. Mr. Benson had a slight limp, and the family moved at their own slow pace.

"I liked the movie," Drew said. "But I don't understand why the Old Man hated the Portuguese man-of-war. They're nothing but floating globs of jelly, and the purple filaments are beautiful in the water. Why did he hate them so much?"

"The filaments are poisonous," Mr. Benson said.

"But that's how they get food."

"Yes, but the filaments never turn off. They drift along with the current, looking harmless and beautiful, and kill everything they touch. They can even paralyze and kill humans."

"Then I hate them, too," Drew said. His thoughts went from the man-of-war to the fifteen hundred pound marlin that pulled the old man and the boat for three days.

As they neared the parking lot, Drew told his dad that he had never seen a fish that big. His dad said they would visit Uncle Ken in Montana again and catch a bigger one. His mom laughed. Drew asked his dad why the old man was alone with no one to help him catch the big fish. His dad said that sometimes the hardest things in life you have to do by yourself. Drew wasn't sure he understood.

His mom said old people shouldn't have to work so much. Then she added they shouldn't have to suffer so much. His dad said she had nothing to worry about. When she asked him why, he just said there was a reason why the name of the movie wasn't *The Old Woman and the Sea*. He said women didn't have to work hard at all. They both laughed. Drew said the movie should be called *The Little Boy and the Sea*. He would show them both what he could do. His mom said he could start tomorrow by cleaning his room. His dad thought that was hilarious.

Tim Benson drove daily down the Schuylkill Expressway to his job as a loan manager at the Wachovia Bank on Market Street in Philadelphia. Nancy, on the other hand, stayed at the house. She loved being at home when Drew was growing up. She saw the changes in his character and was amazed at the intelligence he showed while working with her around the house. But he grew up too fast, and when he started school, the home was quiet and empty. Nancy applied and got a job as a receptionist at the Phoenixville Hospital. She was excited about the work. The traffic and variety of people kept her busy until Drew came home from school.

The only people left walking around the mall were late moviegoers. The Benson family reached their car, and Drew said "Happy Thanksgiving" and opened the door for his mom. She smiled and thanked him. Closing the door, he got in the empty roominess of the back seat. They had to wait a few minutes before Mr. Benson was able to slip into the line of cars leaving the parking lot.

Outside, the sky was black, and Drew saw lightning flashes over the distant hills. It was eleven o'clock when Mr. Benson made a right turn at the mall exit onto Route 23. Soon, they left the traffic behind, and Route 23 became a narrow road that snaked through the hills and valleys of Valley Forge Park.

It was raining harder now, and the windshield wipers made a rapid clicking sound that sprayed water high in the air and over the sides of the car. Slouched in the back seat, Drew listened to the sound, and the steady rhythm began to make him tired.

Drew was a thin boy with little muscle on his five-foot-seven-inch body. Like his dad, he had thick black hair that covered his forehead and ears. His nose was straight, almost pointed, and his blue eyes were large and slightly recessed into his forehead. They gave his boyish face a meditative, intelligent expression.

Ever since he started school, Drew was a straight-A student. His fourth-grade teachers at Ben Franklin Elementary School were frustrated in their attempts to find material that would challenge him. Drew finished all his work and handed it in days before the other students. His parents were proud of him and always showed their love and interest by showering him with praise and attention.

Drew's best friend was Shane Collier, and they had many sleepovers where they stayed up playing games until the morning hours. The Collier family and the Benson family had known each other since they went to George Washington High School together. The Colliers' house was just two blocks down the street. Drew often visited there, but most of his time was spent working hard to please his parents. He loved to talk to them. He loved their company.

Listening to the radio, Mr. Benson and his wife sat quietly in the front seat humming along with the music of *White Christmas*. Then Nancy interrupted the song and commented on how the local businesses started the Christmas season earlier every year. A few minutes later, when a car, bright lights still on, raced toward them, she commented on the crazy young drivers in the park. Drew looked up and slid to the middle seat as the bright flash lit up his face. The lights of the racing car moved down the road, and Drew heard a muffled popping noise and another one.

"What was that?" he asked.

Drew leaned forward and pushed his head between his parent's shoulders. The sound of the windshield wipers and the lyrics, "I'm dreaming of a white Christmas," ran together in his head. Drew stared at the crystal drops of rain that fell from the darkness and spattered circles against the windshield.

The jogging path through the park was on Drew's left, and there was a large hill along the road on his right. Drew peered through the flickering car lights at the dark, almost foreboding, shadow of the hill. Annoyed by the loud spattering noise of the rain, his mother turned up the volume on the radio. Bing Crosby's voice filled the confines of the car.

> I'm dreaming of a white Christmas
> Just like the ones I used to know
> Where the treetops glisten,
> And children listen
> To hear sleigh bells in the snow.

Leaning back comfortably, listening to the sleigh bells ringing with the music, Drew heard another popping sound, louder and closer than the first two. He sat up just as a massive animal form appeared at the top of the hill. In disbelief, Drew watched the animal leap high in the air, and as it descended into the glare of their car lights, a gigantic antlered head dropped toward them out of the darkness. The buck's hoof crashed against the front hood, sending sparks flying in the air.

There was a brilliant flash of lightning, and at the top of the hill, momentarily outlined in the diminishing glow of light, Drew saw a dark, solitary figure, head shrouded in red flames. The figure dropped out of sight, and thunder echoed across the night sky.

In the midst of the thunder, the black form of the buck seemed to expand and double in size. It hit and shattered the windshield, and Drew heard the roaring noise of the storm enter their car. Silver beads of rain and jagged pieces of glass shredded the closed interior. Shielding his face, Drew shouted to his mom on the front seat. She had just turned and was reaching a hand to him when a large section of glass sliced into her throat.

The buck's head, red tongue swinging grotesquely from its mouth, large, watery eyes streaming blood, came right at Drew, and something sharp brushed against the side of his face. As Drew fell backward, fear constricting his voice and paralyzing the muscles in his body, he watched the antlers of the buck slide into his dad's shoulder and chest. Blood spurted in the air and dripped onto the glistening brown hairs of the buck's elongated head.

There was heavier pressure on the gas pedal now, and their car picked up speed, raced off the road, and collided into the side of a cannon. The cannon was lifted into the air, and one of the large spoked wheels broke off and rolled slowly across the field.

Still moving forward at a fast speed, the car slammed into a large pine tree. As steam billowed high in the air, some dead branches broke loose in the tree. The weight of falling branches split away others, and the accretion of wood and needles crashed onto the hood of the car. Breaking the remaining glass in the windshield, branches flared around the buck's bloated belly and covered the bodies in the front seat with needles and large, black pine cones.

Drew was crushed in the back of the car when the driver's seat folded over his body. Fighting the pain in his neck and back, Drew looked up and saw his mom trapped under the pine branches. And then he saw the antlers and bloodied head only inches from his face. The large oval eyes moved, and there was a gurgling sound from the buck's mouth. The sound became louder, and a silky flow of foam and bubbles cascaded toward Drew. He struggled to move, his hand reaching through the pine for his mom, and then he began to scream as pools of blood covered his face.

Drew was unconscious when the emergency workers ripped off the roof of the car and lifted him from the wreck. The medic strapped Drew's body to the gurney and wheeled him to the ambulance. Red lights flashing and siren blaring, the ambulance raced past the holiday traffic now stopped at the side of the road.

The driver reached Phoenixville Hospital in eight minutes and parked the vehicle in front of the emergency room entrance. Drew was lifted out the back doors of the ambulance and rushed inside. Most of the hospital staff had come in when they heard about the accident. The concern was for Drew. Tim and Nancy Benson had been killed instantly.

When Drew opened his eyes, he saw a blur of lights and a circle of hazy figures. There was a ringing noise in his ears and the soft sound of Christmas music in the background. Drew didn't feel any pain. He didn't feel anything at all. Trying hard to focus, he began to see the outline of Shane's face right in front of him. Shane looked white as a ghost, and his eyes were filled with tears. Drew watched the tears drop onto the sheet. Then large hands appeared on Shane's shoulder and moved him to the side.

Holding a small light in his hand, an older man bent over Drew. The light in the man's hand began to grow brighter and brighter. It hovered right over his eye, descended closer, and blinded him. Drew started screaming and swinging his arms. Strong hands grabbed him tightly and held him down. Then there was a slight burning sensation in his right arm, and everything in the room became distant and faint and then disappeared in darkness.

The next morning, the Collier family was there in the waiting room when Drew was discharged. On the phone, the doctor told them that except for the cut under his lip Drew had no physical injuries. The doctor also told them Drew was still in a mild state of shock.

Standing with his parents, Shane was very apprehensive. He watched the door open and saw Drew walk out with the two nurses. Each one held onto a hand and steadied him. When Drew looked up, his face pale and void of emotion, Shane could see the small cloth bandage on the side of his lip.

Mr. and Mrs. Collier finished the paper work at the desk. The receptionist had tears in her eyes. The nurses bent down and kissed Drew before letting go of his hand. Mrs. Collier thanked them, and she and her husband walked down the corridor to the exit. Drew and Shane followed close behind. Along the corridor, the doctor, a group of nurses, and the custodian, wet mop in hand, stood quietly at attention. Mr. Collier shook hands with each one of them, and then he opened the door for his wife and the boys. The custodian waited a few seconds, and when he saw the door swing shut, he began wiping the wet shoe prints off the floor.

The Colliers drove straight home. Throughout the evening and early morning hours, neighbors had helped make space for an extra bed in Shane's room. They drove to the Benson house and transported all Drew's belongings down the street. The manager of Mark's Furniture rushed to his store at midnight and delivered a new bed and dresser to the Collier house. They were placed near the window, opposite Shane's bed. One of Colliers' neighbors, Mrs. Jablonski, an elderly lady, who always waved to Drew from her porch, had folded his clothes neatly in the new dresser. She waited hours in the Collier living room to see Drew, but at three in the morning, she left and walked home alone in the dark.

On the day of the funeral, the temperature dropped below freezing, turning the rain into light snow squalls. All the relatives and family members came for the funeral. Looking through the window, Drew saw a taxi stop on the street, and a man in a black suit stepped out. Drew thought the man's face was familiar, but he wasn't sure where he had seen him. He concentrated hard, but nothing happened.

Then somehow, Drew remembered it was his Uncle Ken from Montana. The family had visited him two years ago. He had a small house on the side of a mountain, and the clear, cold water of Rock Creek was in walking distance. After four days, Drew caught his first trout there. That was the only excitement on the whole trip, and Drew was glad to get back home. Drew watched as his uncle and Mr. Collier, still talking quietly, climbed the steps to the front entrance.

Friends of the Bensons from work, all the neighbors, and most of Drew's classmates filled the Burke Funeral Home. Many had to wait outside in a double, sometimes triple, line that wound down the street and around the corner. They wore heavy coats and hats and shifted their faces to the side when the winter wind blew down the street.

Since Drew was weak and still recovering from the accident, he didn't stand in the receiving line. He and Shane sat in chairs in front of the two closed coffins. The huge baskets of color from the flowers and the green canopy of the hanging ferns gave Drew the impression he was in the middle of a large garden. Sitting quietly and breathing the fresh aroma of the flowers, he felt the small bandage at the side of his mouth where the antler had ripped into his skin. Sometimes, Drew found himself picking at the bandage. He stopped when he saw blood on his fingers.

The blood began to worry Drew, and he tried hard to think of other things. Momentarily, he thought of Uncle Ken and Montana and saw the racing waters of Rock Creek. The waters emptied into a deep pool, and when his uncle had waded out of sight around a bend, his dad pulled Drew aside. Cutting the fly off the line, his dad tied on a small hook and told Drew to go in the field and catch a grasshopper.

Drew knew from listening to his uncle that using live bait was somehow illegal, but he returned with a large brown grasshopper spitting chew and scratching legs against the palm of his hand. His dad slipped the hook under the grasshopper's wing, and giving the rod to Drew, he told him to hurry up and cast it and catch a trout before Uncle Ken returned. Drew quickly swung the line into the water and watched the grasshopper, legs kicking up little circles, descend with the current into the large pool.

The sudden explosion in the pool surprised Drew. The grasshopper disappeared inside the mouth of a huge, curved rainbow shape leaping high above the water. He heard a whirring sound and realized it was the line escaping from his reel. The hooked trout jumped again and again.

Bent to the breaking point, the fishing rod shook in Drew's hand. He struggled and tried to lift it higher in the air. But when the trout jumped again and Drew could see how huge it was, he became too excited. Forgetting everything he had ever been taught about fighting a fish, he grabbed the rod with both hands, turned, and ran wildly up the bank.

Drew continued to run, and the trout was pulled to the surface of the pool and surfed all the way to the bank. When he saw the trout's body flopping against the stones, Drew ran back to the stream. His dad took the trout off the hook and held it high in front of Drew. Water splashed in the air from the swinging tail, and bright rainbow and silver colors glistened in the light. Laughing and reaching out to touch the fish, Drew saw the absolute joy on his dad's face.

Then his vision blurred, and Drew closed his eyes and wiped at the tears on his face. When he opened his eyes, he saw the casket and the somber faces watching him from the receiving line.

During the funeral, there was much talk about what to do with Drew, but in the end, his relatives hurried to return home for the holidays and their family celebrations. Drew shook hands with Uncle Ken and watched him get into the taxi.

After his departure, Drew and Shane stood on the side porch of the funeral home for a long time. Wind howled around the corner of the house and spun thin circles of snow and dead leaves across the open space of the porch. The door opened, and Mrs. Collier and a man walked across the porch to Drew.

"Do you want to come inside?' Mrs. Collier asked. "Pastor Sanders would like to talk to you where it's comfortable."

"I'm fine here," Drew said, looking up at the man next to Mrs. Collier. He was tall and heavyset and dressed in a black suit. There was a stiff, white collar around his neck. Thick glasses angled down slightly on his nose, which was swollen and pink from the cold. He reached out and shook Drew's hand.

"This is a very troubling time, my son." Staring at Drew intensely, holding tightly onto his hand. "I can help you understand what happened and maybe why it happened," Pastor Sanders said.

"I understand what happened," Drew said slowly, his words barely audible in the noise of the wind. He tried to twist his hand to get free of the painful handshake.

Standing at his side, Shane was watching Pastor Sanders and Drew closely. He saw the tightness of the pastor's grip and how Drew struggled to step away. When the pastor closed his other hand over Drew's, holding him firmly in place,

Shane stepped forward. He grabbed the pastor's wrist and pulled the hand away, forcing him to release his grip on Drew.

"They're things we should talk about," Pastor Sanders continued, ignoring Shane's presence. With his hand free now, he took a black handkerchief from his pocket and wiped at his nose and coughed. He put the handkerchief back in his pocket. His voice was quiet, but his eyes were stern and unmoving. "God saved you for a reason. He has a purpose for you."

Drew's face was numb from standing out in the cold for so long. He was sliding his shoes on the porch, but he couldn't feel where his toes were. Drew made a great effort to stop his body from trembling.

"God didn't save me," Drew said. "My mom did. She stopped the antlers from reaching me."

"Still, Drew, you must see God's work in this."

"There was something else on the hill. It was red and fiery, but it wasn't God." Drew was quiet for a moment, the wind chilling his face. "I will never think about God when I think about the death of my parents."

"Then what else is there? What will you think about if not God?" the pastor asked. There was mild irritation in his voice.

"I will think about my mom and how she moved in front of me at the last moment. I will think about how much she loved me," Drew said. Then he added, "And how much I love her."

Drew spoke softly and clearly, the force of the wind muting his words. Pastor Sanders moved closer and was about to say something, but Drew stepped back against the railing. His face was pale, and his lips were trembling. He held onto the railing with both hands to stop the shaking.

"Come in soon, Drew," Mrs. Collier said. She stepped in front of Pastor Sanders and waited for him to return inside the funeral home.

Mrs. Jablonski came out on the porch and kissed Drew on the forehead. She spoke something, but her voice was so soft that Drew didn't understand her. A few school friends came out and shook his hand. When everyone was gone, Drew went in the side door by himself. He walked down the hallway and into the viewing room of empty chairs and elaborate floral display.

There, head bowed, Drew stood between the two coffins. His nose was stuffed, and his body was cold and there was a sharp pain deep in his chest. Tears dropped freely from his face and formed wet stains on the floor as he whispered his final words to his dad. Then he shifted his feet and turned to the other coffin, and another smudged circle began forming on the floor. He was sobbing when he talked to his mom. Shane shuffled up and stood next to him.

Mrs. Collier watched Drew closely. When she saw his shoulders collapse and his head drop lower, she came up and took his hand and walked with him and Shane to the door.

It was dark when they returned to the house. Drew had a glass of water and went upstairs. The bedroom looked strange to Drew, and he wasn't accustomed to the large window and the light coming in from the street. Drew pulled at the curtain but couldn't close it completely. A line of light crossed the center of the bed. Drew lay there motionless, unblinking in the light. The door opened and Shane came in the room.

Shane didn't say anything. He changed and got into his bed. Sliding under the sheet, he glanced at Drew for a moment. The wide band of light from the window slanted downward across Drew and ended in the middle of the floor. Shane saw the lost expression on Drew's face and the pain and hurt in his eyes. Feeling helpless and more troubled than he had been all day, Shane turned on his back and stared at the ceiling for a long time.

CHAPTER 2

The nightmare always began in total darkness. There was complete quiet except for the soft, distant sounds of holiday music from the car radio. After the words "May your days be merry and bright," the first flash of lightning cracked open the night sky, and the dark outline of the hill came into view

Lying in bed, Drew felt his body stiffen and jerk involuntarily. His hands reached out for Mom, but she wasn't there. Frantic and alone, he searched the darkness. The next bolt of lightning was bright and severe and knocked him backward. He thought he had screamed, but he couldn't hear anything now except the music. There was a cold dampness on his face, and his T-shirt was completely saturated. The view outside was menacing, but no matter how hard he tried, Drew could not turn away from the car window.

The darkness behind the hill was alive, forming a sinister pattern of shadows that swirled in circular forms over the hill. Then he saw the red glow of the eyes. They were distant at first and seemed to float above him. Attached to nothing solid, they darted quickly to the right and left. Then, focusing their beady stare on Drew, they became stationary and seemed to grow larger. The eyes settled in the dark swirling shapes on the hill, and Drew knew they were watching him, waiting for him. The air was sucked out of his lungs, and his body was frozen with fear.

It was twelve thirty in the morning. Awakened by the noise, Shane sat on the edge of his bed across the room and looked at Drew. The moonlight gleamed through the window and shone on the figure curled tightly in the fetal position. Drew's face, strained with fear and dripping perspiration, looked out from under the curve of folded arms. His eyes were expanded wide, and in contrast, Drew's mouth was closed tightly, his lips blood red from the pressure.

Muscles straining, Drew's whole body was tense now. He knew it would come for him when the soft strains of the Christmas music reached a certain

56

point. It was the waiting that was horrible. He crunched deeper inside himself. His eyes searched nervously from side to side, and his mouth became dry. He couldn't speak. He couldn't warn his mom. His fear heightened. His heart slammed against his chest as the words of the familiar refrain sounded through the speakers.

> I'm dreaming of a white Christmas
> Just like the ones I used to know
> Where the treetops glisten
> And children listen

It was then that the heavy, black body crashed sparks on the hood of the car, and the glowing eyes and the sharp jagged spikes of the antlers cracked through the glass. Motionless on the hill, the solitary figure, head obscured by a red incandescent light, stared down at Drew. The figure disappeared when the mammoth head of the buck knocked Drew backwards. Brown nostrils pulsated and flared a hot mist into Drew's face. The heavy musk scent mixed with his mom's sweet perfume created a putrid stench that suffocated Drew and overwhelmed his senses. Gagging and trying to catch his breath, Drew jumped up in bed and began screaming.

"Drew!" Shane shouted. He grabbed Drew around the shoulders and began shaking him. Perspiration sprayed from Drew's hair and face. Trapped and alone, Drew tensed his body and struggled to break clear of the back seat. Using all the strength he had, Shane held onto him with both arms.

Drew felt the pressure on his shoulders and opened his eyes. The buck's head and rack of antlers were gone. Not sure of what had happened, Drew touched the scar on his face. The door to the bedroom opened, and Mr. and Mrs. Collier rushed into the room. Mrs. Collier switched on the light, and Drew covered his eyes against the brightness.

"He's all right, Mom," Shane said. "It's another nightmare."

"Did you hear anything?"

"Nothing I could understand," Shane said. He removed his arms from around Shane and stood up. "But when he's sitting there, you can see he's hiding from something."

"What?" Mr. Collier asked.

"I don't know," Shane said. "It's something red and scary."

"He's been through so much," Mrs. Collier said. She rested her hand on his head and smoothed the hair down. "If he can't get any rest, he'll never get better."

"Give him some time," Mr. Collier said. "He's a strong boy."

"I'm sorry," Drew said, looking up. His body felt chilled, and he began to shake a little. He got up and walked past them to the bathroom. He stripped off his wet T-shirt and shorts and turned on the hot water. After waiting a few seconds, steam rising up from the basin, he splashed the water on his face and over his chest. The water was hot and left red marks on his chest. Drew toweled himself dry and returned to the room.

The Colliers were gone. Mrs. Collier had left a dry T-shirt and shorts on the covers. Drew changed into them and got into bed. He pulled the covers up to his chest and sat there, looking at the moon through the window.

"Drew."

"Yes."

"Don't worry," Shane said. The words sounded steady and unwavering. "If it comes again, I'll be here. I'll always be here."

Drew was silent. He didn't know how to answer. He didn't know what it was and how it got inside his head. Maybe Shane could help. Or maybe it was too much for even Shane. Maybe it would always be there waiting for him. Drew wasn't sure of anything. He pulled the pillow under his head, and closing his eyes, he tried to sleep.

The nightmares continued for the next three years. By the time Drew began his seventh-grade classes, he wasn't sure if they were getting worse or not. One night, he turned comfortably in bed, and without any music or warning noise, the monster was there, eyes burning red, inches from his face. Drew felt the heat and the putrid stench of its body.

Jumping out of bed, he broke running, shirtless and in his boxer shorts, down the steps and out the door. Shane chased after Drew and found him shivering on the porch of his old house. Mrs. Jablonski was holding him in her arms. Her little collie dog Tippy was licking Drew's hand. Drew's feet were scratched and bloodied from the rough pavement.

At other times, Drew would go for weeks without any nightmares. He would sleep peacefully the whole night and wake up rested and cheerful. Periodically, maybe three or four times a month, the dark dreams would appear out of nowhere. He was helpless against them, but slowly, as he got older and fought for more control, the darkness in his dreams became less severe.

Drew's life really changed for the better when May Wiggins appeared in his dreams. May was in the eighth grade, and Drew couldn't stop from looking at her. She was five feet ten inches tall, and Drew admired the way her body was growing in all the right directions. Although they seldom talked, actually never talked, she was always smiling and happy to see him. Every day during the first week of school, he waited in places where he knew she would pass. Only then would he go to his class. Often, he would run through the door just as the late bell rang.

In the evening, in bed, he knew that if he saw May's beaming face and bright smile, he would be in for a good night. Every dream was the same. Drew always watched her from a distance. When they walked past each other in the hall, she smiled but never said anything. It didn't matter to Drew that they never talked.

The best part of the dream was when he saw her stretching on the floor in physical education class. Once he saw her changing clothes in the locker room. Drew was embarrassed but couldn't turn away. Waking up with a start, he felt the wetness in his shorts and ran to the bathroom. But when accidents like that happened, it didn't really bother him too much.

That same week after watching May walk by from the top of the steps, Drew was running late to his third period class. The bell had stopped ringing, and the hall was empty. Drew was in the middle of the hall and only had to turn the corner to reach his class when the principal's door opened. A man stepped out and began walking toward Drew. His shoes made a steady, clicking noise that became louder. The man was tall, a Negro, very young looking, and he was dressed professionally in a blue suit, blue shirt, silky blue tie. The clicking noise stopped, and when Drew looked up, he saw the man standing directly in front him.

"Drew Benson," he said.

"Yes."

"Drew Benson, I'm Homer Matthews." He reached out his hand, and Drew shook it. "I want to talk to you."

"Right now?" Drew asked. "I'm late for class."

"I know that," Mr. Matthews said. "I'm assistant principal, and I have the bell schedule memorized. When I hear the last bell, I love to look down the hall and see it completely empty of student bodies. Follow me, Drew. We can talk in my office."

Mr. Matthews and Drew walked down the hall to the main office. They went inside, and Drew was ushered into a small room next to the principal's. The room was windowless, and there was only one picture of a Negro baseball player on the wall. Drew saw number 42 on the man's uniform.

"Sit down, Drew." Mr. Matthews pointed to the nearest chair. Crossing his arms over his chest, Mr. Matthews sat on the corner of the desk and hovered over Drew.

"I'm sorry I was late," Drew said.

"This has nothing to do about being late," Mr. Matthews said. "I'm also the football coach at George Washington, and football is what I want to talk to you about. I want you to go out for the team."

"I don't know anything about football," Drew said. He looked up at the imposing figure in front of him. "I'm not very big."

"That's not a problem. You're only in seventh grade. By the end of the year, if you work hard, you'll be twice that size."

"My parents . . ."

"I know your guardian, Wayne Collier, very well. In fact, we talked about this. He would like you to play football." Mr. Matthews took a paper from the top of his desk. "Take this form home, and he'll sign it."

"But I never played sports," Drew said. "I don't . . ."

"Give it a try," Mr. Matthews interrupted. "We'll see how it works out." He held the piece of paper toward Drew.

Drew took the form, folded it, and put it in his pocket. He didn't say anything. Mr. Matthews reached behind the desk and picked up a large blue gym bag with Patriots Football stenciled in gold letters on the side.

"This is your practice gear and your game uniform." Mr. Matthews swung the bag over the desk and dropped it in Drew's lap. "The uniform may seem big now, but you'll grow into it. You'll be a real Patriot in no time."

"Thanks," Drew said. "I've never had my own uniform before."

"Let me explain something, Drew. I was acquainted with your father. When I graduated from George Washington, I didn't have any money for college. I was turned down by every bank in Phoenixville and Pottstown. Then your father called me. We went to the same church, and he heard about my problem from the pastor. The next day, I was in Philadelphia signing the loan papers. That's why I have this job. And basically, that's why I'm talking to you now. Are you OK with that?"

"Sure," Drew said. The gym bag was uncomfortable on his lap. "It's really heavy."

"Your dad played football for George Washington. He injured his knee the first week of his senior year. Because of that, he only got in one game all year, the last game. He never complained. He never quit. He stayed with the team. His number was 21. And that's the same number on your jersey."

"I never knew why he limped," Drew said. "I guess I never asked him."

"Your dad was a quiet person," Mr. Matthews said. "He never talked about the injury. Also, he never told anyone what he did for me." He ripped out a yellow late slip from the pad on his desk and wrote the time and Drew's name and signed it. "You'll begin practice right after school tomorrow."

"My friend Shane began practice two weeks ago," Drew said.

"So you're a little late," Mr. Matthews said, handing Drew the pass. "There's one last thing, Drew. You'll have to catch up with the conditioning. I go jogging in the morning at Valley Forge Park four times a week. I'll pick you up at six thirty, and you can run with me. Go on to class now."

Drew got up out of the chair. He shook Coach Matthew's hand and walked to the door. In the hall, he was in a hurry and struggled with the gym bag. When he reached the boy's restroom, he pushed the door and went inside. Zipping open the gym bag, he took out the blue-and-gold football jersey. Drew stepped in front of the mirror and pulled the jersey over his head. As he stretched the jersey over his polo shirt, he watched the number 21 slowly unfold.

"Wow," Drew whispered. He rubbed his palms over the numbers, trying to straighten them. The bottom half of the jersey reached down to his knees.

A few minutes later, Drew opened the door to the classroom and walked in. Mrs. Henderson was at the blackboard. She was a soft-spoken, elderly woman who always found books for Drew to read. When she finished writing, "Anyone can be a fisherman in May," Drew handed her the late pass. His body was almost completely covered by the drooping football jersey.

"That's a different look for you," she said. "See me after class for a few minutes."

Drew nodded his head, turned, and began dragging the blue bag down the aisle to his seat. It caught between the legs of a desk and stuck there. Drew struggled to get it loose. A few students in the row began to laugh. Drew's face reddened, but he worked the bag loose and got to his seat.

Watching everything from his seat in the back of the room, Shane had a wide smile on his face. When he caught Drew's attention, he gave him two big thumbs-up. Drew answered with one thumb high in the air and sat down. When the bell rang ending the period, Drew made his way back to Mrs. Henderson's desk.

"I'm sorry I was late," he said.

"It's all right," she said. "I like your new jersey."

"I'm starting football tomorrow," Drew said. He looked at the assignment on the board. "I saw the movie *The Old Man and the Sea* years ago, and I've already finished reading the book. I don't know if I agree."

"Agree with what?"

"Hemingway says that life is easier when you're young, like in the spring when things are growing," Drew said. "But I think young people really take a beating. I think they have it tougher than anyone."

"Wait until you're old," Mrs. Henderson said. "You might change your mind." She pointed to his jersey. "I saw that number in this room years ago when I first started teaching."

"You taught my dad?"

"And your mom," Mrs. Henderson said. "That is, I taught them when I could get their attention. They were always looking at each other, passing notes, making their plans. But they both managed to get outstanding grades. I was so proud when I attended their wedding. They were a beautiful couple." Mrs. Henderson started to say something. Looking directly into Drew's face, her eyes focusing on the thin line of the scar, she hesitated. Her lips trembled slightly when she began speaking.

"You're so much like your dad," she said. "He really loved football. He was so excited about playing his senior year. Seeing you in that uniform and with that number will really make him happy."

"Do you think he knows?"

"Sure, he does," Mrs. Henderson said. "And Coach Homer Matthews is a good man. I know because I had him in class, too. His number was eighteen. Listen to everything he says."

"I will," Drew said. Waving his hand, he thanked Mrs. Henderson and walked to the door. He wore the jersey the rest of the day, walked around the block a few times, wore it during dinner, and went to bed with it on.

The next morning, Drew was sound asleep and at first didn't know what was happening. He opened his eyes to a darkened room and felt himself being pulled out of bed. He resisted and pushed the hands away, and then the light was turned on and blinded him. He raised his hand to his face and staring through his fingers, he saw Shane at the switch.

"What?" Drew mumbled. "What's going on?"

"Didn't you agree to start a conditioning program with Coach Matthews?"

"Yes."

"Didn't Coach tell you it would be in the mornings before school?"

"He mentioned something."

"Well, he's waiting outside," Shane said. "You better hustle. You don't want to get him angry."

Getting out of bed, Drew pulled his football shirt off and changed into a sweatshirt. He went to the bathroom, dressed quickly, and ran outside. Parked in the driveway, motor idling, Coach Matthews stared through the windshield. Drew got in, and remembering that everyone in the house was still sleeping, he closed the door quietly. When the car backed down the driveway, Drew looked up and saw Shane standing at the bedroom window.

"It'll be hard at first," Coach Matthews said without taking his eyes off the road. "The hardest thing may be waking up every morning."

Coach Matthews drove the nearly empty road to Valley Forge Park and stopped the car opposite the Memorial Arch. They stepped outside, and after he showed Drew how to stretch, they walked to the jogging path. Coach Matthews took off running, and Drew sprinted to catch up.

The sprint lasted a few minutes, and Drew struggled to find his breath. Holding onto his side and jogging slowly now, he pushed himself to keep moving and stay within sight of Coach Matthews. But the coach's figure got more and more distant and then disappeared completely around the bend of the jogging path.

After ten minutes of fighting the cramps in his legs and the mounting pain from a headache, Drew settled into a slow walk. He didn't know what to do when he discovered that the slightest movement sent spasms of pain through his body. Drew crested a small hill, heard a light stepping noise, and watched Coach Matthews race past him going in the opposite direction. Drew turned and stumbled down the hill. He didn't know how he made it back to the car.

When the second week of conditioning began, Drew was only sure of one thing. He was either going to survive or die somewhere in the park. The act of running only created pain in every part of his body. And it wasn't really running. At first, he grabbed his side and had to stop every few minutes to rest. Then, glassy eyed and sweating, he began to walk. Coach Matthews never slowed his pace so Drew could catch up. Usually he waited for Drew at the halfway point.

Sitting on the bench opposite the Washington Memorial Chapel, Coach Matthews looked impatient, and then when Drew reached the bench, Coach Matthews got up and began running back to the car. Drew was left at the bench, bent over and panting, his mouth dry and parched. He forced his legs to move forward, and he was always amazed he finished the jog. Although not steep, the hill before the parking lot was a very painful experience.

"It's murder," Drew said, sliding into the car, catching his breath at the same time. "I hate that hill."

"Mount Joy," Homer said, driving the car out of the parking lot. "You'll get used to it."

"No way is that Mount Joy," Drew said. Feeling the burn in his legs and the gnawing emptiness in his stomach, Drew sat back in the seat and looked through the window at the steep slant of the jogging path.

"Mount Hell would be a better name," he said seriously.

By the middle of the second week, Drew began to feel more comfortable running, and he also was able to pay more attention to his surroundings. Mad Anthony Wayne's statue was what Coach Matthews called the first landmark on the run. They ran past rows of cannons, the rugged log cabins built for General Conway's Pennsylvania regiment, and then past the most impressive statue, Coach Matthews said, in all of Valley Forge.

In regal military uniform, right hand folded across his chest surveying the expanse of empty Grand Parade ground in front of him, Baron von Steuben stood on a white granite pedestal. For some reason, Coach Matthews always saluted him. This was the first time that Drew was close enough to see him do it.

When Drew got back to the Memorial Arch, Coach Matthews was standing by the car. He gave Drew a thermos, and Drew took a long drink of ice water. The cold morning air and the ice water were refreshing to Drew. He gave the thermos back to Coach Matthews.

"I have a question, Coach. Why do you always slow down and salute that statue?"

"Baron von Steuben, he's one of my heroes," Coach Matthews said.

"Why's that?"

"The baron left a good life in Prussia, and he came to America to help train Washington's army. And he was a volunteer. He did it for free. The baron actually stood there on the Grand Parade ground in freezing weather and drilled and marched the army into shape. The men didn't have shelter, enough food, and uniforms, but they knew how to load a musket and march in proper formation."

"Why make soldiers march when they're hungry and cold?" Drew asked.

"It occupied them, gave them discipline," Coach Matthews said. "It also kept them from freezing to death." He took a drink of water and offered the thermos to Drew. Drew shook his head. "It's the same job I have. Occupying students like you."

"Just occupying people," Drew said. "How is that important?"

"When you occupy people and give them the right skills to survive, it makes a big difference. Von Steuben did it with the soldiers in a war. And it was the war that gave us our freedom. That's why I salute him."

"Why occupy me? I'm no soldier," Drew said. "I'm not fighting any war."

"Maybe you are, Drew. Maybe you're fighting a war and just don't know it." Homer opened the car door and got inside. "I think you'll have to get tough fast, Drew."

"Why?"

"Because there are always casualties in a war," Homer said. "You don't want to be one of them." He started the engine and began the drive back to Phoenixville.

After that talk about war and statues, Drew always kept his eye on the baron when he ran past. But what caught Drew's attention more than anything, preventing even a second of boredom, was the quantity and variety of wildlife in the park. There were always squirrels, raccoons, and all kinds of birds.

But mostly, there were deer. There were herds of deer. The animals milled around, sometimes standing stationary, sometimes bending to eat grass. Towering bucks with huge antlers grazed with the doe. Drew eyed them cautiously on his run. Sometimes, he turned and looked back to see if one was after him. But they were never startled. They were never bothered by the running movements of Drew and Coach Matthews.

At the end of that second week, Drew wasn't very far behind Coach Matthews. He saw Coach waiting for him at the bench, but Drew didn't slow down and stop as he usually did. Instead, he waved his hand for Coach to follow him. A short distance past the Washington Memorial Chapel, he stopped and waited for Coach Matthews.

"What is it, Drew?" Coach Matthews asked.

"Over here," Drew said. He led Coach Matthews to a lone piece of artillery. The black barrel of the cannon pointed across a hilly stretch of grass. Drew sat down next to the large spiked wheel and crossed his legs. Coach Williams sat next to him.

"Are we resting?" Coach Matthews asked. Drew shook his head.

"Look here," Drew said. He reached out and touched a thin silver band that was twisted around the bottom spoke of the wheel. "This is where our car hit. I put the band here after the funeral. It's my special memorial for my mom and dad." Coach Matthews looked at the flash of silver around the dark metal of the cannon wheel. He reached over and touched it.

"It takes a brave person to talk about this," Coach Matthews said. "Thank you for showing me." Coach Matthews removed his hand from the silver band and stood up. "Drew, no matter how hard it is, you should talk about things that bother you."

"With whom?" Drew asked, getting to his feet.

"With me," Coach Matthews said. "With Shane, with the Colliers. It will help us understand. It's not good to keep heavy things locked up inside. They just get heavier. And besides." With a smile forming on his face, Coach Matthews looked at Drew.

"What?" Drew asked.

"If you have all that extra weight inside, you'll never be a fast runner. You'll never be able to beat me."

Coach Matthews laughed and took off down the path. Drew tried hard to catch up. As they neared the parked car at the Memorial Arch, Drew was only a few steps behind the coach. He saw a herd of seven deer grazing off the side of the track. Running with a smooth stride, Drew laughed loudly at them and watched their heads jerk up. Drew stopped at the car. He exchanged glances with Coach Matthews, and they both silently acknowledged to each other that maybe Drew had lost some weight.

After the third week of conditioning, Drew woke up early and was on the porch waiting for Coach Matthews. He looked forward to the run. His body was stronger, and his lungs thrived on the cold morning air. He began to keep pace and ran step for step with Coach Matthews. Then on that one Friday, breathing smoothly and his body so relaxed, Drew felt the strength in his legs and had the sudden urge for speed.

Drew and Coach Matthews crossed into the shadow of von Steuben, and when Coach Matthew's lifted his hand to salute, Drew sprinted into the sunlight and kept going. The change of pace was exhilarating, and after a few minutes, he didn't hear any footsteps behind him.

Drew reached the Washington Memorial Chapel, stretched out comfortably on the bench, and waited for Coach Matthews. The coach didn't say anything when he approached the bench. He just turned around and started on his way back. In the car ride back to the house, Coach Matthews turned his head slightly so he could see Drew.

"How did it feel?" he asked.

"What?"

"Beating me for the first time."

"Were you trying?" Drew asked. "I mean was that your best speed?"

"That was as fast as I could run."

"It felt good," Drew said. A school bus pulled out in front of them, and Coach Matthews slowed down. "Thanks, Coach."

"For what?"

"For occupying me. I never knew I could run that fast and enjoy it," Drew said. "It's like a whole new world."

"It's only a start, Drew," Homer said. "I know you surprised me. You probably even surprised yourself. You're going to surprise a whole lot of people before you're through."

Later that month, Drew found out that he wasn't going to surprise anyone on the football team. After weeks of practices and two games, he knew that his only use to the team was as a target. In every drill in practice, the bigger players flattened him. He was even knocked around by the smaller players on the team.

In the one game he got in, the Patriots were winning 36 to 7. It was the fourth quarter, and Coach Matthews told him to go in on the kick-off team. The other coaches were shaking their heads when Drew went on the field.

Crouched down in an awkward stance, Drew was positioned next to the kicker. The whistle blew, and Drew saw the ball go spinning down the field. Drew took off, his eyes on the ball, a gyrating, bloated piece of leather in a cold gray sky. He crossed midfield and was still watching the ball when a big body plowed into him from the side. The impact was so hard that the helmet somehow twisted sideways on Drew's head and stuck there, shutting out the light and his vision.

Drew hit the ground hard and found he had a difficult time breathing. Everything was black and wet, and Drew became alarmed when he slid his hand across the side of the helmet and felt his nose protruding through the earpiece. He heard a muffled whistle blowing from somewhere. Drew struggled to get up and fell backward.

There were some funny comments and laughter as more players from both teams gathered around him. Then hands reached down, grabbed the facemask, and twisted the helmet back into place. Drew felt his nose fill up with liquid, and when he touched it, he saw his hand was covered with blood. More players gathered around and began laughing. Shane growled something, and seeing the anger on his face, the players stopped the ridicule and helped Shane lift Drew off the ground.

Drew's infatuation with May ended in the same kind of failure. The failure this time was total and much worse than any bloody nose. One evening, Drew was surprised and excited to see May walk in the house with Shane. At dinner, with May sitting next to him, Drew was nervous and couldn't speak and barely touched his food. After they finished eating and the dishes were cleared, May and Shane went into the living room to study. They slid the door shut and were in there a long time.

The Colliers went to sleep, and the door was still closed. Drew was watching from the top of the steps when the door opened and Shane and May stepped out on the porch. Shane bent over May, and they began some kind of deep kissing. They were still kissing when May's older brother drove up to take her home. As the car door shut, Drew ran inside the bedroom. He jumped on the bed and covered himself with the sheets.

Drew didn't talk much at breakfast. He and Shane walked to the bus, and sitting together on the ride to the school, Shane made several attempts to start a conversation. Drew stared at the frizzled end of the ponytail on the head of the girl in front of him and was silent. He was in a daze most of the day. He didn't care about anything.

At football practice, all the coaches yelled at Drew for his lack of effort. During a break, Coach Matthews tried to talk to him, but Drew just drank from the water bottle and stared past him. Toward the end of practice, Drew found himself in the middle of the brutal circle drill. Players charged from different angles and knocked him down. One big linebacker knocked him out of the circle. Coach Matthews watched Drew try to get up and then blew the whistle to end practice. Shane ran over and offered his hand to Drew, but Drew ignored it.

"I don't need your help," Drew said. He pushed both fists in the dirt and struggled to his feet. Holding the bruised muscles in his side, Drew limped slowly to the car where Mr. Collier was waiting. Shaking his head, Shane followed a few steps behind.

That night, Drew went to bed early, and within minutes, the darkness of the nightmare began to smother him. There was the same shadow of the hill, flash of lightning, and ghostly apparition. But nothing was the same inside the car. May's face, not his mom's, appeared in front of him. Drew screamed in terror and woke before the Christmas music started.

On Saturday morning, usually a fun time for the whole family, Drew was distant and uncommunicative to everyone. He wanted to be alone. He wandered around for a long time and ended up on the bridge over the Schuylkill River. He walked down to the river and sat on the bank in the shadows of the bridge. It was a colorful fall day. The bright, flowing water reflected the blue sky and the red and yellow leaves of the trees along the bank. A boat with two noisy fishermen drifted by. They stopped fishing and began drinking beer. The younger man in a straw hat drank from his bottle and looked across the water at Drew.

"Hey, Fag!" he shouted. "What the fuck do you think you're doing under my bridge?"

Drew didn't say anything. He studied their faces for a moment, and then he raised his right hand slowly and gave them the finger.

"Fuck you!" the younger fisherman shouted and threw the bottle at Drew.

Spinning through the air, spraying beer on Drew's jacket, the bottle flew over his head and shattered against the cement pier. Drew looked at the spots on his jacket, and raising his left hand parallel to the right, he gave the fishermen two emphatic fingers.

"You bastard!" the older fisherman shouted. Standing up directly in front of his friend, he rocked the boat, steadied himself, and threw his half-empty bottle at Drew. It landed in the shallow water at Drew's feet and sank. Listening to their laughter and incomprehensible profanity, Drew watched the stream of bubbles breaking the surface. When the bottle was filled with river water, Drew picked it up.

"Hey!" he shouted, getting to his feet. "These are returnable!"

Drew stepped back and hurled the bottle towards the boat. The older man sat down quickly, and the bottle hit his friend squarely and solidly in the straw hat and ricocheted into the river. Holding his head and leaning awkwardly, he grabbed for the shoulder of the older man, missed badly, and fell over the side of the boat. After the initial splash and wild beating of arms, the man stood up in the waist-deep river.

Drew watched the straw hat spin in the current and drift downriver. Listening to more profanity and how they were "gonna fuck him up" if they ever saw him again, Drew brushed a chunk of mud from his jeans, climbed up to the road, and began a slow, circuitous walk back to the house. Sitting on the porch steps when he got there, Shane held his nose and told him to stop drinking during the day. Drew ignored him.

During dinner that evening, Shane talked about the movie, *Lawrence of Arabia*, he and May were going to see. He said it was a long movie and that he might be home later than usual. Sitting on his bed after dinner, Drew was pretending to read a magazine, but from the side, he watched Shane put on his most expensive shirt and spray himself with cologne. Shane said something to Drew and was whistling when he left the room.

It was late when Shane returned. Lying in bed, Drew heard the water running and Shane brushing his teeth, and then the lights switched off in the bathroom. There was the sound of his footsteps going across the room and the bedsprings creaking under Shane's weight. Everything became very still in the room. The only thing Drew heard was the slight, soft sound of his own breathing.

"Drew," Shane called from across the room. "Drew, are you awake?"

Drew didn't answer. He stayed motionless under the sheets. The bed creaked again, and Shane walked across the room. He began shaking Drew by the shoulders.

"Drew, wake up."

"I'm up," Drew said, wiping his eyes.

"What's wrong, Drew?" Shane asked, sitting on the end of the bed.

"Nothing."

"Something's wrong," Shane said. "I noticed it right away. Mom and Dad noticed it. You had a nightmare for the first time in weeks. Something is really bothering you. What is it, Drew?"

"You wouldn't understand," Drew said. He sat up in bed, crossing his legs in front of him.

"Try me," Shane said. "I'm your friend."

"My friend," Drew said. He felt the tears welling in his eyes, but he couldn't stop them. He lifted his head and focused his gaze right at Shane. He tried to find the words, but nothing happened.

"What is it, Drew?"

"You have everything," Drew began slowly. "You're popular. Everyone in the school looks up to you. You're strong. You're the best athlete in the school." Drew wiped his face and was silent

"What does that have to do with anything?"

"All the girls love you," Drew said. "You can have any one you want."

"You're not making any sense, Drew. None of that concerns you."

"May concerns me," Drew said.

"This is about May?" Shane asked. "All this is about May?"

"Yes," Drew said. "It's about May. I can't stop thinking about her. I even dream about her."

"I didn't know," Shane said. "May and I met after the last football game. She never said anything about you."

"Because she never sees me. She doesn't know I exist," Drew said. He hesitated, trying to find the words to explain. "Maybe it sounds crazy. But I really love her. Sure, it's like from a distance, maybe a hundred miles away. But I still love her. Can you understand any of that?"

"We just started dating," Shane said. "But, sure, I understand. I have a strong feeling for May, too. I mentioned the word love to her on the way home tonight."

"Then that's it," Drew said. "I don't have a chance."

"There are always chances," Shane said. "May's older. She's in the eighth grade. There are pretty girls in the seventh grade. Haven't you seen anyone you like?"

"A few," Drew said. "But not like May. None of the girls look like her. I guess that's why I feel this way."

"There are more important reasons to love someone," Shane said. "I can help you find a girl."

"No," Drew said. "I'll manage."

"I'm sorry about this, Drew. I really am," Shane said. "I don't think there's anything I can do." Shane looked carefully at Drew. "Are we still friends?"

"I guess so," Drew said. They shook hands.

"There's the perfect girl out there, Drew. I'm going to keep my eyes open." Shane got up and walked across the room to his bed.

During school lunch that Monday, Drew was sitting alone at the end of the cafeteria table. He noticed movement and looked up and saw May. Actually, he didn't really see May. He saw her short skirt and legs and knew it was May. She sat across from him and opened her lunch bag. This was the first time Drew saw her up close, and she looked even more beautiful. He could smell some kind of perfume, sweet and rosy and fresh.

"I made this for you," she said. May took a sandwich out of her lunch bag and unwrapped the tin foil.

"For me?" Drew asked. He hesitated.

"Please, it's for you," May said, and she held the sandwich in front of Drew.

"Thank you," Drew said, taking the sandwich. It was warm and soft in his hand and a thick brown liquid squeezed over the side. He looked at May, and she nodded her head.

"Try it."

Drew took a bite. The sandwich melted in his mouth. He tried to put the mixture of tastes together in his mind and identify the ingredients, but instead, he took another bite. Then with another bite, he finished the sandwich.

"It was delicious," he said. "What was in it?"

"A very special recipe," May said. "Do you want to know what it is? I'll tell you if you keep it a secret."

"I won't tell anyone," Drew promised. Leaning across the table, he maneuvered his body forward and got to within inches of her face. Taking in the secret words from her lips, the warmth of her breath, and still savoring the sweet taste of the sandwich, Drew sat there transfixed in wonder.

"Of course," she said, "I begin with fresh, homemade bread. I spread a thick layer of Pennsylvania Dutch butter on the bread. Then I put on this great-tasting Dutch peanut butter and sprinkle cinnamon over it. I put the honey on last. It's a special Dutch honey made from the queen bee. I keep the sandwich in the tin foil so it stays fresh."

"It tasted great," Drew said, staring at the moist redness of her lips.

"Since you ate my sandwich, can I have yours?" May asked.

"Sure," Drew said. He reached in his lunch bag and gave her the grilled cheese sandwich. After she finished it, he watched her wipe the crumbs from her lips. She took a drink of milk.

"A little dry, but not bad," she said.

"Yours melted in my mouth like candy," Drew said. "I won't drink anything the rest of the day. I don't want the taste to go away."

"Every Friday, I make this sandwich for lunch," May said. "Why don't I make you one too? We can share like we did today. It'll be like a date."

"Great," Drew said, not believing what he heard. "That would be simply great."

"Then it's a deal?" May said. She reached across the table to shake his hand. "Your sandwich for my sandwich."

"It's a deal," Drew repeated.

"And Drew," May said. She still held his hand. "You know that Shane and I are seeing each other. We just get along so well together. He says he loves me."

"Do you love him?" Drew asked.

"I really like him," May said. "Shane's a very special person. Maybe I do love him."

"Then why all this fresh bread and honey stuff?' Drew asked.

"It's not about bread and honey," May said. She smiled and placed her other hand over his. "It's about us. It's important to me that you and I be friends. I want us all to be friends. Can we do that?"

"You and Shane, my friends? I don't know," Drew said. He thought about the idea for a moment, and then his eyes opened wide. "You'll still bring me a sandwich every Friday?"

"Of course."

"You won't make any for Shane?"

"No, just for you."

"I can do that," Drew said. He looked at her face, the beauty of her smile, and had a hard time releasing her hand. The bell rang, and they got up from the table.

"I'll be with Shane at the house a lot," May said. "Will that bother you?"

"No," Drew said. "I'll look forward to seeing you. I'll look forward to seeing both of you." The sweet taste of the cinnamon and honey still in his mouth, Drew threw his bag in the garbage can by the door and walked with May down the hall.

Later that week, after Mr. and Mrs. Collier had gone to bed, Drew and Shane were watching a baseball movie on TV. It was *Bang the Drum Slowly*. When the catcher played by Robert DeNiro died and the mournful ballad *Streets of Laredo* sounded on the screen, Drew began to feel really bad. He felt moisture in his eyes, and tears began forming on his cheeks.

> We beat the drum slowly and played the Fife lowly,
> Played the dead march as we carried him along.
> Down in the green valley, laid the sod o'er him.
> He was a young cowboy and he said he'd done wrong.

"Drew," Shane said, staring at him.

"What?"

"Stop being so emotional," Shane said. "You break down over everything."

"He just died," Drew said, wiping his eyes. "I mean he was a great guy, and he just died."

"It's only a story," Shane said. "DeNiro's still alive. You can't let these things get to you like that. And it's not just the movie. Sometimes you still cry at night."

"I'm sorry," Drew said.

"Forget sorry," Shane said. "It doesn't help any more. Yesterday, Mrs. Jablonski's dog, Tipsy, was hit by a car. You were devastated."

"I fed him every day," Drew said. "And his name was Tippy."

"The name's not important," Shane said. "You came in the house crying over a dog."

"It was sad. She loved that dog."

"Sure, losing your pet is sad. But I'm telling you, Drew. You cry too much. When things like this happen, you have to be strong. I'm tired of seeing you cry over anything."

"Yeah, like you're so tough you never cry."

"One time," Shane said. "I cried one time. And it doesn't help. Sometimes, it makes things worse. I want you to stop it."

"And if I don't?"

"Then I'll give you something to cry about," Shane said. He got up and towered over Drew. "I'll punch you into next week."

"Oh, yeah!" Drew lifted his hands in defense.

"Yeah," Shane said and jumped at Drew. "I'll punch you so far in the future you'll forget what you were crying about!"

"Oh, yeah!" Drew shouted again, laughing at the idea.

"Yeah, that's right," Shane said and began to pummel Drew on the shoulders and chest. Drew deflected the first series of punches, but one bounced off his bottom rib, and Drew stopped laughing.

"All right," he said, putting up his hands. "I won't cry any more."

"Promise."

"I promise," Drew said. "You can punch me like you said into next week if you ever see me cry again."

"I will," Shane said. "You know I will." He grabbed Drew by the arm and pulled him from the couch. They went to the kitchen and drank some milk and shared a sandwich. It was after eleven o'clock when they went upstairs to the bedroom. Drew was in bed only a few minutes when he sat straight up and looked across the room.

"Shane?"

"What?"

"Do you know what I think?

"About what?"

"DeNiro," Drew said. "I think when an actor is killed in a movie, that should be it for him."

"What do you mean?"

"He shouldn't be in any more movies. That's what I mean."

"Why, Drew?"

"Because he's dead."

"OK, Drew, I think I understand. If he's really dead, I mean never coming back, then you could watch these movies and cry and wouldn't feel so stupid. Is that it?"

"Yeah, Shane. That's about it."

"Go to sleep, Drew." Shane turned on his side and pulled the sheet up to his neck. "I'm still going to punch you into next week, maybe even next year, if I see you crying like that again."

"Don't worry," Drew said, falling back into the bed. "I made a promise, Shane. And I keep my promises."

CHAPTER 3

Professor Jack Jefferson taught history at George Washington Junior-Senior High School. He was the only faculty member with a Ph. D. After receiving his bachelor's, master's, and doctorate at Villanova University, Professor Jackson taught at the university for forty-five years. He was an expert on Ben Franklin and the colonial period of American history. Professor Jackson retired from Villanova in 1959, but after one year of quiet inactivity, he was encouraged by his wife to get a job. In 1960, he sent his application to George Washington School District, and after a cursory interview by the superintendent, he was hired immediately.

Professor Jefferson was very relaxed, very precise with his class time, and had a sparkling sense of humor. Since he was assigned mostly academic classes, he found the adjustment to high school education was not a problem. On most days, it was a very exhilarating experience for everyone. The students accepted him and appreciated how much he taught them about the history of Valley Forge and Philadelphia.

The seventh-grade projects for American history class were due in April that year. Drew did his on Ben Franklin and went around quoting from *Poor Richard's Almanac* the whole month. When Shane asked him for a quarter to buy soda after school, Drew reached into his pocket and then changed his mind.

"Where's all your money?" Drew asked.

"I bet Gary I had a better grade than him on the math test," Shane said. "He got an 81, and I had a 79. So now I'm broke."

"A fool and his money are soon parted," Drew said. "Poor Richard wrote that two hundred years ago."

"What's with all this Ben Franklin stuff?" Shane asked.

"Professor JJ said Ben was the first American genius. He was a scientist, inventor, architect, writer, and our greatest diplomat."

"Is that all?"

"He signed the Declaration of Independence. He was our first postmaster. He set up our first hospital and first university." Drew looked over Shane's head at the fire extinguisher reset in the wall. "He organized our first fire department. He did all this, and he only finished second grade."

"Great, you have five more years of education than Ben," Shane said. "What about the quarter?"

"If you'd know the value of money, go and borrow some," Drew quoted from *Poor Richard's Almanac* again.

"I have a quote for you, Drew. Listen to it closely. This is from *Poor Shane's Almanac*." Lifting his fist in the air, he moved around and positioned himself directly in front of Drew. "A big fat lip makes it difficult for a little smartass to speak clearly."

"Here," Drew said, giving Shane the money.

"Poor Richard isn't as dumb as he looks," Shane said. He walked over to the soda machine at the end of the hall, put the quarter in the slot, and pulled out an A&W Root Beer. When he returned, he had already emptied the can.

"What did Professor JJ give you on your history project?" Drew asked.

"C+," Shane said. "On my topographical map of Valley Forge, I had Washington's Headquarters and the Washington Memorial Chapel mislabeled, or else I would have had an A. When are you giving your project?"

"I have to wait for the right conditions," Drew said. "The weather's important."

"Why?"

"I need some clouds and bad weather," Drew said. "I'm doing Ben's kite experiment."

"And Professor JJ approved that?"

"He sure did," Drew said. "You don't want to miss this experiment, Shane. I've put a lot of thought into it."

It was cloudy the next day. By noon, the wind had picked up. At the beginning of history class, Drew asked Professor JJ if he could present his project. Professor JJ walked over to the window and looked outside. Overhead, the sky was gray, and there were dark clouds in the distance. Even though it wasn't raining, Professor JJ told the students to get their umbrellas and raincoats and prepare to go outside.

The class followed Professor JJ and Drew across the parking lot and down to the football field. Drew was carrying a magnificent blue-and-white painted kite. It was man-sized, at least six feet tall and four feet wide at the cross sticks. Thirteen large silver tinsel stars were epoxied across the center of the kite. Sliding along the grass, the tail of the kite was a section of cloth Drew had cut from Shane's bed sheet. Tied to the end of this cloth was a silver key. At times, the wind caught the kite, and it flapped loudly in his hands.

As the group of students congregated at the fifty-yard line, Drew walked over to Gary Evans. Gary was draped with a full-length black raincoat. Both his hands were buried inside, and the empty sleeves of the raincoat flapped in the wind. Drew whispered something to Gary and walked to Professor JJ waiting with his grade book in the middle of the circle of students.

"What did you name your kite?" Professor JJ asked.

"I don't know," Drew said. "I didn't think about it."

"Every kite should have a name before it leaves the planet, Drew. And I need a name for your project."

"OK," Drew said. He looked at the kite and the shiny, silver stars. "I know. The kite is called the **Flying Patriot**." The wind blew harder, and dark mushroom clouds moved slowly toward the school.

"The **Flying Patriot**," Professor JJ said. "That's a good name." He opened his grade book and began writing.

A gust of wind lifted Drew's kite in the air, and he moved quickly to keep it on the ground. Straightening, he saw Frank West Jr. and two friends coming down the field. Frank Jr. was short and thin, and unlike the other boys in his class, he had the dark shadow of a mustache under his flat nose.

Drew and the entire school population knew the principal's son was nothing but trouble. Frank Jr. did whatever he wanted at the school, and the teachers, unless it was a life-threatening situation, had learned to ignore him. They got the message when the art teacher Mrs. Wilson wrote a discipline notice on Frank Jr. for drawing a large penis in the mouth of the *Mona Lisa* in his art book. The next week Mrs. Wilson received an unsatisfactory rating on her class observation.

"You fuckin' nerd," Frank Jr. said, bumping his shoulder roughly into Drew. Frank's two friends began to laugh. Protecting the kite, Drew stepped back. A strong wind blew across the field, and he felt the light spatter of raindrops on his face.

"Hurry up, Drew," Professor JJ said.

The wind was blowing steadily down the length of the field. A sudden gust caught Drew by surprise, and he turned to see a small rip in the side of the kite. Pulling it closer to his body, Drew ran quickly to the end zone. He positioned himself at the side of the goal post, held the kite by the centerpiece, and began to slowly let out the string.

Working alone early that morning, Drew had coiled a thin wire along the length of the string. When he was sure it was tight and difficult to see, he attached the wire to the center cross sticks of the kite. Then using super glue, he pasted a gunpowder and phosphorus mixture on the surface of both cross sticks. Hidden by the long sleeve of his shirt, the other end of the wire was connected to a small transformer taped inside the palm of his hand.

There was a slight crack of thunder from the park, and Drew let out more line and began to run. The *Flying Patriot* lifted straight in the air, swayed back and forth, and then soared directly over his head. Drew released the wired line quickly and ran faster toward Professor JJ and the group of students. White stars shimmering in the light, the kite flapped bravely in the darkening sky, and the sound of the student's cheers began to drift down the field.

Drew raced closer and saw Professor JJ, Shane, Frank Jr., and the large group of students standing at the fifty-yard line. The black-draped figure of Gary stood tall behind them. Everyone was looking at the kite. Caught by a sudden draft of wind, the *Flying Patriot* did a complete loop, thirteen stars spinning brightly, and righted itself. There were more cheers, and some of the students began clapping their hands.

Sweating and catching his breath, Drew reached the forty-yard line. A thin, jagged line of lightning cracked down from the clouds over the park. The thunder was a low, distant roar, but Drew could see the concern on Professor JJ's face. Luckily for his plan, the next lightning flash immediately followed the first, and raising his left hand high in the air to signal Gary, Drew pressed the switch in his palm. There was a spark and a surge of power spiraled up the thin wire coiled around the string.

Almost instantly, the phosphorous and powder on the cross sticks of the kite burst into a bright, radiating flame, and to cheers and loud applause, the *Flying Patriot* was momentarily aglow with a fiery brilliance before it came spiraling down toward the group of students.

At the same time the kite burst into flames, Gary threw open his raincoat, lifted two cymbals high in the air, and cracked them together violently. Originating in the midst of the group of students, the explosion of noise was intense, earsplitting, earth shattering. The thunderous echo was immediately followed by spontaneous, genuine panic. There was loud screaming and a scattering of bodies in all directions. Standing there alone, the folds of the black raincoat closed tightly, Gary was stunned.

Soaring above the hysteria on the ground, the burning kite plunged toward the fifty-yard line. Behind the *Flying Patriot* and released by the flames, the silver stars glittered brightly and seemed to float and dive in the air. Holding the line in his hand, Drew turned and looked at the riot of movement.

Only Professor JJ, Frank Jr., and Shane were left in the middle of the football field. Standing behind them, Gary Evans turned and began running toward the sideline. A gust of wind propelled the *Flying Patriot*, spitting flames in all directions, toward the compact group of three.

Professor JJ dropped to his knees and then fell flat on his face. His mouth still open in bewilderment, Frank Jr. cowered and threw his hands up to protect himself from the burning kite. Then shouting some profanity, he lowered one hand and tried to cover the stain appearing on his trousers.

Watching the burning outline of the kite with the trace of a smile on his face, Shane stood motionless in the mayhem. The **Flying Patriot** made a crazy loop, flew directly over Frank Jr., missing his head by inches, and crashed in a wreck of smoke and flame at Shane's feet.

It began to drizzle, and sparks hissed from the kite. Shane hesitated for a moment, and stepping closer, he began to stomp the debris of wood, smoldering cloth, and black powder into the ground. Soon the only thing left of the **Flying Patriot** was a thin line of smoke rising from the tail, a few twisted pieces of silver tinsel, and the blackened key.

Within minutes, the head custodian Anthony Bartoli, the guidance counselor, a very-agitated Mr. Higgins, and the school nurse Barbara Adams ran down the hill. Shouting loudly to the few people still on the football field, Barbara announced that an ambulance was on the way. Visibly shaken by the disaster, Mr. Higgins gave comfort to Professor JJ, who for some inexplicable reason was laughing.

Mr. West suddenly appeared and saw his son standing there. Frank Jr. was in some kind of shock and unresponsive to the principal's questions. The wet stain on Frank's khaki trousers now reached below his knee. After another crack of thunder hit the field, the principal grabbed his son by the arm and quickly ushered him up the hill to the school.

When the ambulance and fire truck arrived, sirens blaring the length of the field, two attendants jumped out, and even though Professor JJ, a wide smile on his face, was still laughing and trying to communicate to everyone that he was unharmed, they strapped the confused professor in a gurney, lifted him into the back of the ambulance, and drove away. Rumors spread quickly through the community, and parents rushed to the school to pick up their kids. The buses came an hour early, and the school emptied.

Because of the confusion in the stampede of students, no one had a clear picture of what had happened. Drew was grilled by the police chief, fire chief, and a furious Principal West for twenty minutes. He was the last one to leave the building. Shane was waiting for him on the school steps. They began walking down the sidewalk together.

"I saw Gary after the ambulance left," Shane said. "He was pretty worried. Why didn't you tell me about this?"

"I wanted to see what you would do."

"Was it some kind of test?"

"Yes," Drew said. "There are different reactions to fear. But today I don't understand what was so scary. It was only a burning kite. And yet look how everyone was terrified. Professor JJ collapsed on his face. Frank Jr. stood there screaming and he kept pissing his pants."

"You should be proud, Drew. You created a lot of excitement."

"Yeah, but I almost killed one person. And I humiliated another."

"That was only Frank Jr.," Shane said.

"What about the fire chief and police chief? You should have seen how angry they were. I think they wanted to arrest someone." Drew pulled the mix of wire, the kite remnants, and key from his pocket. At the corner, he stopped and dropped everything but the key into the sewer drain. Straightening up and slapping the black powder off his hands, he put the key in his pocket and turned to Shane.

"All the other students ran like hell. You just stood there, Shane. Weren't you frightened?"

"No."

"You're tougher than I thought."

"I probably am," Shane said. He and Drew began walking down the street. "But I think I had an advantage."

"What kind of advantage?"

"I was watching the kite. What did you call it, the **Flying Patriot**? Sure, it was burning. That was cool. But I wasn't paying much attention. And I didn't hear the loud bang of thunder from Gary. I had these stuffed in my ears." Shane reached into his pocket and removed the earplugs. "I was pretending to be Johnny Cash and singing *Ring of fire*. May and I really love that song."

"Then you missed everything!" Drew said.

"No, I saw the show. I just didn't hear anything." Shane said, a smile on his face. "I always thought you were a genius, but this was greater than anything you've ever done. I was humming and singing and watching your **Flying Patriot** swinging these crazy circles in the sky and then suddenly, poof! Right when I'm singing 'I stood in a burning ring of fire', the kite explodes in fire, takes a few perfect loops, and comes crashing down right at my feet. And all those falling stars in the sky! That was pure genius. It was better than the Fourth of July. You and Ben really put on a good show."

"I hope Mom and Dad don't hear about it," Drew said.

"Principal West will call them," Shane said. "But don't worry. I was there. I saw the whole thing. I'll tell them that something strange happened to the kite, and it crashed harmlessly to the ground."

"Thanks," Drew said. They reached the house and climbed up the steps. "I hope Professor JJ's all right."

"He'll be fine," Shane said. "But I don't know about Frank Jr. He really gets crazy sometimes. You watch out for him."

"I will," Drew said. He pushed open the door, and they walked inside. The dinner table was already set, and after washing, they both sat down to dishes full of roast beef, gravy, and French fries. Throughout the dinner, Mr. and Mrs. Collier questioned Shane and Drew about the accident at the school. Drew was silent and never looked up from his plate, but Shane said it was nothing serious.

"Nothing at all," he said. "Just a fast-moving storm that caught everyone by surprise."

The next day, there was a substitute teacher for Professor JJ. After lunch, Drew snuck out the side door, cut across the baseball field, and disappeared in the trees. He was absent from history class, but the substitute was confused with the attendance sheet and counted him as present. Drew got back in the building just as the bell rang to change classes. Seeing Shane down the hall, he ran to catch up.

"Where were you?" Shane asked.

"I was worried about Professor JJ," Drew said. "I went to his house. His wife let me in. She was very kind and appreciative that I came to see him. I told them both I was sorry about the accident."

"How was he?"

"He looked good," Drew said. "His eyes were wide open. He had this huge smile on his face."

"Imagine that," Shane said. "The professor was happy after you tried to kill him."

"I don't think I would call him happy," Drew said. "His wife explained that he had the same smile the whole time in the emergency room, and when they came home, he was still smiling. She said he can't seem to close his mouth. All that excitement somehow froze his facial muscles. The doctor scheduled an appointment with a physical therapist."

"That's terrible," Shane said. "What about your grade?"

"JJ told me it was an impressive project, one that he would never forget. He was smiling all the time, and I began to smile, too. Then he said he wasn't sure what blowing up a kite, burning an American flag, and endangering the whole class had to do with history. That's when I stopped smiling."

"What'd you do?" Shane asked.

"At first I was stuck. I couldn't think of anything to say because Professor JJ was one hundred percent right as he always is. I thought quickly and told Professor JJ that I would keep trying, spend more time, and plan the next experiment better. Then I quoted Ben Franklin. I told Professor JJ 'The masterpiece of man is to live to the purpose.' When he heard this, I didn't believe it, but his smile got bigger. It seemed to fill the whole bottom half of his face."

The bell rang, and Drew and Shane began to walk faster. They reached the classroom and got to their seats just as the teacher turned around from the blackboard. He had written a series of math problems on the board.

"Then he didn't flunk you?" Shane asked, opening his notebook.

"Professor JJ said Ben Franklin had failures too, but he was always looking forward to the next great experiment. And Ben always had a clear purpose to what he did, and like me, he had a good sense of humor. Then he added, 'Ben's life was his final masterpiece.' Professor JJ got quiet for a moment. I could tell he was thinking hard about something. When he looked up, he told me my grade was a 73."

"You got a D+," Shane said. "Mom and Dad will lock you in the room. They'll ground you forever."

"Let me finish. Professor JJ said mine was the most unique of all the projects, and that since I was worried about him and took the time to visit the house to see how he was, I deserved better than 73. Right in front of me, he opened his grade book and changed my grade to a 98."

"Drew, that's the highest grade in the class."

"I know," Drew said. "When I got ready to leave, Professor JJ shook my hand. It was difficult with his smile and everything, but he got very serious and thanked me for coming. Then he quoted Franklin again. He said, 'When you are good to others, you are best to yourself.'" Drew looked at the board and began working the equations in his head. "And he didn't even ask me how I got out of school."

"I'm going over there," Shane said. "I'll take him a get-well cake. I'll bake it myself. No, I'll get May to help."

The math teacher began making his way down the row. Drew quickly copied the last equation in his notebook. By the time the teacher had reached his desk, Drew was finished with all ten equations. He looked over at Shane's notebook and saw an elaborate design for a three-layer cake.

That Friday during lunch May finished eating the grilled cheese sandwich and got up to go to the restroom. Drew was enjoying his sandwich, the sweet taste of honey fresh in his mouth, when Frank Jr. and three of his golf friends approached the table. Frank Jr. was carrying a bowl of chili. He sat opposite Drew and placed the bowl on the table. The chili was hot, and steam vapor rose in the air. Pushing behind Drew, Frank's friends crowded against his shoulders and back.

"Kite nerd!" Frank shouted in Drew's face. "You're one stupid son of a bitch!"

Drew didn't say anything. He tried to move, but Frank's friends grabbed his arms and pressed his hands hard behind his back. The two students sitting across from Drew got up and moved to another table. Frank Jr. leaned closer. Staring through the rising steam of chili, Drew looked at his twisted red face, the uneven line of moustache, and the dark chew stains on the corners of his mouth.

"You stupid son of a bitch," Frank Jr. said again. He hit the table with his fist, rattling the bowl of chili. The blue T-shirt Frank was wearing had some kind of putting green on the front. Drew read **Hole in One** above the flag.

Both armpits were wet with perspiration. Drew watched Frank's thick lips open and curl into an oval shape. Then Frank spat something thick and brown into the chili.

Frank Jr. stood up and grabbed the bowl of chili. Holding him from behind, the golf boys twisted Drew's arms and lifted him to his feet. Frank Jr. reached across the table, unbuttoned Drew's jeans, and stretched them open at the waist. Tilting the bowl, he poured the chili down the opening. Drew grimaced at the sudden burning as the liquid slid down his stomach to his groin. Holding him and pinning his body against the table, Frank Jr. and his friends were laughing.

"Feel good?" Frank Jr. asked. "I hope your balls burn off." Frank Jr. put the empty bowl on the table, and laughing louder, his friends pushed Drew on the floor. They grouped together and walked gleefully down the aisle toward the exit.

Trying to ignore the pain, Drew grabbed onto the side of the table and pulled himself up. He felt humiliation and helplessness and then a sudden rage. He picked up the empty bowl and threw it at the walking figures. It sailed over Frank's head and bounced off the chest of the lunchroom monitor, Mr. Jenks, who was just entering the cafeteria.

Mr. Jenks looked at the wet stains on his white shirt, and flicking off some beans with his fingers, he charged past Frank Jr. and his gang. Shouting at Drew the whole time, he wrote up a discipline report and sent Drew to the principal's office.

Frank West Sr. was a short, heavy-set man in his mid-fifties. He had a black moustache and wore thick, dark-rimmed glasses. Sitting at his desk, Mr. West read the report carefully. Then he looked up at Drew.

"You smell like rotten beans, Benson," he said, a smirk on his face. "It's not a good idea to start a food fight in my cafeteria. You'll go right to detention, Benson, and I'm sorry, but there will be no restroom passes. You can sit in your own stink until the bell rings. I'll take you down myself to make sure there are no stops."

Mr. West Sr. got to his feet and led Drew out of the office and down the hall to the detention room. Six small cubicles lined the wall of the room. Mr. West pointed to the last one and left the room. Sitting in a large desk next to the door, the monitor, a thin substitute with light-tinted sunglasses, was reading the local newspaper and didn't look up. Then he smelled the strong odor of chili, put the paper down, and held his nose.

"Garbage man," he said and laughed as Drew walked past the desk.

Drew went to the last cubicle, sat straight in his chair, and began watching the large minute hand of the clock. It was excruciatingly painful to smell the chili, feel the wetness, and watch how slowly time moved in the sticky confines of the room. The minute hand remained forever stationary, and then it would jerk to the next number with a loud clicking sound. Drew sat watching the minute hand for two hours before the dismissal bell rang.

That evening, Drew was already in bed when Shane came in the room. He shuffled noisily across the floor and stood over the bed. Shane was quiet for a moment, and then he nudged Drew in the shoulder.

"I heard what happened at lunch."

"It was nothing," Drew said.

"It was nothing," Shane hissed the words. "I'll get him, Drew. I'll get that bastard. He'll never bother you again."

"No," Drew said, he leaned forward and looked directly at Shane. "Don't do anything."

"But, Drew."

"Forget it, Shane. If anything comes up in the future, I'll handle it. Now go to sleep." Drew dropped down into the bed and pulled the sheet over his chin.

Shane stared at the bed for a moment and then stepped back. He undressed quickly and got into bed. The moon was full and cast a bright glow of light through the window. Shane was restless and angry, and thinking about Drew and the incident in the cafeteria only made things worse. Lifting the sheet, he looked across the room at the quiet figure on the bed.

"I just want to hit him once," Shane said to the quiet stillness in the room.

"No." The reply was quick and final.

"Damn it," Shane said. He slid back under the sheet. "He's too big for you, Drew."

"I don't care how big he is," Drew said. "I can take care of myself."

"Damn it," Shane said again. Lifting his pillow in the air, he punched it a few times and threw it at Drew. When there was no response, Shane settled back in the bed. A cloud moved over the moon, slowing bringing darkness to the house.

CHAPTER 4

In November 1964, Valley Forge was hit with heavy snow and freezing temperatures. The snow was five inches deep the week before Thanksgiving. That Friday after school, the sky was clear when Homer Matthews drove Drew and Shane to his house. It was in a thick-wooded area on the edge of French Creek State Park.

Carrying a rifle in his hand, Homer led them down a path that opened into a long clearing surrounded by dark pine trees. At the far end of the clearing, there was a target, a brown buck with an enlarged head and massive antlers.

With the wind blowing hard and chilling the skin on his ears and nose, Drew stood next to Shane and Homer. Shane had been hunting for years and was an excellent marksman. For the last two years, Shane had tried to persuade Drew into going hunting with him on opening day. Saying it was too cold and miserable, which was how Drew felt now, he had declined the invitations.

"Drew, you're in ninth grade. It's way past time to learn how to shoot a gun," Homer said. "You can practice on that target."

Drew looked at the brown shape across the clearing. The swirling, frigid wind bent the tops of the trees and rattled dry leaves off the branches. The leaves drifted across the frozen ground, some of them forming jagged piles at the base of the target buck.

Drew stared at the buck's head. Two large, red-painted eyes seemed to meet his stare, and Drew felt the coldness travel down his neck into his hands and fingers.

"I don't know," Drew said. He put his trembling hands into his jacket. The wind blowing across the clearing subsided, and it suddenly became very quiet. The last flurry of leaves settled dry and dead on the ground in front of Drew. In the silence, Drew became aware of his heavy breathing. Homer held out the gun.

"It's a Winchester 270," Homer said. "It's an easy gun to shoot." A crow cawed sharply from a nearby tree. Slightly unnerved by the sound, Drew stepped backward and bumped into Shane.

"I can't," Drew whispered. Focusing his stare on the target across the clearing, Drew watched the buck's head and antlers expand and grow larger.

"I can't do this," Drew said in a louder voice.

Feeling an icy chill sweep through his body, Drew closed his eyes. The outline of the clearing faded into the darkened hill of Valley Forge Park. Drew saw his mom and dad, and he saw the glass-pierced eyes and massive head of the buck. Drew almost shouted out when he saw the ghost figure with the blazing red hair standing ominously on the hill. Quickly, he opened his eyes. Homer and Shane were standing there next to him. Seconds had gone by.

"I'll shoot it," Shane said, taking the gun. He got into position, spread his feet, and fired off three shots. The sudden explosion of sound cleared the last of the images from Drew's mind. The crow emitted a loud squawk and burst out of the branches of the tree. It fluttered black wings and flew across the clearing, disappearing in the trees behind the buck. Drew straightened up and saw the broken holes in the fabric of the target.

"Good shot," Homer said, but he was looking at the pale color of Drew's face, the trembling hands buried deep in his pocket. "Your turn, Drew."

"Go ahead, Drew," Shane said. "It's easy."

"Everything's easy," Drew said, "when you know what you're doing."

"We know what we're doing," Homer said. "Believe me, Drew. We know what we're doing."

"OK, I'll shoot the damn thing."

Drew pulled his hand out of his jacket and took the gun from Shane. Staring at the distant target, Drew stepped forward. He gripped the rifle tightly, and feeling utterly worthless, he looked at Homer for help.

"Stand this way," Homer said. He moved Drew's feet wider. Then he lifted the rifle and cushioned it on Drew's shoulder. "Look through the scope, and when you find the buck's head, aim for a spot in the neck right below the ear."

Drew lifted the rifle upward, and looking through the scope, he saw the buck's head and antlers come into view. It was clearer than he had imagined. He could see the points of the ears and the brushed details of color on the buck's neck. He leveled the gun to that spot right below the ear and closed his finger quickly.

"What the hell!" he exclaimed. Drew was not ready for the explosion that blasted his ear and sent vibrations the length of his arm. He tried to shake the roaring sound from his ear.

"It's nothing, Drew. You missed. It happens on the first time. Try again." Homer lifted the rifle and repositioned it on Drew's shoulder.

"Try to relax," Shane said.

"Shane's right," Homer said, placing his hands on Drew's shoulders. "Soften up. You're too tense." Homer pushed down gently on Drew's shoulders, bending his knees. "Hold it there. You have to be totally comfortable. How does the rifle feel? Not too heavy?"

"No, it's fine."

"Sometimes the shooter is the biggest problem, Drew. You must clear all the nonsense out of your mind. Breathe naturally. Don't think of anything but what's in front of you. Drop your shoulders a little. They're too tight. Loosen up some more. There, that's better. Find the target and squeeze the trigger softly. Are you ready?"

"Yes," Drew said. Looking through the scope, he raised the rifle, and the buck's head came clearly in to view. The rifle began to feel comfortable and solid against his shoulder. He breathed quietly, and on the slight exhale of air from his lungs, he squeezed the trigger. Looking through the noisy discharge of the gun, Drew saw the black hole open in the buck's rear.

"Excellent," Homer said.

"Great shot!" Shane slapped Drew on the back. "You got it right in the shitter. Let me show you the difference between the head and the ass."

Drew gave the rifle to Shane. He took some shots standing, kneeling on one foot, and prone on the ground. All his shots hit the target, widening the tear in the head. Drew studied Shane's easy posture and listened to Homer's every word. When it was his turn, he had a clear picture in his mind and knew exactly what to do.

"I got it now," Drew said, taking the rifle. After he squeezed off the first shots, he didn't hear the roar in his ear any more, and there was no sudden pressure in his shoulder. The shooting became very easy. Drew hit the target every time.

"You're an excellent marksman," Homer said.

"I know why you're doing this," Drew said. Still looking at the buck, he handed the rifle to Homer.

"Doing what?" Homer asked, looking at Drew closely.

"Doing what?" Shane repeated.

"This target shooting," Drew said. "You think if I kill a buck, it'll make me feel better. It might help me sleep at night."

"We kind of thought that way," Shane said. "You have to try something. Maybe your nightmares aren't as bad as those first months, but you still have them."

"You had a terrible experience, Drew," Homer said. "It would have broken a grown man. You don't have to deal with it by yourself. Shane and I can help. We worked out this plan."

"What kind of plan?" Drew asked.

"It's not in any psychology book," Homer said. "But we'll continue this shooting practice until you're a good marksman. When you finish Phase One, you'll advance to Phase Two."

"What's this Phase Two?"

"Phase Two is a trophy buck," Shane said. "Homer and I have been tracking one. It's a monster."

"We'll take you out the night before Thanksgiving, the same time as the accident," Homer said. "We'll put you on the buck, and then it's up to you."

"You're going to take me hunting and you've already picked out my target?" Drew asked. "You go to all this trouble. What if I can't hit it?"

"After our teaching, you can't miss," Shane said.

"And you saw this buck?"

"Yes," Shane said. "It's a real trophy."

"Where is it?" Drew asked.

"Valley Forge Park," Shane said. He had a slight smile on his face. "I know. It's kind of illegal."

"It's one time we ignore the law," Homer said. "Valley Forge is where the nightmare began, and Valley Forge is where it will end."

"It sounds crazy," Drew said. "But I like it. Maybe there's no monster out there. Maybe it's just something inside of me." He lifted the rifle to his shoulder and looked through the scope. The buck's head filled his vision, and lowering the rifle slowly, lining up the target, Drew fired, hitting the buck high in the neck.

"Not bad," Homer said.

"Drew can get more practice tomorrow," Shane said. "I can take him hunting near Morgantown. OK, Homer?"

"Sure. I'll drop you off where we always hunt," Homer said. He took the rifle from Drew and looked at his watch. "Brandy should have dinner ready. Let's go eat."

Dark shadows spread over the clearing. Homer shouldered the rifle, and they turned to walk down the trail. A light snow began to fall between the rows of trees. Homer stepped over a fallen tree, and slowing his pace, he looked back at Drew and Shane.

"You're a fast learner, Drew," Homer said. "You're much better than my first pupil. You should have seen Shane when he started."

"Was he good?" Drew asked.

"Let's just say we had some problems. Brandy made us move to this clearing when he shot a hole in the garage."

"It was an accident," Shane said.

"Nice accident," Homer said. "Shane's very impulsive. Maybe aggressive is a better word. He saw one of those crows fly out of the tree and took a shot at it. He didn't think about the garage and the truck inside."

"The stationary target bored me," Shane said. "But it was a long time before I could hit it. You caught on quick, Drew."

"I just watched what you did. And I listened to everything Homer said. It's easy when you know what to do."

"Most things are," Homer said. "You watch and you listen. That's good, Drew. What you learned today is very important. Being a good marksman will help you in the future."

"Like in the war," Shane said. "I'm in the military right after graduation. I've read everything I could find on the war. Vietnam's waiting for me."

"Let it wait," Homer said. "We just had our first major causalities. Five soldiers were killed at some air base. The *Evening Phoenix* said President Johnson was planning to send more troops soon. Everything's escalating. The Chinese tested their first atomic bomb last month, and that's bad news. It's not a good time to be over there."

"I don't care," Shane said. "I'm going for early enlistment." He looked at Drew, who remained silent. They reached the house and climbed the steps to the porch.

After a dinner of sweet potatoes, black beans, and a steaming plate of meat loaf with a red spicy sauce, Drew and Shane sat in the living room waiting for Homer. A strong wind rustled against the side of the house. Drew looked out the window and saw ice forming on the glass. Homer walked in the room and gave them cups of hot chocolate. Small marshmallows floated on the surface.

"This will warm you up for the ride home," he said.

"Homer," Shane said, holding the cup with both hands.

"What?"

"When did you play baseball?"

"I never played baseball," Homer said. "I hate baseball."

"But your name?"

"You have questions about my name?" Homer asked. "Let me explain this name to you." He pointed his cup to the sofa, and Shane and Drew sat down. They sank deep in the large cushions. "What do you know about Jackie Robinson?"

"The first black player in the major leagues," Shane said. "He's in the Hall of Fame."

"My dad loved the Negro baseball league. When the Dodgers took Jackie, my dad died and went to heaven. He lied and cheated his way into so many games. During that first week of Jackie's rookie season, the Giants and the Dodgers played at the Polo Grounds. My dad dragged my mom to the game. She didn't want to go because she was pregnant with me."

"Was she close?" Drew asked.

"Within days," Homer said. "Dad told her not to worry, that the Polo Grounds were real sanitary."

"You were born at the Polo Grounds?" Shane asked.

"No," Homer laughed. "My parents were sitting far back in the right field bleachers. Jackie was at the plate, and my dad was jumping up and down shouting, 'Hit a homer! Hit a homer, Jackie!' Then he yelled as loud as he could, 'Hit one for me, Jackie, and I'll name my son Homer.' And he kept pointing to my mom's belly. All the fans began staring at her stomach. My mom was embarrassed, but there was no place for her to go. And dad just kept yelling and getting more excited after each pitch."

"Jackie hit one?" Shane asked.

"A white man, Dave Koslo, was pitching." Homer looked at Shane and Drew. When they didn't say anything, he started laughing.

"What?" Shane asked.

"Can't you see?" Homer asked. "Jackie was the only black man in the whole of baseball. The pitcher could be nothing but white." Homer waited a second and resumed telling the story. "Well, on Koslo's next pitch, Jackie hit the first homer of his career. My dad went crazy. He kept pointing to Mom's belly and shouting, 'We got a Homer. We got us a Homer for a son'."

"That's how you got to be Homer?" Drew asked.

"That's the whole story. My mom said that on the drive back, he couldn't stop talking. She was tired and didn't want to hear it. She said I was jumping around and kicking her because of all the noise Dad was making. Dad laughed and told her I was trying to get out so I could run to first base. The next morning, I was born in the hospital. My dad named me Homer like he said."

"That's crazy," Shane said. Squinting his eyes together, Shane shook his head and looked at Drew. "Homer, I think that's a stupid way to get a name."

"No, it's not," Homer said.

"But it is," Shane said. He tried to look serious. "I mean what if Jackie hit a double? Would your name be Double now?"

"Or maybe we'd be calling you Triple," Drew said, laughing with Shane. "Or what if your dad had swung and just nicked the ball, your name could have been Foul Ball." He and Shane began laughing louder.

"Never would have happened. It was Homer or nothing. You two make everything into a joke." Homer got up and took their cups. "Enough of the baseball stories. I got to get you home."

"Wait," Shane said, stopping Homer at the door. "What happened to Jackie?"

"The West Coast offered the Dodgers all this money to leave New York. The ownership took the offer and moved the team to Los Angeles in 1957."

"I'm surprised your dad didn't take the whole family out to LA," Shane said.

"After they decided to leave New York, my dad was done with the Dodgers," Homer said. "That same year, the Dodgers traded Jackie to the Giants. Being like he was, Jackie refused to play for another team and retired from baseball. To this day, Dad won't go to a baseball game. And neither will I." Homer turned and walked to the kitchen.

In the truck on the ride home, Shane kept talking about the baseball story. A light snow was falling, but it turned to slush when it hit the road. Shane reached across Drew in the middle seat and turned down the radio.

"I don't know, Homer, but I think I understand. Your name does make a lot of sense."

"Why?

"It's more than baseball," Shane said. His face was serious, and he was thinking hard now. "It's also about life."

"What do you mean it's about life?" Drew asked. "It's just a name his dad picked because he admired Jackie, and Jackie hit a homerun. It's got nothing to do with life."

"You're wrong," Shane said. "You don't understand anything, Drew. You don't see the whole picture. Homer does."

"I do?"

"Sure you do," Shane said. "I think it's more about sex than baseball. Your dad knew what he was doing. He saw this beautiful woman, got up to the plate, and he hit a homerun. And that's why you're here with us."

"Is that how it happened?' Homer asked, a smile forming on his face. "I never looked at baseball that way."

"That's what I think," Shane said. "I know this game. And poor Drew here is really shy. I think he's really scared around girls. He'll never hit a homerun."

"Yes, I will," Drew said.

"Have you ever been to first base yet?" Shane asked.

"No, but . . ."

"That's it then," Shane said. "You can't hit a homerun until you get to first base. That's how the game is played. I'm afraid you'll always be a virgin, Drew."

Shane began laughing when he saw the look on Drew's face. Then Homer started laughing and accidentally drove the truck into the deeper snow and slush on the side of the road. Homer quickly straightened the tires and spun the truck back on the road. Their laughter grew louder, and Drew turned up the volume on the radio. Listening to Roy Orbison sing *Pretty Woman*, Drew sat there quietly and stared out the window.

Early the next morning, Homer picked up Shane and Drew at the house. They wore wool hats, heavy army jackets, and lined boots. Homer took Route 23 out of Phoenixville, past the snow-covered golf course at Kimberton, and through the small towns of Knauertown and Elverson.

It was cold, and snow squalls blew across the road. Slowing down, Homer turned the truck onto a dirt road that led through the woods. After a few miles, the dirt road narrowed and low-hanging branches scratched across the roof of the truck. Homer stopped the truck and looked at his watch.

"It's seven thirty," he said. "I'll pick you up here around one o'clock. That should give you plenty of time to shoot something."

"It'll give us plenty of time to freeze to death," Drew said. He got out of the truck, and Shane handed him the Winchester.

"Here," Shane said. "You get the first shot."

"Thanks," Drew said. He and Shane stepped back into a snowdrift while Homer turned the truck around. After straightening the truck, Homer stopped beside them and rolled down the window.

"Don't go far off that trail," Homer said. "If you get lost, you're on your own. I'm not leaving the truck to look for you."

"Don't worry," Shane said. "I know this area."

Homer waved and closed the window. The truck slowly moved away, and then the red taillights disappeared around a turn. Shane and Drew walked across the road. Sheltered by the trees, the trail was mostly clear of snow. Feeling excited about his first hunt, Drew followed right behind Shane, his hand tight on the rifle barrel.

After twenty minutes of quiet walking, Shane stopped and pointed to a squirrel in a tree. It was big and black, and its stiff, fluffy tail was thick and seemed suspended in the air. Drew fumbled for the strap, and by the time he raised and sighted the rifle, the squirrel was gone.

"Next time," Shane said. As they went deeper in the woods, the sky grew darker, and large snowflakes filled the air around them. The trail turned white, and then it was covered by a few inches of fresh snow. Drew heard the cawing sound of a crow, and when he said something, Shane shook his head no and kept walking. As the snowfall increased, it became difficult to see the trail. Shane stopped and looked up through the trees.

"This isn't letting up," he said. "We should go back to the road before the storm gets worse."

"We can't go back," Drew said. "I haven't shot anything yet."

"Maybe we can wait out the storm," Shane said. "Follow me. I know a place." The snow was getting deeper, and it was slow trudging through the heavy drifts. After twenty minutes, Drew felt the perspiration drip from the matted hair under his hat. It formed icy lines down the side of his face.

"How much longer?" he half shouted.

"Just up ahead," Shane said. He stepped through some branches that flung backward, and piles of snow flew into Drew's face.

"Watch it," Drew said, spitting out snow.

"Sorry," Shane said. He held the branch back, and he and Drew walked out of the woods into a small clearing. "Look at that," Shane said, pointing to the ruins of a log cabin at the far end of the clearing. A large oak tree slanted out of the rubble. It was white under the steady falling snow, and its top half stuck in the branches of an equally massive pine tree.

"Wow!" Drew said.

Shading his eyes, Drew could see how the oak and pine trees crossed branches high in the pristine white, snow-shrouded morning sky. On the ground below the trees, the two remaining walls of the cabin rose prominently in the air and seemed cemented to the small room at the side by deep layers of drifting snow.

"It's like a chapel," Drew said.

"Let's go in," Shane said. He and Drew walked across the clearing and stopped in front of the cabin. Shane saw an opening in the snow, and ducking his head, he and Drew, sometimes stooping to a crawl, made their way through the maze of logs and sharp, protruding branches. They emerged in a long, narrow open area.

"Here's our shelter," Shane said.

"What a shelter," Drew said. Brushing the clumps of snow off his jacket, he saw how the trunk of the tree and thick overhang of branches had created a natural roof. The ground they were standing on was dry and clear of snow.

"Look here," Shane said. There was a doorway built into one of the remaining walls. He and Drew walked to the opening and looked inside. Bright shafts of light shone through the cracks in the wall, and Drew could clearly see posts and planks of wood on the ground.

"It's a bedroom," he said. "How did you ever find this place?"

"Last spring I was hunting and found it. I saw some apple trees, and then I saw this wall. It's all real old." Shane turned away from the door, and he and Drew walked back to the middle of the small clearing. Raising his hand, Shane pointed to the tree directly over their heads.

"What are you looking at?" Drew asked.

"I saw it the last time I was here," Shane said. "See the burned bark and that black mark on the side of the tree. Lightning knocked the tree down. That's how the cabin was destroyed."

"Lightning," Drew whispered. He looked at the blackened wood, the broken, dead branches, and felt a sudden chill. Lifting his hand, he lightly touched the scar on his face.

"What's wrong?" Shane asked, looking at the pale face.

"Nothing," Drew said. He took a few steps and was about to sit down when Shane reached out and grabbed him by the shoulder.

"Don't sit there." Shane placed his hand on Drew's shoulder and led him back to the bedroom door.

"I don't feel so good," Drew said. "Why couldn't I sit down?"

"Look," Shane said. He pointed to the indentation in the ground. "See the outline, how it forms a rectangle. This ground was dug out and refilled. I think someone's buried here."

"This is a grave?" Drew asked. His heart began to beat faster. The Winchester slid lower over his shoulder, and he grabbed at the strap to prevent it from hitting the ground.

"Yes," Shane said. "The body must have been huge to dig such a wide grave. Do you see that bush at the end? It was covered with yellow and white flowers when I was here last time. Someone planted that a long time ago. And there's something else, Drew."

Shane walked to the bush and picked out a piece of branch. Returning slowly, walking carefully on the outside of the rectangle, he held the branch in front of Drew. There was a silver ring in the middle of the branch.

"Put it back," Drew said, pushing the branch away.

"What?"

"Please, put it back," Drew said. His head began to hurt. He looked outside at the falling cloud of snow, and when he closed his eyes momentarily, he heard a loud crack of thunder. Shaking his head at the sharp ringing noise in his ears, Drew looked at the sunken edges of the clearing.

"I can't stay here."

"What are you talking about?" Shane asked, sticking the branch back into the rounded center of the bush.

"It's not one big body," Drew said. Staring at the ring, he saw the silver and how it sparkled in the dim light. "There are two people buried here. This is like a family cemetery. I can't stay here, Shane."

"There's a blizzard outside," Shane said.

"I don't care!"

Drew brushed past Shane, and lowering his head, he crashed into the opening under the fallen tree. The barrel of the Winchester slid into the branches and stuck there, jolting Drew's body to a sudden stop. Drew struggled, and when he reached around to free the barrel, his finger brushed against the trigger.

Slanted upward into the tree, the Winchester went off suddenly and violently. The discharge exploded in Drew's ear, and he fell to his knees. Alarmed and shaken, he looked up. Thick clumps of snow fell from the branches and pelted him in the face.

"Christ," Shane said, sliding the Winchester from around Drew's shoulder. He put it safely out of the way, and when he began wiping the snow and wetness from Drew's face, he saw a bright line of red.

"Are you hurt, Drew?"

"What?"

"Look," Shane said. He touched the scar on Drew's lip and showed the red smear on his fingers to Drew. "You're bleeding."

Drew's ears and head still hurt, and he couldn't hear anything. Lightheaded and dizzy, he tried to breathe, but everything was clogged up. Drew squeezed his nose, and when he pulled his hand away, he saw the blood on his fingers.

"Nose bleed," Drew whispered. The roaring noise in his ears was diminishing.

"You sure you're all right?" Shane asked.

"I'm all right," Drew said and began crawling through the canopy of branches. When he got outside, he leaned forward and blew hard through his nose. A thick glob of blood sprayed into the snow. Drew stood up and breathed easily. The snow was falling steadily, and he could barely see their original line of footprints.

"This way," Shane said. He stepped past Drew and began walking in the knee-deep snow. An hour later when they reached the dirt road, Shane and Drew cleared a spot under a large pine tree and sat down. As the storm increased, clumps of wet snow would crash through the branches and slide off their jackets.

Shivering in the cold, Drew tried to relax. He closed his eyes and listened to the soft thumping sound of his heart. Lowering his head, he saw the flash of silver at the gravesite. Then he heard again the loud crack of the rifle that had knocked him to the ground.

"Shane," Drew said quietly, opening his eyes and trying to see beyond the white curtain of falling snow. "I'm sorry about the Winchester going off. When you showed me the grave, I got really confused. Then when I saw the silver ring, I knew something terrible had happened in the cabin. All I could think about was Mom and Dad. After the accident when we went to the cemetery and I saw their two graves, I felt it was wrong. I felt they should be buried together. And then I saw that double grave in the cabin, and I didn't know what to think."

"Don't worry about it, Drew."

"But I can't stop worrying," Drew said. "I don't think I can go to the park and shoot the buck. I don't think I can make it work like you and Homer planned."

"You don't have to make it work, Drew."

"What do you mean?"

"I'll be with you," Shane said. He turned his head toward Drew, and his eyes were a glint of green in the white snow. "We'll make it work together. Now be quiet and quit bothering me. Go to sleep or something."

Drew lowered his head. There was no wind, no animal sounds. Sitting motionless, his mind jumping the time barrier from past to present, Drew thought he could hear the quiet whisper of his mom's voice. Sometimes it was just the whisper of the snow brushing against the branches. Straining to hear, Drew kept his head down for the next hour.

The truck horn sounded in the distance, and Shane nudged Drew in the shoulder. Drew looked up and saw the two dim lights moving closer and brighter through the falling snow. When the truck slid to a stop, Homer pushed the door open. Listening to the loud sound of country music, Drew and Shane shook the snow from their jackets and got inside the truck.

It was the last day of classes before Thanksgiving Vacation at George Washington Junior-Senior High School. Many of the teachers showed their favorite educational movies, and the cafeteria staff proudly served the traditional turkey and mashed potatoes. In the hall after lunch, May put a book in her locker, and when she tried to close the metal door, she found it wouldn't move. Looking up, she saw Frank Jr. holding the side of the door with both hands.

"I like you, May," Frank, Jr. said. "We can be friends. You and I could have a future together. We could go to the mall tonight, maybe see a movie."

"I'll be with Shane tonight," May said. "Can you just get out of the way?"

"Why waste your time with him?" Frank asked. Leaning closer to her, he almost spit out the words. "Shane's a real loser."

"And you're the principal's son," May said. "Is that what makes you so important?"

"That's right, May, I am important," Frank Jr. said. He pushed on the metal door slightly, trapping her in the locker opening. "Why not give us a try?"

"Why not get out of the way?" May said. She struggled with the locker door, but Frank Jr. kept her pinned. A group of students stopped in the hallway and crowded around the locker. Some of them were Frank's friends on the golf team.

Drew turned the corner and saw the crowd. Then he saw Frank Jr. leaning his weight on the locker door, angling his face closer to May's. Drew ran down the hallway and pushed his way into the circle of students.

"Can you get out of the way?" May asked again.

"Yes," Drew said, charging to the locker. His heart began beating fast. "Why not get out of the way?"

"Well," Frank said, turning to face him, "if it isn't Shane's baby brother. What are you going to do without Shane holding your hand? Maybe you should just get the hell out of here before . . ."

Drew didn't give Frank Jr. the chance to finish. He swung his open palm into the locker door. It cracked back, the sharp edge hitting Frank on the side of the face. A line of blood appeared on Frank's forehead and streaked red down his cheek. Frank touched the wound, and when he lowered his hand, he saw blood sliding down his fingers.

"You bastard!" Frank shouted. He slammed the locker door out of the way and lunged wildly at Drew. Their bodies collided, and Frank reached back and aimed a fist at Drew's face. Drew turned, and the fist slid off his shoulder. Swinging his arm out, he grabbed Frank Jr. in a headlock. Frank grunted something, stumbled backward, and they rolled to the middle of the hallway. Drew landed on top and punched down, hitting Frank in the neck. He raised his fist in the air to swing again when he was hit in the head. Then someone kicked him in the side.

"Stop!" May screamed. She tried to push away one of Frank's friends. Then rough hands grabbed her and dragged her back to the lockers.

Henry Chuck was the varsity football coach. He was short, stocky, and weighed a bulky two hundred and eighty pounds. His face had deep lines and was dark and weather-beaten, and his nose was thick and bent to the side, broken in a fight in the parking lot after his first high school football game.

Coach Chuck was in the Driver's Ed room when he heard the loud shouting. He ran out, shoved his way through the circle of excited, cheering students, and grabbing Drew by the neck, he yanked him in the air. With his other hand, he turned Frank around and helped him to his feet.

"What the hell," he said. Chuck's face reddened with anger when he saw the blood covering Frank's forehead. "Go to the nurse and get cleaned up." Frank tried to break free of the grip.

"I'll kill the bastard!" he shouted.

"First get that cut bandaged," Coach Chuck said. He pushed Frank into his group of golf friends. They steadied Frank, and one of them walked with him down the hall toward the nurse's office. When Frank was gone, Coach Chuck turned his attention to Drew. He tightened the grip on Drew's neck, pulling him closer. Drew gagged from the pressure and tried to catch his breath.

"You!" he shouted, spraying spit in the air. "You're going to the office!" Still holding Drew by the neck, he began dragging him down the hall. "Jeff and Mike," he said, motioning to the two of members of the golf team. "You come too."

Mr. West Sr. was on the phone when Coach Chuck pulled Drew into the office. The two golfers stood by the door. Drew's shirt was spattered with blood, and the two top buttons were missing. The only marks on his body were the dark bruises spreading on his neck.

"What's he done now?" the principal asked, putting down the phone.

"Fighting in the hall," Chuck said.

"With who?"

"Frank, your son," Chuck said. "Frank was hurt. He had blood all over his face. I sent him to the nurse." He turned and looked at the two golfers. "Jeff and Mike saw the whole thing."

"He hit Frank with the locker door," Jeff said. "Then he knocked him on the floor. We tried to . . ."

"There was no reason for it," Mike interrupted. "Drew went wild. It was lucky Coach Chuck came when he did."

"Drew started the fight. That's all I need to know. I'm sure Coach Chuck can finish the story," the principal said, standing up and moving around the desk to the door. "Thank you. You can go to your classes now."

"Yes, Sir," Jeff said. He and Mike left the office. The principal closed the door and walked back to his desk. He reached up and took a long wooden board from the wall. The paddle was heavy. The length of it was interlaced with holes the size of quarters.

"You may want to stay for this, Coach," the principal said. "It's always good to have a witness for discipline matters."

"Sure," Chuck said. "I want to stay."

"Drew, you've been in here before," the principal said. He was calm and spoke in a low voice, but it was an angry voice. A dark shade of red moved up the front of his neck, and his upper lip began to twitch nervously.

"He's always been a troublemaker," Coach Chuck said.

"Yes, and this time you've gone too far, Drew. Assault on another student is much more serious than your other pranks."

"It wasn't an assault," Drew said. "Frank Jr. was . . ."

"For you information, his name isn't junior, and I don't need to listen to any of your lame excuses," the principal said. Except for the black hairs of his bushy moustache, the principal's face was now a deep-red color. He slammed the paddle against the top of the desk. The noise was like a gunshot.

"I think you need to meet the Board of Education." Mr. West walked to the metal cabinet next to his desk and pulled out a piece of paper from the top drawer.

"This is the school form which prohibits corporal punishment. It must be signed by the parent." The principal looked through a folder and closed the drawer. "You have no such form in your file."

"My parents are . . ."

"I know," the principal said. "Your parents are dead. It's probably good that they can't see what you've become." The principal walked around the desk and looked Drew in the face. "Remove everything from your back pockets."

"They're empty."

"Good," the principal said. "Bend over and put your hands on the desk."

Drew turned around slowly and grabbed the front of the desk. The principal reached over and lifted Drew's shirt out of the way. Except for the principal's uneven breathing, the room was completely quiet. There was a long moment of waiting, and then Drew felt the crack of the paddle.

The force and sharp sting knocked him forward, and a wave of pain went down his legs and up the sides of his body. The principal swung again and again, and after each swing, the loud cracking echo of the paddle resonated more loudly off the walls of the office.

After the fourth swing, Drew's face was pale white, and tears welled in his eyes. His feet became unsteady, but he straightened his legs and waited.

"This last one is the best," the principal said. He lifted the paddle high in the air, but before he could begin his swing, the door burst open, and Homer rushed into the office.

"What the hell are you doing?" Homer shouted. He grabbed the paddle from the principal's hand.

"This has nothing to do with you, Homer," the principal said. The interruption was quick and unexpected. Trying to compose himself, his lower lip twitching nervously again, Mr. West stepped back and glared at Homer.

"Drew was fighting, and he's getting his punishment now. He has no signed waiver for corporal punishment."

"He doesn't need a waiver," Homer said. "He's coming with me."

"We're not done," the principal said. Both lips were twitching now, moisture forming on the ends of his moustache. "I'm going to expel him for this."

Drew straightened painfully and wiped his eyes. The sharp needles had settled in his buttocks and legs. He looked at Homer and the principal. Mr. West was moving slowly to the safety behind his desk.

"You won't expel Drew. But the school board might expel your son," Homer said. "I talked to May Wiggins, and she said Frank Jr. was molesting her. She said Drew stopped it. He was protecting her from your son."

"That's crazy," the principal said. "That's nothing what Coach Chuck and the students saw."

"I don't care what they saw." Homer threw the paddle on the desk. It banged against the telephone, producing a sharp ring, and then rattled to a stop. Homer grabbed Drew around the shoulder and started for the door. "Let's get out of here."

Drew went out of the office first. Homer followed and slammed the door behind him. Secretary Bess Stevens lowered her head and moved some papers to the corner of her desk. The dismissal bell rang, and the hallway became crowded with students. They were noisy and excited and throwing books in their lockers.

Homer nodded to Drew and walked to his office. The pain in his body lessening, Drew stopped at the fountain and got a drink of water. When he looked up, he saw three members of the golf team in front of him. He pushed through them and made his way to the exit. It was Thanksgiving vacation, and there would be no school for two weeks.

CHAPTER 5

There were dark, fast-moving clouds over Valley Forge Park that Thanksgiving night. Drew and Shane sat in the front seat of Homer's truck. They were on Route 23, traveling slowly around the edge of Mount Joy. Mounds of plowed snow were stacked along the side of the road. The song "Hang on Sloopy" was playing on the radio. The Winchester 270 was on the gun rack behind his head.

"I would have killed Junior," Shane said.

"I'm glad you weren't there," Homer said. "It was bad enough. Frank Jr. needed stitches. He'll have a scar for the rest of his life."

"Thanks for helping, Drew," Shane said. "May went over the whole fight in detail. She told me you were swinging like Rocky. Way to go. I never knew you were that tough."

"I saw him trying to get close to May and hated him so much," Drew said. "I didn't think. I just charged at him."

"So many people want to pound his face, but they can't touch him. He's gotten away with bluffing everyone, until today. I'm sorry that bastard of a principal hit you, Drew. Was it bad?"

"The first one really hurt," Drew said. He remembered how the stinging sensation burned, like his skin was on fire. "Then I don't know. It kind of got worse."

"The Board of Education," Homer said. "That's his answer for every problem. And he loves that creep of a son so much he can't see how rotten he is."

"He has to love him," Shane said. "No one else could."

The bright lights of an approaching truck lit up the road, and before the driver dimmed them, Drew saw a large herd of deer grazing on the Grand Parade ground in front of the von Steuben statue. Homer slowed the truck as their lights swept across the field.

"Drew," Shane said. He pointed his arm and finger at the windshield, made a sharp spitting noise, and pulled his thumb back, shooting an imaginary bullet at the deer in the field. He took another shot and nudged Drew in the shoulder.

"You ready for Phase Two?"

"Yeah, I'm ready," Drew said. "I'm like scared shitless."

"You'll be fine," Shane said.

"Look," Homer said, slowing the truck to a crawl. There were five deer on the side of the road; and behind them, in the field, Drew saw some heads lift up, eyes glazed in the light. They were all doe, and then he saw a rack of dark antlers rise high in the air.

"Is the monster buck in there?" Drew asked.

"No," Homer said. "We've seen him on the hill on the other side of the chapel." Homer turned left off Route 23, drove slowly down a curved stretch of road past a picnic area, and stopped the truck at the edge of the woods. "We'll walk from here."

Park Supervisor Henry Wentworth saw the lights of the vehicle coming up Route 23. He was sitting in his van on a side road used only by park service workers. The lights turned off the road, and Henry could see three dark figures sitting in the front seat of the truck. He watched the lights stop in front of a line of trees and then blink off into darkness. Henry heard the doors slam, and everything was quiet. Waiting a few minutes, Henry started the van and drove toward the small picnic area near the parked truck.

Drew looked at his watch. It was eleven thirty. Homer released the Winchester from the rack and gave it to Drew. They entered a dense patch of woods where the canopy of thick branches prevented the snow from reaching the ground. Dry leaves rustled under Drew's feet, and Homer signaled for him to be quiet. Drew tried shuffling his feet. It was hard to see in the dark. He stepped on a dry branch, and the loud crack brought them all to a stop.

"Stop making so much noise," Homer said. "Be quiet and walk right behind me."

Drew nodded. They started off again. Drew gripped the Winchester in his hand and focused his eyes on the dark form of Homer's coat. With Drew measuring every step, avoiding every leaf and twig, they walked for another five minutes.

An opening formed in the clouds, and moonlight streamed through the branches of the trees. Drew saw the tree line ahead and the large clearing beyond it. There were dark shadows in the clearing. When the dim lights from a car appeared in the distance, the shadowy heads lifted in the air. Drew could see the deer very clearly now. The car lights illuminated the top of the hill, momentarily became dimmer, and then reappeared in a bright glow. The glow moved past the clearing and disappeared.

"That's Route 23," Drew whispered. "That's where our car was."

"Yes, just on the other side of the hill," Homer said. He studied the area carefully. "You can position yourself over there."

Homer pointed to a large tree. The trunk was encircled by large waist-high bushes, and beyond the bushes was the open space of the clearing. A strong gust of wind blew against Drew's face, and dark clouds moved across the moon. The darkness was complete. Homer, Drew, and Shane crawled to the tree and sat down.

"How will I know which one to shoot?" Drew asked.

"You'll know as soon as you see it," Homer said. "The herd will move slowly across the clearing. The buck could be anywhere. Sometimes in front. Sometimes in the middle. You'll have one shot."

"Great," Drew said. "That's me. One-shot Drew."

"Just remember one thing," Shane said.

"What?"

"If you shoot the buck in the ass, it'll be easy to track in the snow."

"Thanks," Drew said. He shook his head and slid into position at the side of the tree. There was an opening in the bushes that gave him a perfect view of the clearing. Drew turned and looked over his shoulder. Homer and Shane had disappeared in the darkness of the trees.

Drew stretched out on the ground and crawled slowly, noiselessly under the bushes. Clearing away a pile of snow, he positioned the Winchester in front of him. Everything was cold and dry around him. When the wind blew, the lower branches of the bush scratched against the rifle barrel. Drew studied the black shadows as they moved closer over the white landscape. Gradually, his eyes adjusted to the dim light, and he began to see the details of the deer.

Looking through the scope, Drew saw the smooth brown hair on the neck, the bright oval eyes, the flick of the ears, and then he lifted the scope to the moving rack of antlers. He patiently counted the points. He scoped one body then another. His focus was intense, and he didn't feel the drop in temperature. He didn't notice the passage of time.

A squirrel scurried in the tree above him. An owl screeched nearby, and there was the violent falling, fluttering of wings followed by the weak beeping sound of some caught animal. Drew listened to the activity around him, but he focused all his attention on the snorting of the deer and the slight sounds of their hoofs against the packed snow and ice.

At one in the morning, the sky cleared. In the brightening gleam of moonlight, Drew moved the scope to a small doe and stopped, his arm frozen still, the Winchester firm in his grip. In amazement, he watched the monster shape appear behind the doe. The buck's head moved majestically upward and dwarfed the body of the doe. Elevated high in the air and motionless in front of the line of moving clouds, the spiked tips of the huge rack extended deep into the darkened sky.

Realizing immediately that this was the buck in Phase Two, Drew felt the air escape from his lungs, and his heart began to beat faster. He lowered the scope slowly, carefully, until he saw the slight twitch of the ear, and he zeroed in on the spot right below it.

Forming a clear picture in his mind, hearing the quiet discharge, and seeing the hole open in that spot right below the buck's ear, Drew tightened his finger on the trigger. In that slight moment of pause, he saw the bright discharge of a rifle from the other side of the clearing. The explosion of noise followed, and the buck jerked and fell to the ground. Drew moved the scope to where the flash had been and saw a figure step out of the woods. Drew stood up, and even from that distance, he recognized the blaze of red color on the man's head.

"You fucker!" Drew shouted and jumped to his feet. He threw the rifle down and began a crazy charge across the clearing. His hunting jacket felt heavy, and his boots sank in the deep snow. Panting loudly, Drew struggled to run faster.

Staring at the figure in front of him, Drew hurdled over the dead buck and came down hard on a patch of ice. He slid awkwardly, fell to one knee, and struggled to regain his balance. Looking up, he saw the figure in front of him slowly lift the rifle in the air.

"Drew!" Shane shouted behind him. Drew heard Shane and Homer break out of the woods into the clearing.

The figure standing on the hill heard them, too. He hesitated and lowered his rifle. Then he began to run. Drew was panting louder now, and sweat was streaming down his face. Not breaking stride, he threw off his jacket. Freed of the weight, he began to move faster and quickly closed the distance.

He was close enough to see the man's shoulders, heaving now from the exertion. The man slowed, and Drew caught him halfway up the hill. He hit him with a hard tackle. There was an explosion of air from the man's chest, and he went down.

"You fucker!" Drew said, rolling the man over. He saw the band of bright red cloth around the man's forehand, and reaching down, he ripped it off. Two cords of string hanging from each side, it was heavy and thick, and covered with some kind of red needle-like fur. Feeling a rage that ripped through his body, Drew fisted the cloth around his knuckles and smashed it into the man's face. He hit him again and again. Drew heard what sounded like animal screams and grunting noises. He didn't know where the sounds were coming from until he saw the man's mouth was tightly closed.

"Drew!" Shane yelled.

The shouts from Shane and Homer became louder. Still making wild bellowing noises, Drew punched into the face again. Lifting his fist, he felt the cloth soggy in his hand. He lowered his gaze and saw the whiskered face, the swollen, half-closed eye, and the broken pulp of the nose. The men coughed and spit up a stream of blood. It landed on Drew's shirt.

Then powerful hands grabbed Drew and lifted him off the body. He felt weak and nauseas. Shane held him around the shoulder and supported him. Drew breathed deeply. Cold air began to fill his lungs. His vision clearing, Drew looked down at the figure on the ground.

The man's face was misshapen and swollen, and he began coughing and gagging on the blood in his throat. Drew was surprised to see how thin the man was. He was surprised to see the deep age lines on the man's bloody forehead. Homer pulled the man off the ground.

"Get the hell out of here," he said and pushed him toward the woods. The man wobbled and fell to his knees. Then he got up and walked in a broken line down the hill. Drew watched him cross the clearing and disappear.

"He was the figure on the hill," Drew said. He looked at the cloth wrapped around his fist. "I thought he had red hair. I saw it burning like fire. It was just this piece of rag."

"Let me see it," Shane said. Drew loosened it from his hand, the two long cords falling free from the corners, and gave it to Shane. Shane held it up to the sky and turned it around in the dim light. "I don't believe it," he said.

"What?" Drew asked.

"It's some kind of animal skin." Shane showed it to Homer and Drew. Homer took the skin and rubbed his hand over the matting of fur.

"It's a polecat," Homer said

"What?" Drew asked

"Skunk," Homer said. "The poacher cut the pattern from a skunk and painted the fur red. I guess he didn't like the white stripe and the black color." Homer saw a spot on the skin that was scraped clean. "There's something else here."

"What is it?" Drew asked. He took the skin, and brushing back the fur, he saw a drawing. "I need a light."

"I have one," Homer said. Reaching in his jacket, he took out a small flashlight, flicked the switch, and pointed the light at the scarred piece of skunk.

"What the hell!" Drew exclaimed, looking at the markings. Etched over the scarlet surface of the skin, the black outline of a skull and crossbones appeared in the bright light.

"This guy was one crazy fucker," Shane said.

"He sure scared the hell out of me," Drew said. He rolled up the ends of the cap and stuffed it in his back pocket.

"That was the man in your nightmares," Shane said. He slapped Drew on the back. "Christ, did you beat the hell out of him."

"I couldn't stop," Drew said. "When I saw him standing there on the hill, it was just like the night of the accident. I just wanted to get to him. I wanted to hit him."

"You did a good job of that," Homer said, shining the light on the moisture and blood on Drew's face and shirt. He clicked off the light and put the flashlight back in his pocket. "I think we're finished here. Let's go home."

They walked down the hill. Homer picked up the man's rifle, and a little further down, Shane stopped and picked up Drew's jacket. He gave it to Drew, and Drew put it on. Drew felt better. The light breeze blew cool air on his face. He followed Homer and Shane to the dead buck. Shane leaned over and began to count the points.

"One, two, three . . ."

"Twelve," Drew said. "I already counted them. I knew it was the monster buck as soon as I saw it. I was ready. I was a split second from shooting."

"Remarkable job," Homer said. "I wouldn't have believed it if I hadn't been here."

"But I didn't kill it," Drew said.

"You did better than that," Homer said. "You got the poacher who caused the car accident. He was responsible for everything."

"You beat the hell out of him," Shane said again.

"I'm going back for the truck," Homer said. He took a brown sheath from inside his vest and removed the knife. Homer gave the knife to Shane. "I need you to gut this monster. Drew can help."

Homer slapped Drew on the shoulder and started across the clearing. At the tree, he bent down to pick up the Winchester and then went into the woods. Swinging a rifle in each hand, Homer began to whistle as he disappeared under the darkness of the trees.

Staring at the knife in Shane's hand, Drew stood quietly next to the buck. He reached down and traced his fingers along the tip of the antlers.

"Take your jacket off," Shane ordered.

"Why?"

"I don't want you to get it dirty," Shane said. "After I slice open the buck's stomach, you have to reach in and pull everything out."

"Pull what out?" Drew asked

Shane didn't answer. He rolled the buck carcass on its back and bent down on one knee. Slicing the knife into the skin, he began to cut a circle around the testicles and substantial penis.

"Look here, Drew."

"What?" Drew leaned closer.

"If you were born with these," Shane said, finishing the cut, "you wouldn't still be a virgin."

"Very funny."

Shane grabbed the testicles and penis, and twisting them off, he threw them over his shoulder. Drew jumped out of the way and watched as the sex organs flew by his head and splattered into a snowdrift, the penis sticking vertical and erect in the air.

"Just hilarious," Drew said. He walked over to the stiff penis and kicked it spinning across the field.

"Drew's buck don't fuck no more," Shane said, laughing at the rhyme and stabbing the knife through the hide below the breastbone. Using considerable strength, he slid the knife, pausing once to wipe the sweat from his forehead, the length of the belly to the base of the tail. When he straightened, gas and a moist steam hissed out from the dark, cavernous belly.

"Shit," Shane said.

"What?"

"I went too deep." Shane smiled and shrugged his shoulders. "I cut into the innards. But that's your problem, Drew, not mine." Shane removed the knife and wiped it on the thick fluffy tail. A light snow began falling and dropped glistening specks of moisture on the buck's smooth skin.

Homer walked quickly back to the truck. He opened the door and put the Winchester on the rack. Lifting the other rifle in front of him, he looked at the line of notches curved in the wood. He turned at the sound of footsteps.

"Homer," Mr. Wentworth said. He flashed a light in Homer's face and lowered it. "I heard a gunshot. What happened?"

"A poacher shot our buck before Drew could," Homer said. "Drew ran him down and beat the hell out of him. It all happened pretty fast."

"Where's the poacher now?"

"He's long gone," Homer said. "But you'll recognize him. His nose is flattened, and his face is a bloody mess."

"I think I know who he is," Mr. Wentworth said. "There's a recluse who owns two acres of woodland bordering the park. He's old, kind of crazy, mean-spirited at times, and really thick-skinned. His name's Jeb Wood."

"Has he been poaching here long?"

"Probably, but there's no way of knowing for sure. He's like an Indian. You can't see Jeb if he don't want to be seen. Maybe there is some Indian blood in him. His family goes back for generations. His great grandparents had deed to over two thousand acres way before Washington camped here. Then the family hit hard times and sold off most of their land. The government bought some for the park. Jeb lost the rest of it himself. He was delinquent in taxes, and the bank foreclosed. Local people said the bank president had the paper work done pretty fast."

"Why?"

"Two board members needed the acreage to finish plans for the Lafayette Country Club. They got their land, and they built the clubhouse right where Jeb's barn was. Except they don't call it a clubhouse. They call it a chateau."

"I hear Lafayette's the most private and expensive membership in the East," Homer said. "Is it true the restaurant serves only French gourmet food?"

"It's true," Mr. Wentworth said. "And they only drink champagne and the best imported wines. They got the best of everything at the country club. Jeb was left with nothing but his anger. His acreage juts out onto the golf course at the ninth hole. Once he saw some caddies looking for golf balls in his woods. Right away Jeb threw up some bright-red **NO TRESPASSING** signs. And to make sure the golfers understood, he set out a line of those old Duke bear traps with the sixteen inch jaw spread. He buried a few of them in the ground. No one, not even the sheriff, goes in there now."

"I hope I never see him again," Homer said. "Where's he work?"

"Jeb hasn't had a job for years. I guess that's why he lives off the land."

"Maybe he'll need this back," Homer said. He gave Mr. Mr. Wentworth the rifle.

"I don't think he will," Mr. Wentworth said. "I was in his shack once, and I saw his gun cabinet. It was the only clean, no immaculate, spot in the room. He had cartridges and some expensive rifles in there. He knows what he's doing when it comes to hunting."

"Does he have family here?"

"His brother Joshua died a few years ago."

"The way he lives alone," Homer said. "He could be real crazy."

"You three are witnesses," Mr. Wentworth said. "With your testimony, we can have him arrested and put away for a while."

"He's had enough trouble," Homer said. "I'd prefer not to testify, and it would be awkward for us. I don't think the judge would understand why I was in the park late at night with two hunters and a Winchester."

"You're probably right," Mr. Wentworth said. "I've felt sorry for Jeb ever since the bankers stole his land. He doesn't have a radio or TV. He can't read or write."

"Maybe he never knew about the accident," Home said.

"Maybe," Mr. Wentworth said. "I'll return the gun and tell him to stay on his two acres." Mr. Wentworth shouldered the rifle and shook Homer's hand. "I'm glad the way things worked out, Homer. No one else could have done it. You do work some magic with these kids."

"They do all the magic. I just occupy them," Homer said. "I'll see you and the family at the house for Thanksgiving dinner. If Drew agrees, maybe we'll eat fresh venison."

"We'll be there," Mr. Wentworth said. He turned, and swinging the gun in his hand, he walked up the hill. Homer took a cloth out of his pocket and began to wipe the glaze of snow and ice off the truck window.

In the clearing, Drew covered his nose at the smell. He looked at the line of intestines bulging through the stomach opening. A yellow liquid and blood flowed onto the ground. Drew removed his jacket and threw it aside. He knelt down next to Shane.

"What now?" he asked.

"Reach in there with both hands. When you feel the ribs, grab the intestines and all the guts in there and pull everything out."

"The guts!"

"Everything," Shane said. "And be careful. The bladder and intestines will be full of shit and urine and other good stuff."

"Great," Drew said. He bent closer to the buck and pushed his hands through the slashed, hanging section of skin. His fingers became instantly warm and moist, and the stench was unbearable. Holding his breath, Drew pressed his head against the stomach cavity and slowly maneuvered his hands further into the heavy, slithery mass of viscera.

"Faster!" Shane shouted. He jumped to his feet, raised the flap of the opening, and lifting his foot in the air, he power-kicked Drew in the ass. Drew's head slid smoothly and deeply into the stomach cavity.

Drew opened his mouth to swear, but closed it quickly when thick, foul-smelling liquid splashed against his face. Everything became dark and moist, and his head cracked against the ribcage. Holding his breath against the smell, Drew ripped down with both arms and pulled the mass of innards to his chest. With eyes closed and on his knees, he backed out of the cavity.

"You bastard!" Drew shouted at Shane as soon as he sensed clean air. Getting in a sitting position, he dropped a section of lung, the bladder, and the liver onto the snow. Drew noticed there was a long piece of intestine stuck in his lap. When he looked closer, he saw a tiny rupture in the side of the intestine. On some crazy impulse, Drew placed his hands on either side of the rupture and squeezed. Blood and brown excrement and a muddy yellow liquid squirted from the opening and sprayed onto his shirt and jeans.

"Good job," Shane said. He began to laugh. "Don't worry. It's only buck shit." Trying to hold back the laughter, he reached down and helped Drew up. The intestines dropped to the ground. Drew looked at his jeans and felt the wetness soak through to his skin.

"I'm covered in it," Drew said, looking at the dead buck and the huge rack of antlers. "But I feel great."

Drew leaned forward and rubbed his hands in the shit on his jeans. Lifting his hand slowly, he flicked his finger toward Shane, and a wad of excrement landed on Shane's jacket.

"What are you doing?" Shane asked, scraping away the stain.

"I said I feel great," Drew said loudly, stepping closer, getting in Shane's face.

"Don't try anything stupid," Shane said.

"You started it," Drew said, pushing Shane in the chest.

Shane slid in the wet snow and bloody deer entrails, and as he tried to regain his balance, Drew tackled him hard. Both bodies hit the ground, and their momentum rolled them toward the buck's carcass. Shane went through the ripped flap of skin first, and he pulled Drew in after him.

Legs kicking up mounds of snow outside, their heads buried in the buck's stomach, Drew and Shane began swinging wildly at each other. They wrestled fiercely for a few minutes, and only stopped when Shane managed to spin Drew around and pin his face into the buck's curved, putrid anus.

Drew gagged, swore something, and quit struggling. Exhausted and laughing, Shane pulled Drew out of the buck's stomach. Sitting up slowly, Drew breathed in the cold air and felt the snow on his face. He laughed and pointed at the brown stains that covered his shirt. Then he pointed at the dark blotches on Shane's head.

"What a mess!" Drew said. "And you stink so bad!"

"What'd do you mean?" Shane asked. "I smell great. I smell just like school lunch." He began laughing even harder now. He didn't care about the smell. He saw the change in Drew, the pure happiness in his face. "I think we need to do one more thing."

"What?"

"It's a spiritual Indian ceremony," Shane said. "I have to draw a blood line across your forehead. It will honor the dead buck, and it will make us blood brothers for life."

"There's more shit here than blood," Drew said, looking at his hands.

"Then I'll draw a shit line on your forehead," Shane said. "We'll be shit brothers." Shane stuck his finger through the hole in the buck's intestine, swirled it around a few times, and removed the finger, covered and dripping with excrement.

Shane raised his hand over Drew's face, and thinking about the importance of the ceremony and trying to stifle his laughter at the same time, he pressed his finger into the skin and made an uneven, jagged line across Drew's forehead. When he was done, he lowered his hand and looked at the line with admiration.

"It's good," Shane said. "It looks like a chocolate lightning bolt."

"My turn," Drew said. He stuck his finger in a thick puddle of excrement and traced a darker line across Shane's forehead.

"It tickles," Shane said. They both began laughing, and when Drew took his hand away, Shane fell onto his back in the snow. Drew dropped down next to him, and when he stopped laughing, he looked at the night sky and the slanting circle of pine trees along the border of the clearing.

Amazed, he saw how the branches turned white and heavy and drooped gracefully downward to the ground. And high in the darkness, the snow fell into the towering, twisting branches and covered everything with a pristine, white glow of reflected moonlight.

Where the treetops glisten, Drew whispered quietly to himself. He whispered the words again, his lips barely moving.

"What?" Shane asked, turning to look at him.

"Nothing," Drew said, his eyes bright and wide, staring at the glistening snow dropping out of the black sky.

It was clear and cold, and when Drew took a deep breath, the cold air and heavy, musk scent of the buck filled his nostrils and seemed to reach deep into his lungs. He held his breath for a long time, and when he breathed out, a warm cloud of mist lifted in the air, melting the cascading snow into drops of moisture. Feeling relaxed and at peace, Drew marveled at the beauty of the night.

There was the sound of an engine, and sitting up, Drew saw the dim lights of Homer's truck moving along the edge of the woods. The truck came across the clearing and stopped in front of them. Without turning off the engine, Homer got out, and when he saw the condition they were in, he shook his head.

"You guys look terrible," he laughed. "You smell even worse. There's a tarp in the back. Wrap the buck in it, and we'll get out of here."

It took them a few minutes to slide the buck onto the tarp. They rolled up the tarp, grabbed it on the sides, and dropped it in the back of the truck. The sky was completely dark now. Drew and Shane rolled around in the wet snow a few times before getting into the truck. Homer drove off slowly.

"Crank the windows all the way down," Homer said. "You guys stink."

Drew lowered the window, and cold air and snow blew into the truck. The snow became heavier, and Homer turned on the wipers. Soon, they left the side road and turned onto Route 23. Drew was quiet, watching the snow slide off the windshield. He didn't notice Shane watching him.

"Why so serious?" Shane asked. "You didn't swallow any of that shit, did you?"

"No," Drew said. "I was just thinking. I was thinking about the buck. I think I would have killed it with one shot."

"I know you would have," Homer said. "It's a real trophy, Drew. I'll get the head mounted. I want you to have it."

"Thanks, Homer, but I didn't kill it."

"Doesn't matter," Homer said. "We can cut the head off at the house, and we can save the venison for Thanksgiving."

"Can you get a turkey for Thanksgiving, Homer? I need the buck for something." Drew hesitated for a moment and then continued talking slowly. "And I need to borrow your truck tonight." Drew turned and looked at Homer. "I know I don't have a license. If we get stopped, I'll say I stole it."

"You won't have to steal anything," Homer said. "What are you up to?"

"It's nothing much," Drew said. "Shane and I can handle it."

"Handle what?" Homer asked, looking in the mirror at Shane. "What are you two planning?"

"Don't look at me," Shane said. "I don't know what Drew's talking about."

"Is this important?" Homer asked. He stopped at a red light on the empty street and looked at Drew. The light turned to green.

"It's real important," Drew said. "It's something I have to do."

"OK," Homer said. He drove through the intersection. "No more questions. I trust you. I trust Shane."

"There's something else," Drew said. "I also need your master key to the school."

"Oh," Homer said. "This is getting complicated. Don't tell me anything else."

Homer turned on the radio and drove the truck through the empty streets of Phoenixville. They listened to country music as they headed to French Creek. It was two thirty when Homer stopped the truck at the house. He went inside the garage, and when he returned with a hacksaw, Shane and Drew had the tarp open. The buck's head, antlers scraping into the ice and snow on the driveway, hung over the dropped gate of the truck.

Drew grabbed onto the antlers with both hands, and he and Shane steadied the head. Homer positioned the blade over the buck's neck and began sawing. The blade cut smoothly through the flesh and muscle but stopped at the bone with a grinding noise. Homer gave a stronger effort with the saw, and the head dropped to the ground at Drew's feet. The antlers were thick and heavy in his hands.

"What a trophy," Drew said. He stared in awe at the massive rack. Struggling with the weight, he gave the head to Homer who took it to the side of the garage. Shane and Drew pulled the tarp and headless buck back into the truck and closed the gate. Homer walked over to Drew and gave him a key.

"This master will open any door at the school," Homer said.

"Thanks, Homer," Drew said, pocketing the key, and he and Shane got in the truck.

Breathing heavy, Jeb Wood collapsed in the snow. He struggled to get back on his feet, and it took him half an hour to reach his truck hidden on a back road. Spitting blood and thick mucus, he crawled on his hands and knees the last twenty yards. Grabbing onto the door handle, he pulled himself off the ground, opened the door, and crawled inside the truck.

Having some difficulty making his hands work, Jeb dropped the keys on the floor twice before he was able to start the truck. When Jeb turned on the lights, he saw a thick wall of snow and ice on his windshield.

"Fuck!" he swore. He tried the windshield wipers, but they gave a humming noise and didn't move. Jeb stumbled outside, wiped the windshield with his forearms, and punched at the wipers until they moved. Getting back in the truck and driving forward, he had a hard time keeping the truck on the slick road. His left eye was swollen shut, and his right eye was glazed over with a thin film of blood. Trying to see the outline of the road, Jeb briefly caught a glimpse of his mangled face in the rearview mirror.

"I'll kill the bastards!" he vowed to himself. "I'll kill 'em for sure!"

Losing control of the wheel, Jeb felt the truck slide into a ditch. He accelerated fast, spun out of the ditch onto the adjoining field, and he floored it again. Spraying snow high in the air, the truck careened back into the ditch, tilted sideways for a long distance, and bounced onto the road. Jeb slowed the truck to a crawl, the view of the road turning from red to black whenever he blinked his eye.

Jeb drove out of the park onto a straight stretch of road with flat snow-covered fields on both sides. He knew this road, and although he could barely see, he began to drive faster. Soon he came to a long, diagonal wall that ended at the side of a monumental building constructed in the shape of a castle.

A large sign, words scripted in gold letters, read **Lafayette Country Club**. Under the sign, connected by two short chains, was a larger one that read **Members Only**. The entrance road leading to the golf course went through the center of the castle. The iron gate in front of the entrance was shut, a wide bar locking the two sections together.

Jeb drove a short distance down the road and over a hill. The flat fields gave way to a dark shadow of thick trees. Jeb turned left at the only opening in the tree line, and after a few minutes he stopped the truck in front of a small one-story, one-room, dilapidated cabin. Jeb shut off the motor and sat quietly. When the pain in his head lessened and he could see without the flashes of red, he got out of the truck, walked to the cabin, and pushed open the door.

It was cold in the room. Jeb turned on the light bulb hanging from the ceiling. The brightness dazed him momentarily. When he was sure where he was, he went to the gas heater and turned up the thermostat. There was a sink, a table, a rocking chair, one armrest broken off and hanging loosely from the side, and a cot along the wall next to the heater. Torn and ripped along the edges, a black bear hide was stretched on the floor in front of the cot.

The rest of the room was covered with rubbish. Egg cartons, some with cracked shells inside, open cans, whiskey bottles, a large skillet, dirty cups, and broken dishes were scattered over the floor. The side wall of the cabin was completely covered by rows of trophy antlers. They were stacked high, the pointed tips of the antlers sticking in the cracks of the ceiling. An assortment of shirts, trousers, jackets, red animal skins cut in the shape of caps, one large eagle's talon, and a pair of woolen underwear hung from the tips of the antlers.

A polished gun cabinet was on the opposite wall. There were places for four rifles inside the cabinet, and boxes of cartridges were piled neatly next to them. The first rifle, a Winchester Model 70, .30-06, Jeb used only for bear.

Beside the Winchester was the rifle Jeb called his "favorite toy". It was a World War II sniper rifle, the M1903 Springfield. Next to the sniper rifle was a Winchester Model 94, .30-30. The fourth section of rack was blank, and Jeb cursed when he saw the empty space.

Kicking a bucket half full of urine out of the way, Jed walked to a wooden cabinet leaning over the sink. He opened the door and pulled out a bottle of Jack Daniels. Sitting on the cot, Jeb unscrewed the cap and took a long drink. He sat there, waiting for the whiskey to work, and then he took a dirty towel off the floor. Jeb saturated the towel with whiskey, and then he began to scrape away the dried blood caked on his face.

The pain was unbearable, but Jeb only drank more whiskey. Wiping at his face again, digging the towel deep into the cuts, Jeb thought about what he planned to do to the boy in the park, and he smiled and began to enjoy the pain. Taking one last drink, Jeb lay back on the cot. He experienced a feeling of revolving dizziness and great warmth, and folding the towel over his face, he dozed off.

After starting the engine and showing Homer his most confident face, Drew backed slowly down the driveway. The road was completely covered with snow. Shane turned up the volume on the radio. Jan and Dean were singing *Dead Man's Curve*, and Shane, slapping his hands on the dash, joined them.

"If you've got the nerve, let's race all the way to Dead Man's Curve." Shane was about to begin the refrain when the truck picked up speed going down a hill and slid sideways a few yards before Drew managed to straighten it.

"Slow down," Shane said. "Maybe I should drive."

"I'm fine," Drew said. "But do me a favor."

"What?"

"Stop singing, please. And turn down *Dead Man's Curve*.

It took them twenty minutes to reach the entrance of the school. The brightness of the spotlight at the main entrance was dulled by the cloud of falling snow. It cast a pale glow over the deserted sidewalk and parking lot. Drew stopped the truck at the corner of the building. He and Shane got out and went to the back of the truck.

"What are we doing here, Drew?" Shane asked. He dropped the gate, and they lowered the tarp to the ground.

"I brought this for the principal," Drew said, pointing to the buck. "Today Mr. West gave me something I'll never forget, and in return, I have to give him something he'll remember the rest of his life."

"I guess that's fair," Shane said. Leaving a wide, smooth path in the snow, they dragged the heavy tarp to the side door. Drew took the key from his pocket and put it in the lock. The door swung open. Pulling the tarp behind them, they went inside and walked down the darkened hall. Drew looked back at the tile floor and the wet trail of melting snow and red streaks of liquid. After a few minutes, they stopped in front of the principal's office.

"Here we are," Drew said, unlocking the door. The glow from the outside light streamed in through the large windows. They had to maneuver the tarp between the chairs of the outer office. At the principal's door, Drew dropped his corner of the tarp and reached for the key. He found the lock, turned the key, and pushed the door open. He laughed, and they pulled the buck inside.

The luminous hands of the oval clock on the wall showed 3:10. Drew looked at the cushioned chairs, the line of cabinets, and the large desk. There was a picture of Mr. and Mrs. West and Frank Jr. at the corner of the desk. Shane picked up the picture and held it up to the light.

"I've never met the principal's wife," Shane said. "She's not bad."

"Give me that," Drew said, taking the picture. "I can see why you say she's not bad."

"Why?"

"Because she's the only one in this beautiful family portrait without a moustache," Drew said. "But I can fix that." Taking a magic marker from the desk organizer, he drew a black moustache under her nose. Then he traced long sideburns that curved around the bottom of her chin. "That's much better," he said.

Drew put the picture back on the desk next to an elaborate nameplate of polished wood. Mr. Frank West, *High School Principal*, was etched in gold on the smooth surface of the black shiny plate.

"Where do you want the buck?" Shane asked. He looked around the room.

"I'm not sure," Drew said. He looked at the large desk, and then his eyes focused on the principal's black and the leather swivel chair behind it.

"Let's put the buck in the principal's chair. Ass in the air, facing the door."

"Great idea," Shane praised. They slid the buck across the desk and tried to prop it onto the chair, but there was too much weight. The chair spun away and knocked Drew on the floor.

"Damn it," Drew said. Getting up, reaching around the buck with both hands, and using all his strength, he tried to shove the open neck cavity over the back of the chair.

"Wait," Shane said. He got in front of the desk; and pushing as hard as he could, he slid the desk into the chair, and the chair slammed against the wall. The buck's body lifted in the air, and the impact forced the front hoofs tightly over the armrests. At the same time the flapped opening of the neck cavity slid over the backrest.

The massive body tilted to the side but somehow stayed balanced on the chair. Its back hoofs scratched lines into the wood, and the buck, with its ass and white fluffy tail raised high in the air, stretched halfway across the principal's desk.

"Cool," Drew said, stepping back and studying the angle of the buck's body. "It's like eating the seat cushion."

Drew walked over to Shane. They both jumped in the air, slapped their hands together in a big high five, and gave a loud Patriots victory shout. Still laughing, they rolled up the tarp. When they reached the door, Shane hesitated and looked back at the buck. He dropped the tarp on the floor.

"Wait," he said, walking back to the desk. He picked up the principal's nameplate and handed it to Drew. "You got to do it, Drew."

"Do what?"

"Stick it," Shane said in a loud voice and nodded his head toward the buck's posterior.

"I think I understand," Drew said. He and Shane walked over to the edge of the principal's desk.

"Mr. Frank West," Drew laughed. Reading the nameplate and looking up at the dark, shit-smeared anus, he spoke in a serious, deep voice.

"We, Shane and I, would like to present you with the *Most Distinguished Principal of the Year Award.*"

"*Principal of the Decade,*" Shane corrected.

"Yes, *Principal of the Decade,*" Drew said. He laughed, and stretching his hand forward, leaning away to avoid the stench, he shoved the nameplate in the buck's ass. It stood there, slanted high in the air, the golden words, *High School Principal,* barely visible.

Drew and Shane jumped in the air, and there was another enthusiastic Patriot high five. They admired the scene for a second, picked up the tarp, and started toward the door again. Then Drew stopped and lowered the tarp to the floor

"Wait," Drew said. He walked behind the desk and took the Board of Education from the wall. He dropped the paddle in the blood-stained tarp, and he and Shane rolled the tarp into a tight bundle. As Drew straightened, a fly, wings buzzing loudly, flew out of the corner of the room. Drew turned and watched it.

"Shane."

"What?"

"Look," Drew said. He pointed to the buck's elevated tail and the mutilated anal opening below it. The fly circled once and then alighted on the torn flesh. There was more buzzing, and another fly landed next to the first.

"A few flies," Shane said. "So what?" Suddenly the buzzing sound increased, and in a blur of motion, the second fly jumped on the first. "Shit, they're doing it!"

"Let's make them comfortable," Drew said. He walked to the thermostat by the door, and reaching up, he turned the dial from 65 to 110 degrees. Immediately there was a loud humming noise, and a flow of hot air burst through the vent in the wall.

"I smell bad, really bad," Shane said, swinging his hand at the wave of heat hitting his face. "In a few days, that buck is going to be real ripe."

"Food for maggots and new generations of flies," Drew said. "One happy family."

"Just waiting to greet the principal when he opens the door," Shane said. "I think we've done all we could. Let's go home."

Carrying the tarp between them, Drew and Shane walked out of the office and down the hall. It was still snowing outside. It was a heavy wet snow. When they walked out of the door, the snow was up to their ankles. Leaving deep shoeprints in the snow, they reached the truck and dropped the tarp in the back. Drew got inside, and Shane wiped the snow off the windshield. After most of the windshield was clear, Drew started the engine; and following the thin line of tire tracks in the snow, he drove the truck to the exit.

There was still a strong smell in the truck. When Drew turned on the heater, the smell became worse. Looking through the moving wipers at the snow-covered road, Drew didn't care. He saw the cassette sticking out of the player and pushed it in. Soon the slow, mournful lyrics of *Mr. Tambourine Man* sounded through the truck's cabin.

Driving carefully through the snowstorm, Drew saw the sign for French Creek State Park. Shane was sleeping, his head balanced against the window. Humming the Bob Dylan lyrics, Drew drove past the sign, missing the turn to Homer's house.

> Hey! Mr. Tambourine Man, play a song for me,
> I'm not sleepy and there is no place I'm going to.

"But I'm going some place," Drew said. He went two miles down the road and stopped the truck on the bridge spanning the Schuylkill River. There was no traffic, no sign of life anywhere. He clicked off the cassette, and leaving the motor running and headlights on, he got out of the truck.

The wind and swirling snow stung his face. Going to the back of the truck, Drew opened the tarp and grabbed the Board of Education. He walked to the railing, and for a few moments, he stood there motionless. The thick falling snow swept past him and melted into the black torrents of rushing water. Drew watched a large piece of ice float from under the bridge and vanish in the darkness downriver.

Taking a deep breath, Drew lifted the Board of Education over his head and threw it over the railing. He watched it spin through the falling snow and then splash silently in the river. The small circle of waves disappeared quickly in the fast current. Drew saw the handle bob up for a second, and then the Board of Education was gone.

There was nothing but silence. Drew reached into his back pocket and removed the red skunk-skin cap. It was wet and soaked with blood. Holding the cap by the corner, he shook it once, twice. In the beams of light from the truck, the two hanging cords and the squared design of the cap opened in front of him. Drew saw the drawing, and he saw how the black lines of the skull and bones were smeared with blood.

Drew dropped the skunk cap over the railing, and as it fell, it was caught by a sudden draft of wind. The edges of the cap flapped open, and it descended scarlet and white with the falling snow. The squared cap dropped flat onto the surface of the black water and was quickly, quietly carried away by the current. Brushing the snow off his jacket, Drew backed away from the railing.

Drew walked to the truck and used the sleeve of his jacket to clean the windshield. When he finished, he saw the glass was quickly covered again by large snowflakes. Drew got in the truck and turned on the wipers. Sitting next to him, Shane was sleeping. He mumbled something when Drew closed the door. Squinting through the windshield, now alternating clear and then wet and blurry, Drew had to twist the wheel hard and back up four times before he could get the truck turned around.

Driving slowly to the end of the bridge, Drew turned on the high beams. The light was bright and illuminated a misty, falling wall of thick snow that was surrounded by pitch black darkness. Drew switched on the low beams and swung the door open. Getting out, he walked to the front of the truck and looked down the road. The tire tracks from a few minutes ago were gone, and the road had completely disappeared under a foot of snow.

"Totally erased," Drew said in amazement. Staring at the expanse of snow, which at times seemed to be rising up from the ground, he thought about the hunt, the scarlet headpiece, and how he swung out and busted the man's face again and again. He thought about how old and how small the man was.

In the glow of the lights and falling snow, Drew stood there alone in the storm, and he was only sure of one thing. Lifting his shoulders with a sense of relief, he knew the pain and the black horror of the nightmares were gone.

Buried, he thought, *somewhere deep, like the road, under the flat, undulating mounds of snow.*

Drew heard the steady swishing, clicking sound of the windshield wipers and turned to see chunks of snow spraying off the side of the truck. Shane's slumping head appeared behind the wipers and then disappeared in the wet haze of melting snow. When the wiper swung back and briefly cleaned the glass, Drew clearly saw the dark brown ceremonial line on Shane's forehead.

Drew walked to the open door. Snow had settled onto his seat, and he brushed it off. Getting inside, he sat down and glanced at his face in the rearview mirror. Laughing at his reflection, he saw a mat of excrement sticking in his hair. Pulling off a patch of the stuff, Drew noticed it was soft and stuck to his fingers. He turned to Shane, and reaching over, he smeared it under Shane's nose, forming a thin, brown moustache. Not opening his eyes or moving, Shane only smiled and coughed lightly.

"Thanks, Shane," Drew said. "Thanks for everything."

Drew closed the door and put the truck in gear. The truck moved out slowly, and looking through the windshield, Drew saw only a hazy tunnel of light and falling snow. The walls of the tunnel were shaped by the low-hanging branches of the pine tress along both sides of the road. Even though he felt trapped in the close darkness of the tunnel and once almost slid into an unseen ditch, Drew was in no hurry.

Drew pushed the cassette in and turned down the volume. He began humming the words "jingle-jangle morning." The truck slid deeper into the tunnel, and Drew hummed along with the song.

> Then take me disappearin' through the smoke rings of my mind,
> Down the foggy ruins of time, far past the frozen leaves,
> The haunted, frightened trees, out to the windy beach,
> Far from the twisted reach of crazy sorrow.

"Hey!" Drew shouted loudly at the windshield. "Mr. Tambourine Man!" The words echoed in the cab of the truck.

"What?" Shane yelled, jumping straight up. He stared at Drew for a second and then slumped back in the seat. His eyes closed, and he was asleep again.

"Hey, Mr. Tambourine Man, play a song for me," Drew sang more quietly.

Drew repeated the words again. He looked through the ice-streaked window at the drooping trees and the glistening bed of crystals on the road ahead. At the distant end of the tunnel, the rising sun emitted a dim glow that flashed slanted lines of light through the curtain of white falling snow. Gradually, the sun rose higher in the horizon, and the tunnel disappeared completely. The level stretch of icy road and the fields on both sides reflected the bright morning light, and Drew raised his hand to shield his eyes.

The heater in the truck was running on high. Feeling the strong flow of warmth on his face, Drew turned the heater to low. Shane coughed, and the sound of his snoring filled the front cab of the truck. Then Drew yawned and breathed deeply and yawned again. His eyes began to close and the truck lurched to the side, and he jumped straight up in his seat. Alert now, Drew paid more attention to his driving and maneuvered the truck carefully through the slippery expanse of snow.

It was six in the morning when Drew turned into the drive leading to Homer's house. Wearing blue earmuffs, a George Washington football cap pulled low over his face, and covered by a heavy jacket, Homer was standing on the porch with a snow shovel in his hand.

CHAPTER 6

T he Valley Forge winter was over. As he ran down the stretch of windy beach, Drew realized how happy he was to have finished his freshmen year at George Washington High School. He also realized how happy he was to be at the Jersey Shore. The rising sun burned a sparkling line of light across the surface of the ocean. With each cresting wave, the light shattered into bright frothy bubbles that broke along the long stretch of sand. His feet sinking wet toe-and-heel prints in the glimmering sand, Drew ran easily down the nearly deserted beach. Specks of sand kicked up behind him and stuck to his blue George Washington T-shirt now moist with perspiration and salt water.

Looking down the beach, Drew saw the incandescent, oval lump roll in with a large wave. It stuck there in the sand, and Drew hated it immediately. He remembered how much the Old Man detested the Portuguese man-of-war, and although this was a smaller version, Drew knew what he had to do. He ran faster and than leaped high in the air. Both of his feet landed flat on the jellyfish, and he smashed it deep into the sand. As he stepped out of the hole, he saw the next rolling, cresting wave fill the indentation with water and drifting sand. When the wave drained back into the ocean, the jellyfish, but for two twisted tentacles lying flat on the moist sand, was completely buried. Drew felt a stinging sensation on his right foot, and he took off running down the beach.

There was a gathering of sea gulls in front of him, and Drew raced through them, scattering them squawking through the air. They hovered momentarily, gliding in the wind, and then settled quietly behind him. Drew circled around an elderly couple stooped over at the edge of the breaking waves. The woman stood slowly and held a small shell in her hand.

It was the beginning of summer vacation, 1965. Two days ago on Friday, he and Shane had raced home from school, packed their clothes, and early the next morning, the family was on the way to Wildwood Crest for the annual weekly rental. The traffic down the Schuylkill was moving fast, and there were no delays going through Philadelphia and across the Ben Franklin Bridge into New Jersey. Mr. Collier met intermittent traffic on Route 40, but when they turned onto the New Jersey Parkway, the volume of traffic increased and they experienced long delays. Then the traffic slowed and came to a complete stop at the Ocean City tollbooths.

Sitting in the back seat, both Drew and Shane were restless. Although it was still morning, the sun was bright in the sky. It was hot and humid, and waves of heat radiated around the triple lines of cars backed up at the tollbooth. A horn blew from the nearly empty northbound side of the parkway, and Drew looked at the tanned faces of the kids in the convertible exiting from the toll.

A boy was driving, and the girl sitting next to him showed only the slightest bit of fabric of yellow bikini across her upper body. There were three more girls in skimpy bathing suits in the back seat. They all wore dark glasses and beach hats, and the girl in the front seat waved her hands at the line of cars.

Shane was immediately alert. He waved and shouted something through the open window. Sitting back, he complained to his parents that they were a week late and had missed all the fun. Mrs. Collier said they were only sophomores now and not ready for Senior Week. Mr. Collier said they would never be ready for Senior Week. Then Mrs. Collier said that she had lasting memories of her Senior Week, and they both laughed.

Mrs. Collier turned up the radio, and the two adults reminisced about their graduation bash at the Shore. Drew heard something about encountering the Wildwood Beach Patrol at two in the morning. When Shane asked them what they were whispering about, Mrs. Collier ignored him. At the end of a ten-minute wait, she threw the quarters in the cage, and they had clear road in front of them.

After running two miles, Drew stopped at a lifeguard station. Breathing easily, he relaxed and felt the warm ocean breeze begin to evaporate the moisture from his body. He stretched his hands behind his neck and looked at the crowds of people walking down from the boardwalk. Some families set up big umbrellas and placed folding chairs on the sand. One lady with three small kids unfolded a huge blanket that was a bright orange color. She sat on it, and the three kids went splashing in a shallow pool of tide water.

Drew finished stretching and began his run back. The Collier rental was a big three-story house at the end of the boardwalk. They had the whole top floor to themselves. When Drew saw the outlines of the balcony, he ran into the breaking waves. High-stepping furiously, he felt the muscles in his legs begin a slow burn, and he dove into the ocean.

The water temperature cooled and then turned colder as he descended. Feeling chilled and greatly refreshed, he swam hard for the surface, and within seconds his body broke clear of the water into bright sunshine. Drew took a deep breath and swam back to the beach. Straightening up, putting his hands over his head and squeezing the water from his hair, Drew saw Shane and the Colliers on the balcony.

That afternoon Drew and Shane waved to Mr. and Mrs. Collier sitting on folding chairs on the roasting sand and began the trip down the boardwalk to the arcades and souvenir shops. This was the third trip to the Shore for Drew, and he knew what to expect. He was relegated to observer, sometimes admirer, of the Shane technique on how to hook up with cute girls.

Shane could quickly pick out the girls who he said were ready for a good time. He made sure they were in pairs and one of them was stunningly beautiful. When he got through all the preliminaries and introductions, Shane walked off holding hands with the beach beauty. Drew was left to socialize with the other girl, who was usually pretty bland, sometimes overweight, sometimes with a mouth full of silver braces.

Drew was resigned to the situation. Whereas he was thin, immature, and still clumsy around girls, Shane could have passed for a college student. He had built up his body with a year of weightlifting. His trim muscular features combined with the clear innocent face and penetrating green eyes presented a lethal attraction to the summer girls at the Jersey Shore.

Scoping the movement and great variety of bodies on the boardwalk, Drew became very interested, even excited, when he saw two girls standing in a line for funnel cakes. The one girl was beautiful with a nice body and a decent but average-sized chest. The great thing for Drew was that the homely girl next to her had bigger breasts, and she smiled at him.

"Those two," Drew said, nudging Shane in the side. Shane ignored him and kept walking.

"What was wrong with them?" Drew asked.

"Just wait a few minutes, Mr. Horny, and you'll see," Shane said. They continued their leisurely pace down the boardwalk, and Drew did see. May was sitting with Joyce Thompson on a bench.

Even with the parade of beautiful bodies on the boardwalk, May was stunning. She had a clear, flawless face, bright lively eyes, and a youthful smile that seemed out of place on her sharply defined, very sensual body. Her breasts were large and her nipples were clearly outlined by the stretched fabric of her bathing suit. Drew stared. That's all he could do as a friend.

May and Joyce saw them and jumped up. They seemed genuinely happy as they greeted Shane and Drew. Shane had met Joyce a few times during the school year. She was average looking, and her face had a dull appearance.

Then Drew suddenly realized that any girl standing next to May would look dull. Joyce was always friendly, and she laughed easily. She surprised Drew by hugging him, and when the four of them walked down the boardwalk, she placed her arm around his waist.

They spent some time at the amusement pier. Joyce and Drew got on the Ferris wheel, and when they spun up to the highest point, the ride stopped, jerking their carriage back and forth. With people screaming below them, Joyce jumped and dropped her body sideways in his lap. Rocking with the motion of the ride and enjoying the extra weight, Drew laughed nervously and looked at the miniature people on the sand and the endless breaking waves along the beach.

Drew's laugh reached a higher pitch as the weight of her body slid forward. Drew felt the sudden stirring and growing lump in his swimming trunks. He moved slowly upward against her body, and the pleasure he felt made him catch his breath. Then Joyce turned to him, blocking his view of the ocean, and kissed him. She kissed him again, deeper this time, just as the attendant kicked the handle and sent the carriage in motion. The spinning Ferris wheel was descending too fast, and Drew let out a groan when it stopped and the tanned hands of the attendant lifted the bar. Drew wanted to get in line for the ride again, but Shane directed them to the big, noisy arcade.

In the arcade, the four of them jammed into a picture stall, and closed the curtain. Joyce was squeezed hard against Drew's groin, and he had a bewildered look on his face when the flash went off. Waiting outside, Shane pulled the picture out of the slot and held it up in front of them. They all laughed at the expression on Drew's face. Arcade games occupied them for the next half hour. Then Drew saw May and Shane at the entrance holding each other tightly and whispering and laughing.

Drew and Joyce walked over, and Shane said it was time to leave and play better games. The temperature outside was in the high 90s, and the wooden planks of the boardwalk were hot. The sand at the bottom of the steps was hotter. Holding Joyce by the hand, Drew thought they were going to make a run for the water and the breaking waves. But Shane called to him and disappeared under the steps of the boardwalk. He and Joyce followed.

Sunlight streamed through the cracks on the boardwalk and crisscrossed bright lines of light on the layer of sand and the scattered beach debris of cups, dirty napkins, and cigarette butts. Drew saw something yellow next to a broken piece of driftwood, and looking closer, he saw it was a condom. He hastily kicked sand over it.

Drew and Joyce bent lower as the beach began to slope upward. Shane and May moved off to the right behind a wooden piling. Drew watched as they spread the blanket deep in the shadows of the boardwalk. He saw Shane hesitate, pick up a stick, and trace something in the sand. Then he pulled May onto the blanket, the pocket of sand shaping to the weight of their bodies.

Listening to the distant sound of the gulls on the beach, Drew helped Joyce spread their blanket on the sand. The blanket was blue with a large yellow flower in the middle. Joyce stood up and removed the top half of her bathing suit. She held it between her fingers and slid both hands down Drew's waist. He felt the softness of her fingers and the intoxicating warmth of her flesh against his. She pulled him closer, her small breasts touching and rubbing and growing firm against his chest.

They stood there silently between the lines of dark shadows and bright light, their heads inches from the wooden planks of the boardwalk. Drew wrapped his arms around her. He could smell her hair and the slight fragrance of her tanning lotion. Joyce slid her hands under his shorts and squeezed his buttocks, and his entire wet body pressed forward against hers and the remaining, thin fabric of her bathing suit. Drew was now enormously erect, and his legs began to weaken. Directly over his head, on the boardwalk, the noise and laughter of people and the shuffling sound of feet became more and more distant.

Joyce untied the bottom half of her bathing suit, and it fell to the blanket. Dropping to her knees, she pulled Drew's nylon shorts to his ankles. He felt the sudden freedom from his bathing suit and had a sense of his total, rigid nakedness. Then she grabbed him there and squeezed with a gentle twisting motion, and Drew sensed a sudden urgency. He pulled Joyce quickly, gently, onto the blanket. Lowering his body over hers, the beads of perspiration and tanning lotion lubricating their skin, bonding them together, Drew made a hasty, clumsy attempt to get inside. His body was moving too fast, sliding out of control. With a giant effort, he willed himself to slow down, to relax. He began to fantasize, his mind racing in all directions.

Then remarkably, Drew pictured himself at home plate wearing a Phillies uniform. He gripped a Louisville Slugger, and the bases were loaded. Listening to the roar of the noise, Drew swung wildly at a pitch, and then feeling unbelievable pleasure, he felt Joyce gently grab him and slowly guide him with her hand. He slid his body slightly forward, and he was finally there.

The sudden roar of applause and booming cheers from around the stadium were deafening. Feeling a bit dizzy, Drew gasped and watched the pitcher throw a fast ball. He saw the threads of the baseball spinning closer, and he swung with amazing strength.

The contact was pleasurable and beyond anything he had ever experienced, and the fans were up and cheering louder as the ball soared into the center field bleachers. Listening to the echo of noise, Drew didn't make any attempt to run to first base. He was back with Joyce on the blue beach blanket, and his body was rocking uncontrollably.

It was then, between his second and third hard, downward thrust, that Drew heard the scream. It wasn't Joyce. It was a shrill, high-pitched, little-girl scream from above. The small body smacked down on the boardwalk, and her drink flew out of her hands. A stream of cola and crushed ice flowed between the boards and spattered on Drew's buttocks.

Drew's muscles tightened, and he shouted something as the icy hot sensation flowed between his legs, covering his testicles with fire. He momentarily saw the look of surprise and concern on Joyce's face. Then the burn of heat and ice shook through his lower body. Thrusting downward, he shuddered at the strength and force of the rushing fluid, and he came again and again. It was over in seconds. With perspiration and Coke streaming down his body onto hers, Drew was red-faced, embarrassed, drained of all energy. Everything hurt inside. Leaning closer to Joyce, he lowered his lips to her ear.

"I'm sorry," he whispered softly.

Drew rolled over on his back and looked up. Rays of heat and light, broken by sliding sandals and small kid's feet, beamed down through the cracks. Behind him, he could hear Shane and May panting to some kind of rhythm. There were occasional higher moans from May.

"It's all right, Drew. I enjoyed it," Joyce said. She turned her head and looked right in his eyes. "Shane said you were a very special person. He was right. I really like you, Drew." Joyce sat up and reached for her bathing suit. "Let's go for a swim."

They got dressed, and Drew shook out the blanket. He looked at the dark stain on the yellow flower and folded the blanket quickly. When they stepped out on the beach, the bright glare of light flashed across his face and blinded him. Feeling the muggy layers of heat settle over his body, he rubbed at his eyes.

Seeing better now, Drew looked at the hundreds of bodies spread out on the sand. Then he grabbed Joyce by the hand, and they ran a zigzag line between the blankets and beach umbrellas. Reaching the surf, they splashed through the shallow line of foam and slammed their bodies into the middle of a cresting, breaking wave.

Later that evening, after taking the girls to their rental house, Drew and Shane walked up the nearly deserted boardwalk. Most of the shops and arcades were closed, and there were only a few stragglers left. Some were couples, whispering and holding onto each other in the shadows between the shops. The moon was bright in the night sky, and a hot wind blew off the ocean. Drew slowed when they approached what he now considered his section of the boardwalk. He looked down and saw the dark smear freshly ingrained in the wood.

"Cola," he said. "Really freezing, burning, stupid Cola."

"What?"

"Nothing," Drew said. He looked at Shane. "You knew May and Joyce would be here."

"I knew," Shane said. "May asked Joyce to come with her. We hoped you two would, you know, like each other."

"I think we do," Drew said.

"Then you had a good time?" Shane asked.

"Good time," Drew said. "It was great."

"That's the important thing," Shane said. "You've had a tough life, Drew. You deserve some good times."

"I had a good time. But don't tell anyone," Drew said. He looked straight ahead, averting Shane's gaze. His voice became low and serious. "It was my first time."

"I kind of figured that," Shane said.

"I don't know for sure," Drew said. He was smiling now. "But I think I hit a home run."

"Great," Shane said. He began laughing and pushed Drew into the railing. "Only one problem, Drew. It was over so fast. I think you missed first base and second and third. May asked me why you and Joyce got up and left so soon."

"It was my fault. I was really getting into it," Drew said. "I mean I was feeling so strong. There was this amazing buildup of energy and heat, and I began fantasizing. Then some kid spilled ice and cola on my ass. I can't explain why. I felt I had died and gone to heaven. Well maybe a few seconds of heaven. Then it was all over."

"That fast," Shane said. "It'll be better tomorrow."

"No," Drew said. "It'll never be better."

"Then, maybe longer," Shane said. They were laughing again. When they settled down and things were quiet, Drew nudged Shane in the shoulder.

"I have a question," Drew said. "When you and May picked your place under the boardwalk, you got that stick and made some marks in the sand. What was that about?"

"It was nothing?"

"Tell me."

"I said it was nothing. I just made a big circle around the blanket."

"Why?" Drew asked. He studied Shane's face, looking deep into the green eyes, and then he remembered and he laughed.

"It wasn't a circle. It was a ring. It was a *Ring of Fire!*"

"I love that song," Shane said and began singing loudly, his words echoing off the boarded arcade and store fronts.

> Love is a burning thing
> And it makes a fiery ring
> Bound by wild desire
> I fell into a Ring of Fire

"I fell into a burning ring of fire!" Drew joined him, and they tried to out shout each other on the empty boardwalk. After a few minutes of singing and joking around, Shane became quiet and turned a serious face to Drew.

"What?" Drew asked.

"You know how Mom always has something to worry about. Well, she asked me to ask you." Shane hesitated. He began walking more slowly. "She asked me to . . ."

"Ask me what?" Drew looked at Shane closely.

"She was worried that your parents hadn't talked to you about sex, about having babies, and that kind of stuff. She was going to bring it up, but she didn't know how to approach you. So she asked me. She said I could talk to you about anything. So if it's all right."

"Go ahead," Drew said. "It's all right."

"OK then. Did your parents ever give you the big talk about sex?"

"No," Drew said. "But you can tell your mother not to worry. I know the baby story."

"I'll tell her that," Shane said. "It will make her feel good." Shane stepped closer and put his arm around Drew's shoulder. His eyes were wide and bright, and there was a mischievous half smile forming on his face. "And if you ever have any questions about, about you know what, ask me."

"What questions?"

"Come down here," Shane said. He pulled Drew down the steps to the sand. Shane picked up a stick and drew a curved line in the sand. Then slicing the stick into the sand again, he closed the oblong shape.

"What's that supposed to mean?"

"I overheard Joyce telling May it was great for her, but you had a hard time getting it in." Shane jammed the stick into the middle of the oblong shape in the sand. "Stick your dick right there."

"You bastard," Drew said. He lunged for Shane who jumped up the steps, howling with laughter, and running at full sprint. There was an empty boardwalk in front of them. Drew easily caught up to Shane, and they ran down the center of the boardwalk, their bodies casting long, dancing shadows against the planks of wood.

Drew didn't believe how fast the week went. On Saturday morning while the Colliers were preparing the final breakfast, he burst out the door and took off running down the boardwalk. Twenty minutes later, his T-shirt soaked wet and dripping moisture, he saw Joyce sitting on the bench in front of the rental. He ran to her, and as she stood up, he grabbed her and hugged her tightly and kissed her for a long time, just as he saw Shane do with May. He was trying for a longer kiss, but Mrs. Thompson called from the house and he had to stop.

Without saying a word, and feeling stronger than ever before, Drew waved at Joyce and began racing past the joggers and bicyclists, his shoes barely scraping the wood of the boardwalk. When he reached their rental, he saw Mr. Collier loading the last suitcase in the trunk of the car. Shane walked down the steps, handed him a bagel, and gave him a contorted "you're crazy for running in the morning" look. Then sunburned and tired, they all got in the car, and Mr. Collier drove away.

When school began in September, Drew and Joyce did everything together. They rode the bus together, ate lunch, did homework, and in the evenings put their change together to buy pizza and burgers. Occasionally, although she professed it was boring, Joyce would run with Drew in the park. On the weekends, they had double dates with Shane and May.

At seven o'clock on Thursday morning, just three days into the school routine, Drew and Joyce were standing under a tree near the bus stop when Shane came running down the steps of the house. The bus had stopped down the block, and Drew could see its red lights flashing. Shane grabbed him and Joyce by the hand and pulled them around the corner. Standing there, back out of sight, Drew watched the bus slow down, stop, doors flap open. The bus driver looked out, and seeing no one, closed the doors, and drove away.

"That's our ride," Drew said. "What's going on?"

"We're taking a day off from school. It's almost like a snow day," Shane said. "I think missing school when the weather's terrible is a waste of time. Students should have a day off when the weather's great, like it is today."

"What you're saying is that we're not going to school. We're unexcused. We're breaking the law."

"No, Drew, we're taking a skip day," Shane said. "Just a skip day."

"I think skip days are for the older students," Joyce said. "They have cars and can go anywhere to hide."

"That's right," Drew said. "Where can we go?"

"May's waiting at the train station," Shane said. "I have it all planned. We're going to Philadelphia. We're going to see the Liberty Bell and the old houses and cemeteries. But mostly we'll just have fun."

"We'll have a lot of fun if the school finds out," Drew said.

"Don't worry so much, Drew. If we have time, we'll go to Ben's birthplace. You don't want to miss that, do you?"

"Ben wasn't born in Philadelphia," Drew said. "He was born in Boston."

"That's close enough," Shane said.

Shane, Drew, and Joyce walked quickly down the street, and when another school bus turned the corner, they ran in a side alley. They stayed on the back streets until they saw the train tracks. Except for May and an elderly couple, the Phoenixville Train Station was empty.

It was a forty-five-minute train ride to Philadelphia. Most of the commuters had gone earlier, and the nine o'clock train was not crowded. Because of past visits with his parents, Drew knew downtown, and he became the understood leader of the group. They walked with the crowds down Market Street, and when Drew saw the front entrance to the Wachovia Bank where his dad had worked, he walked by quickly without looking up.

With the morning sun and bright blue sky and cool dry air, it was a pleasant walk to Independence Mall. Large tour busses and some horse-drawn carriages were parked at the corner. A group of tourists exited one of the busses, and Drew and Shane and the girls got in the end of the slow-moving procession. They followed the tourists down the wide sidewalk to the Liberty Bell Pavilion. It was a long building in the middle of a large grassy field. The walls of the pavilion were made of thick glass.

At the entrance, they walked through a detector of some kind and past the security guard. There was a room to the side filled with pictures and historical information, but Shane led Drew and the girls right to end of the pavilion. More security personal stood near the simple rope barrier tied to the silver posts that circled the bell.

Shane moved carefully through the crowd until he was next to the rope. Drew had managed to keep close to Shane, but May and Joyce were two people behind. Sliding along the rope, Shane positioned himself right in front of the deep, vertical crack in the great bell. Surrounded by the bodies of tourists and looking right and left, Shane reached slowly over the rope.

"Hold me," Shane said. Drew grabbed onto his shirt as Shane stretched further over the rope. With one last effort, he put his hand on the side of the bell. Then he slid his fingers into and down the length of the crack. When Shane tried to do it again, the security guard pointed a black club at him and told him to move along. Drew was at his side when they left the building.

"What were you doing?'

"I was touching history," Shane said. "The crack felt kind of funny. It was wide and deep and smooth to the touch. It was almost sexual."

"You're crazy," Drew said. "All you think about is sex." They stood off to the side for a moment, and the girls caught up and joined them.

"The security people move you through pretty fast," May said. "You could hardly get close to the bell."

"Shane got close," Drew said. "He got close enough to put his finger in the crack."

"Enough about the bell," Shane said. "Does anyone want a drink?"

"No," Drew said. "Joyce and I will wait over there." He pointed to the benches along the side wall.

"Be right back," Shane said. He took May's hand, and they started toward the corner of the mall where there was a line of vendors. Joyce and Drew walked to the wall and sat down on a bench away from the crowd.

"It's been a fun day," Joyce said, brushing the hair from her forehead.

"I could spent the rest of it right here with you," Drew said. "Since that week at the shore, I really like your company. You're a special person, Joyce.

You don't talk too much, you don't complain, you don't ask silly questions. All in all, you're just great to be with."

"I feel the same way about you," Joyce said. "I only regret we didn't meet sooner."

Searching for food, a squirrel scurried under the bench and stood up at their feet. Making chirping noises and with eyes open wide, it flicked its tail in the air. Joyce laughed.

"You look like that some times," she said. "I mean you have those big blue eyes that look so innocent."

"They are innocent."

"Maybe," Joyce said. "Maybe not." She leaned closer and touched his face. "And I love this scar. When you smile, it makes you look different, I think, handsome." She leaned closer and kissed him. Drew felt her lips and then her tongue move around the edges of the scar. Putting his arm around her, he returned the kiss. Just as he was getting real excited, Drew heard loud, scraping footsteps in the leaves. The squirrel hissed sharply and raced for a tree.

"We're back," Shane said and pointed his finger at Drew. "Don't be grabbing each other like that in public. This is a skip day, not a sex day." He handed each of them a soda in a plastic Liberty Bell container.

"Thanks," Drew said. He released his hand from Joyce and took the drink.

Tail jutting in the air, the squirrel dropped down from the tree and approached the bench cautiously. Shane took a package of cheese crackers from his pocket. He ate a few pieces and gave the rest to the squirrel. Two other squirrels and some pigeons appeared out of nowhere. Then a whole flock of black birds came squawking toward them from the telephone wires. Soon they were sitting in the middle of a zoo.

"The animals are out of control," Drew said, standing up quickly. "Let's get out of here." They walked through the scattering of birds. There was a tourist booth at the corner of Third Street and Market. Drew stopped and looked at the large map on the wall.

"Do you want to visit Christ Church or the Betsy Ross House?" he asked.

"Betsy's house," Shane said. They walked down Third Street and saw the house as soon as they turned the corner onto Arch Street.

There was a large courtyard in front of the Betsy Ross House. Dressed in colonial clothes, one of the guides stood on a wooden bench and was talking to a group of elementary school kids. Straining to hear, an elderly teacher hovered in the back of the group. The teacher had a blue hat on her head, and she wore a blue dress adorned with miniature flags. The colonial guide paused for a moment in his lecture and wiped the perspiration from his forehead. He looked up and saw Shane waving his hand in the air.

"Yes, you have a question?" the guide asked. He had a thin face, and he wore thin Ben Franklin spectacles that slid to the tip of his nose. Some of the students turned their heads when Shane spoke.

"Did Ole Ben ever hump Betsy Ross?"

"What?" the guide asked. The legs on the bench wobbled, and the guide seemed a bit uneasy standing there.

"My friend told me that Ben Franklin and Betsy spent a lot of time together working on the flag." Shane hesitated. "My friend also told me they spent some time under the flag." Shane stared patiently at the guide. The small faces of the students also turned and looked at the guide. "Is that true?" Shane asked.

"I don't know what you're talking about," the guide said. He jumped down from the bench. Soon, he had the group of students and confused teacher moving across the courtyard toward the entrance to the house.

"That was embarrassing," May said when they reached the sidewalk. "How can you talk like that around children?"

"It was Drew. He told me Ben was the P and P lover."

"What's that supposed to mean?" May asked.

"It means that Ben loved all the beautiful women in Philadelphia and Paris—P and P. Drew said he banged them all."

"I didn't say it that way. I said Ben was popular with the ladies even when he was old."

"Same thing," Shane said. "Learning history is fun some times."

They walked down Arch Street and turned onto Second Street. There was a crowd of people standing around the entrance to Elfreth's Alley. Many of the women wore colonial blouses and large skirts. Most of the men wore the uniforms of the Continental Army. Drew read the historical marker on the corner.

"The oldest, continuously inhabited street in Philadelphia. The first people were here in 1702." Drew was still looking at the marker when a tourist holding a camera bumped into him.

"Excuse me," the tourist said, looking annoyed. He pointed the camera at the marker and waited.

Drew stepped quickly out of his way. He took Joyce's hand, and they followed Shane and May down the cobblestone alley. Shane stopped in front of a small, narrow house that was three-stories high. Climbing the porch step, Shane looked through the window.

"There's only one room," he said. "How do you live in that?"

"It's a trinity," the elderly colonial lady next to him said. "The house has a total of three rooms, one on each floor. The clever colonialists saved money living that way."

"How?" Shane asked, looking at the top story.

"They were taxed by how wide the house was and not how high," she said. "So they build tiny, tall houses."

"What a way to live," Shane said. He took one step past the house and was out of the shadow of the building.

Two doors down a colonial soldier, a very pompous, bearded man, was talking to a tourist family of two parents, two grandparents, four children, and one baby in a stroller. In his tricorn hat, light blue tunic, knee-high stockings, and buckle shoes, the soldier was impressive. The musket over his shoulder was more impressive.

In a slow, monotone voice, the soldier was explaining something about the Battle of Brandywine when the baby began crying. It was a loud, shrill cry, and the family circled the stroller and pushed it away.

Drew, Shane, and the girls took their spot directly in front of the soldier. Coming up to the man's chest, Drew studied the shiny buttons on the soldier's tunic. Looking closely, he saw something else there.

"What's that?" Drew asked, pointing to the thin wire that was connected to a radio on the ground. The wire wound under the soldier's coat and reappeared at his neck connected to what looked like large earmuffs.

"The Phillies pre-game," the soldier said. He looked around and then began speaking with enthusiasm. "We're doing great. We're six and one-half games in first place with only twelve left to play. We're going to the World Series."

"That's very strange," Shane said. He got a smart look on his face. "I didn't know there was much interest in baseball during the Revolutionary War. I think you're wasting our tax dollars. Listening to a Phillies game when you should be helping us students learn history, you're nothing but a fake. There's nothing authentic about you except maybe that potbelly."

Drew felt pressure from behind, and turning, he saw people beginning to gather around them. The soldier's loud voice attracted more people from across the street. A small girl pushed forward and stuck her head through the crowd.

"Does this look real to you?" Unbuttoning his tunic, the soldier pulled it open. Wrapped tightly around the protruding belly was a blue belt, and the silver buckle in the center was adorned with a large red-and-white Phillies logo. "The World Series, that's what's important. Now, if you don't have any questions, you can move on so I can listen to the game."

"I have a question," Drew said, stepping closer to the soldier. "Were you at Valley Forge? I heard it was bad there."

"You bet I was there," the soldier said. He turned his attention to Drew but kept a hard stare on Shane. "And it wasn't bad. It was terrible. We had no uniforms and no food. But mostly, it was the cold that done us in. We lost twenty percent of the army."

"But you had cabins."

"Not at first," the soldier said. "We built them in a hurry, and the cold wind blew right through. You young people wouldn't understand. You couldn't have taken it. You're too soft and spoiled. You would've deserted and gone home and given America back to the redcoats. We'd all be eating fish and chips now instead of burgers."

"You're exaggerating," Shane said. "It couldn't have been that bad." The little girl stepped next to Shane. She was nodding her head in agreement.

"But it was," the soldier said. "One winter night, we used up what little wood we had, and the fire in the cabin went out. The three soldiers by the door froze to death. Hard as a rock they were the next morning."

"What'd you do?" the little girl asked in a timid, quivering voice.

"We did the only thing we could at the time," the soldier said. "We propped them up outside against the log wall so they could do guard duty and we ourselves wouldn't be freezing to death." The soldier's voice was serious and his face was stern. "And when the wind come howling and knocked them down like dominoes, we took turns going out and straightening them up."

"That was wrong." The girl spoke in a loud squeaky voice. "You should have buried them."

"How could we do that? The ground was frozen. And besides, the soldiers didn't care any more, did they?" the officer asked. "They stayed on guard until spring came, and then they thawed, and only then did we bury them. And I will tell you this for a fact. Standing there bravely like that in the freezing cold, they probably saved our lives many times. And I salute them for that."

The soldier straightened his body to attention. The girl screamed something and ran to her parents. Drew looked at the circle of disapproving faces and turned back to the soldier.

"And is that why you're alive now telling this story?" Drew asked.

"Most certainly," the soldier said. "It was the soldier's sacrifice that kept the army alive. It's why we defeated the British."

"I like that story," Drew said. He raised his hand and saluted the soldier. "It's inspiring."

"That's my job," the soldier said, returning the salute. "To make you young people appreciate this great heritage you have. Don't you ever take it for granted. And don't forget to give a loud cheer for the Phillies."

"I love the Phillies," Drew said. He joined the others waiting at the corner. They walked back to Chestnut Street and followed it to the busy waterfront area.

"I'm hungry," Shane said. "Let's get a burger." He was looking at the Burger King down the street.

"Since we're here, let's try different food," Drew said. "Let's try something exotic."

"I guess we can," Joyce said. "We eat burgers all the time at school."

"And this is our skip day, and I don't want to be reminded of school right now," Drew said.

They were surrounded by a variety of shops and restaurants. Drew pointed to a gaudy, brightly colored sign, Middle East Restaurant, hanging over the sidewalk across the street. They crossed between the traffic of cars, double-deck tourist busses, people hanging over the sides, and horse-drawn carriages. Drew opened the large wooden door carved with half-moons and strange symbols and ushered them inside the Middle East Restaurant. It was cavernous and empty of customers.

There were round tables in the middle of the room, and booths lined both sides. Shaded lamps in the corners of the booths gave out a very dim light. Looking at the plush hanging carpets on the wall and the large pictures of seaports and marketplaces with colorfully dressed but foreign-looking people, Drew led Shane and the girls down the floor into the deeper recesses of the Middle East.

Incense burned in oval glass holders and filled the room with smoke that rose slowly and clouded the high ceiling. When they reached the last booth in the corner, Shane and Drew stood back, and the girls slid inside. Joyce and May coughed and tried to wave the smoke away with their hands, but Drew was looking through the smoke at a large picture of a belly dancer. He marveled at her curved, sensuous features.

"I can't breathe," May said, coughing again in her hand.

"The smoke's not that bad," Drew said, straining to find the belly button in the picture.

Wearing a black uniform and a white shirt with ruffled cuffs, the waiter came to the table. He was bearded and had a long black moustache that twisted up on the corners. He gave Drew and Shane menus, and when Drew opened his, he saw pictures filled with brightly colored vegetables and meats and sauces. The words describing the dishes were just a strange mixture of lines. Drew lifted the menu in front of the waiter and pointed to a dish that had some kind of meat, small tomatoes, and onions skewered on a pointed stick. It rested on a bed of yellow rice.

"Four," Drew said. When the waiter just looked at him, Drew wiggled four fingers in his face and pointed to the picture and the people in the booth. The waiter mumbled something and took the menus.

"What did you order?" Shane asked.

"Chicken," Drew said. "Barbequed chicken on a stick."

Shane believed it was really chicken, but Joyce and May weren't sure. They were still bothered by the smoke and strange incense smell that seemed to be getting stronger. Fanning a napkin across her face, May said something about the Burger King down the street. They talked for a while, coughed across the table at each other, went to the rest room, and waited. Twenty minutes after the order, the waiter returned with four dishes of steaming food. Drew tasted the meat first.

"This is good," he said.

Everyone took a large forkful, but May tried a very small bite. After tasting and swallowing it, she broke off a bigger piece of meat. Drew took a dark piece of meat from a different plate and ate it quickly. The curried taste was sweet and spicy. The food was delicious and disappeared fast. Except for some of the vegetables they couldn't identify, they ate everything on the plates. At the end of the meal, Drew was stuffed and felt good about the selection.

"I know my exotic foods," he told them.

When the waiter brought the bill, they put their money together. Luckily, May dropped twenty dollars on the table, and they had more than enough money to cover the food and the tip. After he cleared the dishes, the waiter brought cups with a very dark liquid in them. Joyce tasted hers and made an ugly face.

Then a high-pitched, kind-of-weird music began playing from the wall speakers. Drew looked up at the sound and saw a hand slide through the red-and-black curtain next to the booth. The hand was followed by a naked arm and a nearly naked body.

Clicking the golden cymbals on her fingers, the belly dancer slid from behind the curtain into full view. Shane turned quickly at the sound, and his mouth dropped open when he saw her. She was a big woman, her stomach rounded and very substantial. She wore a slight black bra with flesh bulging from the edges, and there was only a dark string with hanging beads around her waist.

The belly dancer clicked her way around to the front of the booth and began a slow, hypnotic type of dance. Her body mass flowed back and forth and moved gracefully with the music. Shane and Drew watched every inch of motion while May and Joyce sulked safely back into the corner of the booth.

The dancer's hands rose straight over her head, and her body spun circles in the shifting clouds of smoke and incense. It was a painfully slow dance that went on for minutes. Then after a swirl of her body, beads swinging to a stop on her glistening skin, she bent closer and presented her butt cheeks to the two boys now sitting mesmerized at the edge of the booth.

Staring at the smooth, oily skin, now so close and completely exposed, Drew gasped for air. The buttocks wiggled in front of him, and the beads made a slight jingling sound. The dancer turned and showed him a bright smile with amazingly white teeth, and then she wiggled her butt again. Drew began to see beyond the mass of flesh and thought he understood what he was supposed to do.

Reaching into his pocket, he took out the last bill he had, five dollars. It was his lunch money and snack money for the week. It was all the wealth he had, and he reached over and slid the green bill under the black silk string. Feeling the oil and warmth of the dancer's skin, he slowly, ever so slowly, maneuvered the bill deeper into her flesh, and he then folded it neatly back over the string.

Drew patted it twice, but it still protruded at a funny angle. He patted it once more ever so gently; and removing his hand, Drew slid his fingers together, feeling the smooth oil. He lifted his hand to his nose and smelled it. It was sweet, and a pleasant feeling began to warm his body.

Green eyes open wide, Shane had an amazed expression on his face. Frantically, he began to search his pockets for money. He found a quarter, and turning it slowly in his hand, he looked thoughtfully at the dancer. She wiggled her butt again, and the beads quivered musically. Shane's face began to glow in the dim light, and he leaned forward. Holding the silver quarter in his fingers, he reached his hand toward the two voluptuous mounds of quivering, cream-colored, Jell-O smooth buttocks.

Drew stared in disbelief as Shane was about to slide the coined image of a solemn-faced George Washington into the center of the oily cleavage. But May screamed something, and swinging out her arm, she smacked down on Shane's wrist. The quarter flipped in the air and landed on the floor. When the spinning coin slowed and stopped flat at the dancer's feet, the silver profile of George Washington's face shown clearly in the dim, smoky light.

Drew attempted to get the quarter, but the dancer reached down quickly, and the quarter disappeared in her hand. Beads swinging wildly, she danced around the booth and slid behind the curtain.

"I don't believe you!" May shouted. She slapped at Shane.

"What?" he asked incredulously. "What'd I do?"

"You were going to . . ."

May didn't finish the sentence. She pushed Shane out of the booth. Drew and Joyce slid out of their seats, and they all walked quickly to the door. Drew didn't realize how hot it was in the Middle East until cool air hit him hard in the face. He could still feel the oil on his fingers.

"I guess you didn't see what Drew did with his money?" Shane asked.

"I was being respectful," Drew said. "I left a tip like you're supposed to."

"See, May, don't yell at me. Drew started it."

May was still angry, and Shane tried to mollify her as they walked down the street. Finally, when the girls had finished criticizing and had found something else to talk about, Shane stepped close to Drew and whispered softly in his ear.

"There was no contest," he said seriously. "Her crack was way better than the Liberty Bell's." Drew had to laugh. Joyce and May looked at him suspiciously, and then they turned and pretended to ignore both Drew and Shane.

Walking in the sun totally oblivious to the crowds of people brushing past and the honking noise of the traffic in the street, Drew drifted away and entered a quiet world he had never experienced before. Holding Joyce's hand and gently rubbing the last of the oil into her palm, he felt really good. It was their first skip day, and Drew began to sense how great life was, how great it was to be young and free and with his best friends, Joyce and May and Shane.

On the Saturday after skip day, Drew and Joyce were in the park. They had just finished jogging past the Memorial Arch and across Mount Joy. It was nearly noon, and the weather was pleasant and warm. Crowds of picnickers and tourists were filing into the more popular areas of Valley Forge. Drew was feeling good about the run when they stopped near the von Steuben statue. He looked at the traces of perspiration on the front of Joyce's George Washington T-shirt.

"I like the shape you're in," Drew said, hesitating when he saw the look on her face. "I mean running's getting you in great shape."

"I could never do this by myself," she said. "But with you, I don't notice the running so much."

"What do you notice?" he asked, observing how the perspiration formed a clear outline of her breasts.

"You," she said. "How easy you run. Maybe how much you enjoy it."

"I enjoy it even more now," he said. "The view is much better. I mean there are more things to look at."

"I know what you've been looking at," Joyce laughed. "Mom will pick us up soon. I'll be right back. I'm going to the rest room." She waved and crossed Route 23, heading for the Varnum Picnic Area.

Drew watched her disappear behind the log cabin. Then he turned and walked toward the large statue of Baron von Steuben. On a stone pedestal, black cloak reaching to his boots, his arm folded across his chest, the general fixed his eyes resolutely on the parade ground of tall grass and rolling field. There were three wooden benches on either side and sitting alone on the left bench was an old man, his body leaning slightly to the right. Drew recognized him immediately.

"Professor JJ," he said, approaching the bench. "How are you doing?"

"I'm fine, Drew." He stood up, and they shook hands. "I'm really enjoying my retirement. I saw you and Joyce running."

"She went to the rest room," Drew said. "Do you come here often?"

"Oh, yes," Professor JJ said. "Next to Independence Hall, the park is my favorite place. This view overlooking the Grand Parade ground is the best in Valley Forge. This is where the baron did most of his work. It must have been something when the soldiers and officers first trained and marched here in the snow and cold. And at the other end of this field near the Memorial Arch, that's where the officers ensured that the baron would have his army to train."

"How did they do that?"

"According to the official war journals, the Memorial Arch is where the tree was located. It was a huge oak tree, one of the few left standing."

"I don't understand," Drew said.

"It was where the military tribunal passed judgment and hanged deserters."

"They hanged deserters!"

"The army was disintegrating, and the officers had to do something. They needed to establish control, and General Washington was ruthless when he had to be. That was good for this country or else we would have lost the war."

"I never thought about that," Drew said. "I remember seeing this painting of Washington kneeling in prayer next to a tree. He looked so calm."

"The picture in the forest. The famous picture of General Washington at Valley Forge. I think the artist took some liberties, Drew. There was no forest at Valley Forge. Most of the trees were cut down to build the cabins and then to heat the cabins. It was a tough time. No, it was worse than tough. It was a horrible time for the army. Come over here, Drew."

Professor JJ moved away from the bench and led Drew across the grass to a flattened piece of stone set into the ground. It was rectangular, anchored in the earth by nails in the four corners and on the sides. A thin series of horizontal and vertical lines formed square patterns across the face of the stone. In the middle of the pattern of squares was a longer rectangle shape.

"What is it?" Drew asked.

"The first monument in Valley Forge," Professor JJ said. "It's the Chicken Thief Monument."

"Who's the chicken thief?" Drew asked.

"Just a hungry soldier trapped by the Valley Forge winter. The local farmers were losing their livestock. The order came out from Washington's Headquarters that thieves would be shot. And that's exactly what happened to this soldier."

Professor JJ looked at the memorial. He knelt down and scraped some dirt and dry grass off the stone surface.

"The history is clear on this one. In 1901, a local farmer, Francis Wood, found a human skeleton on his land. Family diaries from 1778 recorded that a young colonial soldier was killed trying to steal chickens. Wood concluded this was the soldier's skeleton, and he offered to bury the remains in the park. With amazing good sense, the park superintendent at the time, Mr. Bowen, accepted the offer, and consequently, this stone marks the burial place of a soldier who was also a chicken thief."

"It's hard to imagine a soldier would be killed over a chicken," Drew said.

"But try to imagine it," Professor JJ said. "There was a period of time during that winter that no supply wagons came in. There was no food but what the soldier could scrape up on his own. This soldier stole a chicken and was killed. Can you picture this soldier, Drew? Can you see him clearly?"

"I can see someone who hasn't eaten in days, but I don't feel anything. I've never experienced starvation."

"No, you never have," Professor JJ said. "But you've grown up in this park so you've seen many pictures of soldiers at Valley Forge. And you've gone through cold winters here so you can imagine him freezing. Can you do that?"

"Kind of," Drew said. Willing himself to feel hunger and the sting from an icy winter wind, Drew closed his eyes. On numerous occasions in the past he realized he could project himself easily, and with a high degree of cogency, into imaginative situations that seemed to be entirely real. As he listened intently to Professor JJ's quiet, almost hypnotic words, a chilling darkness engulfed him.

"The chicken thief soldier was young and probably a farmer. To leave his home and volunteer to join the army at Valley Forge, he must have loved the idea of freedom. Or maybe he came because he hated the redcoats because of some past injustice."

"Maybe both," Drew said.

From visits and his daily running, Drew knew every part of the Valley Forge encampment. His memory produced a flashing kaleidoscope of images of soldiers in all manner of attire, officers in splendid uniforms, log cabins, large artillery pieces, horse-drawn wagons, the Colonial flag with the circle of stars, and the encampment itself, shrouded and waiting death under a thick blanket of ice and snow. From these images emerged a solitary figure standing alone on a snow-swept hillside.

"And our chicken soldier was starving, Drew. The new army had no organization, no supplies. So if he arrived hungry, he stayed hungry. The soldier knew there was food on the farm. He would go there at night, and he would wait until there was dead quiet. It would be freezing, especially if the moon were full. When he could no longer take the pain, he would sneak into the barn. There's no way of knowing how close he actually came to catching a chicken."

"I think he got hold of one," Drew said. His eyes tightly closed, Drew saw a bright orb high in the darkness over the farmhouse and barn. "And there was a full moon like you said. It was freezing, but it wasn't quiet like it should have been. There was noise everywhere."

Drew visualized the open clearing covered with glistening white snow. He heard and then saw chicken feathers thrashing wildly. But there was a figure on the porch, and he had a red covering over his head. Drew was confused, and his breathing became irregular. There was a thundering noise behind him, followed by bright flashes and total darkness. Opening his eyes, Drew grabbed at his throat and muttered something.

"What did you see?" Professor JJ asked.

"He did have a chicken," Drew said, shielding his eyes from the glare of the afternoon sun. "It was crazy. I saw feathers and a chicken. I can't explain it. I felt like I was there."

"You've always had this vivid imagination, Drew, maybe too vivid," Professor JJ said. "But because you have that gift, you probably understand better than others that the chicken thief was a good citizen, a good soldier, and even though he wasn't killed in some famous battle, he died bravely and honorably. He died for our freedom like all the soldiers in the Colonial Army." Professor JJ looked at the stone and then fixed his gaze on Drew. "I think he was a lot like you."

"I'm not a farm boy, nor a soldier," Drew said. "And I don't think I'll ever have to steal any chickens."

"Probably not," Professor JJ said. "But when I envision the chicken soldier, for some reason, I don't know why, I see your face." They walked back to the bench and sat down under the dark shadow of General Baron von Steuben.

"The general was an exceptional soldier," Professor JJ said. "Before he came to Valley Forge, he fought in the Seven Year's War and was an aide-de-camp to Frederick the Great. Do you know who Frederick was, Drew?"

"No."

"He was King of Prussia."

"The name of the mall," Drew said. He laughed and shook his head. "What happened to the general? Was he killed in the war?"

"No," Professor JJ said. "He died an old man at the age of sixty-four. He died on his land in the Mohawk Valley in Upper New York State. It's kind of ironic, Drew."

"What is?"

"Von Steuben died alone in a log cabin. I think as an officer and a general he had better accommodations here at Valley Forge."

"That's sad," Drew said.

"I think the chicken soldier's story is more depressing," Professor JJ said. "Do you remember Katczinsky?"

"Kat," Drew said. "From *All Quiet on the Western Front*. Sure, I remember him. It was a great story."

"Kat always brought food to the soldiers in his company," Professor JJ said. "He went out and found geese, all kinds of farm animals. That was World War I. What I'm getting at, Drew, there are chicken soldiers in every war, and they're important. They're the ones who do all the fighting. They're the ones who win wars."

Drew didn't say anything. He looked at Professor JJ and sensed that he wasn't finished. A big blue-and-white tour bus went by, and the Professor waited for the noise to subside.

"That's why I don't understand these monuments, Drew. Generals get these huge statues." Professor JJ pointed at the massive figure of Baron von

Steuben. "What does the common soldier get? He gets dead, that's all. No big monuments are built for him, yet he suffered the most. Especially, here, in this park, the suffering was unimaginable. I really think the chicken thief soldier was as big a hero as the baron. I think he should have a bigger statue than von Steuben's."

"I think so, too," Drew said.

"Sure, von Steuben was an impressive officer. He taught the army the tight marching that was so important to form strong lines of fire. He taught the quicker gun-loading motions and the proper firing positions that were critical in a battle. But do you know what Ben Franklin said about fighting with muskets in close quarters like that?"

"No," Drew said, smiling that Professor JJ was on his favorite subject.

"Ben put forward the proposition that bows and arrows would be better than the muskets in fighting the British. And of course he had done his research. The arrows were more accurate and thus more deadly, but Ben had also established one important fact that was conclusive, Drew. What do you think it was?"

"I don't know."

"What have I taught you to do?"

"Like I just did with the chicken soldier," Drew answered. "You said to always form a clear picture or nothing would make any sense." Drew focused his thoughts quickly and could see the congestion of soldiers on the field and how they knelt and fired and reloaded and fired again until there was a black cloud over everything.

"What do you see?"

"It's the smoke. With all that smoke, it's hard to see what to shoot at." Drew shook his head. "But arrows wouldn't change that. I don't know."

"It's true our soldiers wore blue, distinctive colors, and the English wore bright red so they wouldn't shoot at each other," Professor JJ said. "But Ben was more concerned with efficiency. He stated the soldier could fire off four arrows to every musket shot. Did you know it took fifteen motions to fire and reload a musket? On the other hand, it took no time to place an arrow in the bow, aim at the stationary line of red jackets, and fire. That four to one ratio would have been devastating to the enemy. Of course, the military officers laughed at him."

"Of course," Drew said. He looked across the parade ground and pictured the red lines of the British and the blue lines of the Continental Army. There were alternating volleys of musket fire from the red line, and thick clouds of smoke soon covered the soldiers. But the individual soldiers in the blue line were clearly visible, and they shot hundreds of arrows into the smoke across the field.

Soon the musket fire stopped, and when the smoke had cleared, the British soldiers were on the ground, feathered arrows jutting at awkward angles from their red coats. Drew smiled at the absolute destruction in the picture and how mathematically sound the bow-and-arrow strategy was. He then remembered the classroom and the value of everything Professor JJ had taught him.

"I wish you were still teaching, Professor JJ," Drew said. "I wish you were still in the school. I'm sorry about the kite accident."

"Don't feel sorry for me, Drew. I never told you the truth about that day."

"The truth was simple," Drew said. "I did a stupid thing. It was stupid and dangerous. I read later that Franklin was knocked unconscious two times while experimenting with electricity."

"Yes, but that didn't deter him," Professor JJ said. "And he was wiser and a lot older than you."

"How old was he?"

"Let me think," Professor JJ said. "Franklin's kite experiment was in 1752."

"When?" Drew asked, watching the serious expression of Professor JJ's face.

"To be more precise, it was on June 15, 1752," Professor JJ said. "Exactly one hundred and two years ago. And since Franklin was born in 1706, that would make him forty-two years old." Professor JJ looked at Drew and smiled with admiration. "You did the experiment at a much younger age, Drew."

"It wasn't the same."

"You had all the same materials," Professor JJ said. "You had the kite, the metal key, the lightning, and you also had the innovative sound effects. But there was one thing you didn't have that Franklin had. Franklin had the sense to make sure he was insulated. Without insulation, your experiment was potentially very dangerous."

"I know. I'm sorry I caused so much trouble."

"That's what I wanted to tell you, Drew. It wasn't your fault. Remember, I approved the experiment. I was there on the football field with you. I knew what you were doing, and I let it happen. I was responsible for everything."

"I don't understand."

"It's hard to explain, Drew." Professor JJ hesitated. His face was pensive, and he squinted his eyes against the glare of the bright sunlight. "Seventy-five people every year are killed by lightning, so I knew there was danger. I knew it as soon as you told me about the experiment. And there on the field with the kite and silver key twisting in that dark sky, I felt the danger, and somehow, it made me feel more alive than ever." Professor Jackson paused and looked out over the Grand Parade ground.

"I was really excited, too excited for a man my age. Then there was that first glow of lightning in the distance, and I should have cleared the field. I should have gotten everyone inside. I counted twenty seconds when I first saw the lightning and heard the thunder. I thought we had more time."

"Everything got kind of crazy," Drew said.

"It was the same with Ben's experiment, Drew. Science is crazy sometimes. I felt the danger, and it gave me a sense of what Ben himself might have felt.

I was finally living that dream of being close to this genius of a man. It was a magical time for me." Professor JJ turned away from the sun's glare and looked seriously at Drew. "There was one thing I was never sure of, Drew. Did the lightning really hit the kite? Did you feel anything?"

"I think it hit," Drew said. With his eyes open wide and a sincere expression on his face, Drew lied. He lied completely and honestly, and while he was lying, he rubbed the palm of his right hand where he had held the string. "I felt a shock, and my hand was numb. But it didn't hurt much. It went away as soon as I dropped the string."

"You and Ben," Professor JJ said. "Remarkable."

"It was remarkable," Drew said.

"Here's some kite information that will interest you," Professor JJ said. "There are plans to build a sculpture in Philadelphia to honor Ben Franklin and his kite experiment. It will be called the Bolt of Lightning. It should be finished in a few years. I hope you get to see it."

"I can't wait to see it," Drew said.

"One other thing I should tell you, Drew," Professor JJ said. "I've loved teaching all these years. But this is the first time I've felt a genuine sense of triumph. Sometimes, teachers imagine they see a part of themselves in a student. At first, I thought it was intelligence we were identifying with, but I was wrong."

"What was it?"

"It's the imagination, Drew, the strength of the spirit in the student. I see that strength in you. That's why I hope you will consider becoming a teacher."

"I've already considered that, Professor JJ," Drew said. "I'm going to school to get a degree, a degree in history. It's what Mom wanted me to do." He heard a car horn and turned to see Joyce in the parking lot. She was standing next to her mother's car.

"I have to go now, Professor JJ. I'm glad to see you healthy and well. I'll never forget the things you said and everything you taught me. Even today I learned so much. And I'll never forget the story about the chicken thief soldier."

Drew shook hands with the professor. He noticed the smile and the brightness in the eyes. The car horn sounded again. Drew turned and walked quickly to the parking lot. He greeted Mrs. Thompson and squeezed in the front seat next to Joyce.

"Isn't that your old teacher?" Mrs. Thompson asked.

"Yes," Drew said. As they drove out of the parking lot, Drew looked back at the towering black statue of Baron von Steuben, the grove of trees, and Professor JJ sitting straight and tall on the park bench.

CHAPTER 7

O n a hot spring day in 1967, Mr. Collier celebrated his fortieth birthday. Mrs. Collier didn't mention anything that morning, but she had been secretly preparing for the birthday for weeks. She contacted the caterers and sent out invitations, and that night at the house, she treated him to a surprise birthday party.

Neighborhood friends, fellow workers, and even the store manager and his wife from Devon came to the party. The driveway was filled, and the street was lined with cars. The caterers from King of Prussia brought two trucks and four servers. They set up a big tent, strings of colored lights, tables and chairs, and an arrangement of potted plants around the yard.

The menu started with an appetizer of six grilled shrimp on a stick coated with a zesty Thai sauce. The main course was filet mignon with wild mushroom gravy, mixed fresh vegetables, and Mr. Collier's favorite side dish, sweet potato fries, which he and his wife had first eaten on their honeymoon at Seneca Falls.

There was a big, rounded cream-colored birthday cake at the end of the serving table. It had one large red candle stuck in the middle of it. There were glasses filled with champagne on the tables. The celebration was loud and delightful, and the noise drifted over the neighborhood. Once, a police cruiser went down the street, slowed in front of the house, and then continued on its way.

Shane and Drew met everyone as they entered, and sitting with their parents, they greatly enjoyed the meal and the champagne. Shane congratulated his dad again, and he and Drew walked inside the house. The party was still going strong at ten o'clock when Shane got up from watching *Gunsmoke* on TV and left the living room. A few minutes later he returned carrying a small cooler.

"Let's go," he said to Drew.

"Where?"

"To celebrate," Shane said. "It's my dad's birthday. And we're juniors now. We graduate next year."

"We can wait and celebrate with the rest of our class," Drew said. He followed Shane out the door to the car.

"I can't celebrate with them," Shane said, sliding the cooler in the back seat. "I'm scheduled to fly out right after graduation." He and Drew got in the car, and he was able to maneuver out of the tight parking space.

"That early enlistment was your decision," Drew said. "What's in the cooler?"

"Some ice-cold Sam Adams?" Shane said. "All the champagne's gone."

"Where are we going?"

"To Valley Forge," Shane said.

"No way," Drew said. "That's government property. Let's just go to the covered bridge. Or we could go that park behind the mall."

"We're going to Valley Forge," Shane said. "Relax, Drew. It's late. No one will be there."

Shane drove into town and stopped at the first red light. Reaching into the cooler, he pulled out two bottles of Sam Adams and gave one to Drew. Shane clicked off the cap, looked around, and took a quick drink. The light changed, and he drove slowly to the next light where he took another drink.

"What are you doing, Shane?" Drew asked, still holding onto his unopened bottle. It was moist and cold in his hand. "You can't drink and drive."

"I'm not drinking and driving," Shane said. "I'm only drinking and stopping. I mean I'm only drinking when the car is stopped."

"I don't care how you try to explain it; it's against the law. And you can't have open bottles in the car."

"Just relax, Drew."

"How can I relax?" Drew asked. "We're committing every crime in the book."

"Look," Shane said. "Like I've been telling you all along, our senior year will end before we know it. Then I'll be gone. I'll be in the war. I think we should take every opportunity to have a good time. OK?" He drove slowly out of town and over the bridge at the Pickering Creek Dam. The water flowing down the spillway was sparkling in the moonlight.

"No, it's not OK," Drew said. Reluctantly, he opened his Sam Adams and took a drink. When he lowered the bottle, he burped quietly and looked both right and left for any vehicles hidden in the trees or back out of sight on the side roads.

Five minutes later, Shane drove the car into Valley Forge National Park. The light at the intersection next to Washington's Headquarters was red, so he and Drew lifted their bottles and drank quickly. They both emptied their bottles at the same time. Shane turned off Route 23 and took the back road. He parked the car at the cobblestone entrance to the Memorial Arch. The sky was clear, and bright moonlight streamed over the top and through the center of the monumental arch. Shane and Drew each picked up a handle of the cooler and walked to a large tree.

Looking at the oval moon and the silhouette of the arch, Drew sat down in the shadows of the tree. Shane took a bottle from the cooler, shook it behind his back, and gave it to Drew. When Drew opened his bottle, a spray of beer and foam spurted over his face,

"That's real funny," Drew said, wiping his face. "Why not just pour the beer on the ground?"

"I'm sorry," Shane said. He took another Sam Adams, shook the bottle, and opening it quickly, he was hit by a thick burst of foam. Bubbles stuck to his nose and cheek. Laughing and trying to drink, he sat down next to Drew.

"I still don't think we should be here," Drew said.

"Why?"

"This is hallowed ground," Drew said. "This is where soldiers of the Revolutionary Army starved and suffered, and," Drew pointed his Sam Adams at the Memorial Arch, "that is the monument that honors their courage."

"Is that your only reason, Drew? I don't get it. I'm sure those soldiers, if they weren't all dead, would love to drink with us."

"It's sacrilegious," Drew said. "And we're breaking local, state, and all kinds of national laws."

"Laws, laws, laws," Shane said, burping little beer bubbles from the side of his mouth. "We don't live in the past, Drew. We're celebrating the present. We're celebrating our last year together. And we're celebrating my dad's birthday." He lifted the bottle and took a drink. "Happy birthday, Dad. Come on, Drew. Drink a toast to our dad. You know how much he cares about you. He put you first in his will."

"Sure he did," Drew laughed, raising his Sam Adams in the air and clicking bottles with Shane. "Happy birthday, Dad." Drew finished his bottle.

"Now, you're talking," Shane said, reaching into the cooler. "Have another one. We're just getting started."

"Thanks," Drew said. "I believe Sam Adams is my favorite beer."

"What are you talking about, Drew? You've never had Sam Adams," Shane said, holding the bottle back. "You've never had any alcoholic beverages before."

"I know," Drew said, taking the bottle. "But Sam's a hero. He organized the Boston Tea Party. And at the Continental Congress, he signed the Declaration of Independence with Ben Franklin."

"So that's why it tastes better?"

"That's right," Drew said. "It's a beer for us Patriots."

Opening another bottle, he threw the cap in the cooler. The cap made a clicking noise when it hit the ice, and then Drew heard something else. It was a light scraping sound coming from the direction of the Memorial Arch.

"Quiet, Shane," he whispered. "There's something at the arch." Getting quickly to his feet, Drew looked into the dark shadows at the side of the memorial.

"Sit down, Drew. You're hearing things. That's what happens when you have a few drinks and worry about all those laws. Your friend Sam Adams didn't worry about laws when he dumped the tea in the harbor."

"Be quiet, Shane. I really heard something."

Drew listened to Shane burp again. The only other sound was the shrill cricket noise that echoed periodically from the high grass. The sky was clear, and the moonlight around the arch grew brighter.

"Come on, relax," Shane said, dropping an empty bottle in the cooler and reaching for another one.

"If we get caught, we're dead. Let's go back to the birthday party."

"We'll go back," Shane said. "After we empty the cooler."

Drew looked at the green eyes and the determined expression on Shane's face. Shrugging his shoulders, he was about to sit down when he heard another scraping noise and a heavy grunting sound. The sound came from high up, and then glancing at the curved center of the arch, Drew saw the sudden movement.

"Ahhhhh!" The screaming sound exploded in front of them. Drew watched in disbelief as a figure fell from the arch and began swinging slowly back and forth in the moonlight.

"What the hell!" Shane shouted. Tossing the bottle, he jumped to his feet, and he and Drew began running across the cobblestones toward the car. As they neared the car, Drew heard a loud grunting, coughing noise. He stopped and turned and looked back toward the Memorial Arch. There, clearly in the bright rays of moonlight, he saw the dark line of the rope swinging from the center of the arch and the thick noose around the man's neck. His hands grabbing at the rope, his feet kicking wildly in the air, the man wore a brown army uniform.

Feeling lightheaded, Drew shouted incoherently and sprinted back to the arch. He lost his balance, slipped, and was up again, running faster. Getting directly underneath the swinging figure, he grabbed the man by the ankles and tried to push up on the shoeless feet. He pushed harder, and the man straightened, releasing some of the pressure around his neck.

"Come on!" Shane shouted from the car. He started the engine, and in an explosion of spinning wheels and flying stones, he spun the car around.

"He's alive!" Drew shouted. "Bring the car here!"

"You're drunk!" Shane shouted back

"Hurry up!" Drew shouted. Perspiration poured down his forehead and burned into his eyes. He was still pushing up on the man's feet and was thrown off balance as the right leg kicked out wildly. The lights of the car grew brighter, and Shane blew the horn and shouted at him from the window.

"Get out of the way!"

Holding onto one leg, Drew stepped backward quickly, and Shane drove the car under the hanging man. Leaving the engine running, he jumped out of the car and helped Drew onto the roof. The roof cracked loudly and bent under his weight. Drew got to his feet and grabbed the man around the chest. Struggling with his grip and exhaling a massive burst of air, Drew managed to lift the body a little. The man gagged, and his head leaned slightly forward. Tightening his grip around the chest, Drew bent his knees and strained upward again. Under the extra weight, the crack in the roof became larger and stretched from door to door.

"I need help!" Drew shouted. "Get your . . ."

But Shane was already climbing onto the roof with the pocket knife in his hand. He reached up, silver blade bright in the moonlight, and sliced through the rope. The man in the soldier's uniform dropped motionless and heavy into their arms. After Shane loosened the noose from around his neck and threw it over the side of the car, they lowered the man to the roof, down the trunk, and onto the ground.

"Go call an ambulance," Drew said, bending over the man.

"I can't leave you alone like this," Shane said.

"Hurry up, Shane, I know what I'm doing," Drew said. "Remember? I had that lifeguard training last summer."

"You had one day of training, and you've never saved anyone."

"Just go down to the main road and see if you can find some help." Drew knelt closer to the pale, lifeless face and pinched his fingers over the man's nose.

Looking nervously from Drew to the soldier, Shane jumped in the car, and spinning a deeper rut through the cobblestones, he raced away from the arch. After a few minutes, he skidded the car to a stop at the Route 23 intersection. Almost immediately, he saw a dim glow of lights and heard the sound of a car engine on the road ahead.

In the bright rays of moonlight beaming through the arch, Drew blew bursts of air into the man's mouth and pushed down on his chest. There was little sign of life in the soldier's body. Alone now and becoming more afraid with each futile pumping movement, Drew began to have a feeling of helplessness. Looking up at the arch, his vision now beginning to blur, he saw the rope swinging freely in the breeze.

Jumping out into the middle of the road, Shane waved his arms frantically in the air, and the car came to a quick stop. The woman hesitated, studying the excited teenager, and then rolled the window down a few inches. Shane began to shout at her in a voice that was too loud, and when he saw the alarmed expression on her face, he slowed down and explained what had happened at the Memorial Arch. She lowered the window all the way and told him she would drive to the gas station at the park entrance and call the ambulance and police.

After thanking the lady, Shane ran to his dad's car and raced it back up the road. When he stopped the car, the lights shone brightly on the cobblestones and the stationary rope hanging from the arch. Squinting through the glare, Shane couldn't see Drew or the soldier. Then he saw two figures in the shadow of the tree, and shutting off the engine, he slammed open the door and ran to them.

"He's OK," Drew said softly. Perspiration covered his face, and his T-shirt was soaked. "His name's Jackson. He's from the veteran's hospital." Drew's hand rested on Jackson's chest, and he could feel the weak, rhythmic beating of his heart. "Did you get anyone?"

"A lady's calling the hospital," Shane said. He sat down next to Drew and the soldier. The man's eyes were open. He stared blankly at Shane, and his lips began to move.

"They wouldn't discharge me from the hospital. I don't know why." Jackson coughed little bubbles through his tight lips. Swollen red abrasions circled the side of his neck. "I wanted to die, but your friend wouldn't let me." Jackson coughed weakly again and closed his eyes.

"My friend, the lifeguard," Shane said, slapping Drew on the back. "You did it. The soldier is alive because of you. You're the man!"

Shane reached into the cooler, grabbed the last Sam Adams, and gave it to Drew. Drew took a drink and then drank some more. Then he put the bottle to Jackson's mouth, and the soldier gulped the remaining beer down with a loud gasping noise.

Beyond the hills of the park, Drew heard the distant sound of sirens. Soon, the flashing red lights, twisting with the curves of Valley Forge Road, began to grow brighter. Shane got up quickly and ran the cooler to the car where he locked it in the trunk. Realizing what was happening, Drew reached for the empty bottle in Jackson's hand. Jackson held on tightly and wouldn't let go. Drew pulled harder, but he couldn't get the bottle.

"Friggin' death grip," Drew said, surprised at the man's strength. "Damn it, Jackson. You're going to get us arrested."

With a strong effort, Drew twisted the bottle free, and in one motion, he threw it into the trees. It hit the low-hanging branches with a crashing sound just as the ambulance, siren blasting the night air, stopped next to Shane's car. The doors swung open, and two medics rushed towards the tree.

A Phoenixville police car and a jeep pulled in behind the ambulance. A young lady dressed in a blue miniskirt got out of the jeep. She looked over the scene, and taking a camera from the seat, she walked to the front of the Memorial

Arch. Standing there in the moonlight, she took a series of flash pictures of the arch and the rope swinging below it. Then she took some pictures of the medics lifting Jackson onto the gurney.

Holding a note pad, a police officer motioned Shane and Drew to the side. Shane explained to the officer how he and Drew had just happened to be driving past the arch on their way home from King of Prussia. Then to be more honest, Shane said they were hoping to see some of the big bucks in the park. The officer said it was a lucky thing for Jackson that they had this strong curiosity for natural things. But then his expression suddenly changed, and he got right in their faces.

"Just remember one thing."

"What?" Shane asked.

"This land is federal property. It's alright to look, but don't ever come hunting the big buck we got here." The officer looked at their faces and began to laugh loudly. Shane and Drew laughed with him. Drew couldn't stop laughing. Shane grabbed him by the shoulder, and they were about to go when the officer stopped them.

"Hold on a minute!" he ordered.

"Yes," Drew said. He and Shane faced the officer, who was now very quiet. The officer inhaled deeply, sniffed the air a few times, and studied them carefully, his eyes shifting from one to the other.

"I caught a whiff of something strong just now," he said. "Has either one of you been drinking tonight?"

"No," Shane said. He glanced quickly, furtively at Drew. "But I think that old veteran was drunk."

"He was," Drew said, nodding his head in agreement. "He threw up over by the tree. Boy, was he wasted."

"Well, the important thing is that you got to him in time," the officer said. "Maybe this experience will keep him from getting drunk again."

"I hope so," Drew said. "I really hope so." They both shook the officer's hand and walked quickly to the car.

"That was close," Shane said. He and Drew got in the car and slammed the doors shut. Looking back at the police officer who was now talking to the reporter, Shane backed up the car and drove slowly away from the Memorial Arch.

"Can an underage drinker be arrested for saving someone's life?" Drew asked.

"Probably," Shane said. "You were damn lucky tonight?"

"Why me?"

"Why you?" Shane asked. "Why you, Mr. Beer Breath! You were laughing and spitting beer in his face the whole time. I could smell it from where I was. Any real officer of the law would have cuffed you right there."

"I didn't know it was that bad," Drew said.

"It was bad," Shane said. He stopped the car at the red light at Washington's Headquarters, and the bottles in the cooler rattled back and forth.

"I don't even know why I was laughing at him," Drew said. "He wasn't funny with his stupid joke about hunting buck."

"I thought he was hilarious," Shane said. "But then I don't have a guilty conscience." He turned and laughed at Drew. A vehicle pulled in behind them, and Shane saw it was the police car. "Close the window, Drew. Don't breathe or laugh or spit any beer on the windshield. The law's right behind us."

Shane watched the light turn green, and he drove slowly through the intersection. The car hit a pothole, and the bottles rattled noisily in the trunk.

"Slow down," Drew said nervously. He watched the police car through the side mirror. The car moved closer, and Drew could clearly see the officer's face. Suddenly, the siren blasted, and the red lights on top of the police car whirled into brightness.

"Oh, shit," Drew said. His heart began beating fast, and he slouched low in his seat. The police car swerved around them and slowed momentarily while the officer smiled and waved his hand. Then the car did a wheel squealing u-turn and raced back toward Valley Forge. Drew watched the lights grow dim and disappear around a bend.

"You OK, Drew?"

"I'm fine," Drew said. "I'm fine now." He sat up and turned on the radio. The sergeant-composer was singing the #1 song in America. As Drew listened to the military tempo of the *Ballad of the Green Berets*, he looked at Shane.

> Fighting soldiers from the sky
> Fearless men who jump and die
> Men who mean just what they say
> The brave men of the Green Beret

"Are you still planning to enlist?" Drew asked, turning down the volume a little.

"Yes," Shane said. "Nothing's changed."

"Is May still worried?"

"A little," Shane said. "But she understands. I'll be back for her."

"Gary says he's enlisting."

"This is Valley Forge," Shane said. "We're Patriots. The whole class is enlisting except you."

"I'm still a Patriot," Drew said.

There were blaring sirens and flashing red lights ahead of them, and Shane pulled the car to the side of the road. A police car, two fire trucks, and an ambulance raced past them. The *Green Beret* song ended, and the announcer began talking about hot bargains at a local car dealership. Drew turned, and looking through the back window, he saw a bright red glow in the sky over the park.

"A big fire," Drew said. "Want to go?"

"We've had enough excitement for one night," Shane said. He pulled onto the road and drove across the Pickering Creek Bridge. After a few minutes he reached Phoenixville. Stopping at a blinking red light, Shane turned off the radio.

"Drew."

"What?"

"That was a great thing you did tonight," Shane said without taking his eyes off the light. "I think you're a real hero, but when we get home, we need to have a plan. Let me talk to Mon and Dad and you can dispose of the bottles in the trunk. Dad can't go to work tomorrow with all that rattling."

"Why should you do the talking if I'm the hero? Why can't you be the garbage man?"

"Drew, I was hero first.'"

"How do you figure that?"

"Because nothing would have happened without me, Drew. I got the idea to go to Valley Forge, and I had to drag your lazy ass out of the house. Jackson would probably be dead now if I hadn't developed this great taste for Sam Adams."

"Maybe Sam Adams is the real hero."

"Maybe he is," Shane said. "Just let me do the talking."

"OK," Drew said. "You do the talking. I'll take care of the bottles."

Drew was quiet as the car approached the house. All the birthday guests had gone, and the driveway was empty. The house was dark except for the porch light. Shane parked the car and shut off the engine. He opened his door, but Drew didn't move.

"What's the matter, Drew?"

"When you left to go for help, it was pretty scary. I don't know what I did, but somehow Jackson survived. After Jackson began to breathe, I was the one who threw up by the tree."

"That's nothing to worry about. Alcoholics throw up all the time. You did great tonight, Drew."

"There's something else."

"What?

"That officer really got to me. I almost threw up again. Can we hold off drinking until I can figure out how to make the beer smell go away."

"Sure," Shane said. "I think there's a special spray you can buy."

"I'll need something strong," Drew said. His eyes opened wide, and he had a bright smile on his face. "Did you see that reporter? She wore that miniskirt and had some great legs. I wonder what she wrote. Do you think the paper will make a big story out of this?"

"I doubt it," Shane said. "He was just some crazy old vet."

There was noise in the house, and the front door swung open. Mr. and Mrs. Collier walked onto the porch. Mr. Collier had a smile on his face, and he had to hold onto the banister with both hands. Waving to them and shouting "Happy Birthday" in a loud voice, Shane walked to the porch. Drew waited, and when the family disappeared inside the house, he got out of the car and walked back to the trunk.

The next day, when Drew looked at the front page of the *Evening Phoenix*, he saw a half-page picture of fire and smoke rising from the chateau clubhouse at the Lafayette Golf and Country Club. The caption under the picture stated the clubhouse was completely destroyed and that arson was suspected.

Drew turned through the newspaper, and on the last page he saw a picture of the Memorial Arch. The picture was stark and simple. The dark shadow of the rope hung ominously from the center of the arch. Drew was surprised to see the noose was now attached to the end of the rope.

"Trick photography," he said to himself. In the background the oval moon was distant and cold. The only colors on the page were the two school pictures of Drew and Shane inserted in the bottom right-hand corner of the page. Shane had a big smile on his face, and his green eyes sparkled in the light.

CHAPTER 8

VALLEY FORGE   1967

It was Drew's senior year and a bitter winter day in December. Snow had been falling throughout the day, and a cold wind plastered frozen patches of ice against the windows and doors of George Washington High School. Drew was on his way to the exit when he heard Homer's voice. He stopped and turned around.

"Drew, I hope you're not busy tonight."

"No," Drew said. "Shane said you talked to him about some kind of project. You needed both of us to be there."

"It's kind of a get-tough project," Homer said. "I want to see if you two are tough enough to graduate."

"What does that mean?"

"You'll see," Homer said. "I'll pick you up at nine o'clock. We'll be out all night so plan to be back home in the morning."

"All night," Drew said. He shook his head as Homer walked back to his office. Drew zipped his jacket up to his neck and pulled his hat down over his ears before walking out the door. A blustery wind of snow and cold air hit him hard in the face.

It was ten minutes after nine when Homer's truck stopped in front of the house. Drew saw the lights and then heard the horn. He and Shane ran down the steps and squeezed in the front seat, slamming the door shut. The heater was on high, and hot air circulated through the truck's cab.

"Where are we going?" Drew asked. The truck moved forward, and he stared at the snow sliding off the windshield. Heavy flakes pelted the glass, and between the downward rotations of the wipers, there was a brief, blurry view of the streetlight and rows of houses.

"To the park." Homer drove slowly, and at the intersection he slid the truck past the stop sign and turned onto Route 23. Because of the treacherous road conditions, it was after ten thirty when they reached the entrance to Valley Forge. The wind was blowing harder now, and long sections of road were covered with drifts.

"There's a winter storm warning tonight," Homer said. "Not a car on the road."

"Only us crazy people," Drew said. "We're always out in a storm."

Homer turned left into the parking lot adjacent to Washington's Headquarters. The truck's tires left deep tracks in the snow. Homer sped the truck to the far corner of the parking lot, jumped the curb, and drove down the walking path. Drew put both hands on the dash and looked at Shane. Shane just shrugged his shoulders.

"Hold on tight," he said. There was a smile on his face.

"Relax," Homer said. He braked, turned the wheel sharply, and slid the truck to a stop next to a log cabin.

"This is it?" Drew asked.

"This is it," Homer said. He shut off the engine and opened the door. They got out of the truck. The wind lifted clouds of snow around them, and Drew felt the tingling sensation as the snow melted and then quickly froze on his face. Homer took a flashlight out of his pocket and pointed it on the truck.

"Can you get the hay out of the back?"

"Hay," Shane said. "What are we, cows?"

"Just take it inside," Homer said. "We're not going to eat it."

Drew and Shane got the two bales of hay from the truck and followed the beam of light to the front of the cabin. Homer gave the flashlight to Shane, and taking a key from his pocket, he unlocked the padlock and pushed open the door. It was black inside.

"The commander in chief's guard hut," Homer said. "Go on in." They went inside, and Homer closed the door, shining the light slowly along the walls. On both sides of the room, there was a row of bunk beds, uneven planks of wood fitted across the top of each bunk. The floor was hard clay, and there was a fireplace at the end. Some newspapers and two stacked piles of wood were next to the fireplace.

"I brought the wood in last night," Homer said, his words forming clouds of misty vapor. "Let's build the fire right away."

The frigid night air enveloped them, and when Drew took a deep breath, he felt a tightness in his chest. He breathed again slowly, and rolling some newspaper in his hands, he dropped it into the fireplace. Shane scattered some pieces of wood over the paper, and then they put on a few bigger logs. Homer struck a match, the flame quivering brightly in the darkness, and lit the paper. The paper burned quickly, lifting fire over the sides of the logs. Smoke began to fill the room, and Drew coughed.

"There's something wrong with the chimney," Drew said, covering his mouth. Clouds of black smoke seemed to boil out of the bottom of the fireplace. It was a cold smoke that burned into his nostrils. "It's not working," he repeated, sitting down on the bale of hay. He looked up through the smoke at Homer.

"I heard you," Homer said. He threw another log on the fire, and sparks flashed in the air. "When the soldiers first built these log cabins, there wasn't much ventilation. But they had no choice. They had to stay warm. They lived and slept in this smoke. Soon most of them suffered from what they called 'smoky eyes.' Their eyes were all bloodshot and covered with a gray mucus."

"Like mine," Drew said, trying to wipe the burning sensation from his eyes. "At the school, you said something about all night. You were joking, weren't you, Homer?"

"I wasn't joking," Homer said. "One night in the guard's cabin. A week before Christmas when most people are out buying stuff, you and Shane get to experience what the soldiers went through in 1777. The army came here on December 17. They spent the holiday here."

"Is this like a living history lesson?" Shane asked. He sat down next to Drew. "I never liked history class."

"It's more than history," Homer said. "This Vietnam War that's going on, you already did early enlistment, Shane. You're going to be in it. Drew, you're going to college, and I hope the war's over by the time you graduate. You may never have to fight. Either way, I want you both to see what the soldiers did here."

"I can't see anything now," Drew said, wiping his eyes. He coughed again and watched Homer drop a huge log on the fire. His whole body was chilled, and his feet were shaking from the cold when the wave of heat rolled past him and blushed his face. The front of his body was suddenly hot, and all the cold relocated to his back and neck. Drew leaned forward and shuddered, his gaze on the wispy lines of smoke rising from the singed pieces of hay at his feet.

"Homer, the front of me is cooking, and my back is freezing. My eyes are burning. I can't breathe. I know what you want to teach us. I get a really clear picture of some soldiers freezing and being miserable in these cabins. Can we go home now?"

"They weren't just soldiers," Homer said. "They were old men and boys, hunters and farmers. A few of them were former slaves. Many didn't have coats or blankets. I imagine the elite Virginia Guard in this cabin were better taken care of than most. But to stay alive, they had to keep the fire going. And that's what we're going to do. We're going to keep the fire going and sleep on the hay."

"Sleep on this?" Drew asked, hitting his hand against the side of the bale of hay.

"Yes," Homer said. "We'll take turns on the fire. We can't let it go out, or we'll freeze to death." Homer stood up and untied the twine on the bale of hay. "Pick out your bed and throw the hay on top of the wooden planks. The insulation will help keep you warm."

Drew and Shane moved off the bale. Drew threw some hay on the bottom planks closest to the fire. Shane covered the planks on the top bunk and climbed up, dropping strands of hay and dust through the cracks onto Drew.

"Watch it," Drew said, scraping the hay off his jacket. "Homer, I can't sleep here."

"You'll be just fine," Homer said. He threw double layers of hay on the middle section of planks directly opposite them.

Outside the cabin, the wind tore through the pine trees, rattling the branches. In the open holes on the sides of the cabin where the clay between the logs had fallen off, the wind burst through the chinks with a low whistling noise.

Drew curled his body on the hay. There was a sudden gust of wind, and Drew watched a flurry of snowflakes shoot from the wall and settle lightly over his face. He grabbed a handful of hay and stuffed it in the chink. His fingers were numb from the exposure to the outside temperature, and he rubbed them and held them out to the fire.

"It's freezing," Drew said.

"You don't remember anything from your science classes," Homer asked.

"Remember what?"

"Heat rises," Homer said. "The bottom bunks are the coldest."

"I remember that," Shane said.

"This is miserable," Drew said, looking up at the clouded haziness of the upper bunks. He rubbed at his eyes. "Heat rises, but smoke rises with it. I'd rather freeze to death than go blind from mucus eyes."

"It's cold up here, too," Shane said, looking down through the smoke.

"You've taken field trips here since elementary school, but I don't think you understand the kind of suffering the men experienced."

"I understand," Shane said. "When I freeze to death up here, just prop my body outside the door, and I'll stand guard till spring comes." Shane lifted his head and coughed. When he looked down again, he saw the smile on Drew's face.

"What's that mean?" Homer asked.

"Just some Valley Forge history few people know about," Drew said

"Let's see how much you know about Valley Forge," Homer said. "What do you remember about the size of the army?"

"About twelve thousand men," Drew said. "It was a test question, multiple choice."

"How many soldiers died in camp?"

"Twenty percent of the army," Shane said. He gave Drew a quick look. "I know my history, too."

"That's two thousand men," Drew said.

"Yes," Homer said. "They died from disease, malnutrition, exposure."

"They were special, weren't they?" Shane asked. "I mean they had nothing. The British were safe and warm in Philadelphia, and the American soldiers were suffering and dying right here in Valley Forge. And yet we won."

"We won," Drew said. "And here we are, reliving it." The wind blew stronger, and a chill filled the cabin. A cold draft of air hit the fire, and the moving flames flickered shadows along the wall. "It's spooky. I wonder if any soldiers died in this cabin."

"Three of them," Shane said. "They were buried outside when the ground thawed in the spring." He was laughing and trying to keep warm.

Homer looked at Drew and Shane and shook his head. He got up and put more wood on the fire. With his back to the fire and clouded in smoke, Homer was a dark silhouette in front of the burning logs.

"It's getting late," he said. "But I need you to get serious and pay attention before you go to sleep."

"What is it?" Drew asked.

"It's this connection I made," Homer said. "It might be hard to understand, but I'll try to explain. The connection I see is between us and Vietnam. Here at Valley Forge and in later battles, we were able to beat the British and win the war because we fought harder. We fought for freedom. That's what's happening over there."

"You mean like the Vietnamese are fighting for freedom?" Drew asked.

"That's their strength," Homer said. "They want to be free."

"But they're a tiny country," Drew said. "We're the strongest country in the world. How can they win against us?"

"We would crush them," Homer said. "Except that Russia and China are supporting them. It was the same here at Valley Forge. Our alliance with the French government gave us supplies and a navy to fight the British. And then there were foreign officers like General Baron von Steuben."

"I see his statue every day," Drew said.

"The general really helped us," Homer said. "The Vietnamese have the same kind of help from the Russians and Chinese. And that's who we're really fighting over there." Homer reached down and threw a log on the fire. Then he sat down on the straw covered plank of wood. "We're fighting communism, and that's the worst kind of government there is."

"And the Vietnamese?" Shane asked.

"Caught in the middle," Homer said. "To get their freedom, they need help from the communists. And they're getting all the help they need."

"So they have a good chance of winning the war?" Shane asked.

"Yes," Homer said. "We can win but only if we are as strong as they are. That's what you must know, Shane. You have to be stronger. And you have to have good people around you. Right now, there's no safe place in Vietnam.

You'll have to find new friends who will cover your back." Homer looked at Shane and was quiet for a moment. In the silence, a burning ember cracked out of the fire and landed on the dirt floor.

"I'll never find friends like here," Shane said. He was looking at the smoke rising from the dirt.

"Maybe Shane shouldn't go," Drew said. His eyes burned from the smoke, and a clear liquid dripped from his nose. He rubbed it off with his jacket sleeve. "Many people say Vietnam is a bad war. They just had those peace demonstrations in New York and Philadelphia. The police arrested over five hundred protestors in New York."

"Spock was one of the ones arrested," Homer said.

"From *Star Trek*?" Shane asked. "That's impossible. Spock and Captain Kirk would never quit. They always fought and won."

"Not that Spock," Homer laughed. "I'm talking about the baby doctor."

"What does a baby doctor, a diaper-changer know about war?" Shane asked. "How can he protest anything, except maybe some new baby formula?"

"Everyone's protesting," Drew said. "We have over four hundred thousand troops there now. Too many are getting killed. War doesn't solve anything. Even Ben in his *Almanac* wrote that there never was a good war or a bad peace."

"But think about it, Drew," Homer said. "Franklin was for independence and supported the war. He's the one who convinced von Steuben to come to America and fight for us. Franklin knew the Revolutionary War was a good war."

"Homer's right," Shane said. "Sometimes you have to fight."

"I think the only bad war is the one you lose." Homer turned away from the fire and got into his bunk. He looked at both of them. Coming from the shadows, Homer's voice sounded distant and strange. "And we can't lose this one. We have to outlast the communists and leave a strong government. There's no alternative. If the communists win, thousands of people, maybe millions, will be killed."

"That's why I'm going to Nam," Shane said. He jumped down and sat in front of the fire. "You guys sleep first. I'll keep the fire going."

Drew listened to the words in the smoky darkness. His body was freezing, especially his hands and feet. And his nose and eyes still hurt. Drew remembered Shane trying to explain something about how they could enlist together in some kind of buddy system. At the time, Drew didn't pay too much attention because graduation seemed so far away. But now it was a few months away.

Worrying about Shane and the war, Drew lay awake and stared into the flickering shadows on the cabin wall for a long time. He rubbed at the burn in his eyes, and the shadows grew larger. With the cold shaking through his body, he buried his hands inside his jacket. Soon he drifted into a restless sleep.

In the morning, bright rays of sunshine illuminated the inside of the cabin. The fire was still burning, and the pile of hot coals radiated heat off the walls. Drew sat up, stretching in the warmth and rubbing the smoke out of his eyes. Shane was curled up, sleeping next to the fire. The two large stacks of wood were gone. The door opened, light flooding the cabin, and Homer stepped inside.

"Time to get up," he said. He walked over and nudged Shane in the shoulder. "The fire was burning all night. You guards were great. Ole George would have been real proud."

"Shane did it all," Drew said. "I fell asleep. I didn't hear anything. I didn't know hay could be comfortable."

"We have one more thing to do," Homer said. "Then I'll buy you breakfast at the Vale Rio Diner."

"What's next?" Shane asked, turning to face Homer. "Any thing will be easy compared to last night."

"It's a beautiful morning. We're going to walk to the river." Homer sat down on the plank and started unlacing his boots. "First we have to remove our shoes and socks."

Drew and Shane looked at each other. Shane hesitated and then slowly untied the laces on his tennis shoes. Drew removed his shoes and placed them next to the fireplace. Homer walked through the door, and they followed. After taking a few steps in the snow, Drew shouted something and began jumping up and down.

"What's your problem?" Homer stopped and turned to look at him.

"My feet are freezing," Drew said, kicking snow in the air. "No, they're burning up."

"Will you just be tough," Shane said. "I don't feel a thing."

"And you're full of shit," Drew said. He reached down in the snow, rubbed his toes gently, and straightened up with a pained expression on his face. Homer pointed toward the train station and river, and the three of them began walking through the knee-deep rounded mounds of snow.

"Why can't we wear shoes?" Shane asked. "Can anyone tell me why we can't wear shoes?"

"I know why," Drew said. His feet buried deep in the snow, he began to feel the burning sensation travel up his leg.

"You were always good at history," Homer said.

"History's easy," Drew said. He looked back at their ragged line of footsteps in the snow. Then he looked at Shane's feet when he lifted them out of the snow. They were a bright rose-red color up to the cuff of his jeans. When Drew lifted his foot out of the snow, he saw an even brighter shade of redness. The burning sensation was not as severe, but there was a tingling cold that traveled the length of his legs.

"We don't have any shoes," Drew said "because many of the Colonial soldiers were poor and didn't have shoes. When they marched here, George Washington stated the British could have tracked his army by following the bloody footprints in the snow. Of course, George was riding a horse."

"You're the general here, Homer," Shane said. "Where's your horse? Or maybe you should have a snowmobile."

"I don't need anything," Homer said. "We're only going to the river."

"How far did the army have to march?" Shane asked.

"From White Marsh," Homer said. "It's about twenty miles from here."

"Damn," Shane said. "I could never do that."

"My feet aren't burning like they did," Drew said. "At first, it felt like I was walking on needles. Now everything's just numb."

Stepping into Homer's footprints, Drew and Shane crushed the snow deeper and deeper. They walked along a picket fence that had rounded piles of snow on the top logs. Behind the picket fence was George Washington's Headquarters. A scattering of black trees threw shadows against the brown and gray brick walls of the colonial house. High in the sky above the tree branches, two red chimneys rose out of the snow-covered roof. Drew looked at the top floor of the house where the sun reflected off a stained glass window that was shaped like a wagon wheel.

Drew and Shane followed Homer the length of the fence. When they reached Valley Creek, Homer walked carefully down the steep grade. The drifted snow was deeper here, and there were smooth patches of ice. Shane was watching Homer's slow descent when he heard Drew shouting something behind him.

Shane turned and saw Drew trudging through the snow toward a small shed. He disappeared behind the shed, and when he reappeared, he was pulling a brown toboggan. Kicking up large clumps of snow, Drew made quick progress toward Valley Creek.

"Get over here, Shane," he said, stopping the toboggan a good twenty feet away from the bank. With the rope twisted in his hands, he sat down and slid up to the front of the sled. Shane walked over and looked down at Drew.

"What?"

"Give us a running push and jump on," Drew said, his face red with excitement. "We're going down the fast way."

"I wouldn't do that!" Homer shouted from the creek. "You can't stop . . ."

"We'll be fine!" Drew shouted loudly. "Let's go, Shane."

"OK," Shane said. He crouched low, grabbed onto Drew's shoulders, and began running through the snow. The toboggan picked up speed quickly. As it neared the top of the bank, Shane gave one last tremendous push, jumped on, and knelt behind Drew, his hands digging deep into the folds of his jacket.

"Hang on!" Drew shouted.

The toboggan lifted high over the edge of the bank, was airborne, and then slammed down onto the snow. The impact knocked Shane into Drew, and Drew's forehead smacked into the curved front of the toboggan. The weight buckled his knees, and his toes crushed hard into the wood.

"Sorry," Shane said and pulled on Drew's jacket.

"I'm OK!" Drew looked up. Cold air blew across his face and stung his eyes. He blinked away the cold, and when he opened his eyes, he saw the flowing waters of the creek and Homer standing there waving his hands over his head.

"Oh, shit!" Shane said.

The toboggan hit an ice slick, made a loud grinding, scraping noise, and propelled faster down the bank. Homer's figure grew instantly larger. There was a look of panic on his face, and he flung his body out of the way. As the toboggan sped closer to the deep, glistening waters of Valley Creek, Drew felt hard pressure on his shoulders.

"Jump!" Shane shouted and grabbed Drew around the shoulders. Drew released his grip on the rope and half jumped, half rolled off the toboggan. His face and chest hit the snow and stuck there. Shane landed behind him, and his body slid forward, burying Drew's face deeper in the snow.

"You're both lunatics!" Homer said. He rushed over and pulled Drew out of the snow.

"He'll survive," Shane said. Brushing snow off his jacket, he looked at the front end of the toboggan buried in the middle of the creek and began laughing. When he saw Drew roll over and spit up a mouthful of snow, he began laughing louder.

"That was great," Drew managed to say.

"You're both certified lunatics," Homer said. He pulled Drew to his feet, and they began walking down the creek.

"We should do this again, Homer," Drew said. "I love winter sports. But I can't feel my toes anymore. I think they broke off in the toboggan."

"Don't worry," Homer said. "I can see your footprints. All your toes are still connected."

Valley Creek flowed under a large train trestle before it dropped into the Schuylkill River. As they entered the tunnel, the snow disappeared, and they slapped their feet against the cold mud along the creek bed. Jagged, white icicles streaked down the dark walls of the tunnel. A train went by overhead, and the engine created a thunderous roar of noise.

A large stalactite of an icicle broke loose from the ceiling, and Drew watched as Shane ran forward and punched the falling icicle with his fist. It shattered into bright pieces of shiny glass, and Shane laughed. The train sped by, leaving the tunnel in silence. With Homer a few steps ahead, Shane and Drew left the shadows of the tunnel and walked into the bright morning light. They stood in the deep snow on the banks of the Schuylkill River.

"I don't know how, but we made it," Homer said. He brushed away some snow, sat down, and stretched his feet in the warm sunshine. Shane flopped down next to him. Drew walked to the river's edge, knelt down, and splashed water over his face.

"It's freezing cold," he said.

"What are you doing?" Shane asked.

"Clearing the mucus from my smoky eyes," Drew said. He splashed more water on his face and joined them on the bank.

The river in front of them was wide and shallow. It streamed around snow-covered brush, fallen trees, and piles of large rocks. Clear, icy waves splashed along the bank at their feet.

"This is a fantastic river," Homer said.

"Homer, I've seen it all my life," Shane said. "The Schuylkill's just a river like any other river."

"It's not like any other river," Homer said. "The Colonial Army was starving. They had no food. But the Pennsylvania soldiers knew the Schuylkill. One day according to the journals, the soldiers began shouting up a storm. Everyone broke ranks and ran to the river. What they found at the Schuylkill gave them enough food for the rest of the winter."

"What do you mean?"

"The shad run," Homer said. "Fish everywhere. They caught them with their hands; they caught them in makeshift nets. They caught fish for weeks. What they didn't eat, they smoked. The shad may have saved the army."

"That's a good story," Drew said. "But talking about food is making me hungry."

"Then let's get breakfast," Homer said. "It was a long night."

There was a loud booming noise, followed by another. The shots echoed the length of the river, and everything became deadly quiet.

"A hunter?" Drew asked.

"See what you started, Drew. Now everyone poaches in the park."

"The way sound travels, the shots could have come from the other side of the river," Homer said. "That's legal hunting there. Let's go. We're still hungry."

Homer stood up and reached out his hands, pulling Shane and Drew out of the snow. They turned away from the Schuylkill and walked to the tunnel. Except for some deer watching them from the edge of the trees, the park was deserted. They tramped through the same deep footprints in the snow. After reaching the cabin, Drew put on his heated shoes. The numbness slowly left his feet, and the burning sensation returned quickly.

Homer turned on the engine to the truck and then took a shovel from the back. While Drew and Shane began cleaning the snow off the windshield, Homer took a shovelful of snow in the cabin and threw it on the red coals of the fire. Watching the steam and smoke flow through the numerous cracks in the cabin, Drew reached for the door handle and saw the two holes.

"Homer," he called. Homer finished locking the cabin and started walking to the truck. "Look at this."

"What?" Homer asked. He tossed the shovel in the truck and looked at the door. "Well, I'll be . . ."

"What?" Shane asked, walking from the other side of the truck.

"Someone shot my truck," Homer said. Brushing off the snow, he traced his hand over the two jagged holes in the side of the door. "Those were the two shots we heard."

"How could this happen?" Drew asked.

"Who knows?" Homer said. He turned and studied the thick grove of trees behind the log cabin. "It's nothing to worry about. I'm covered. I got good insurance. Let's go eat."

Shane and Drew got in the truck, and Drew clicked the heater to high. A gust of hot air hit him in the face. Basking in the heat, he turned on the radio and relaxed. Homer got in the truck, slammed the remaining snow off the door, and drove up the walking lane to the parking lot. A bright glare of sun reflected off the fresh snow. Homer gunned the truck across the parking lot and spun smoothly onto Route 23. After a few minutes, he reached over and turned off the radio.

"I heard talk in church last Sunday about some major changes at the school," Homer said. "One board member thinks George Washington might close down and consolidate with the neighboring districts. Students always find out the news first. Did you two hear anything?"

"No," Drew said. "What are they saying?"

"Washington's an old school, but we're in a rich district. There's talk about building one big school for the whole Valley Forge region," Homer said. "Some of the smaller school districts are looking for help."

"I can't imagine George Washington School not being here," Drew said. He watched a plow truck speed by, throwing high arching clouds of snow in the air. With the road cleared in front of them, Homer drove faster.

"When I was freezing and couldn't sleep last night and watching you two playing with the fire, do you know what I thought about?" Homer asked.

"What?" Shane asked.

"Your last football game when you scored the winning touchdown in the final seconds and beat the Eagles."

"Drew scored the touchdown," Shane said.

"Yeah, I did," Drew said. "It's hard to imagine, but I did. I think it was the best night of my life."

"You both did amazing things that night. Gary was outstanding, too. That football game on Senior Night was the best game in any sport I've ever seen," Homer said. "Thinking about it kept me warm. I'll never forget it." Homer drove through Phoenixville and parked the truck in the lot behind the Vale Rio Diner.

The Vale Rio was an old train-car diner built in the forties. Climbing the steps and going inside, Drew saw that there were only two customers sitting in the red-topped stools that lined the counters. The booths on the window side were all empty. Homer pointed at the second booth, and they slid inside. When the waitress came with the menus, Drew didn't open his.

"Two number 10 breakfast specials," Drew said. "You should get the 10 special too, Homer."

"What is it?"

"T-bone steak, hash browns, and eggs," Drew said. "It's the most expensive, but it's the best."

"I guess we earned it," Homer said, giving the menus back to the waitress. "And coffee and orange juice for all of us."

"I love this place," Drew said. "I came here often with Mom and Dad. The hamburgers are double-sized, and the omelets fill the whole plate."

The waitress returned with the coffee. It was hot and black. Homer lifted his cup and took a long drink. Shane put a quarter in the booth jukebox. There was a clicking sound from the rows of speakers, and the voice of Johnny Cash filled the empty dinner.

"*Ring of Fire*," Shane said. "My all-time favorite song."

They listened to another Cash song, *I Walk the Line*, and talked for a while. Shaking snow off their coats, the morning customers began to arrive. One elderly man carrying a worn black Bible walked by them and sat at the counter. He opened the Bible and began reading. The waitress brought their dishes. The plate was filled with steak and hash browns, and the eggs folded over the sides. They began to eat seriously, and it was a few minutes before Shane looked up from the plate.

"Drew, do you remember skip day and that old soldier tourist guide?" Shane asked, chewing on a piece of steak.

"Yeah. What about him?"

"He was wrong about everything. He said the Phillies would win the World Series. After that day, the Phillies lost ten straight games. He must have been a very sick soldier when Philadelphia missed the playoffs by just the one game."

"I remember that year," Homer said. "That losing streak made a lot of people sick."

"And the old soldier was wrong about us, too. He said we couldn't take it. He said we were too soft. But there were no problems. We survived last night."

"But it was only one night," Drew said. He soaked a piece of toast in his egg and lifted it to his mouth. "Five months would have been pretty hard."

"If you can survive one night, you can survive the whole winter," Shane said.

"I don't know if I could," Drew said.

When the waitress came with the check, Drew asked Homer if they could have a piece of lemon meringue pie. Homer's mind raced back years ago when he was sitting in the Benson's kitchen, and Mrs. Benson had placed a dish of lemon meringue pie in front of him. While he was eating the pie, Mr. Benson explained how the bank would give him a loan. It was the best pie Homer had ever eaten.

Looking at the dark smudges of soot on Drew's face and the streaks of red lines in his bloodshot eyes, Homer told the waitress to bring three pieces of pie. When she was a few steps away, he called her back and told her to bring the whole pie. In a few minutes, she returned with three dishes and placed them on the table. She put the pie, carefully sliced into six large pieces, in the center of the table. Then she put a slice of lemon meringue pie on each one of the dishes. Thin lines of heat rose from the plates, and Drew could smell the sweet aroma of lemon.

"Enjoy," she said. "It's just out of the oven."

"Great," Drew said, reaching for a dish. Shane and Homer grabbed for their dishes, and by the time Homer had the fork in his hand and was ready to start eating, Drew had finished his piece of pie. A crust of white meringue was stuck to his lower lip.

"It's delicious," Drew said, starting on his second piece.

"Take it easy, Drew," Homer said. "This isn't a race." Homer ate more slowly, and when he was finished, he cleaned the crumbs off his plate. "That's enough for me. One of you can have my second piece." Drew quickly slid the pie plate between him and Shane.

"We'll share," Drew said, slicing the pie in half. In a few seconds the dish was empty, and Drew was licking the side of his fork. Lifting his glass, Homer finished the rest of his coffee.

"Shane, you're going to leave right after graduation?"

"The next day," Shane said. "I can't wait to get out of here."

"And you, Drew? You're going to college like you planned?"

"I'm going to be a teacher. I'll get a minor in biology." Drew took a napkin and cleaned the meringue from his face. "But my major will be history."

"Like Professor JJ," Shane said.

"I'll never be as good as Professor JJ," Drew said. "And I'll never be as good as you, Homer. I wouldn't be here but for you and the professor. I'll just go out and do my best. It's what Mom and Dad wanted. Dad thought I should go to a business college, but Mom always said I would be a teacher."

"My parents said that, too. When I talked to them about you going to the army with me, they told me to drop it. I mean really drop it. I understood what they were doing, but you and I are a team, Drew. I really wanted us to go in together."

"I'll enlist after college."

"Four years," Shane said. "The war will be over by then."

"I hope so," Homer said. He looked up at their faces. "I hope the war will be over."

At the counter, the old man closed his Bible and reached into his pocket. He dropped some change next to his coffee cup, and holding the Bible against his chest, he scrutinized both Drew and Shane as he walked past their booth. When he opened the door, a blast of cold air blew into the diner. Taking out his wallet, Homer slid out of the booth and went to the register to pay the bill. When he returned, he left a five-dollar tip on the table. Waving to the waitress, Drew and Shane followed him to the exit.

"Thanks, Homer," Drew said, holding the door open. "Breakfast was great."

"Yeah, thanks, Homer." Shane said.

"You're welcome," Homer said.

Outside it was still snowing, and the truck was completely covered. Drew and Shane began cleaning off the windshield. Homer got inside and started the engine and heater. As soon as Drew and Shane got inside, Shane turned on the radio. The sound of *Jingle Bells* immediately filled the cab. Homer pulled out of the parking lot onto Route 23.

"Merry Christmas, Homer," Drew said.

"Yeah, Merry Christmas," Shane said. "And, Homer, don't bother getting us any presents this year."

"Why not?" Homer asked. "You two are family. I always get you something."

"No, don't," Shane said. "You already gave us our present."

"He did?" Drew asked. "How come I didn't see it?"

"You did see it, Drew. It was great. It was an overnight stay at the plush Valley Forge Resort with complementary breakfast included." Shane laughed. "I'll never forget it."

"That's right," Drew said, laughing with Shane. "It was a great Christmas present. But I'm glad you reminded me, Shane, because I really didn't see it. I had this 'smoky eye' disease and couldn't see much of anything."

"But you did manage to see the lemon meringue pie?" Homer asked.

"I did see the pie," Drew said, nudging Shane in the shoulder. "But only for a second." He and Shane began laughing again.

Listening to the noise, Homer began humming to the music of *Jingle Bells*. Shane and Drew joined in. They were singing loudly, shouting in each other's face, slapping the dash for sound effects, as the truck moved slowly down the snow-covered streets.

After a short drive, Homer stopped in front of the Collier house, and they all shook hands. Shane and Drew got out of the truck and walked to the house. When they reached the top porch step, they both turned and waved, almost simultaneously, like they always did. Homer waved back, put the truck into gear, and drove down the road.

"Considering that we almost froze to death, that was a good time," Drew said.

"You better enjoy it now," Shane said. "It'll never be like this again."

"What are you talking about. Shane?"

"We're graduating soon. We're done here. Get the jingle bells out of your head, Drew. I'm going to the war, and you're going to college. Don't you understand? It'll never be like this again."

"That's crazy talk," Drew said. "You'll see. We're both coming back." Putting his arm around Shane's shoulder, Drew opened the door, and they walked inside the house.

Watching, listening from the tree line, Jeb Wood, a scarlet patch over his left eye, was motionless for a long time. He was completely covered by the falling snow. Jeb studied the tire tracks and the line of footprints that went around his cabin and onto the porch steps. When he knew there were no intruders, Jeb stepped out of the woods and shook the snow off his jacket and trousers. Jeb walked to the cabin and went inside. Going first to the gun cabinet, he placed the Winchester 70 onto the rack.

Jeb went to the cot, and folding the bear rug out of the way, he reached for the recessed handle and lifted the trapdoor. He stepped on the top rung of the ladder, and sliding the bear rug back in place and closing the door, Jeb descended into his cellar. Reaching the floor, Jeb struck a match and lit the lantern hanging from the ceiling. Then he took off his cap and jacket and removed his army boots.

It was a large cellar. Three rows of wooden pillars supported the planked ceiling. Three of the walls and the entire floor were covered with animal skins. One wall was pitch black with heavy bear skins. Grooves between the skins showed the outline of a door. The door opened to a long tunnel that ended behind the ninth hole of the Lafayette Golf Course. The buried exit there was covered with brush and circled with bear traps. Built during the Indian years, the tunnel was sturdy and old and web filled. The other two walls in the cellar were covered with a patchwork of deer skins.

The remaining wall was smooth clay with a reddish-brown tint. A square indentation the size of a casket was cut in the center of the wall. A picture of a bearded, deeply wrinkled, stern-faced man was nailed to the clay.

There was a bed with sheets and blankets, a table with a metal dish and large spoon and silver-bladed machete, two chairs, a wash basin, three extra lanterns, and there was a wooden cabinet along the deer-skin wall. The cabinet was filled with cans of baked beans, macaroni, and chicken noodle soup. One shelf of the cabinet had six bottles of Jack Daniels neatly lined up in a row. On the floor next to the cabinet was a case of champagne.

Jeb opened the cabinet and grabbed one of the bottles. Walking to the bed, Jeb sat down and took a long drink. The temperature in the cellar was always moderate, and Jeb began to feel very comfortable. He leaned back against the matted wall of deer skin and looked across the room at the picture in the clay.

"I just spooked them today, Joshua," he said. "Just put two holes in their truck." Jeb was in the habit of talking to his brother like he was alive and standing at the wall. "I could have had anyone of them, but it's not time yet." The lantern flickered, and the light in the room dimmed. Jeb took another drink and stared at the face on the dirt wall. Joshua stared back at him, and Jeb knew that his brother was there with him all the time. And he knew that he had to keep doing the right thing just like Joshua taught him.

Jeb was so proud of his older brother. Joshua was in the big war, and although he never got the medals he deserved, he never got nothing at all from the U.S. Government, Jeb knew that Joshua was a big part of winning the war.

He and Joshua were sitting on the porch that night and drinking all that Jack when Joshua talked about how his best sniper student, a poor black kid from West Philly, had stopped the whole German army in that battle in France.

"Gerard had nothing going for him," Joshua said. "Except he kept his mouth shut and did everything so slow and careful until he got it right."

"Like me?" Jeb asked.

"Exactly like you, Brother," Joshua said, and Jeb smiled and emptied his glass of whiskey, the cool burn in his throat sweet and pleasurable.

"The German tanks were coming across this open field," Joshua said. "Gerard was way out of sight, like he was taught, and he was watching them. The lead Tiger tank stopped, and this general popped open the hatch and stood up looking at his map.

"Gerard wasted no time. He blew the side of the general's head off. Then Gerard began shooting the soldiers trying to hide behind the tanks. The tank gunners were firing away, but they couldn't find him. No one can find you when you're good at what you're doing."

"Like you taught me?" Jeb asked. "Am I good like that?"

"You're the best," Joshua said. "You and Gerard were the best I ever had. Well, Gerard kept on killing until he ran out of ammunition. Then he walked back to Bastogne. He said he was starving so he ate three cans of rations and was looking for more."

"How many Germans did he kill?" Jeb asked.

"Gerard told me he was sick of himself because he ran out of ammunition so fast. He only had thirty-eight rounds. And Gerard never did miss what he shot at."

"That's why I know you helped win the war," Jeb said. "Your good teaching done it. Your snipers were everywhere killing just like you taught them."

"My boys learned fast, and they were all good," Jeb said. "But Gerard was the best. He knew how to fight and how to win. He didn't let the distractions get in his way."

"What distractions?"

"The stupid stuff, Jeb. Like the people back home and how they think killing and dying for your country is bad. But there's worse than that. There's the politicians campaigning and going in all directions to be popular. Gerard understood like I taught him that you just go after the enemies at all times and with all you got. You must never stop until you kill all the bastards. That's how you win a war." Joshua was quiet for a moment. "And we dropped the big bomb and won it. That's for sure." He raised his glass to Jeb.

"To the big bomb," Joshua said, and they drank the toast silently.

Jeb loved remembering and retelling that story to himself. It was always the clearest after he did a killing and began drinking the Jack. And he loved all the other stories with what he and Joshua did together. The stories and the memories were all he had now. He took a drink and glanced at the wall.

"I have to stay out of sight for a while. There's still a small problem with the locals," Jeb said. "Ever since I torched that castle of theirs, the police have been snoopin' around. I wished you could have seen the way the castle flared up so fast. You could have watched from the tunnel like I did." The wick in the lantern burned lower, and soon there were only dancing shadows in the room. They cast intricate shades of light and dark across Joshua's picture.

"The bastard bankers stole our land, Joshua. And now they got dogs comin' after me. But I can take care of them. No problem. Those money bankers don't know what they're getting themselves into. Like that boy should never have stole my buck and come after me with his friends. He got my eye, but I'm in no hurry. I got skins to sell. I need money to buy more Jack and live the good life. I'll get to them when I'm ready." The lantern flickered a few times, and then the room went dark.

"Good night, Joshua," Jeb said. He put the bottle on the floor and lay back in the bed.

CHAPTER 9

In 1975, George Washington High School was demolished and a new building was constructed on the site. It took the school board members only seven minutes of discussion to change the name of the school to Valley Forge High School. They talked about a new look, a new start, a new direction, but the overriding reason for the name was Mr. Henry Wentworth, the new school board director. As supervisor of Valley Forge Park, he insisted that the park, the veterans hospital, and the school all be united under one name.

Valley Forge High School was a modern two-story building constructed in the form of an elaborate horseshoe. The ends of the horseshoe pointed in the direction of Valley Forge National Park. The building had rows of large windows that presented clear views of the historical countryside. A green lawn with a shiny metal and glass bulletin board in the middle was in front of the school. Written in blue letters with gold trim on the bulletin board, *"Patriots vs. Eagles for League Championship"* was on the first two lines, and *"Friday, October 28, 7:30"* was on the last line.

Two large student parking lots were to the right and left of the main building, and behind the school the high-rising bleachers of the football field dominated the area. On the hill behind the football field, the roofs of buildings that made up the Valley Forge Veterans Hospital made a compact circle. There was a huge American flag in the circle, and beyond the flag and hospital buildings was Valley Forge National Park.

It was almost midnight, Sunday evening, and there was only one car in the parking lot of the school. Loud music blared from the speakers in the car. Leaning against the side of a canary yellow Jaguar XL, senior Leroy Schaffer was a 235-pound linebacker on the undefeated Patriots football team. His face bloated red, his flat nose a darker red, he drank from the bottle and made a wheezing sound from his nose.

"That was the greatest game," he said.

"You had eighteen tackles," Chester said. "How the hell did you do that?" Chester Greenwood was another senior starter. He was black, played safety, and was the fastest player on the team. His muscular six-foot-two-inch, 190-pound frame looked small standing next to Leroy.

"Hell, those runners were so dumb coming into Leroy Land. I had to give them my best welcome." Leroy took another drink and gave the bottle to Chester.

"Nice welcome," Chester said. "Two of them were carried off the field." After draining the bottle, Chester threw it high in the air and laughed as the bottle shattered, sending jagged pieces of brown glass across the parking lot.

Sophomore Sally Grimes laughed, too. She was a slight, dull-faced girl who donated the money for the drinks and owned the Jaguar XL. Her father, Attorney Sam Grimes, the school's solicitor, had given the Jaguar to her for her birthday. Sally enjoyed being with the football players, but more importantly, she enjoyed all the partying and all the attention she received from the football stars. Even though the celebrations of Friday's 45-6 victory over Great Valley High School were over, she and Leroy and Chester had managed to drag the party into Sunday night.

"Lightning Leroy," she said. "That's what you are."

"The hell with lightning," Leroy said. "It's Bad Leroy. As bad as you can get Leroy." He reached into the car, clicked on the ignition, and slid a cassette into the player. Jim Croce's song *Bad, Bad Leroy Brown* boomed through the speakers.

"Damn, this is great," Leroy said. He began throwing his arms in the air and gyrating his body to the music. When he attempted a slurred sing-along, Sally clapped her hands and joined him in the dance.

> Well, the South side of Chicago
> Is the baddest part of town
> And if you go down there you better beware
> Of a man named Leroy Brown
>
> Now Leroy more than trouble
> You see he stand about six foot four
> All the downtown ladies call him treetop lover
> All the men just call him sir

When they reached the chorus line, Leroy and Sally began singing louder. The noise echoed across the empty parking lot. "And he bad, bad Leroy Brown, the baddest man in the whole damned town." Chester watched their clumsy drunken movements. Before the end of the song, Leroy hit the button, and the cassette popped out.

"What about the rest of it?" Chester asked. "The part after the fight when Leroy looks like a jigsaw puzzle with some of the pieces missing?

"Fuck that," Leroy said. "I'm no puzzle. I'm too bad. That could never happen to me."

"We're out of beer," Sally said, looking at the empty cartons of six-packs scattered on the seat and floor of the car. "What'll we do? I can't go home now. It's too late."

"I don't want to go home either," Leroy said. "I'm not done celebrating. Hell, one more win and we have the first undefeated season in school history."

"There is no school history," Chester laughed. "We've only been open one year."

"He means one year of new school and thirty-five years of old George Washington School," Sally said. She counted five and one on her fingers. "That's thirty-six total years. Let's celebrate all night. We can sleep in the park and go to school at noon."

"We need money for food," Leroy said. "I'm starving after all that drinking."

"I don't have any," Chester said.

"Let's go see what we can find on the turnpike," Leroy said. "It's been good to us before." Excited about his idea, he became energized and ran around the car. Opening the door on the driver's side, he jumped in the Jaguar.

It took them twenty minutes to get to the Valley Forge Interchange of the Pennsylvania Turnpike. Driving up to the tollbooth and pulling the ticket from the slot, Leroy raced the Jaguar around the sharp curves and headed west toward Harrisburg. At two in the morning, the traffic was light in both directions. After ten minutes of nearly empty turnpike, Chester looked over at Leroy.

"Too quiet," he said.

"The best time," Leroy said, studying another pull-off in the distance. He saw reflector lights and slowed down. The car was parked next to a picnic table and trash can.

"See, I told you," Leroy said, pulling the Jaguar quietly behind the black Honda. There was a small figure slumped down in the front seat of the Honda.

"How do you want to do this?" Chester asked.

"Sally,'" Leroy said, opening the door. "You go knock on his window and ask him for his money."

"What?"

"Just joking," Leroy said, laughing at the expression on her face. His nose made a loud wheezing noise. "Wake him up and ask him for help. Tell him all the red lights on your dash are lit up. Give him your saddest face."

Sally got out of the car and walked around to the Honda. Leroy and Chester crept down between the two cars. She tapped on the door and tapped again, louder. A truck raced by, and Sally looked up at the flash of bright lights. The front window of the Honda lowered a few inches and stopped.

"What?" a tired voice asked through the opening.

"I need help," Sally pleaded, a worried look on her face. "All my red dash lights are on, and I'm afraid to go any further. Can you look at them?"

"Where you going?" the sleepy voice asked.

"Alexandria," Sally said. Pushing down on the handle, she saw the door was unlocked. Slowly she opened the door and smiled sweetly at the man. "Please, I'm all alone. Can you help?"

"Maybe it's nothing," the man said. He slumped out of the front seat. An elderly man, he carefully straightened up and followed Sally to the Jaguar. When he got to the front fender, Leroy jumped up in a blur of motion and hit the man squarely on the side of his head. Leroy grabbed him before he went down and pulled him behind the Jaguar.

A horn sounded, and there was a flash of bright lights. With Chester and Sally standing together in the glare of light, the car slowed momentarily and then sped down the road. It disappeared in the darkness. The only light in the rest stop was the dim glow from the Honda's interior.

Looking into the glow, Chester and Sally watched the moving shadows as Leroy hit the man again and again. His fist was covered with blood that spattered onto his shirt. Sally turned away, but she said nothing. The wheezing noises became louder and then subsided.

"See what he has in the car, Chester," Leroy said, massaging the knuckles on his right hand.

Chester walked around the body to the front of the Honda. He slid into the front seat and saw a gold chain looped around the mirror. There was a replica of the Liberty Bell swinging from the chain. Chester uncoiled the chain and put it in his pocket. Then he opened the glove compartment, saw a set of maps, and slammed the compartment shut. Turing around, he began looking through a suitcase in the back seat.

"Poor dumb bastard," Leroy said. He bent over the unconscious figure and reached into the man's back pocket. After taking his wallet, a black leather billfold thick with bills of all denominations, family pictures, and three credit cards, Leroy dragged the man to the picnic table and propped him on the bench. He dropped his head on the top of the table, blood flowing over the cracked wood.

"Is he dead?" Sally asked, walking with Leroy to the Jaguar.

"I don't think so," Leroy said. He took the money out of the wallet and then threw the wallet over his shoulder. Counting quickly, he began laughing loudly.

"How much?"

"We did good, Sally. One hundred and sixty-five dollars." Leroy looked back at the figure slumped over the picnic table and laughed again. "Thank you, old man."

"Nothing in the car," Chester said, returning from the Honda. They all got in the Jaguar, and with a squeal of tire and cinder, Leroy spun onto the turnpike. Sally turned on the radio, and music rocked the car. Leroy drifted into the passing lane and cranked up the Jaguar to ninety. They were all singing and trying to clap their hands to the rhythm of the music when Leroy slowed the car for the Pottstown exit.

"I hit that man so bad!" he shouted above the music. "That was the best tackle I made all weekend. That's what I'm going to do to the Eagle players next Friday." Turning the Jaguar sharply onto the exit ramp and thinking about football and food and how much money he had in his pocket, Leroy was excited and began singing loudly.

Sitting in the tollbooth at the Pottstown Exit, John Weller leaned back on the chair. But for some loud crickets, it had been very quiet for the last two hours, and he was in a half-asleep, comfort zone. Then he heard the slight strains of music. The exit ramp was a sweeping curve that came back over the turnpike to the tollbooth. John heard the shrill squeal of tires on the curve, and the music became louder and clearer. In the still night air, the cricket noise disappeared, and John heard Jim Croce's voice,

> And he bad, bad Leroy Brown
> The baddest man in the whole damned town
> Badder than old King Kong
> And meaner than a junkyard dog.

Looking up, John saw two lights racing toward him. He saw that the car was yellow, and then the bright lights flashed on and blinded him. The car skidded to a stop inches from his window, and *Bad, Bad Leroy Brown* shattered the quiet of the booth. From the darkness of the car, a hand reached out and handed him a ticket. John rubbed at the glare in his eyes and tried to read the blurred exit names.

"He got a .32 gun in his pocket for fun; he got a razor in his shoe." The laughter and singing in the car grew louder. Rattled by the noise and music, John lifted the ticket in the light and studied it closely.

"Hurry up, Asshole!" a voice shouted through the window.

"Excuse me," John said. Lowering the ticket in his hand, he squinted into the darkness of the Jaguar and shouted over the noise of the song. "This tollbooth is run by the Pennsylvania Turnpike Commission, and we follow certain rules. You don't use that kind of language here."

"Fuck you," Leroy said. He threw a crumpled five-dollar bill out the car window. It hit John in the chest and rolled to the corner of the booth.

Leroy focused his gaze on the squared signal box on the side of the booth. The glaring red light began to annoy him and tired of waiting, he slammed his foot on the gas. Tires spinning smoke and hurling fragments of stone, the Jaguar exploded sideways, swiped sparks against the signal box, straightened, and raced down the road.

John stepped quickly to the back exit and saw the brake lights of the yellow car grow smaller and smaller. The Jaguar turned onto Route 100 and disappeared. Getting back in the booth, John looked at the spot of red on his shirt where the five-dollar bill had hit. He reached for the phone and dialed his supervisor.

It was five thirty Monday morning, and Valley Forge National Park was deserted when Drew Benson pulled into the parking space in front of the National Memorial Arch. Just returned home from Vietnam, Drew was twenty-five years old. With the clear, smooth features of his face, he looked younger than twenty-five. His black hair was neatly trimmed and dropped slightly over his forehead. There were no blemishes or developing age lines on his youthful face; the only distinguishing mark was the small scar below his lip. He was wearing a blue George Washington sweatshirt.

It's been a long time, Drew thought.

Sitting there in the car, Drew focused his gaze on the Memorial Arch across the road. The monumental shape rose out of the ground, its massive stone facade a towering outline in the gray morning light. Drew got out of the car, took a deep breath, and began a series of stretches. After he worked the tightness out of his muscles, he began to run.

Moving smoothing, his Reeboks gliding quietly over the cement surface, Drew ran effortlessly. He raced by the familiar log cabins and stone memorials, and as he ran, he noticed the glassy eyes of the deer as they lifted their heads from feeding. The cold air filled his lungs, and Drew felt strong and ran even faster.

I can do this, he thought. *I can get through this. Nothing has changed.*

But after twenty minutes of the fast pace, Drew began to lose his concentration. He began to feel the presence of the past, the close proximity of the war, and his muscles began to tighten. In the brisk morning, his breath forming steam in the cold air, Drew began to feel the sweltering tropical heat.

Then there was a sudden blasting crescendo of gunfire. Breathing deeply and slowing his stride, he tried to relax, but the deafening sound stayed with him. Drew stopped at an artillery piece next to the jogging trail. Wiping the perspiration from his forehead, he stared blankly into the depths of the black barrel.

When Drew checked into the base camp outside of Saigon, Shane informed him that his training in the States would be useless. It would be hard, but he would educate Drew himself. After days of listening to Shane explain what he had to do when the helicopter landed, what he could expect from the Vietcong, and most importantly, how to avoid the stupid things that would get him killed, Drew was not sure of anything. He was on his first mission, and he was lost.

The roar of the helicopter filled his senses. Crouched at the side of the helicopter and caught in the swirling water and grass from the rice paddy, he waited for the stretchers. Flying cover overhead, fighter jets sprayed the tree line with napalm. Soldiers came splashing across the rice paddy, and Drew helped lift the first stretcher, a man bandaged at the neck, blood covering his shirt.

Drew secured the stretcher, and hearing a gunshot and turning quickly, he watched a hole open up in the side of the helicopter. Catching his breath, Drew heard another shot. He saw a blur of a body diving at him, and he was hit hard from the side and knocked off his feet. Releasing his arm, Shane looked at him from the broken stalks of rice.

"Stay down," he said. There was a slight rip on the sleeve of his shirt. "That bastard is keyed on you."

Shane moved away slowly and disappeared over the side of the rice paddy. Except for the whirling noise of the helicopter, the shooting had stopped. Drew lifted his head slightly, and another bullet smacked the mud next to his shoulder.

"Fuck," he said, slamming his face down in the mud and water. There was a loud burst of gunfire from his right, and looking up, he saw the bullets kick up the water along the far patty. Then he saw a green form roll over the mud-caked side of the paddy, crush through the rice stalks, and lie motionless in the water.

Running in a zigzag line, Shane raced back to the helicopter. They loaded the last stretcher and were about to take off when four Marines ran up with another wounded soldier. Even though they had too much weight, Shane lashed the stretcher onto the side and gave the thumbs up. When the pilot tried to lift off, the chopper rose and thumped back to the ground.

Drew saw the look of terror in the eyes of the wounded man. The helicopter struggled, shook violently side to side, and lifted slowly off the ground. Drew looked across the row of stretchers and saw the smile on Shane's face. The rip in his sleeve was wet and smeared with a dark red stain.

After the helicopter landed, Drew went with Shane to the hospital. Shane seemed embarrassed by the scratch, but the doctor cleaned the wound and bandaged it carefully. Shane then went to the PX, and Drew returned to the barracks alone. Lying there on the bunk, his hands crossed behind his head, he realized that Shane was right. Drew knew nothing. He had spent four years in college, and he knew nothing.

Thinking how useless he was, Drew remembered the notice posted on the bulletin board. It suddenly became very important. Making a quick decision, he ran to the hall and took the piece of paper from the board. Approaching the row of phone booths, Drew read the first line of the advertisement, **Learn How Not To Die In Vietnam**. And on the line below, he read **Kim Lee, Expert Fight Instructor**. Drew got in an empty phone booth and called the number on the paper. After talking with Kim Lee for a few minutes, he had the schedule for his own private fight class.

Drew's instructor, Kim, was part Vietnamese and part Chinese. He was tall, five feet ten inches, and when Drew first saw him, he looked thin and unassuming. Then later after the introductions and the lesson began, Drew saw the agility, the power, and the explosive quickness. On that first day, Drew formed clear pictures of Kim's arms and legs as being flexible bands of rubber that were somehow hidden and compressed deep within his body. They struck out effortlessly and with blinding speed and stung Drew before he saw any hint of movement.

The classes took place on a soccer field in front of a bombed-out French lycée. The roofs and all but one of the walls of the classrooms lay in piles of rubble. Only one goal post stood on the field that was covered with weeds and clumps of grass. Between the helicopter missions and some field exercises, Drew trained for six weeks with Kim, and the grass around the goal post became matted smooth.

After the two-hour workout on the seventh week, Drew was exhausted and thirsty. Sweat rolled down his face and saturated his green T-shirt and shorts. He was bent over, looking at the ground, trying to catch his breath.

"You're not very good at this, Drew," Kim said, standing stationary next to him. He gave him a bottle of water, and Drew drank it quickly. What was left in the bottle, Drew poured over his head.

"But I've worked hard. I can do everything you showed me."

"Yes, you're tough that way. You keep trying no matter what. But there's something you don't have. There's something missing inside."

"What's this missing stuff about?" Drew asked. "I don't understand."

"There are skills you are born with, and without them, you have nothing to work with, nothing to build on." Kim sat cross-legged on the ground, and Drew sat opposite him. "I don't know if I can explain it. Sometimes, hours into my practice routine, when I am really sharp and focused, I find myself doing different patterns, shadow patterns that I have never practiced before. But they are challenging and strong patterns. I think they are from a past life."

"You're a Buddhist?"

"Yes," Kim said. "I believe I had past lives, and they influence who I am now."

"And you were a great fighter in one of your other lives? That's why you're so good."

"Something like that," Kim said. "At times, I can study people and see what their past lives were." He was quiet for a moment, studying Drew's face, staring into his eyes. "I thought I saw yours."

"What was it?"

"At first, because you were so weak and clumsy, I thought you had been a homeless person at one time. But now I don't think so. Your spirit is stronger than your body. Your strength is inside. You have been a fighter in one of your lives. I think a soldier, a good soldier."

"Thank you," Drew said. "That's the first compliment you've given me. But as a fighter, I'm not improving very much. Have I been wasting our time?"

"No, this practice has been valuable to you," Kim said. "And you have learned the skill to handle an average, slow opponent."

"All these weeks I worked so hard," Drew said, "and you say I can handle a slow opponent. How slow? Maybe like your grandfather."

"No, he would probably hurt you," Kim said, missing the joke. "But it's not your fault, Drew. This instinct to be a great fighter is something rare. Like I said, you must be born with it. Did you do any physical sports in the U.S.?"

"I played football in school."

"Were you good at it?"

"I was terrible," Drew said. "I guess I'm terrible at everything."

There was a slight wind across the field. Filtering through the clouds, the sunset cast an orange glow on the line of palm trees, and the moving branches formed long shadows across the soccer field and the solitary wall that jutted high out of the rubble from the school.

"You're not terrible, Drew. You have some quickness. Your hands and legs are strong." Kim stood up and motioned Drew to do the same. Looking totally relaxed and smiling, Kim walked behind Drew. "Let me show you something."

"What do you want me to do?"

"Nothing, don't move," Kim said. "How do you feel now? Do you sense anything, any danger?"

"No," Drew said. "But with you, there's always . . ."

Drew didn't have a chance to finish. Kim's hand clasped down onto Drew's shoulder, and he buried his thumb deep into a pressure point. Drew felt sudden, great pain, and his whole arm down to his fingers went numb.

The pain was unbearable, but Drew clenched his lips shut and suffered through it silently. Feeling his legs weaken and not sure if he would collapse, he felt tremendous relief when Kim released him from the grip.

"You're stronger than you think, Drew. Most people could not tolerate that pressure. They would be crying in pain."

"It hurt like hell," Drew said. "But I don't cry any more."

"Good," Kim said. "Let me show you how this works. If done correctly, it will stop any opponent."

In the evening light, Kim identified the important pressure points and showed Drew where to place the hand and thumb. He went over everything carefully, and hours later as a warm drizzle began to fall over the soccer field, Kim told Drew he was ready to practice the move.

"You're sure you want me to do this to you?" Drew asked.

"I'm sure," Kim said. "Please don't worry about me."

Kim placed Drew's hand over his shoulder, and guiding the thumb into position, he told Drew to apply the downward pressure. Drew clamped down hard, and exerting as much force as he could, Drew watched Kim's face for any sign of emotion. There was nothing. After a few moments, Kim told Drew that his thumb was in the right location and he could release his grip.

"But you didn't feel anything," Drew said.

"I've done exercises to strengthen these muscles since I was a child," Kim said. "But I did feel something like a tingle. You have strong hands."

"A tingle," Drew said. "Let me try again." Drew exerted more pressure on the muscle, but the result was the same. Kim showed no discomfort at all. They repeated the practice over and over again until Drew could find the pressure point in the dark.

"What if an expert fighter won't let me get this close?" Drew asked. He was opening and closing his fingers of his hand, trying to relax the tightness he felt.

"That is an excellent question. You must remember this, Drew. It's very important for your good health. If you have any suspicions that your opponent is an expert fighter, you must never try this maneuver."

"What should I do?"

"You must take your gun and shoot the man or woman from a safe distance," Kim said.

"Even a woman?" Drew asked.

"Even a child," Kim said. He had a calm, serious look on his face, and Drew didn't ask any more questions.

When Drew returned to the barracks, Shane was at a table, concentrating on a letter he was writing to May. Drew walked past some crumpled drafts of paper on the floor. He told Shane he wanted to show him something, but it might hurt a little. Without looking up, Shane nodded his head slightly. Drew stepped behind him and clamped his fingers and thumb deep into the shoulder muscle on Shane's right side. Shane dropped the pen on the table, and Drew watched it roll over the edge and bounce on the floor.

Drew knew he had the spot and felt the muscle tighten under his grip. He applied more pressure, and Shane's body seemed to give up and then collapse weakly in his grip. There was tightness in the skin on Shane's face, and he squinted his eyes shut and clenched his lips together.

Then Shane screamed out profanity after profanity and lifted his left hand, extending the middle finger in the air. Drew saw the finger as a sign of surrender and released his grip. Shane let out a loud roar.

"What the hell!" Shane shouted at Drew. "What the hell!" he shouted again. "Don't ever do that again."

"I wanted to show you my new move," Drew said. "Kim taught it to me today. I call it the Tiger Claw."

"You and Kim and your Tiger Claw can go to hell," Shane said, massaging his neck.

"Kim said it would disable the strongest man. That's why I wanted to see what you would do with it."

"Thanks," Shane said. He had an irritated look on his face. "How did I do?"

"You did fine," Drew said. "But you screamed, didn't you? When I first experienced the move, it hurt a lot, but I kept my mouth shut. I kept my pain inside."

"That's great for you," Shane said. He reached down and picked up the pen. Straightening up, he looked closely at Drew. "I would like to see you use that new Kim move when a VC is pointing his AK47 at your chest. Maybe he'll wait while you walk behind him and get your hand into position for your Tiger Claw. Or maybe you should sneak silently away and come back in the night and Tiger Claw him in his sleep. Did Kim explain how useless the Tiger Claw would be in the jungle?"

"He explained a little," Drew said. He watched Shane straighten the stationary on the table. "I think I know what I'm doing. And I think I know why it bothers you."

"It doesn't bother me, Drew."

"I can finally do something better than you. That's what bothers you."

"If it bothered me, I'd take that Tiger Claw and shove it up your ass."

"See," Drew said. "You're upset."

"Go away," Shane said. "I'm busy." He began writing on the stationary.

"Tell May I still love her," Drew said. "Tell her to airmail me her special honey sandwich."

Shane ignored Drew and continued to write his letter. Drew looked over Shane's shoulder for a few moments, and then he walked down to the recreation room where a group of soldiers were sitting in front of a TV.

All in the Family was on the screen, and the soldiers were laughing and making loud comments about the show. Drew heard Archie Bunker yell at Edith to shut up, and to loud laughter from the TV audience and the group of soldiers, Archie grabbed a newspaper and slouched down in his favorite chair.

The jocular image of Archie Bunker still in his mind, Drew stepped away from the empty barrel of the cannon. He began to run fast, and with the sound of the soldiers' laughter growing dimmer and dimmer, he broke into a hard sprint. Breathing heavily now, his arms pumping with his lengthening stride, Drew ran the length of Mount Joy. Twenty minutes later as he turned the corner of the jogging path, he saw the statue of Baron von Steuben rise dark and ghostly into the morning sky.

Drew slowed, and walking past the statue, he stopped at the small memorial buried in the ground. Moisture and an intricate pattern of silky spider webs covered the surface of the Chicken Thief Monument. Drew hesitated for only a moment, and seeing the image of the chicken soldier and feeling a sudden chill, he took off running again.

Sprinting at his fastest pace, Drew slowly but determinedly cleared his mind of all images, and looking ahead, he saw the circular dome of the bell tower. Drew crested the hill across from the Washington Memorial Chapel, and perspiration running down his face and drenching his sweatshirt, he stepped off the jogging path and stood there exhausted.

Drew wiped the sweat from his face. Hearing the engine, he looked up and saw the lights of a car coming down the far hill. The lights disappeared momentarily and then reappeared. Blasting music in all directions, the car raced closer, lights swinging wildly across the road. Lifting his hand to shield his eyes, Drew recognized the Croce song.

Now Leroy he a gambler and he like his fancy clothes.
And he like to wave his diamond rings in front of everybody's nose.

The resonating sound of music grew louder and shredded the morning air, and then the lights turned to high beams. Suddenly, the car, a blur of yellow, swerved off the road and headed toward him. Drew was frozen in the brightness of the light.

"Asshole!" a voice shouted over the laughter and loud sounds of *Bad, Bad Leroy Brown*. The Jaguar came within a few feet of Drew and swerved back on the road. Drew didn't move. He studied every detail of the white faces of the driver and female passenger in the front seat and the black face of the big figure in the back.

The rush of air and roar of music against his face sent an icy shiver the length of his body. Drew looked down the road and watched the red brake lights grow small and disappear. The thin echo of Leroy Brown music disappeared with the lights. Drew stood in the sudden stillness for a moment. Then stretching his hands behind his neck and breathing easily, he walked slowly down the jogging path.

There was a rustling noise and some movement behind him. Drew turned quickly. Snorting misty clouds of steam that seemed to freeze in the air, the herd of deer stood half hidden in the deep grass. There were six of them. One was a buck, a towering rack lifting high in the air.

"Eight points," Drew counted in a glance. The glassy oval eyes, sometimes clouded by the rising steam, focused on him. Drew's heart began to beat faster, and for a moment he felt a jolt of anticipation and excitement move through his body.

Then the distant sound of a car horn shattered the morning silence. The buck bolted into motion, and the herd trampled past Drew, their hoofs lifting sparks from the surface of the cement road. Seconds later, the brown forms disappeared into the dark line of trees behind the chapel.

Leroy blew the horn again and laughed. Bloated with double cheeseburgers, he was feeling good. His favorite song blasted through the four speakers of the Jaguar, and he had a full bottle of beer in his hand.

"The dumb fucker didn't hardly move!" Chester shouted.

"The baddest damn man in the whole damned town," Leroy was singing loudly and looking at his face in the mirror. He drove the Jaguar down a dirt side road and parked it behind a small maintenance building. Leroy shut off the motor, killing the music. He looked around surprised by the sudden silence. Lifting the bottle in his hand, he gulped down the beer.

"Fuck 'em," he said. "Fuck 'em all." He leaned back on the seat, dropping the bottle on the floor, his head rolling against Sally's shoulder. Soon the wheezing sound filled the car, and he was fast asleep. Pushing his head carefully aside, Sally slid away from the sleeping football player.

"Come sit with me," Chester said, pushing the door open. Sally squeezed into the backseat. Chester pulled her closer and had her Patriots T-shirt off in seconds. Soon grunting sounds joined the uneven wheezing noise in the car.

Drew sat down on the bench opposite the Memorial Chapel. The morning sun was bright now, the rays warming his face. Drew heard the harsh sound of a heavy vehicle. The yellow school bus, engine grinding noisily, turned the bend, and when it passed him, he read Valley Forge High School on the side. The noise from inside the bus was loud, and the animated faces of the students stared from some of the windows. As the bus went by the Washington Memorial Chapel, one of the boys in the back seat, a very plump boy with thick glasses, leaned out the window and gave him the finger.

Laughing at the stupid-looking kid, Drew took a small audio recorder from his back pocket. It was a Sony, the newest and smallest model on the market. He had purchased it at the PX before he left Saigon. Holding it on his palm, he pressed the play-record button.

"This is my first time back in the park, Shane. I parked at the arch. Then I ran two miles, and even in the morning darkness, I could see every log cabin, every piece of artillery, and every statue before I got there. Nothing had changed. It was cool thinking of all the fun things we did here. Then I don't know why, but I started to hear the choppers. I thought of that evacuation at Quan Tri where we could hardly get off the ground. I began to see the faces of the wounded. I saw the bullet you took for me.

"Oh, and I saw a huge buck. I'll never forget what happened when we went hunting the trophy buck our freshmen year. After that night, you said I would never have nightmares again. And you were right. I never had another nightmare.

"But the park was real crazy this morning. A car with some young kids came right at me. I didn't move, and for a moment I felt they were going to hit me. I felt like I was back in Nam."

Throwing loose gravel in the air, a big construction truck rolled by the bench. There was a white van, Valley Forge National Park painted in big blue letters on the side, behind the truck. As it went by, the driver rolled down the window and stared at Drew on the bench. Drew clicked the stop button on the Sony and put it in his pocket. Standing up and taking a deep breath, he crunched his shoulders into his neck.

Drew stretched again and walked slowly down the jogging path. He saw the black artillery piece next to the tree. Bright rays of sunlight reflected off the moisture on the grass and lifted a cloud of mist through the spokes of the wheel and along the length of the barrel.

Kneeling next to it, he saw the crusted silver band. Drew reached his hand between the spokes and wiped off the dirt and grime. When he finished, the band glistened in the sunlight. Drew looked into the dazzling light for a moment. Then he straightened and began the slow jog back to the car.

CHAPTER 10

Frank West, Valley Forge High School principal, stood at the window next to his desk. The former George Washington High School principal wore an expensive suit now, and he occupied a large, elaborately furnished office. Mr. West Sr. watched the line of school busses and student cars backed up on Charlestown Road. Caught in the morning traffic, the students turned up the volume of their stereo systems and tried to out blast the other cars. With the blaring music, the loud base sound thumping against the sides of the building, and the harsh sounds from the bus engines, it was a noisy, uncomfortable time for the high school principal.

"Damn it," Mr. West said. One of the school busses had stopped in front of the building, and behind it was the Valley Forge Park ranger's van, lights spinning red and blue. He watched the school board president exit the van and walk to the open door of the bus. He was holding a silver-and-blue can in his hand. After a few minutes, Mr. Wentworth left the bus and walked toward the main entrance of the building. The lights of his van were spinning colors behind him.

Mr. West sat down and cleared some papers off his desk. Looking at his school security monitor on the wall, he saw the students leave the bus and walk in broken lines to the front building. There was a knock on the door, and Mr. Wentworth entered his office. He and the principal did not exchange any formalities. Instead, Mr. Wentworth walked across the room and slammed a can of Pepsi on the desk. Some brown cola and bubbles dripped down the side of the can.

"We don't teach littering at this school," Mr. Wentworth said. "A student in your bus threw this can on the grounds of George Washington's Headquarters." He glared at the can of Pepsi on the desk. "Washington's Headquarters! This is the foundation of our country, and your kids trash it."

Mr. West was quiet. His face reddened, and there was a nervous twitch on his mouth that seemed to quiver around the edges of his neatly trimmed moustache. Looking past Mr. Wentworth, he saw Homer Matthews walk in the office and give the secretary a slip of paper.

"We're working on it," he told Mr. Wentworth. "We've had daily announcements about behavior on the bus. All we have to do is catch one kid."

"Well, there's your evidence," Mr. Wentworth pointed at the can, which now had a pool of cola forming a circle on the bright glaze on the table.

"I understand what the problem is."

"Then solve it," Mr. Wentworth ordered. "I have more important things to do than return your trash." The school board president stormed out of the room, leaving the door open.

"That's his fourth visit this month," the secretary said, coming in the room. Bess Stevens had worked with the principal for twenty-one years and understood his moods. She picked up the can and placed it next to the three others on the shelves by the window. "Your delinquent student is a Pepsi lover," she said.

"I'll hear about it again at the board meeting. Tony found some cases of beer and trash in the parking lot this morning. That would really give Wentworth something to talk about." The principal wiped the smear on his desk and replaced the papers.

"I saw Homer come in the office," he said. "What did he want?"

"Mrs. Deal called in. Her sister died in Monaca. That's near Pittsburgh. She'll be out this week. You know the substitute situation is getting worse."

"How many teachers are out today?"

"Eight," Bess said. "Homer said he could cover her class this morning, but he had to get someone this afternoon."

"Who?" the principal asked.

"Homer said he tried to call Drew Benson. He was going to try again."

"Oh, hell," the principal said. "Why does Homer do this crap all the time? How did Benson's name get on the substitute list?"

"He has a degree in history and biology. He's a veteran, and he graduated from here."

"No one graduated from here yet," the principal corrected her. "He graduated from George Washington. Benson was nothing but trouble, and Homer always backed him up. I almost had him suspended a couple of times, but he was sneaky smart. I'm convinced he was the one who trashed my office and stole school property."

"There's no one else," the secretary said. "Homer said he called the others, but they're already scheduled."

"Bullshit!" Mr. West couldn't control his irritation. He picked up his phone and dialed a number.

"Homer," he shouted. "I don't want Benson teaching in this building!" The principal listened for a second. "You did what?" He slammed the phone down.

"Homer's already scheduled him this afternoon and the rest of the week." The principal looked at Bess. There was a note of determination in his voice. "This will be Benson's last time in my building. Type a memo to Homer. Clearly state that the principal will assign all substitute teachers."

"More work for you," Bess said.

"It will be worth it if I can keep trouble out of my building." The principal stood up. He looked out the window and saw a car pull into one of the few empty parking spaces. A girl stepped out, took a long inhale from her cigarette, and then flipped it into the grass.

"This is a new start, a new beginning," the principal said. "We don't need problems from the past to mess the school up. And Benson is a problem."

The phone rang again in the office. Bess turned and walked through the door to her desk. The 8:10 bell rang, and the morning assembly began. The sounds of the National Anthem echoed through the halls of Valley Forge High School.

On Drew's drive back from his morning run, he was slowed by the heavy traffic. It was nine thirty when he turned into Valley Park Homes. Drew parked his car on Betsy Ross Street. All the streets in the new housing development situated on the edge of Valley Forge National Park were named after Revolutionary War figures.

His blue-painted house with red-framed windows and two large elm trees on the front lawn was one of the two original residences that had not been taken over by the developers. His elderly neighbor, Mrs. Jablonski, owned the other house.

Closing the door to the car, Drew stood on the walk and looked at the rows of identical houses on the treeless street. Beyond the house on the corner, he could clearly see the hill in the distance and the large American flag that flew over the Valley Forge Veterans Hospital. He climbed the steps to the porch, and the door to the house opened slowly in front of him. Whin stood there next to her daughter NuWhin. The girl was two years and six months old. Drew kissed them both on the cheek.

"Morning," she said. Still struggling with the English language, Whin spoke only in short phrases. "The phone came for you today."

Whin looked up at Drew, seeing if he understood. She was a trim, slender woman, twenty-six years old, and was strikingly beautiful. She had a light complexion, which was highlighted by the black hair that flowed neatly to her shoulders. When they first met, she told Drew that her father was in the French Foreign Legion and her mother was a teacher. They were both dead; her father killed in the final days of Dien Bien Phu, her mother when her school was destroyed by American bombs.

A secretary from the French Embassy in Saigon had told Drew that the French-Vietnamese children were the most beautiful children in the world. He saw some truth to this when he was in Vietnam. But he also saw what some American blood did in the mix. The girl, NuWhin, was more striking than her mother. She swung her arms in the air and laughed at him. Her green eyes blinked with excitement. Drew marveled at the delicate features of her face. He marveled at the peace and contentment and pure joy in NuWhin's smile. Thinking about the fear on her face a few months ago, Drew remembered clearly their last day in Saigon.

In April 1975, Saigon was flooded with refugees. One hundred thousand North Vietnamese troops were advancing on the city. At the end of the month, on April 29, Drew and Whin were scheduled to be married at the consular office. He carried the girl in his arms, and taking detours and routes that Whin knew, it still took them two hours to get around the crowds of people and through the gate of the American Embassy.

Drew led Whin through the busy groups of employees and armed military personal straight to the consular's office. Mr. Abrams, a good friend from Pennsylvania, said he had no time for the full wedding, but for Drew he could manage a shortened ceremony. It was total confusion in the embassy. People were running folders around and pushing each other in and out of his office. Paper shredders ran nonstop on three of the desks. After finishing the wedding certificates, Mr. Abrams motion to Drew and Whin. When Drew was next to him, he spoke quietly.

"I'm sorry about Shane."

"Was it as bad as they said?"

"Worse," Mr. Abrams said. "Let's get done with this wedding."

Drew and Whin were hastily married in a simple ceremony. Right after the wedding, the speakers on the wall clicked on. There was a humming static, and then he heard the voice of Bing Crosby, and the sounds of *White Christmas* filled the office.

> I'm dreaming of a white Christmas
> With every Christmas card I write
> May your days be merry and bright
> And may all your Christmases be white

"What's going on?" Drew asked nervously. His heart began racing, and he leaned against the wall for support. Holding NuWhin in his arms and clutching

Whin with his other hand, he watched as the hurried activity in the office came to a complete stop.

Distracted by the song, the people were frozen in place. The embassy personnel, some in uniform, some in short-sleeved shirts, stood staring at each other as the words, "I'm dreaming of a white Christmas, just like the ones we used to know," resonated from the speakers. The music sounded in the halls and all the offices and echoed across the grounds of the embassy. Drew noticed perspiration dripping onto NuWhin's dress, and he handed her to Whin and wiped his forehead. His face was heated and flushed red.

"What's the matter?" Mr. Abrams asked.

"The song," Drew said.

"I'm surprised you don't know," Mr. Abrams said. "*White Christmas* is being broadcast on every radio signal in the country. It's the code signal. Everyone in Saigon will be racing to the two assigned evacuation locations. The embassy is one of them. You're lucky you're here already

Mr. Abrams grabbed Drew by the shoulder and ushered him, Whin, and the girl to his desk. Unlocking the top drawer, he pulled out red priority passes and attached them in a clearly visible spot on their clothes. Then he pointed down the hall to the side staircase that led to the roof.

"Helicopters are waiting on the roof," he said. "Get on the first one you can."

"Thanks," Drew said, shaking hands. The music ended suddenly, and there was a brief silence. Then the noise and hectic movement of activity began again. Mr. Abrams returned to his desk and was soon surrounded by people.

"We have to leave Vietnam now," Drew said, leaning closer to Whin,

"But our money. Everything we have is at the house."

"We can't go back," Drew said.

Whin lowered her head. The rush of people around them became more feverish and noisy. Holding NuWhin in his arms, Drew took Whin by the hand and led her down the crowded corridor to the staircase. The two armed Marines at the door scrutinized their red passes and let them advance with the others.

After a stressful hour of waiting in line, listening to the mounting voices of anger and frustration and the sporadic sound of gunfire from the street, Drew stepped into the helicopter with his new family. As the helicopter lifted away from the embassy, NuWhin began crying. Her sounds were drowned out by the thundering echo of noise from the helicopter. Drew held her tightly, and he could feel her chest heaving up and down against his. Her screams became louder, and he saw the fear in her face.

"It's OK," Drew said, whispering in her ear.

Looking from the helicopter, Drew could see the mad rush of people surrounding the walls of the American Embassy. All roads leading to the embassy were blocked with crowds and stalled vehicles. As the helicopter ascended in the sky, the city of Saigon became smaller and smaller and disappeared. There was only the glistening waters of the Mekong River flowing through a patched, smoky landscape of burning fires and destroyed villages.

"It's over," Drew whispered. He tried to comfort NuWhin, who was still sobbing.

A car drove by the house. NuWhin pointed at it and began to laugh. Feeling a cool breeze in his face, Drew looked up at the sound of laughter. He saw Whin standing there and waiting for a response.

"The phone came for you today," she repeated.

"The phone came for me," Drew said, a smile on his face. "It'll come again." He went to the kitchen and opened the refrigerator. Drew took the plastic container and drank the cold spring water. When he finished drinking, he heard the ringing noise in the living room.

Putting the container on the kitchen table, Drew went to the living room and picked up the phone. He listened to Assistant Principal Homer Matthews explain about Mrs. Deal's emergency leave. He listened to how Homer needed him to cover her class. Then Homer corrected himself and said he had actually assigned Drew to cover and he would start that afternoon.

"Why so soon?" Drew asked.

"Because," Homer said, "teaching will help you forget about the war, Drew. You have to get busy fast, and that means this afternoon." Homer finished talking, and there was a short pause. "Did you hear me?"

"Yes, I heard everything," Drew said. "I'll be there as soon as I get cleaned up." Drew put the phone down.

"What is it?" Whin asked, standing next to him.

"I'm going to teach today," he said and then corrected himself. "I'm going to teach all week."

"Teacher," she said. "Good."

Drew went upstairs to the bedroom. After he showered, he put on brown pants, brown shirt, dark brown tie, and he carried his tan sport coat in his hand. He kissed Whin and went to the car. The school was only a mile from his house. It was eleven in the morning.

The Lafayette Country Club had been promoting its yearly membership drive for a week, and Jeb Wood had plenty of time to plan his own surprise promotion for the new members. At the corner of the ninth hole, he sat unseen in the shade of trees. Moving the M1903 Springfield slowly, comfortably, he scoped the distant, gentle grade of hill as it dropped down to the green. There was a slight breeze, and the flag moved lightly in the wind.

Studying the hill of dazzling bright, perfectly cut grass that stretched across his land, Jeb felt the sudden rush of anger, and he lowered the Springfield. His eye began to hurt, and he closed it against the light and the pain.

He saw Joshua then. It was a cool, spring morning, and they sat camouflaged in the same deep brush and trees. Except for a small clearing near the crest, the hill was overgrown with pine and brush and dogwood. They both studied the clearing for the slightest movement, the slightest sound.

Then Joshua began the turkey call, and it was the sweetest music that Jeb ever heard. Enjoying the sound, Jeb kept waiting and concentrating on the clearing. After a few minutes, Joshua was quiet and brushed next to him.

"Get ready," he whispered softly. "They're close."

Jeb strained so hard to hear what Joshua heard, but there was nothing. He was about to lower the Springfield when the first turkey stepped into the clearing. Another huge gobbler followed and another and then the entire flock. There were so many of them that the ground was soon covered by a moving black blanket of bobbing red heads and fan-shaped feathers. Jeb was always amazed when that happened, and waiting as long as he could, he aimed at the largest gobbler.

Jeb shot, and as the turkey fell, the blanket exploded into an ear-splitting, fluttering, crashing confusion of bodies and feathers. But for the one dark lump, the clearing was empty in seconds. Jeb walked through the brush and picked up the dead turkey. He only killed what he and Joshua needed. And every year, the flock came back, thick in number and fat and healthy.

Jeb heard the distant noise from the engine and opened his eye. Lifting the Springfield and looking through the scope, he saw the golf cart bounce into view and begin a speedy descent down the hill. There was a driver and two passengers. Golf bags and golf clubs were swaying with the motion of the cart.

Jeb shot the Springfield, and with flaps of black rubber flying in the air, the front tire and rim of the golf cart exploded in pieces. The driver catapulted high over the front of the golf cart and landed solidly on his face and chest and didn't move. The other two golfers held on briefly, but on the second roll, they were thrown awkwardly onto the splendid grass. Golf clubs and white golf balls were flying everywhere.

Delighted with the view, Jeb watched the race of golf balls down the hill for a few seconds. Then he turned silently and walked to the hidden entrance of the tunnel. He moved the bear trap out of the way, pulled the door open, and replacing the trap and brush covering, he crawled down the steps. The tunnel was cool and dark. The great picture of the wrecked golf cart and bodies flying in the air was fresh in his mind.

Christ, this is fun," Jeb thought. He began to laugh, a hard crusty gobble-laugh that came from deep in his throat. Soon Jeb was coughing and laughing at the same time. He began coughing so hard, his stomach hurt, and he had to sit down and take a breather.

There was little traffic, and Drew reached the school in a few minutes. After completing two circles around the building, he found an empty space in the back row of the faculty parking lot. Closing the door, he saw a yellow car race down Charlestown Road and turn into the school entrance. Drew stood there and stared at the three faces when the yellow Jaguar drove past.

"Valley's best," he said. The car spun into the student lot and disappeared. As Drew reached the sidewalk, a black-and-white sheriff's car drove by slowly. It stopped, and the driver put it in reverse and came back to him. The window slid open, and the driver lowered his dark glasses and looked at Drew.

"I never forget faces. I remember you from somewhere," he said. "I'm Sheriff Quincy Hess." He reached out through the window and shook hands with Drew. "Do you teach here?"

"This is my first day here," Drew said. "I'm a substitute."

"You look so familiar," the sheriff said, studying Drew's face. "I remember now. Didn't you used to play football for George Washington?" The sheriff's eyebrows lifted, and he looked closely at Drew. "Did you score that touchdown?"

"Against the Eagles?" Drew asked.

"Yes," the sheriff said. "The one that won the game."

"Yes, I scored that touchdown," Drew said. He smiled, thinking back to the game. "Were you there?"

"I was there," the sheriff said. His voice became irritated. "I was there on the field. I was the Eagles kicker." The sheriff's face reddened slightly. He slid away from the window and kicked the cruiser in gear. Without another word, he peeled his tires and drove toward the exit.

Drew stood there for a moment. The cruiser's revolving lights flashed on when it turned onto Charlestown Road. Drew walked to the main entrance of the school, and at the front door, he immediately recognized the short, elderly, wiry man sweeping the steps. The man looked up at him, and a wide smile covered his face.

"Drew," he said, walking over and hugging him. "I heard you were back."

"Tony," Drew said. "It's great to see you. You must be head custodian by now."

"No, same old clean-up job," Tony said. "Two more years and I'm done." He considered what he had said. "Maybe one more year. This new Valley Forge School is not too good for me. I miss George Washington School so much. We must talk together like the old days. We must talk about Shane, too."

Drew looked at the lined face of Anthony Bartoli. The custodian had worked at George Washington High School since it first opened in the forties. Drew and Shane hung out with Tony throughout their school years, but mostly during their senior year. When they cut class or needed a place to hide, he would always open the door to his maintenance office and let them in. Surrounded by brooms of all sizes and large, black cans of cleaner, they ate lunch together. It was garlic bread smothered in olive oil and huge helpings of his wife's spaghetti or lasagna every day for nine months.

Tony was always laughing and telling stories about how hard life had been in Sicily. It was through prayer and God's goodness that he came and found a wife in America. Now he had a big house in Collegeville, drove a new Buick, and his two kids went to private schools.

Shane often talked to Drew about Tony's situation. He never understood how a janitor's salary could cover all those expenses. Shane was convinced that Tony was connected to one of the powerful Philadelphia families. He spread the word around school that Tony was a hit man, and all the students, even the dropouts, showed him more respect than they did the teachers.

"And how are your wife and children" Drew asked

"More headaches," Tony said. "Little Tony and little Maria hate each other, and they hate school even more. They want to quit and work somewhere." A loud bell rang inside the building, and there was a rush of students in the hall. "First lunch. I have to go to the cafeteria, Drew. I will see you again?"

"I'll be here this week," Drew said. "I'm teaching biology for Mrs. Deal. I'll find you for lunch sometime."

Drew shook hands with Tony, and they went inside the building. The lobby was a large circular area crowded with students. Many were moving up and down a wide spiral staircase that led to the second floor. There was a three-sided log cabin in the back of the lobby, and standing guard in front, a ten-foot Patriot soldier had his musket raised high in the air. In the brightly lit, open side of the log cabin, a student receptionist sat behind a log table. The table had a computer, telephone, and school pamphlets. A blue-and-gold Patriots banner curved around the whole wall of the reception center.

Before continuing toward the cafeteria, Tony pointed Drew to the right corridor. Drew walked down the corridor, past the principal's office, and opened the door that read Assistant Principal, Homer Matthews. The secretary looked up from her desk behind the counter.

"I'm scheduled to sub this afternoon," Drew said.

"You must be Drew Benson," the secretary said, coming to the counter with some papers in her hand. "Biology for Mrs. Deal. Here's the folder with everything you need."

"Is Mr. Matthews busy?" Drew asked, taking the folder.

"He's with a student now," she said. "He shouldn't be too long if you want to wait."

Drew sat down at a table to the side of the counter. The *Evening Phoenix* was on the table, and he opened it. On the second page of the newspaper, he saw the heading "Another Turnpike Victim." Drew read the article about an elderly man in the hospital. The victim had pulled over to take a nap early that morning and was beaten and robbed by some kids. The only thing he remembered was trying to help a young girl fix her car. Drew finished the article and turned the page.

"Valley Forge Dominates!" The heading was spread across the top of the sports page. There were pictures of varsity football coach Stanley Chuck and interviews with some players. Drew recognized the picture of Gary's younger brother. The caption under the picture described Terry Evans as the best quarterback in the East. Next to Terry's picture was a grim-faced picture of Leroy 'the Crusher' Schaffer. The reporter described Leroy as the hardest hitting linebacker in the state.

"The Crusher," Drew said, remembering the face he had seen screaming Leroy Brown lyrics out the Corvette's front window.

Drew laughed and began reading the two-column article below the pictures. He was interrupted by loud shouting, and the assistant principal's door slammed open. Moving at a fast pace and swinging his arms in front of him, Leroy burst through the door and rushed out of the office.

"Drew," Homer said, appearing at the door. Shaking Drew's hand and then hugging him, almost lifting him in the air, Homer had a big smile on his face. "It's great to see you. Come inside."

"You haven't changed," Drew said, taking a deep breath. He straightened the chair in front of Homer's desk and sat down. "You almost crushed my chest."

"I feel great. You're back safe. The worst day I've ever had was at Gary's funeral." Homer took a chair behind his desk. "I had hoped you'd get a teaching job and forget about going to Vietnam. But you were gone right after college."

"What can I say? I was a Patriot. Shane told me to enlist and volunteer for this special program he was in, and I did. Right after training, I flew to Saigon, and he was there to welcome me."

"But in 1973, Nixon withdrew the last American troops. I remember the president saying 'The day we have worked and prayed for has finally come. There will be peace with honor.' Brandy and I and everyone else in Valley Forge thought you and Shane would be home then."

"All troops did leave, but Shane wanted to stay," Drew said. "He got us transferred out of the military. We did the same flying, but we worked out of the American Embassy."

"Why stay any longer than you had to?"

"Shane was worried about his Vietnamese friends. He thought he could help them."

"Shane was like that. He would never quit," Homer said. "Have you heard anything? How's he doing?"

"He's still in a coma," Drew said. "He was discharged from the military hospital in Tokyo yesterday. He's now on route to Dover and could arrive here at Valley Forge anytime."

"He'll be home. That's the important thing." Homer looked across the table at Drew. He studied his face for a moment. "You're home, too, and I can see a major change. You have that same innocent expression on your face, but you look different. There's a strength there I didn't see before."

"That's because I'm much tougher than I was." Drew leaned back in his chair and smiled. "I took some Asian self-defense classes while I was in Nam. I had a good teacher."

"Bruce Lee?"

"No," Drew laughed. "Kim Lee. He was good. He taught me pressure points and how to disable attackers. Kim said I was an adequate student for a foreigner."

"You always were a fast learner. I remember when you beat me in the park. And then how fast you learned to handle a gun."

"You and Shane did that."

"It seems a long time ago," Homer said. "So much has changed since you and Shane were in school."

"How is it here? I mean, this place is huge."

"Three times the size of George Washington," Homer said. "And three times as many problems. Students transferred here from four other districts. And in some cases, some districts unloaded their troublemakers. I've never seen so many head cases."

"Like the Crusher who just stormed out of here?"

"Leroy Schaffer," Homer said. "Defensive lineman of the week. He's the team captain. Coach Chuck loves him. You know Chuck is undefeated?"

"I read some of that," Drew said. "When did you get out of coaching?"

"Last year."

"Do you miss it? There's all this excitement of being undefeated."

"Undefeated, unscored on," Homer said. "It's all bullshit. You saw one of the Patriots leaders. Leroy, he's a bum. He's late for school two, three times a week. You can't discipline him. Chuck treats his players like NFL stars. The school board and community support the team. The players can't do anything wrong. Winning football games is the greatest thing for a new school."

"It's nothing like the Patriots team I was on," Drew said. "We were all losers. Except for that one game we won against the Eagles."

"On Senior Night when George Washington beat the Eagles, that was the proudest day of my life. The whole team, you, Shane, and Gary were the best." Homer paused. "I can't help thinking about Gary's death."

"It was pretty sudden," Drew said.

"The army should never have taken him. Since his dad ran out on the family, Gary was the only man left in the household. I don't understand it. But his younger brother Terry is doing great. He's the biggest star on the team."

"I just read that. Is Terry that good?"

"He's that good. Except for Shane, he has more natural talent than I've ever seen here," Homer said. "But something's wrong. Terry's a total jerk sometimes. You put him and Leroy together, and there's no one in control. I think Coach Chuck has them all on a strength enhancement program."

"Probably steroids," Drew said. "I saw some muscle freaks on the base. They were real fucked-up. Oh," Drew said. "Excuse the language. I forgot I'm back in school. The principal will suspend me again."

"You're used to military talk," Homer said. "Your right, though. The players are fucked-up. I don't know what's happening with them, but I do know Chuck will do anything to win. He was never qualified to coach. It was pure luck that some good athletes transferred to our school. And we hired a young coach from Penn State who does all the hard work. Of course, Chuck takes all the credit."

"How do the players feel about Chuck?"

"They put up with him," Homer said. "And they're not all like Leroy. There are some talented athletes on the team. I worked with a place kicker, Wesley, who kicks the ball out of the end zone. He'll go Division 1. There's a farm boy, Randy Allen, who lives down the road from me. He set a league record in receptions. And Riley, on special teams, is an all-state long jumper in track. They all come from good families." There was an annoying buzzing sound from the large clock on the wall behind Drew. Homer stood up and slid his chair away from the desk.

"Lunch will be over soon," he said. "I'll take you up to your room."

Homer and Drew left the office and were approaching the front lobby when the door to the main office opened and the principal stepped directly in their path. He stood there flatfooted, his hands on his hips, a stern expression on his face.

"Mr. Benson, I need to talk to you." Mr. Frank West Sr. spoke in a loud over-bearing voice. The corner of his mouth twitched when he spoke, lifting his moustache in motion.

"Mr. Benson, we have a shortage of substitutes now, but the problem will be fixed soon. What I'm getting at is that we won't need you very long. The only reason you're here now is that Mr. Matthews made a mistake."

"There was no mistake," Homer said, staring directly into the principal's face. "Mr. Benson was approved by the board. He's as good as any substitute on the list."

"Maybe your list, Mr. Matthews. Not mine. I don't want him in this building." Mr. West hesitated, struggling to find the right words. "I don't know how you managed to graduate, Mr. Benson."

"Mr. Benson graduated with a 4.0 GPA," Homer said, his voice showing some annoyance. "And he had 1245 on his SAT."

"That's not what I'm talking about," Mr. West said, ignoring Homer and looking at Drew. "You were always a troublemaker. If you cause any problems here, anything at all, I'll see that you'll never teach again." Mr. West, his face flushed red, turned, and disappeared in his office.

"That's the kind of welcome I like," Drew said. "I imagine it might have something to do with that buck's ass he found on his desk."

"There were swarms of flies in the building for weeks, and Tony, no matter what disinfectant he used, he couldn't get rid of that rotting buck stench," Homer said. He smiled and slapped Drew on the shoulder. "Whenever our principal left the office and walked down the hall, the smell followed him. He knew where his nameplate was, but he wouldn't get it, and no one else would either. He ordered the woodshop to make him another one. And they never did find the Board of Education."

"They never will find it," Drew said.

Talking loudly at each other, three older students came down the corridor and walked in the principal's office, slamming the door shut. Drew watched them approach the secretary's desk and begin a heated argument.

"Homer, I don't see how this is going to work," Drew said. "Do you think this is a good idea?"

"You teaching here? Sure it is," Homer said. "You won't see the principal again. He never leaves his office unless it's to skip out early and go golfing. So don't worry about him. But there is someone else. Frank West Jr. is on the staff. His father says his education in Canada made a man of him. Junior teaches American History, your favorite subject."

"Junior was so fucked-up in high school, I don't think he'll ever be a man," Drew said. "Excuse my language, but that's how I'll always see Frank."

"He had some cosmetic work done on his scar, but it only made it worse."

"Good," Drew said.

Homer and Drew began walking down the corridor into the main lobby. As they approached the log cabin reception center, Drew saw a familiar figure standing at the desk. Coach Chuck was still short and stocky, but he was over three hundred pounds now. He turned to walk away, but stopped suddenly when he saw Homer and Drew. A shaggy beard and moustache covered his face, and an old RAVENS football cap was pulled low over his forehead. His blue coaching jersey bulged out at the belly.

"Benson," he said. His voice was loud and gruff. "I'm surprised to see you here?"

"Why's that?"

"You were nothing but trouble," Coach Chuck said. "You and Shane never did a damn thing for the school. And I'll tell you something else. When you both graduated, things around here got better fast. Especially the Patriots football program. We're the best in the East and setting all kinds of attendance records. I bet Mr. Matthews regrets quitting the team.

"I regret a lot of things," Homer said. "Working with you isn't one of them."

"You don't admit it, but you probably cry when you read the sports page. After Friday's game with the Eagles, Valley Forge will be undefeated and the #1 team in the state." Chuck shuffled his football shoes forward and stood face to face with Drew. "The only problem we have to worry about is you, Benson."

"I'm in the building for twenty minutes, and suddenly I'm your only problem. How did you come to that conclusion?"

"The Eagles want revenge for what you did. You scored that touchdown and ruined their undefeated season eight years ago. They want simple payback." Chuck was talking faster now. Drops of spit and tiny flecks of foam began to form on the sides of his mouth.

"They want to ruin our undefeated season just like you did theirs. That's all Coach Fielding talks about in the papers. He said he never forgot that game. The bastard knew what an undefeated season meant to the school, meant to his program. He's using that game as motivation. The Eagles have been fired up all week."

"I'm sure you'll have the Patriots fired up, too," Homer said. "You have real skills at motivation."

"A great motivator," Drew said. "That's why we ran the hospital hill every day rather than practice football."

"You ran because you needed discipline."

"No," Drew said. "We ran so you could sit on your lazy ass and do nothing."

"You disrespectful, little shit!" Red-faced and seething, Coach Chuck stepped forward, but Homer was already between him and Drew.

"Excuse us, Coach. We have a class to teach." Taking Drew by the arm, they walked to the staircase.

"Coach really likes you, Drew."

"I'm not very popular here; first, the school principal and now Chuck goes ballistic. I did talk to Tony. He was happy to see me."

"He's the only one who matters," Homer said. "Tony and his maintenance crew run the school. That's who you go to if you want something done right."

Drew and Homer started up the wide, circular staircase. It curved around the roof of the log cabin to the second floor. As Drew climbed the steps, he looked through the large two-story window and saw Valley Forge National Park and the top half of Memorial Arch on the distant hill.

"It's a great view," he said.

"Ole George would be proud of Valley Forge," Homer said. "I forgot to tell you, Drew. Easy day tomorrow. It's probably in Mrs. Deal's lesson plans."

"What?" Drew asked.

"An all-day field trip to the park," Homer said. He and Drew continued up the steps to the second floor corridor. "The bus leaves at eight o'clock in the morning and returns at two in the afternoon. The sophomores will concentrate on litter pickup. The upper classmen will go on the usual tours, which they've been doing since kindergarten. Some of the gifted students will work on their own individualized projects. We've been going out to the park a lot. You know, getting ready for the big bicentennial."

"What will I do?" Drew asked. "Pick up litter?"

"Last year, Mrs. Deal's biology class did water testing on the Schuylkill River. It was a hot day, and there was a water fight at the river. Some students had stomach cramps and got sick.

"They swallowed the water?" Drew asked.

"They accidentally had their heads shoved in the river by two of Chuck's linemen," Homer said. "They began to throw up. Chuck said it was all a little fun for the team. But the river's so polluted. Who knows what chemicals the kids drank? One eighth grader threw up in his mother's car. So no one will be testing water quality this year. You'll probably just walk around and keep order."

"I can do that," Drew said. They reached the end of the corridor, and Homer opened the door to the biology classroom.

"Here we are," Homer said. "If you're lucky, the students will show up at the bell. Relax and enjoy your first day."

"Thanks," Drew said. He shook Homer's hand, and Homer walked back down the corridor. Drew went in the room. The front wall had a large blackboard with bulletin boards on each end. Drew saw a long worktable and the teacher's desk in front of the blackboard. There were five rows of student's desks, and to the right of the desks, there was a large window that was broken into sections by silver frames. Heavy yellow drapes were folded into the corners. On the other side of the room, there were glass display cases and a series of science charts on the wall.

Looking through the window, Drew saw the football stadium, and beyond the bleachers of the stadium on the far hill, Drew could see the buildings of Valley Forge Veterans Hospital. There was no wind, and the colors of the flag dropped toward the ground.

Hearing the distinct sound of bubbles, Drew looked at the large aquarium in the back corner of the room. He walked between the rows of desks and stopped in front it. The aquarium was huge, at least five feet long. Not as high as it was long, the top of the aquarium came to Drew's chest. Bending down and looking inside, Drew watched the myriad varieties and colors of fish swim between the green, red, and yellow clusters of plants twisting up from the dark gravel bottom.

The crystal-clear water was loudly displaced by lines of bubbles rising upward from the buried air stones. Enormous rocks with cave-like holes and a large sunken ship, masts extending to the surface of the aquarium, gave additional color and structure to the aquarium.

"It's fantastic," Drew said. He was bent over, admiring the aquarium when a form slid quietly behind him.

"Drew," she said, and a hand touched him on the shoulder. He stood up and turned as a body squeezed against his.

"May," he said, surprised as she kissed him on the lips. Drew returned the kiss and became aware of a sweet, flower-scented perfume.

"I heard you would be back soon, but I didn't know when," May said. "I looked in the room, and there you were. I couldn't believe it. It's great to see you, Drew."

May Wiggins was genuinely excited. Her face lit up, and she smiled and kissed Drew again. He breathed in the lingering scent of perfume as May stepped back. She was dressed neatly in a blue dress with white flowers, and she was still very beautiful. The bell rang, and there was the sound of opening doors and traffic in the halls. Drew and May walked to the front of the room.

"Fifth period," she said. "You have a good group of juniors. My class is across the hall. I'm free next period and so is Mrs. Deal. I'll come right over. I have so many questions about Shane." May turned and walked out the door as a group of students wandered in and took their seats.

Drew quickly opened the folder with the lesson plans. He found the seating chart, introduced himself, took attendance, and read the instructions for a chapter test. The students took the test and worked quietly on the next chapter until the bell rang. A few minutes after they left the room, May came through the door.

"That was a great class," Drew said, sorting the test papers on the desk.

"Forget the classes for a second, Drew. I want to know about the rumors. Did you get married over there? Do you have a wife and baby?"

"Yes, they're at the house now. It feels really strange to have a family." He put the last test inside and closed the folder. "Does Joyce know?"

"Yes," May said. "She's pretty upset."

"I'd like to see her."

"You're a family man now, Drew. She's really angry."

"Are you angry too?"

"I can't be angry with you." May's smile returned to her face. "Joyce is helping her parents at the antique store in the Kimberton Mall. She still wears the sapphire ring you sent her."

"It's crazy how things work out," Drew said. "Marriage was the furthest thing from my mind, especially marriage in Vietnam."

"You'll have some explaining to do," May said. She was silent for a moment, looking out the window past Drew. "Can you tell me something, Drew?"

"Sure," Drew said. "What is it?"

"What was it like over there?" May turned away from the window and looked at Drew. "I mean when you weren't fighting. I saw on TV about the bars and nightlife. Did Shane do any of that?"

"No," Drew said. He lowered his eyes and began to feel uncomfortable. "He always talked about you. He read your letters and kept them and read them over and over. He always talked about what he would do when he came home."

"What was that?"

"He wanted to marry you," Drew said. "He wanted to marry you and have a family with . . ."

"Three kids," May laughed. "He always wrote about the family in his letters. I just never knew for sure. He was away for so long." May's smile disappeared, and she looked distant and hurt. "He did bring Gary home. But that was a sad time. We didn't talk about anything. We were just together for the funeral and that night. Then he flew back."

"He's always loved you, May."

"I didn't hear too much about his injury. Is it bad? I mean he's not a cripple or anything like that."

"He's in a coma. That's all I know. Unless they have problems at Dover, he should be here in the veterans hospital soon."

"I called at lunch," May said. "The nurse or whoever answered the phone said the hospital received his papers and he might be admitted tomorrow. I want to see him. I want to see how he is. Do you know anything, Drew? Do you know what happened to Shane?"

"He was on a mission that went bad."

"You were there, weren't you?"

"No," Drew said. He looked at May, not volunteering any information.

"Shane said you two were a team. You always flew together."

"We always did, but it was the last week. It was in April. Saigon was surrounded by the North Vietnamese. The war was all but over. We were just waiting to get our clearances to come home. Sure, you could go out if there was an emergency, but no one was flying out. We were waiting to go home."

Perspiration forming on his forehead, Drew looked at the clock on the wall. It was midway through the sixth period. With the bright light and warmth from the afternoon sun reflecting through the windows, it was beginning to feel hot, almost stifling, in the room. Loosening his tie, he looked at May.

"I need something cold to drink," he said.

"There's a water fountain by the staircase," May said. They walked to the door and down the hall to the fountain. The wall above the fountain was covered with Patriots football figures. Drew pushed the foot lever, and a spray of water arched in the air. He took a long drink. The water was warm at first. Then it turned icy cold. Drew splashed some water on his face and turned to May.

"I'd better check the lesson plans for the next period."

"Mrs. Deal has a lot of trouble with this group, Drew. They're mostly football players, and they won't do any work. They just fool around and wait for the bell to ring."

"I used to do that at George Washington, and I played football, too. Maybe I can relate to them."

Drew and May walked back up the hall. He waited for her to go in her classroom, and then he returned to his. In the room, he closed the heavy curtains, blocking out the bright sunlight, and then sat at the desk. The lesson plans called for a video series that would last through the week. There were worksheets for each video.

Drew found the first video and the remote for the video recorder in the top drawer of the desk. There was a twenty-seven-inch TV with a Sony VCR on a stand in the corner of the room. Drew turned on the machines, put in the video, and dimmed the room lights.

The only noise in the room was the bubbling sound from the aquarium. The hood light was on, and in the darkened room, the water in the aquarium flashed with the bright colors of the swimming fish. Drew sat down in the shadows of the back row and hit play on the remote. The TV screen lit up.

Shrill bird cries filled the room as the green canopy of a jungle flashed on the screen. In yellow letters, *Animals of the Rain Forest* appeared over the jungle view, and the film credits scrolled up the side of the trees.

Drew listened to the jungle sounds and saw the first animals, monkeys with long tails that curled high in the air. Drew only watched the monkeys for a short time. Then he heard May's voice, and her words were damaging in their clarity.

"Shane said you two were a team. You always flew together."

We did. Drew whispered to himself. *We always flew together.*

Drew closed his eyes, and the scene of the jungle and monkeys was replaced by the noise and smoke and heat of the Bamboo Bar in the center of Saigon. Being an important participant of the hastily organized Drew & Shane Farewell Party, he was sitting at a large round table with friends, soldiers, and embassy people.

Since Shane hadn't shown up yet, the party started without him. By late afternoon, the bar was packed, and the resultant clamor echoed out into the street. The air conditioners whirled noisily and created a cool, recycled, toxic mix of smoke and moisture. Wearing only g-strings, the bodies of the hostesses were covered with sweat.

Some of the more pretty girls took turns dancing on the tables. When they jumped and spun around, drops of perspiration and oily perfume spattered on Drew. He laughed and wiped his face with a dirty napkin. His table was the noisiest, drunken faces shouting toasts to each other. Shane's chair was still empty, and everyone drank to Drew and then had another drink to the empty chair.

Drew was dizzy, and his head hurt. The topless dancer moved gracefully, seductively on the table above him. Listening to the blaring CCR lyrics of *Who'll Stop the Rain,* he watched the smooth brown breasts spinning in front of his face. With a sudden burst of energy, Drew lunged up awkwardly for the closer one and missed, knocking half-empty bottles of Heineken on the floor. There was another toast, and then two figures pushed through the circle around the table.

"Benson!" Drew heard his name being called. "Benson!" He heard it again, louder and closer.

A drunken body standing beside his chair was pushed aside, and strong hands began shaking Drew's shoulders, trying to lift him. A voice shouted something about a mission, something about flying out.

It was all jumbled and confusing to him. He heard the words "Stupid drunk," and the hands roughly released him, his head hitting the table. The sudden shock momentarily sobered him.

Drew stumbled to his feet and pushed his way to the exit. He reached the porch exhausted and stumbled down the steps. A light rain fell from the sky, and a misty fog covered the street. The flashing red lights of the bar were vague and troublesome. Drew struggled to stay on his feet. He searched the fog for the two figures who had called his name, but they were gone. All he saw were the jeep's rear lights moving away at a fast speed.

Listening to the strains of the music from the open door, Drew began to comprehend what the voices meant about flying out. He ran forward, tripped, and fell. He had trouble moving. Lying there on the wet asphalt, he felt the rain beginning to seep through his uniform. When he tried to get up again, he saw figures run from the bar. Laughing and shouting orders at each other, they picked Drew up by the shoulders, pulled him back inside, dropped him in the chair, and filled his empty glass.

Drew heard a sharp ringing bell and jumped up in his chair. He looked around the empty room. The heavy smoke, dancing bar girls, and noise were gone. Putting his hands over his head, Drew looked at the lines of graffiti on the desk. His thoughts became clouded with guilt and anger.

I was drunk, Drew admitted to himself. *That's what I wanted to tell you, May. I couldn't fly with Shane because I was drunk.*

Drew heard the bell ring again. Looking up, he saw the blank screen on the TV. Drew got up quickly, rewound the video, walked to the front of the room, and turned up the lights. He took his seat at the teacher's desk and waited.

Groups of students walked casually into the room. Looking at him and whispering comments to each other, they began to fill the empty chairs. When the late bell sounded, Drew heard loud talking and laughter in the hall. The last group of five students pushed into the room. Drew recognized Leroy and his friend from the yellow Jaguar. Behind them were two short, bulky football players. Then quarterback Terry Evans walked in the room.

Checking the seating chart but looking at Terry over the top of the page, Drew saw that Terry had his brother's height. He was more muscular than Gary, and his hair was longer, falling loosely over his forehead. His face had the same handsome features; but whereas Gary always had a casual smile on his face, his brother's face had a tense, almost angry expression. Then Terry laughed at something, and Drew saw the happy, carefree expression he knew.

"Damn," Drew whispered and thought back to the funeral. He looked down the receiving line and saw Terry standing next to his brother's casket. Terry seemed small, even fragile. He shook hands with an elderly lady and began crying. The elderly lady grabbed him and hugged him.

Drew looked up and saw the football players, making jokes and laughing at each other as they strutted to the back of the room. Terry knocked a boy's book off the desk and sent it sliding across the floor. Leroy slapped Terry on the back. The players laughed with approval. After checking the names, Leroy Schaffer, Chester Greenwood, Terry Evans, Rusty Jones, and Junior Henderson, Drew put the seating chart down.

Pushing students out of their assigned seats, the football players grouped together in the last row. Terry sat in the chair next to the fish aquarium. His face cocky and gleaming with amusement, he turned around and looked at Drew. There was no sign of recognition.

For this last class of the day, Drew skipped all the substitute formalities. He didn't introduce himself. He didn't comment on Mrs. Deal's absence. After he checked attendance, he explained about the movie and distributed the worksheets.

"I'll collect the papers at the end of the class," Drew said. He turned off the lights and started the movie. On his way back to his seat, *Animals of the Rain Forest* appeared on the TV screen. The music was interrupted by a series of monkey calls from the back row. Drew hit the remote button and increased the volume.

After about five minutes, the door opened and a figure slid into the darkness of the room. Drew watched her move slowly down the rows of students. There was some loud whispering and muted laughs, and she disappeared into the bodies in the last row. The laughter from the back row increased and mixed with the loud bird cries from the rainforest.

Drew shut off the video with the remote. He walked to the door and switched on the lights. Startled by the brightness, some students rubbed their eyes. There was more laughter from the back of the room. Most of the students turned their heads to look. The girl who had entered the room was sitting on Leroy's lap. Her cheek was pressed against Leroy's, and she had a bright, wide smile on her face.

"What are you doing here?" Drew asked, looking at the girl, recognizing the same laughing face in the front seat of the yellow Jaguar.

"My schedule was changed," she said. She straightened and removed her hand from around Leroy's neck.

"What's your name?"

"Sally," she said. Her smile broadened. She made a strange giggling sound and rubbed her body against Leroy's lap. "I was just transferred to this class."

"I'm sorry, Sally. You don't belong in this class. You'll have to leave."

"But I can't just leave."

"Yes, you can leave, Sally. I saw you all this morning, and I saw you come in with the football players at noon. You're all still wearing the same clothes."

"What are you talking about?"

"I mean that spending the night with the football team doesn't mean you're enrolled in their biology class."

There was a gasp from some of the girls in the room. Then everything became very still. Drew walked slowly to the back of the room. Sally studied him nervously.

"I'm staying here," Sally said.

"I'm sorry, but you have to leave now."

"You can't order me around," Sally said. "My dad's the school attorney. I'll tell him . . ."

"Tell him what?" Drew interrupted.

"This is bullshit." The football player next to Leroy turned suddenly. The legs of the desk made a grating noise against the floor, and he moved to get up.

"Chester." Drew said, remembering the name on the seating chart. He put his hand lightly on Chester's shoulder. "Don't get up if you want to play football this Friday."

"Fuck you," he said, glancing at Leroy and Terry. "Are you going to take this?"

"Hell no!" Leroy said, but Terry leaned across the aisle.

"We can't get in any trouble now," Terry said. "Our last football game is Friday. Remember it's the championship."

"That's good advice," Drew said. "I would concentrate on playing and winning the championship."

Leroy was too angry and frustrated to say anything. His face was bloated, and the veins on his neck were thick with blood. He straightened slightly and looked at Sally.

"Maybe you should go now," Leroy said. He lifted Sally off his lap. She bent low and whispered in his ear.

"The bastard insulted me!"

"We'll fix it later," Leroy said. "I guarantee it."

"This isn't over," Sally said, turning to face Drew. "I'll tell my dad. He'll get you fired!" She walked down the aisle past Drew. Opening the door quickly, she looked back at Drew and slammed it. After the echo of noise subsided, Drew walked to the front of the room.

"Sorry for the distraction," he said. "Let's finish the movie." Drew shut off the lights and hit the remote for the TV. The room was completely quiet as the black form of a monkey appeared on the screen. It jumped from the tall branches of a tree and seemed to fly across a clearing. The monkey hung in the air and then crashed into the branches of another tree.

During the movie, Drew occasionally took his gaze off the TV and watched the door and hallway. Toward the end of the movie, he heard hushed talking and saw some movement in the back corner of the room. Drew looked again, but everything was still.

The movie was over just as the five-minute bell sounded. Drew turned on the lights and gave the class time to finish the worksheets. Walking down the aisle, he noticed something strange at the aquarium. The sound of the bubbles was louder. Drew saw that the top cover of the aquarium was slid open. He also saw that there were no shadows or movement through the streams of bubbles.

Drew walked to the aquarium and looked inside. The dull colored bodies of the dead fish floated on top of the water. A few remaining fish flopped and swam in circles. Leroy coughed, and he and Chester laughed while writing on the worksheet. Terry gave a muffled laugh.

Drew looked at the open bottle at the side of the aquarium. He read the label, zinc sulfate. There was some powder on the floor and some specks of powder on Terry's tennis shoe. A large red fish jumped out of the poisoned water and landed flopping on the floor. The dismissal bell rang. The students began to get out of their chairs.

"Put the papers on the front desk," Drew said. He moved next to Terry and put both hands on his desk. Drew spoke in a slow, measured voice.

"Terry, stay here. I want to talk to you."

"Something wrong?" Leroy asked. Looking at Drew, he stood up and pushed his desk away.

"No," Drew said. "I want to talk to Terry. You can leave."

"Go ahead," Terry said casually. "I'll meet you in the hall."

Leroy shrugged his shoulders. He took his worksheet, crushed it in his fist, and dropped the ball of paper on the desk. Chester did the same. They walked away, and Drew followed them to the door. When they left, Drew closed the door, and with a snapping sound, he locked the bolt in place. Then he walked back to the aquarium. Terry looked up from the desk. He had a half smile, half smirk on his face.

"They listen to the quarterback," Drew said. "I like that."

"It's the training," Terry said. "What's this about? Why do you want to see me?"

"The fish."

"What about the fish?"

"It looks like you killed them," Drew said, talking in a soft, serious voice.

"I didn't do anything," Terry said, sensing something strange, something menacing in Drew's voice. "I was just watching the video like everyone else."

Terry looked at the swirling bodies in the aquarium, and a nervous, almost agitated, expression formed on his face. The handle of the front door turned and rattled. There was a loud knocking sound that echoed through the room. Then it stopped, and except for the steady bubbling sound from the aquarium, the room became quiet.

"Maybe you were watching the video," Drew said. His eyes glared into Terry's face. Moving behind Terry, he pointed to the floor. "But maybe you got careless. When you unscrewed the cap, some of the powder fell on your shoe."

"I didn't do anything," Terry said, looking at the powder. His voice quivered. Although Drew didn't have a large body size, he seemed to tower over him.

"The powder says you did."

"I have witnesses," he said. "They'll tell you I was working."

"The hell with your witnesses," Drew said. With practiced quickness, he grabbed Terry high in the shoulder and forced his thumb deep into the muscle.

"No!" Terry winced with pain. He felt his body go numb, and he was lifted out of his seat. Drew slid the aquarium cover all the way to the side and forced Terry's head over the top of the aquarium.

When Terry opened his eyes and looked down, he saw the colorless bodies of fish floating on the water. There was unbearable pain in his neck and shoulder. He was helpless as strong hands pushed his head downward. The bodies of the dead fish grew larger and bubbled inches from his face. Terry began to scream, and his spit and heavy breath splattered circles against the watery surface.

"Let's see how you like it," Drew said. He forced Terry's head lower and then shoved it beneath the surface of water. The water in the aquarium rose. Dead fish floated up, became stranded on the top of Terry's head, and then slid slowly down his hair to the water.

Terry shook his shoulders and tried to move, but he couldn't. He gasped, and large bubbles of air boiled to the surface. The doorknob rattled, and the angry sound of pounding fists filled the room. Drew held Terry there until the pounding stopped and then lifted his head out of the water.

"That's what it feels like," Drew said, releasing his grip from Terry's neck. Terry's eyes were open wide, and the veins crisscrossing the pupils were thick and bright red. The rattling on the doorknob became louder.

"That's what it feels like when you can't breathe. That's what it feels like to die."

Drew held Terry up by the shoulder. His chest gave a heaving sound, and Terry coughed and spit water on the floor. Drew took a towel from the back wall and threw it to Terry. Terry wiped his face and dried is hair. His breathing slowly returned to normal. When Drew saw that Terry was steady and most of the shock was gone from his face, he began to walk Terry down the aisle to the door.

"You won't get away with this," Terry said.

"Away with what?"

"Drowning me like that," Terry said. "Teachers can't grab students and drown them."

"Drown who?" Drew asked. "Drown a tough football player in a classroom? Who would believe a story like that?" He took the towel from Terry and unlocked the door. "Just get the hell out of here." He opened the door and nudged Terry into the hall.

"Terry," Leroy said. He and Chester jumped around the side of the door. "Is everything OK?" Leroy looked at the wet hair and collar. There was a green strand of aquarium grass on Terry's neck.

"Let me get that," Drew said. As he reached over and picked off the grass, Terry flinched backwards.

"We'll be late for practice," Chester said. He had no idea what was going on. He stepped along side Terry and Leroy, and then becoming clownish, he turned and smiled, throwing a finger at Drew.

"For you, motherfucker," he mouthed the words.

Drew watched them walk down the hall. Leroy was talking to Terry, who was shaking his head back and forth. Drew went back into the room. He found a plastic bucket under the front counter. Dipping the bucket in the aquarium, he poured the dead fish and poisoned water down the large drain in the sink. Then he changed the filter pads and refilled the tank with water. After he replaced the stones, artificial plants, and large sunken ship, he turned on the pumps, and water began to circulate in the lifeless aquarium.

Drew took the Substitute Report form from the folder and sat down at the desk. He filled out the student work that was done in each of the classes. With the last class, he explained about removing Sally from the room and that the fish had accidentally died. When Drew left the room, it was five o'clock. He went to Homer's office, and turning the knob, he saw that the door was locked. Drew slid the report under the door.

Drew walked outside. The parking lot was nearly deserted. On the way to his car, he heard a shrill whistle from the direction of the football stadium. He looked at the field in the distance. Figures in shoulder pads and helmets ran from their positions and formed a circle around the coaches.

There was a loud roar, followed by two more loud roars. Blue-and-gold helmets began swinging wildly in the air. After more cheering, the circle broke up, and the players and coaches began walking toward the school's locker room. Drew watched Leroy and Terry and Chester in the last group pushing and punching each other. Then he got in his car and drove to the exit.

CHAPTER 11

As he drove down Charlestown Road, Drew stopped at the first red light. Sitting there somewhat distracted, he thought about school and sensed he may have made a mistake on his first day of teaching. In his four years of teacher training, he couldn't remember reading anything that explained how or why a teacher would want to submerge a student's head in a fish aquarium. Even Kim Lee had preached restraint.

I can't figure it out, Drew thought. *It just seemed right.*

A horn blared behind him. Drew saw the light had changed to green. Ignoring the second angry horn blast, he went slowly through the intersection. He went past the Vale Rio Diner, drove three blocks, and stopped at another red light. After it changed, Drew turned left into the Kimberton Mall. There was a scattering of cars in the parking lot. Drew parked in front of the antique store and turned off the engine. Sitting there in the darkness, he looked through the store window.

Mr. and Mrs. Thompson were working with some papers on the front counter. There was movement to the right, and Drew saw Joyce putting something on a table. She had not changed. The white blouse she wore opened low in the front, and her skirt was short to her knees.

Even from that distance, Drew could see the brightness in her eyes, the slight, upward turn of her nose, and the moist color of her lips. Her face radiated warmth from the soft light in the room. She leaned forward, picked up a figurine, and began cleaning it with a cloth. The phone rang, and Joyce turned slightly to the side. Drew could see the curve of her breast and the trim lines of her waist.

A heavyset lady crossed in front of the car and walked into the antique shop. The door closed behind her. She stood in front of Joyce. Drew leaned to his right but couldn't see anything. The lady kept talking. Mrs. Thompson walked over and showed her a green vase.

Shaking his head, Drew started the car. He turned out of the parking lot and drove slowly past the store. When he looked inside again, he thought he saw Joyce staring out the window. Caught off guard, Drew jerked the car forward and continued driving. He stopped at the intersection, waited for the light, and turned onto Route 23.

The Collier house was a few blocks away. Approaching the front lawn, Drew saw their car in the driveway and the lights on in the living room. He pulled in behind the parked car and stopped. Drew sat nervously in the front seat.

After a few minutes, Drew got out of the car and walked to the porch like he had done a million times before. But this time he stopped and rang the door bell. Shifting his feet back and forth, he watched the door swing open.

"Drew," Mrs. Collier exclaimed. Tears formed in her eyes, and she kissed him on the cheek and hugged him. Mr. Collier came and shook his hand. They ushered him into the living room and sat him down on the couch.

"We heard you got home safely," Mr. Collier said. "The TV news had us all worried. We saw what happened at the American Embassy and how many people were left behind. It was horrible to watch."

"I was in that emergency evacuation," Drew said. "I spent some time in Thailand, got discharged, and arrived home Saturday. I should have stopped in sooner."

"That's OK, Drew. You need time to settle in. Wait here a minute. We'll get you something to drink." Mr. and Mrs. Collier walked through the door into the kitchen. The room was very empty and quiet.

Drew went to the mantle and looked at the pictures of Shane. He was kneeling at the goal line in his blue-and-gold football uniform; he was standing on the stage, a big smile on his face, in his cap and gown; he was in front of an American flag, face stern and serious, in his military uniform.

There were other pictures of just Drew and Shane on family vacation at the shore, posing in front of the go-carts at Wildwood, holding two small sand sharks over their heads on the beach. There was a color picture of them standing in front of the Memorial Arch holding up a copy of the *Evening Phoenix*. At the end of the mantle was a square plastic case holding Shane's blue football helmet. The number 17 was stenciled in bright gold letters on the side.

Next to the helmet, there was a larger picture of their best Wildwood vacation ever. The four people in the picture were squeezed together in the booth. Shane was laughing, and he had his arms wrapped tightly around May.

Drew heard footsteps from the kitchen. Mr. Collier was balancing three cans of A&W Root Beer, and Mrs. Collier had a tray with some sandwiches. She put the tray on the table next to the sofa. Drew walked over and sat down opposite them.

"Here's something to drink," Mr. Collier said, handing the root beer to Drew.

"Thank you." Drew took the can.

"We thought about you often," Mrs. Collier said. "We're so glad to see you."

"We just came back from the Veterans Hospital," Mr. Collier said. "Shane was admitted an hour ago. We took some clothes over and got to see him for a short time, but the doctor said no visitors for a few days."

"He looked fine," Mrs. Collier said. "But he didn't say anything. He didn't move. May was there, too. He didn't recognize her either."

Drew drank some of the root beer. He listened to them. Their voices sounded nervous and unsure. Mrs. Collier gave him a sandwich.

"The doctor said it was a coma," Mr. Collier began talking again. "That's all he would tell us. They would feed Shane, take care of him. They said he didn't seem to be in any critical danger now. When we asked our doctor, Dr. Stevens, he said the critical time for a coma was not very long, something like four weeks. Then the patient could relapse into a permanent state."

"Something bad happened to him," Mrs. Collier said. She became emotional again and wiped tears from her eyes. "It hurt him, and now he can't wake up. Do you know what happened to him, Drew?"

"I remember we were waiting to come home. The war was over for us. In fact, we had scheduled a big farewell party." Drew looked past the Colliers at the picture on the mantle. With the angle of the light reflecting off the frame and the slight tilt of his head, the two green eyes seemed to be staring directly at Drew. Drew hesitated, took a bite of the sandwich, and drank some soda.

"The embassy assigned him to fly out on some mission. I heard it was near the Cambodian border. It was a total disaster. Shane was injured. It had to be serious because Shane was evacuated straight to Tokyo." Drew put the remainder of the sandwich on the tray. "I called the hospital and talked to a doctor there. I said I wanted to fly over and see Shane. He said Shane was in rehab and there were no visitors allowed."

"We talked to Shane once," Mr. Collier said. "It was weeks after he started rehab. Shane told us his helicopter was blown up on his last mission. Only he and an officer, a Lieutenant Davis, survived. The lieutenant had been shot in the arm. Shane didn't talk about his own injuries. We don't know if he was shot or anything. He just said the doctors planned to keep him in rehab for months. He said it was nothing to worry about. But his voice sounded weak and so strange. We kept calling, but no one would talk to us. Finally we found a doctor who knew something. He said Shane's condition had deteriorated. He was in a coma."

"We don't understand any of it," Mrs. Collier said. "We don't know why he's in a coma. We're just happy he's alive and back home." Mrs. Collier took a drink from her glass and looked across the table. "And you, Drew. We're so happy you're back safe."

"May told us you're married and have a baby," Mr. Collier said. He had a smile on his face and reached over and shook Drew's hand. "Congratulations."

"Thank you," Drew said.

"You must bring the family over for dinner soon," Mrs. Collier said. "This will be your second home again."

"As soon as we get settled," Drew said. He put the can of soda on the tray and stood up. "I'm going to try to get in the hospital tonight."

"Be careful, Drew. The nurse looked mean," Mrs. Collier said. "Shane's in the big building on the left side, the one right on top of the hill. He's on the fourth floor, Room 402."

"It's a nice room," Mr. Collier said. "You can see the school and football field from his window."

"I'll find it," Drew said. "He shook Mr. Collier's hand again and hugged Mrs. Collier. She held him tight against her body and was crying when she let him go. Drew returned to the car, and backing down the lane, he slowed and waved at them. They stood on the porch, hands around each other's waists, and waved back.

At Valley Forge High School, the new stadium lights were bright over the football field, and there was a line of cars at the far end of the parking lot. Drew drove slowly past the school, crested the hill, and saw the Veterans Hospital. There was a black Sherman tank next to the entrance. Spaced in a half circle on a grassy knoll behind the tank, two rows of flags were lit up by bright spotlights.

Drew slowed the car and saw the blue flag with its circle of thirteen white stars enclosing the United States Air Force insignia. Next to it was a white flag with a red United States Army 1775 banner on the bottom. The bright red flag in the center had the United States Marine Corps banner at the bottom, and the globe, anchor, and eagle were golden in the light. The white United States Coast Guard flag and the blue United States Navy flag finished the back row.

There were only two flags in the front row. The blue Pennsylvania State Flag had two black draft horses on either side of the coat of arms. The red banner below opened with the breeze, and Drew could read the words virtue, liberty, and independence.

Black and at times invisible against the dark sky, the POW * MIA flag was the largest flag. The wind unfurled it, and Drew saw clearly the bowed head of the soldier, and the bleak, menacing silhouette of the guard tower. Drew read the phrase in white letters at the bottom of the flag.

"You are not forgotten."

Drew drove past the spotlights and flags and turned left into a parking lot in front of a large four-story building. He walked to the entrance. The sign on the glass door read, *Visiting Hours: 1:00-3:00 PM and 5:30-7:30 PM.*

Drew looked at his watch. It was 7:20 PM. He pushed open the door, and the nurse at the counter looked up immediately. She stood and watched him walk across the room.

"We don't permit visitors after 7:15," she said.

"I have a friend here." Drew said. "He was admitted today. I just need to see him for a few minutes."

"What's his name?"

"Shane Collier," Drew said. He watched the nurse pick up some papers. She flipped through them and returned to the first sheet.

"He's restricted," she said, putting down the papers. "Come back in two days."

"I was with him in Vietnam."

"Come back in two days," the nurse said. "He'll still be here."

"It's important," Drew said. "I promise I won't be long. Can I see him for a few minutes?"

Drew watched her make a hard face and shake her head. Staring at her, he backed away and pushed through the door into the night air. As he walked to the car, he saw movement at the corner of the building. A man stepped into the light. He was well groomed and dressed in a blue hospital staff uniform. The man walked up to Drew and stopped in front of him.

"Hi, Jackson," Drew said.

"Hi," he said. "So you remember me." Jackson smiled.

"I'll never forget that night," Drew said.

"Neither will I," Jackson said. "I was here when they brought your friend in. I saw his face and recognized him right away."

"I came to see him."

"I know," Jackson said. "I heard you and Nurse Bitchy in the lobby. Follow me. I can take you to your friend."

Jackson motioned to the exit door where light gleamed from the side. Holding the door open, a broom handle was sticking out of the crack of light. Drew followed Jackson to the door, and they stepped inside. There was a staircase leading to the upper floors. Next to the steps, there was a short hallway that led to the lobby. Jackson pulled the door shut and turned facing Drew. For a few seconds he was quiet, and then he spoke in a slow, quiet voice.

"That night in the park, I saw you both. Your car comes squealing up the road and you two drinking and laughing. I didn't want nobody there. I wanted to be alone for what I planned to do. I waited and waited, but you were in no hurry to go."

Jackson looked down at his feet. He shuffled around a little. When he straightened, Drew saw the rough line of scars around his neck.

"There was no foothold on that damn arch. It was hard leaning against the wall, and my arms and legs began to hurt bad. I began to sweat. Worst of all, I got real thirsty. And you two were just drinking and drinking." Jackson stared at Drew. He shifted his body and stepped forward.

"I don't know what happened. Even now I can't explain it. I forgot about wanting to die. The only thing I wanted was some of your cold beer. It was driving me crazy. Then when I turned to climb down, I slipped and felt myself falling."

Jackson reached up and moved his fingers over the scar on his neck. He shrugged his shoulders and began twisting his head in a crunched circle. As Jackson moved, the features on his face grew hard, and his eyes were white and glassy.

"And then I was swinging through the air. I grabbed for the rope, but my hands slid off. My neck was crushed by the weight. I couldn't breathe. My head was all hot and felt like exploding. It did explode. And for an instant, I saw something bright all over the sky above the arch. It was coming toward me."

"Shane put the bright lights on," Drew said.

"What?"

"I was blinded, too. The car lights were dim at first, but Shane turned on the bright lights."

"Was that it?" Jackson asked. "I thought the light was an angel or something. I'll be damn. Are you sure?"

"I'm sure," Drew said.

"I'll be damn," Jackson said, a stubborn expression forming on his face. "Well, after the angel came and untied the noose, the next thing I remember, I was looking up and seeing your face. You amazed me. You were just a boy."

"I was in high school," Drew said

"You gave me the drink. It tasted so good. Then I saw your friend standing there. And then the doctors came."

"We were lucky," Drew said.

"You saved my life." Jackson moved closer and studied Drew's face. "You know, you still look like a boy."

Jackson turned and limped up the steps. Even with the limp, Jackson handled the steps easily. After a few minutes of steady climbing, he pushed open the door to the fourth floor, and Drew followed him into the empty hallway. Jackson walked down the hall and stopped at the second door, Room 402. He opened the door and motioned Drew inside.

"Thank you," Drew said. He walked in the room and waited for Jackson. But Jackson stood at the door.

"I go to the park every day," Jackson said. "I saw you this morning. This car stopped in front of the arch, and then I saw you get out. I was expecting you. I knew you'd come back. You just began running like before." A smile formed on Jackson's face, exposing chew-encrusted teeth.

"I enjoy it," Drew said. "Running relaxes me."

"Just being in the park relaxes me," Jackson said. "I have to go to work now." Taking a glance at the bed, he closed the door.

The room was lit from two angles. There was a soft light shining down over the front of Shane's bed, and the brighter football stadium lights glowed through the large window. Drew walked over to the bed and looked at Shane. It was warm in the hospital room. Shane wore his old, blue varsity T-shirt, the golden Patriot figure etched in the left corner. His hair was trimmed, and he was cleanly shaven. The smell of aftershave was strong in the air.

"Shane," Drew whispered. He bent closer and looked at the face. Shane's green eyes were wide and watery bright, staring somewhere past him.

"Can you hear me?" Drew asked. The room was so quiet. Drew listened to his own heart beating. There was a slight dim of noise from the football field.

"Blink if you can hear me." Drew studied the face. He could see the tiny reflection of his face in Shane's pupils.

"Shane," Drew said louder. He put his palm on Shane's chest and felt the steady movement of his lungs. He pressed down slightly, and Shane coughed. Drew jerked his hand away.

"I'm sorry," Drew half shouted. Shane coughed again and then was quiet. Drew watched him breathing for a few minutes. When there was no change, he walked to the window and opened it. After a few deep breaths of fresh air, he studied the rusty fence and the sharp slant of the hill.

Drew remembered the sharp steepness of the hill and the big hole in the chain-link fence at the top. The bleachers and the football field were at the bottom of the hill. There was a crowd of spectators in the center rows of bleachers. The players on the field looked small in the large shoulder pads and blue-and-gold helmets. The scoreboard at the end of the field was bright in the darkness. When the official blew the whistle, a piercing, loud blast, to start the game, the kicker lofted the ball high in the air. The spectators stood up and cheered.

"There's a junior high game going on," Drew said, walking back to the bed. He talked to Shane quietly. "The field's the same; the bleachers are all metal and much bigger, nothing like the warped wooden planks we had. And they put a lot of money in the new scoreboard." Drew pushed a chair to the side of the bed and sat down. He took the Sony recorder from his pocket.

"I bought this in Bangkok. I wanted to make sure you heard everything that happened. So whenever I see or think of something, I record it on the Sony. Like this morning I saw this huge buck in the park and I recorded that. And I recorded everything about Whin and NuWhin. I know you want to hear about them. There's so much to tell you, Shane."

Drew was about to turn on the Sony when the horn sounded from the scoreboard. It was a resounding blast that vibrated against the bleachers and echoed up the hill to the hospital.

"The noise is louder with the new bleachers," Drew said, sliding the Sony in his pocket. He moved closer to the bed and looked at Shane's face staring at the ceiling. Drew reached his hands under the pillow and shifted Shane's head so the green eyes looked at him.

"That's better. You can see me now." Drew settled back in the chair.

"I met Gary's brother today. I remember you talking to him at the funeral. You told him he would have to be the man in the family. Well, I don't know if that will ever happen. He's a star quarterback now. But Gary was way better. Gary was the best.

"His brother seems like a real jerk. He killed some fish in biology class today. There was no reason for it. I guess I got angry. I used my Tiger Claw for the first time. But that wasn't enough. I also tried to drown him. Coach Chuck will probably hear about it. I met him today, too. He really hates us. I mean he really hates us. I know we won only one game for him, but still . . ."

Drew paused for a moment. Shane's head was stationary in the pillow, and he looked totally relaxed and comfortable. The bright green eyes looked mischievous to him, and Drew had to smile.

"Maybe it was your fault coach hated us, Shane. Maybe it was that name you called him. Remember when you saw him stumble out of Walt's Bar that night? He was drunk and threw up in the street. You always called him Up-Chuck after that. Coach Up-Chuck." Drew laughed, picturing Coach's red face.

"Some kids in the gym class began calling him that. Someone, I think it was you, spray-painted Up-Chuck on his windshield. That really made things worse for everyone. When he found out you gave him the nickname, he made practice hell for us.

"We kept losing games. I mean some of the scores were 35-0 and 40-0. We didn't score a touchdown all year. Chuck began to call us losers. He hated us. All we did was sprint and run. And the hospital hill here. How many times did we run up to the fence and back? And the scores only got worse."

A whistle sounded from the football field. There was some cheering from the fans. Drew looked at the window and then turned back to Shane.

"Who would have thought the season would end like it did? The unscored on, untied, undefeated super-team Eagles, the big red-and-white Eagles coming to George Washington to win their championship.

"It was Senior Night. We wore our blue uniforms with gold numbers. I walked with you and Mom and Dad across the field. The Eagles fans packed into their side of the bleachers, but there were too many of them. They filled their bleachers, and hundreds more wandered over to the Patriots' side. They all stood up and cheered for us seniors.

"But it wasn't for real. The Eagles people cheered because we were their final victim. We were a joke to them. It was the most noise ever at George Washington. I know they heard us here at the veteran's hospital, and I bet even in the park.

"You were angry at all the cheering and ridicule. You said they were making fun of us and our families and that you would shut the bastards up. And you did shut them up. They couldn't run the ball because you hit their star halfback in the backfield. They couldn't pass either because you sacked their star quarterback. It was great how you destroyed their offense. And it got so quiet. The thousands of Eagles fans just sat there with nothing to cheer about.

"It was that way until the end of the fourth quarter. That last minute, Gary ripped the shirt off that star halfback on the two-yard line and stopped a touchdown. Gary cracked some ribs or something and still wouldn't leave the field. Then the Eagles kicked a field goal with nine seconds left in the game. That was the only time the Eagles fans cheered all night, but it was so loud. It went on forever. The game should've been over. Coach Chuck was going crazy, so Homer told us where to lineup for the kick return.

"You never played there before, but Homer wanted you to receive the kickoff. He ordered me in front of you to block, and all the other Patriots were up on the line. When the ball sailed over my head and you caught it, I began running wildly. I just wanted to hit someone. But suddenly, players were rolling on the ground, and a big hole opened up in front of me. It was so easy. I just ran through it, and then you ran past me into the open field.

"It all happened so fast. I tried to catch up to you, and that's when I saw the kicker and their big safety standing on the fifteen-yard line. The safety stepped forward and got low, and you went right at him, Shane. And just when you two were ready to collide, you turned and tossed the ball back to me. I was so surprised, and the ball slipped a little in my hands, but I caught it.

"You didn't break stride when you cracked into the safety. He was knocked way in the air, and then there was only the kicker. He heard how hard you hit the safety, and he put his forearm in front of his helmet and just sat down. But you plowed into him anyway, and I ran past you both and crossed the goal line. I never heard so much noise in all my life.

"I think I went crazy. I mean I lost it. I started jumping and screaming and swinging the ball in the air, and when the horn blasted and I saw the number 6 fill the empty square on the scoreboard, I was buried under a mountain of blue-and-gold bodies."

For a moment, Drew was back in the end zone. It was dark, and he was crushed under the pile of players. Excited and scared at the same time, Drew remembered he had a hard time breathing.

"Then you were there, Shane. You pulled me out of the pile and lifted me on your shoulders. Surrounded by the whole team, you ran me down the field. There was this tremendous cheering, and all the Patriots were standing. But I was crying so much I couldn't see too clearly. Everything was so blurry and crazy and out of control, but I swear I saw my dad in the stands cheering like everyone else. It was the happiest moment of my life."

There was the sound of a car horn from the school parking lot. Then another longer answering horn. Wiping the perspiration from his forehead, Drew took a deep breath. There was a bright flash of light through the window, and the stadium lights blinked off, darkening the side of the room. Drew looked up and saw the glow from the bed light. It cast a soft circle around Shane's face and shoulders.

"You could have scored the touchdown," Drew whispered. "You could have won the game and been the hero. But you gave me the ball."

Drew turned and walked across the room. Opening the door, he stepped outside. The hall was empty and quiet. Drew walked to the exit. He went down the back stairs and pushed the door open to the night air. His was the only car in the parking lot. Drew got in, started the engine, and drove diagonally across the large empty lot. Jackson stepped out from the shadows of the building. He watched the lights move through the darkness and disappear at the exit.

CHAPTER 12

The next morning at six o'clock, Drew was putting on his jogging shoes when the phone rang. He answered it quickly. At the other end, Homer sounded wide awake and alert.

"Are you still running in the morning?"

"I'm just getting ready to leave."

"Can you come over to the football field?"

"Is that where you run now?" Drew asked.

"No," Homer said. "Bad back. I'm done running. Come on down to the football field. I want you to meet some students."

"I'll be right over," Drew said. He changed into his school clothes, drove to the school, and parked at the gate to the football field. The air was cool, and the sky was just turning light. There was a misty fog rising over the field. Looking through the mist, Drew saw Homer and two students wearing blue-and-gold football jerseys and blue shorts standing near the equipment shed on the side of the track.

"Drew," Homer called. "Over here." As Drew walked closer, he saw the players were holding two large tackling dummies.

"Good morning," Drew said. "You said you weren't coaching any more."

"This is volunteer work," Homer said. "I read your discipline report. I'm sorry about that. Yesterday you met the assholes of the football team. Now I want you to meet the better half. This is Wesley Foote, our kicker." They shook hands. Wesley was short, had powerful muscular legs and upper body, and his head seemed small for his build. He had a serious, grim look, and there were deep blemishes on his face.

"And this is Riley, our special team's everything." Drew shook hands with Riley.

"Just Riley?" Drew asked. Riley was as tall as Drew. He face was clear and smooth, and he was relaxed, more loose than Wesley.

"Just plain ole Riley, Mr. Benson," Riley said, with a smile on his face. "Coach Matthews said you scored the winning touchdown against the Eagles."

"I did," Drew said.

"That's great," Riley said. "I wish I could do that Friday night. I'd remember it the rest of my life."

"Good luck," Wesley said. "You're not even on offense."

"I'll recover a fumble and run it back," Riley said. "Defense wins games."

"Kickers win games," Wesley said. They argued back and forth for a few minutes and then Homer told them to carry the dummies to the forty-yard line and warm up.

"I've coached them since fifth grade," Homer said. "Wesley picked up on the kicking early, and he's in his own league now. On his kickoffs, everything was way out of the end zone, and he was getting really bored. So we worked on the onside kicks. Coach Chuck only understands the high-arching, dead-duck kicks, but Wesley and I kept practicing the line drives and the recovery. Wait till you see what he does."

"Is he good?"

"Wait till you see."

"What about Riley?"

"Riley has real talent. He has the state record in the high jump. He's already accepted a full scholarship at Bucknell."

"What's he doing in football?"

"He's good friends with Wes, and I guess he wants to stay in shape and get more physical. At safety, he can get up high and catch anything in the area. They're both pretty fired up about the game on Friday."

"They should be."

Wesley and Riley ran four laps and returned to midfield. Homer held one of the dummies, and Riley dragged the other one closer to the sideline. Wesley took the football and teed it up on the forty-yard line. Then he walked back, turned, and stared at the dummies.

"Ready?" he asked.

"Wait one second," Homer said. He went behind the dummy and knelt down. Riley did the same. "Stand over there out of the way," he told Drew.

Drew walked off to the side. Homer signaled with his hand, and crouching low to the ground, Wesley ran at the ball. He kicked it with such force that Drew heard the impact, but he didn't actually see it hit the dummy. The dummy tilted backward, and the ball spun high in the air. Homer straightened the dummy and laughed.

"See what I mean, Drew."

"Amazing," Drew said. He watched Wesley crush the ball off the two dummies for ten minutes. The last few times he was able to focus on the ball clearly. Once the impact was so hard it knocked Riley to the ground. He got up laughing.

"Pussy," Wesley said and walked to the bag. The two players joined Homer and Drew.

"Those feet are a great weapon," Drew said. "You can hit anything with the football. And you're so accurate!"

"Dad didn't believe me when I told him what we were doing," Wesley said. "He wanted me to listen to Coach Chuck and practice the stupid high kick. And then he said I could do it if I could prove to him that it really worked. So one Sunday afternoon he came and stood right there where the dummy is."

"I'm glad I wasn't here to watch this," Homer said, looking at Wesley.

"I kicked the ball, I guess it was pretty hard, and before Dad could close his hands, the ball smacked him in the chest and knocked him on the ground. He actually rolled over once. He was breathing hard when he stood up. I saw the imprint of the football on his T-shirt. He told me to stay here and practice some more. Then he wrapped his arms around his chest and walked to the car."

"He never bothered Wesley after that," Homer said.

"I understand why," Drew said.

"Why don't you try it, Mr. Benson?" Riley asked.

"OK," Drew said. He walked to the dummy, and Wesley took the football to the forty-yard line and teed it up. When Wesley was in position, Drew stepped in front of the dummy.

"No, Mr. Benson, get behind the dummy," Riley said.

"I'm fine right here," Drew said, relaxing his body, raising his hands slightly. "Go ahead, Wesley, give it your best shot."

"But, Mr. Benson."

"It's OK," Drew said. He glanced at Homer and smiled. "My old football coach told me I should never stand behind a dummy."

"Are you sure?" Wesley asked. "My dad . . ."

"I'm sure," Drew said. "Go ahead and kick it. Oh, and, Wesley, don't you dare let up."

Wesley looked at Homer, and Homer just shrugged his shoulders. The sun was higher now, and shone brightly on Wesley's face. Getting in his stance, Wesley ran and kicked the ball cleanly and powerfully. Hitting Drew's hands, the ball made a loud smacking noise.

Drew's hands collapsed inward, straightened quickly, and the ball stopped inches from his chin. Lifting the ball in the air, Drew turned and passed it to Riley. Standing openmouthed, Riley let it bounce off his chest. Homer laughed and slapped Drew on the shoulders.

"I know one thing, Mr. Benson," Riley said. "I'm glad you're on our side. I'm glad you're a Patriot." He and Wesley picked up the dummies and carried them back to the equipment shed.

"You've got great reflexes," Homer said.

"My instructor Kim taught me how to focus," Drew said. "And Professor JJ always had me form these clear pictures in my mind. I saw myself catching the football, and it was easy."

"That was not easy," Homer said. "Believe me or talk to Wesley's dad, but that was not easy."

Homer and Drew walked up to the parking lot which was now filled with cars and trucks. They turned the corner to the main building, and Drew saw a line of yellow busses in front of the entrance.

"Have a good day in the park," Homer said as they walked into the lobby.

"Thanks," Drew said. He went up the steps to his classroom and waited for the students. They entered the room in groups of two and three. Some of them walked back to look at the fish aquarium. After morning ceremonies and attendance, Drew went with his class to the buses. Most of the students ran to sit with their friends. Drew got on Bus 10 and sat down in the front seat opposite the driver. She was an elderly woman with a sweet smile. Drew returned the smile, and looking out the window, he saw Frank West Jr. get on the bus in front of him.

It was a noisy ten-minute ride to Valley Forge National Park. Some of the windows were down, and cool morning air filled the bus. Bright sunlight reflected off the black asphalt as the busses pulled into the parking lot next to George Washington's Headquarters. The door swung open, and Drew stood up.

"Indian summer," the bus driver said. "You'll have beautiful weather today."

"It's warming up fast," Drew said. He stepped off the bus. The rush of students followed him. Showing her friendly smile again, the bus driver waved at Drew and closed the door. The line of busses pulled slowly toward the exit. After some searching and running around, the students found their teachers and joined the assigned groups. The teachers gave final instructions, and the various groups left the parking lot walking in different directions.

An older group of students were laughing and pushing into each other when they walked toward Drew. Leroy and Chester and two girls were at the end of the group. Dressed in loose-fitting blouses and tight pants, Sally and her girlfriend were clinging to the football players. The group stopped in front of Drew.

"Mr. Substitute," Leroy said. He was unshaven, and there were dark circles under his eyes. The smile on his face was forced and stupid looking. "I didn't think they would let you back in school."

"Why would you think that?" Drew asked.

"Because you're a pervert," Sally answered for Leroy. "My father called the principal. He said it was student abuse what you did to me."

"And you're very incompetent," Leroy added. "You let all the fishes die." He laughed and put his arm around Sally's waist, nudging her into motion. "Let's get away from this fish head. We have a fun day ahead of us."

"The fishes must smell so bad," Chester said, walking away. "Maybe they smell like you, teacher."

Chester pinched his nose with his fingers, and he rushed to join the main group of students. When they reached the far corner of the parking lot, Leroy and the football players slowed down and separated from the group. Drew watched them walk down a dirt path toward a secluded log cabin on the edge of a clump of trees.

Drew turned and walked in the direction of Washington's Headquarters. He reached the row of log cabins, the commander's guard huts. The door of the first cabin was unlocked. Drew went inside, and taking out the Sony recorder, he sat on the corner bunk.

Drew clicked on the record button, and looking at the fireplace and wooden bunks, he began talking in a quiet voice. Even after eight years, Drew remembered everything about the get-tough adventure. He talked to Shane about the freezing cold, the mucus eyes, the shoeless walk in the snow, and about the wild sled ride.

Drew was about to turn off the recorder when he remembered the bullet holes in the truck and the great feast at the Vale Rio Diner. He talked about the breakfast and how the whole lemon meringue pie disappeared so fast. Then shutting off the small recorder, he put it in his pocket and walked outside.

Shielding his eyes from the sun, Drew saw Terry Evans coming toward him. Terry carried his blue varsity jacket covered with large gold VF letters on the front. The blue varsity T-shirt he was wearing showed the smooth flow of muscles in his chest and shoulders.

"Hey, Mr. Benson, I heard you were here," Terry said. "Can I talk to you?"

"Sure," Drew said. He looked at the smile on his face and unblinking shift of his eyes. "Is it about the fish tank?"

"No, nothing about the fish tank," Terry said. "You knew my older brother?"

"Gary was one of my best friends," Drew said. He saw the wooden bench under the tree near the parking lot. "Let's get out of the sun."

They walked over and sat across from each other in the shade of the tree. Shadows of dark and bright light moved across Terry's face as the wind rustled the leaves.

"I remember Gary's funeral," Terry said. "You helped carry the casket."

"I came back from college for the funeral. When I saw Gary, I couldn't believe it. He was in Nam for only a few months."

Through the shifting pattern of shadows, Drew looked at Terry and saw how closely he resembled his brother. Drew recognized the brown eyes, sharp nose, square jaw, the thin growth of hair on his chin.

"Coach Chuck said you two played football together."

"Three years."

"Coach said you only won one game your senior year. He said Gary had real talent, but he never got better because he always fooled around with you and Shane."

"Coach Chuck said a lot of things," Drew said. "I never listened to any of it."

"I listen to him. Coach told me I could be what Gary could never be. He said I could be a real winner. And Coach was right. I hold two state passing records and have five scholarship offers from D1 schools. I'm leaving now to meet with the head coach of Maryland."

"Good luck," Drew said. "But you want to know something, Terry?

"What?"

"In your wildest dreams, you'll never be as good as your brother."

"I'm not afraid of you, Mr. Benson." Terry stood up and stared at Drew. "Coach said you were a loser here, and you were a loser in Vietnam, too. He said Vietnam was the only war America ever lost." Terry started to walk away but turned and looked back at Drew.

"And you'd better stop messing with the football players. We're going to win the championship game on Friday. And I have a good idea for you, Mr. Benson. Why don't you come to the game? You'll see who I am. You'll see I'm way better than Gary ever was." Terry laughed, threw his varsity jacket over his shoulder, and walked to his car.

As Terry drove away, a school van pulled into the parking lot, and cafeteria workers began unloading boxes of bagged lunches. A group of students gathered up the large boxes to deliver them to the designated lunch areas. One student reached the corner of the parking lot when two large figures jumped in front of him. They pushed the student hard, and he dropped the box. Leroy and Chester grabbed a handful of bags off the ground. After kicking the empty box, they walked quickly across the field toward the log cabin.

Drew went over to the student and helped him put the remaining bags in the box. The student was red-faced and nervous. He picked up the pieces of a smashed hoagie and threw them into the field.

"Thanks for helping," he said.

"I saw what Leroy and Chester did," Drew said. "I can report it."

"No," the student said. "They would lie about what happened. I'm nobody here. The school would believe them."

"I'm a substitute nobody," Drew said. "Maybe the school would believe two nobodies."

"They'd just come after me. And maybe you," the student said. "Thanks again. Here, have a lunch." He gave Drew a bag and hurried up the path.

Drew opened the bag and unwrapped the hoagie. It was ham and cheese. Watching the student disappear around the bend of the jogging path, Drew took a bite of the hoagie. He took another bite and threw the rest of the hoagie and bag into a trash container. Looking at the log cabin in the distance, he saw two doe break running across the field.

Drew started walking, and when he reached the middle of the field, he heard the broken rhythm of rap music and laughter. The sun was directly overhead now, and there was no wind. Drew's forehead was beaded with perspiration when he reached the log cabin. The front door was closed. Thin lines of smoke rose from the dark cracks along the side and roof. The noise and laughter became louder. Drew pushed the door open and stepped inside, and everything became quiet.

"What the fuck do you want?" Leroy asked, looking up through the smoke. His arm around Sally's waist, he was stretched out on the bottom bunk. There was a joint dangling from the corner of his mouth. Chester and the other girl were sitting next to the fireplace. Placed on a thin pile of hay, Chester's shirt was folded neatly in the shape of a pillow.

"Shouldn't you be with your class?" Drew asked.

"It's lunch," Leroy said.

"Yeah, it's lunch," Sally said. "It's our time."

"Smoking joints and making out," Drew said. It was hot, almost stifling, in the cabin. Slanting lines of light from the cracks in the wall filtered through the thickening clouds of smoke. The light spread across Leroy's eyes and mouth. His lips moved, shaking ashes from the joint. A slight wheezing noise came from his nose.

"Fuck you," he said. "I think you should get the hell out of here."

"Yeah," Sally said. "You're disrupting our lunch time. And you're alone. No one would believe any of your stories."

"No one would," Drew said. "You're probably right. Enjoy the rest of your lunch." He stepped out of the cabin and pushed the door shut. There was laughter from inside.

"He's not so fuckin' dumb," Chester said.

"Maybe I won't kick his ass," Leroy said loudly.

Drew listened to the ridicule and laughter. He saw the glint of silver in the grass by the side of the cabin. He picked up the heavy lock and pulled it open. Then he slid the latch into place, put on the lock, and snapped it shut.

Drew went to the back of the cabin. In the shadows of the trees, he took the audio recorder from his pocket and put in a new tape. Turning on the recorder, he placed it into a large crack between two weather-beaten logs. He could hear the students talking and moving around inside.

"Give me some of that shit," Chester ordered in a loud voice.

After checking the recorder, Drew retraced his steps, and in a few minutes, he joined the group of students outside George Washington's Headquarters.

The busses returned to the parking lot at two thirty. The students and teachers loitering under the shade trees began to join their bus groups. In the older group, Frank West Jr. was still taking attendance when a football player ran past the students and stumbled to a stop in front of him.

"I heard shouting from inside the cabin," he said. "When I got there, I saw the door was locked."

"You think some students are locked in a cabin?" Frank Jr. asked.

"Yes, Sir."

"Do you know who they are?"

"I think Chester and Leroy," the student said. He hesitated for a moment. "And maybe Sally and Judy."

"It's banging time!" someone shouted. There was excited talk and loud whistling.

"Everyone, be quiet!" Frank Jr. shouted above the noise. Just as he finished, a few students and then the whole group broke away and ran up the path. Drew watched them reach the field and begin a wild race toward the cabin.

"Come back!" Frank Jr. shouted.

The students ignored him and began to run faster. Frank Jr. saw a ranger van drive into the parking lot, and he hurried over to meet it. After a brief conversation with the ranger, Frank began a mad dash toward the cabin. Soon, there was a mass of teachers, students, and bus drivers around the log cabin. Drew was one of the last ones to get there. Standing in the shade of a tree, he watched the excitement build as the cries for help from the log cabin grew louder.

It was 3:00 PM when Mr. Wentworth's van reached the parking lot. Lights spinning red and blue, the van jumped the curb, raced across the field, and skidded to a stop behind the circle of people. The engine shut off, the door slammed open, and Mr. Wentworth stepped out, swinging a ring of keys in his hand.

"Get out of the way!" Frank Jr. shouted. He and Mr. Wentworth pushed through the crowd of students. At the front of the circle, the students were noisy and excited. Some of them were pounding and kicking on the door.

Mr. Wentworth quickly unlocked the door with his master key, and he and Frank Jr. went inside the dark entrance. There was some talking, loud coughing, and then the students came out. They instantly raised their hands to shield their eyes from the bright sunlight. Their faces were pale, and their shirts and blouses were drenched wet. Sally's blouse was stretched tightly against her body, exposing the outline of her breasts. Leroy made a loud wheezing noise every time he took a step.

Mr. Wentworth led them to the van, and the students climbed awkwardly inside. Moving around the side of the van, Mr. Wentworth got in the driver's seat and slammed the door shut. The rotating emergency lights came on as soon as he started the engine. The engine roared loudly, and the tires spun on the grass as he exited. After the last group of students started across the field, Drew went behind the cabin and took the audio recorder from the crack in the walls. The two-hour tape had run out.

CHAPTER 13

There was a crowd of parents waiting in front of the entrance to Valley Forge High School. The busses arrived at the school forty minutes late. The students were noisy and animated when they left their friends and joined their parents. Some mothers were concerned about the long delay and waited for an explanation, but most of the parents were in a hurry and began a brisk walk to the cars. There was some congestion and loud horn blowing as they rushed to get out of the parking lot.

Drew watched the line of cars grow smaller. It was late, and the security lights around the building blinked on. The yellow school busses joined the end of the line of cars. Drew glanced at the large American flag at the Veterans Hospital on the hill behind the school. It was slowly being lowered.

As Drew was about to get in his car, he saw Frank Jr. race out of the school entrance. He was swinging his arms and shouting in Drew's direction. Frank slowed to a fast walk as he neared the car.

"The principal wants to see you," Frank said. His face was red and wet with perspiration. The thin line of the scar ran white down his forehead.

"School's over," Drew said. "I'm going home."

"This can't wait. He wants to see you now. The students said you locked them in the log cabin. You're in a lot of trouble, Benson."

"Is that right, Frank Jr.? Are you still a teacher here, or did your dad already promote you to assistant principal? Whatever your position, Frank Jr., I don't have to listen to a word you say."

"You always caused trouble in school and got away with it. But not this time. Sally's father is preparing a lawsuit."

"So I'm going to be sued, is that it?"

"You put students' lives in danger. You'll be fired. And then you'll be sued. You'll never teach again."

"I'm really impressed. Frank Jr. has everything figured out."

"There was nothing to figure out. Students are under the teacher's supervision and protection. You can't lock them in cabins." Frank Jr. looked up at Drew. His face was still flushed with anger. "I hope they send you to jail."

"Jail is for losers, Frank Jr."

"And that's what you are. You were a loser before. And the war only made you a bigger loser." Frank's voice became louder. There was a slight bulge under his lip. As Frank spoke, the bulge moved outward, and Drew watched a dark brown stain appear at the corner of his mouth.

"Did you enjoy it over there, Benson? The killing? The torture? How about the napalm burning up all those people? Agent Orange was a good idea, too. It's still killing farmers. You and Shane did a great job over there."

"You never made it to Nam, Frank Jr., so how do you know so much about the war? I mean you're using all the keywords."

"I read the newspapers. I saw the stuff on TV."

"The daily news headlines, two-minute TV video clips, none of it showed the real Vietnam. But maybe the news was more accurate in Canada. How was it up there where you were hiding, Frank Jr.? Was it more accurate?"

"It was the same," Frank said. He turned away and looked at the school. A sturdy figure in the window of the principal's office stared at them.

"Some of us fought and died in the war, Frank Jr. And some of us ran away to Canada. At any other time in our history, we would call these people cowards. At Valley Forge you would have been hung as a traitor and a deserter. But the TV news was on your side. The TV said it was OK to be a coward. The reporters portrayed the war so bad that they had no choice but to portray the cowards protesting the war as the good Americans. And these good Americans lived in comfort and safety. Were you safe in Canada, Frank Jr.?"

"It wasn't like that," Frank said.

"It took President Ford's pardon to permit you cowards back in the country. What a clemency program! You had to repeat the Pledge of Allegiance, which you had already broken. And you had a few years of community service. What was your service, Frank Jr.? Did you cut the grass somewhere? Did you clean the streets?"

"Sure, I cut grass at the park," Frank said. "I painted some buildings."

"Unbelievable," Drew said. "I was sick when I saw you teaching students at the park this morning. You shouldn't be allowed near Valley Forge. There were real soldiers at Valley Forge." Drew stepped closer until he was inches from Frank.

"You didn't have the guts to fight for your country. The only wound you'll ever have is that scar from the locker. Being tough with a girl. Then when it really counted, you ran away to Canada. Maybe instead of Frank Jr., I should call you Benedict Jr. Every time you see your face in the mirror, you'll be looking at a coward, so don't talk to me about Vietnam." Drew turned away and opened the door to his car.

"My dad wants to see you now."

"I'm going home, Frank Jr. Tell your dad to sue me tomorrow."

Starting the engine, Drew drove past Frank West Jr., who stood there motionless. He lifted his fist in the air and spit a hunk of chew onto the pavement.

Drew exited the parking lot onto Charlestown Road. He drove to the outskirts of Phoenixville and turned onto a narrow tree-lined road. After passing through a two-mile section of big houses, each having its own acre of lawn, Drew entered a heavily wooded area.

Drew slowed for a sharp curve, and when the road straightened, he saw the rolling hills and green pasture.

There was a large, three-story house on the nearest hill, and below it the clear waters of French Creek cut a deep, meandering line through the pasture. The pasture was covered with weeds and shrubs and a scattering of blueberry bushes. Drew stopped the car at a covered bridge that spanned the creek. It was a weather-beaten wooden structure, and the road narrowed to one lane going through it. Birds flew out of the shadows.

Three bicycles were dropped down randomly at the side of the bridge. The owners of the bicycles were at the bottom of the hill on the bank with fishing rods in their hands. The boys were fishing at the only deep hole on this stretch of French Creek. Wearing a blue denim jacket, one boy was taller and older than the other two. They all sat under a large tree, one twisted branch stretching high over the bank. The remains of a frayed rope were tied to the branch. Odd-angled planks of wood, some broken and pointed downward, were nailed to the side of the tree.

Closing his eyes, Drew leaned back in the seat, and his thoughts raced back to that perfect afternoon. He and Shane and Gary were running through the pasture to the creek. He was struggling with the planks of wood. Shane was swinging the rope over his head. And Gary was carrying the hammer and nails.

When they reached the tree, Shane hammered the first two planks into the trunk. Then he climbed up and hammered the third plank. Drew followed him up the tree and kept handing up planks of wood. When Shane grabbed the tenth plank and held it against the tree, high off the ground, he balanced himself precariously and swung the hammer with incredible force. Hanging onto Shane's ankle, Drew felt the impact vibrate into his ears. Shane shouted for another plank, and they continued to inch their way up the side of the tree.

A hot wind blew and rustled the branches above Drew. The planks of wood scraped against his ribs, and Drew could see thin lines of blood on his T-shirt. After five more planks, Drew blinked and looked down at the water. The creek was dark and small and seemed a great distance away. He swayed backward slightly and grabbed Shane's leg for support. The loud croak of a bullfrog lifted up from the muddy bank.

Shane nailed the last board to the tree, and Gary climbed the planks and gave him the end of the rope. Drew held it up to Shane who crawled out and wrapped it tightly around the middle of the huge branch. Then he tied a thick knot at the bottom of the rope and released it. The rope dropped down and swung back and forth, the knot skimming the surface of the water.

Drew climbed to the ground and stood there with Gary. Shane jumped from the fourth plank and landed softly in front of them. After they stripped to their shorts, Shane grabbed the end of the rope and pointed it at Gary. He said Gary should jump first since it was Gary's land and Gary's covered bridge. Gary didn't want to take the rope. Then Shane said it was also his creek, and Gary took the rope.

Shane led Gary to the designated starting point. Gary turned and stood there facing the water, his hands twisted around the rope. He hesitated, an empty expression on his face. He began to make some kind of excuse, but Shane ordered him to hold on. He lifted Gary by the waist, ran him down the hill, and swung him over the edge of the bank.

Gary started yelling as he spun across the surface of the water. At the high end of the arc, his body stopped momentarily, suspended over the far bank, and yelling louder than before, he fell back toward the water. Drew and Shane began shouting at him.

Listening to the loud shouts to let go of the rope, Gary only tensed his body and lifted his knees high in the air. Shane was waving his hands and shouting even louder. Gary became quiet when he saw Drew and Shane and the steep edge of the bank. He clenched his mouth shut, closed his eyes, and let go of the rope.

Drew watched Gary spin over the deep hole in the middle of the creek, and with a mighty splash, his body hit the water near the bank. But his body didn't stop there. His momentum slid him forward, and shouting in a loud voice, Gary bodysurfed head first into a shallow pool of mud and lily pads. His face disappeared. His shorts slid down to his knees, muddy water streaming over his white skin.

Shane was laughing and clapping his hands. He slid down the slope of the bank and lifted Gary by the shoulders. He was coughing and spitting out mud. Struggling to stand, Gary pulled his shorts up and fell backward into French Creek. Resurfacing quickly, he glared at Shane through the streaks of mud and water

"I got to try that again!" Gary laughed, running up the bank.

Drew was startled awake by loud shouts from the tree. One of the fishermen was yelling something. Drew looked at the three boys through the car window.

"Got the bastard!" the older boy shouted. He stood up and lifted a fish from the creek. It landed jumping and flapping on the grassy bank. Grabbing it and ripping out the hook, he held the fish high over his head so the other boys could see.

"It's a fuckin' sucker!" he shouted and threw the fish at the tree. The body smacked against the bark and fell heavy to the ground. The boys were laughing. The older boy picked the fish up by the tail and, still laughing, smashed it into the tree again. Then he stuck its gills through the jagged plank of wood and left it hanging there, the silver body streaked red in the light of the setting sun.

Drew started the engine and drove through the bridge, the tires making a loud rumbling sound that echoed off the wooden walls. Some pigeons flew out through the bridge opening and circled toward the house. Drew drove up the hill and turned into the driveway. The gravel road to the porch was filled with potholes and weeds.

When Drew stopped the car, he saw the screen door open. Wearing a plain green dress, Mrs. Evans walked down the steps. Her brown hair was loose and cut natural to her shoulders. Recognizing Drew immediately, she called out his name and smiled. Drew walked over and hugged her.

Mrs. Evans asked him about Shane. Drew told her about the coma and that Shane was at the Veterans Hospital. She said she was sorry, and they went up the steps into the screened porch. There were two wooden chairs with oversized brown cushions. In the corner was a table covered with a red-and-white striped cloth. A row of three lit candles was in front of the table. Pictures of Gary were arranged behind the candles. A large one of him in military uniform was in the center.

"I'll get some ice tea," Mrs. Evans said.

Drew looked across the porch and thought about all the nights he had slept here. Mrs. Evans treated him and Shane as family. They stayed up all hours of the morning and always woke to a huge breakfast of ham, sausage, scrambled eggs, and tall stacks of blueberry pancakes. They were the best pancakes he ever had.

Drew walked closer to the memorial table. It was spotless. There were a few badges and awards from training and a Purple Heart in the middle of the table. Under the Purple Heart was the red piece of Eagle football jersey from Senior Night.

Drew recognized all the pictures. He, Shane, and close family members were in the last picture. They were carrying Gary's casket from the church.

Mrs. Evans returned from the kitchen with two glasses of ice tea. She gave one to Drew. The ice clinked against the glass. Drew and Mrs. Evans sat down in the cushioned chairs that faced the front yard and covered bridge.

"The memorial is very nice," Drew said.

"Gary was the greatest son," Mrs. Evans began. "When his dad took that trip to Atlantic City and never came back, Gary changed overnight. He went to school and still got all the farm work done. He helped take care of Terry. I guess he wanted to prove to me that he was the man of the house. He proved that the first week, but it was too much work for a boy. He never took time to have fun. I could see it was wrong. I didn't know what to do." Mrs. Evans looked down the pasture at the wooden bridge. "Then you and Shane changed everything."

"How?"

"It started that afternoon you and Shane and Gary showed up on this porch. All of you were wet and muddy and couldn't stop laughing. After that, Gary began acting like a normal teenager."

"We had the best times here," Drew said.

"I'll always appreciate what you and Shane did for Gary," Mrs. Evans said. "He had so much catching up to do. You took him everywhere. You even talked him into playing football. Then when the team lost all those games."

"We were terrible," Drew said.

"No," Mrs. Evans said. "You weren't terrible. It's easy to be happy if you win all the time. But you were losing games, and it didn't change anything. You were all best friends. But most important you stayed together. You helped each other. In the middle of the season, Gary sat on this porch and told me he was having the best time in his life. And you hadn't won a game."

"Gary always did play hard," Drew said. "He really enjoyed football."

"That senior game had me in tears," Mrs. Evans said. "At the end of the fourth quarter when Gary caught that star running back and ripped part of his jersey off, I was in the stands cheering and crying like a baby."

"We all did some crying that night," Drew said.

"It means so much to me now," Mrs. Evans said. "Knowing he had that before he went to war. Knowing how much he enjoyed his last year." Mrs. Evans held her glass in both hands. She shuffled her feet back and forth and lowered her head. When she spoke, Drew could barely hear her words.

"I'll never forget that day. It was late afternoon and just a beautiful, peaceful day. I was sitting here on the porch, listening to the radio and relaxing. I happened to look up and see the black car turn the bend. The driver was taking his time, going so slow, like he was lost, like he didn't want to get here. The car hardly made any noise going through the bridge. It took a long time in there. Everything became so quiet. There are always pigeons, but I remember none of them flew out. The car pulled into the drive. I could see it was a government car, and when the two army officers got out, I watched them and I couldn't breathe. I couldn't move. They talked, but I couldn't hear anything."

"It was a shock to all of us," Drew said.

"I can't seem to let go, Drew," she spoke softly. "I can't seem to get on with my life. I know I should. I should be doing more with Terry. I really love him. He's gifted, and football comes easy for him. I go to the games, but it's not the same. I can't forget Gary. And I think Terry knows. I think he resents it."

"Terry's doing well. He said he has a scholarship."

"I don't know," Mrs. Evans said. "He doesn't talk much. His friends never come up. They blow the horn, and he runs to the car. There's always loud music and shouting. I think they're his football friends but not like you and Shane were to Gary. They don't care about him. Could you talk to him, Drew?"

"Talk to Terry?"

"Yes," Mrs. Evans said. "Maybe you can help."

"I've met him twice already," Drew said. "It didn't go very well. But it might have been my fault. I didn't give him much time. There are so many things going on now."

"It needn't take long. Just a few minutes to see how he is."

"Sure," Drew said. "I'll talk to him." He finished the tea and gave the glass to Mrs. Evans. "I should be going."

"Thank you, Drew, for visiting." Mrs. Evans stood up and walked with Drew to the steps. She hugged him. "I'm so sorry about Shane. I hope he gets better."

"Shane will get better," Drew said. "I'll tell him I was here."

Drew walked down the driveway and hesitated at the car. The setting sun cast a glow that sparkled a crimson light deep into the moving waters of French Creek. In the center of the pasture, the covered bridge was dark and solitary. The line of crimson flowed under the bridge and emerged brighter and wider and seemed to burn a path across the field.

Drew got in his car and drove down the hill into the cover of the bridge. As he exited, he saw a car parked in the shadows. Drew drove past the car and looked down at the tree. A figure was sitting there. It was Terry. Drew drove forward a short distance and stopped. He hesitated for a moment. Then he put the car in reverse and parked it behind Terry's. Getting out of the car, he walked down the slope to the tree.

With the sun setting, the air became cooler. There was the chirping of crickets and the soothing, lapping sound of the water over the stones. As he approached the creek, Drew saw the dried body of the sucker stuck on the tree, and below it, a fish head was spiked on a sharp plank of wood. A circle of flies buzzed around the tree. Drew stopped next to Terry, and when Terry remained quiet, Drew sat down on the grassy bank next to him.

"I saw you here," Drew said. He hesitated, not sure how to begin. There was an awkward silence. The waters from the creek swirled into the deep hole in front of him. "I wanted to ask you how the meeting went with the Maryland coach."

"If Friday's game goes well, I'll get a full scholarship." Terry spoke in a matter-of-fact voice. He didn't look up. "Even if it doesn't, I think they want me. I was on my way home to tell Mom. I stopped here first. I wanted to tell Gary. I can't talk to him in that room with the candles. That's her place."

"She'll be glad to know."

"She doesn't care about me. Ever since Gary died, she lost interest in everything. I tried so hard to help. I tried to talk about it, but she looked past me. It was like I didn't exist anymore."

"It was a bad time for her," Drew said.

"It was bad for me, too. I was just beginning to know Dad. Then he ran out on us. No one told me why. Then Gary became like my dad. We played together. We threw the ball in the yard. It was great being with him. Gary was my brother and my dad. Then he got killed. In a way it killed Mom, too. The house became empty. I hated coming home. I began to hang out with the football players. They took me in. Maybe we did things, stupid things. But I had a place with them."

At the top of the hill, there was a dim light from the porch. The sky was a red glow now. A light wind carried the smell of berries and mint from the pasture. Terry's voice broke the silence.

"I remember it was January. The pool was frozen. Gary and I ran down the hill. I reached the pool first and pretended to skate. I was laughing and doing crazy jumps. I slipped and fell and the ice broke. I saw the crack coming right at me, and then it opened up. Before I could do anything, I slid into it. The water soaked through my jacket and sweater. My pants became heavy and pulled me down. Within seconds, I was completely under. The water really began to burn into my face and hands."

Drew looked at the deep pool of water in the middle of the stream. With the fading light, the current turned black. Bits of floating debris, leaves, sticks, a feather, swirled around on the dark surface, were pulled under, and disappeared.

"I was freezing," Terry said. "I looked up at the jagged hole filling with slush and saw streams of light shining down. Then a dark shadow shut out the light and crashed through the ice. I saw this explosion of bubbles and these black boots dropping toward me. They were Dad's hunting boots. I really panicked. I began to think Dad came back for me. I guess I really missed Dad. When I saw Gary's face in front of me, I went crazy. I swung and punched him hard in the nose. He didn't move. He just looked at me in disbelief. A small bubble of blood filled his nose and seemed frozen there."

Terry was still for a moment. Drew could see the tears forming in his eyes. There was only the slight buzzing noise of the flies. The hint of mint was strong in the air. Wiping his eyes with the palm of his hands, Terry took a deep breath and forced a smile on his face.

"I didn't even see it coming. Gary hit me so hard. I was stunned. Then he grabbed me and pulled me to the hole. But I was too wet, too heavy. He couldn't lift me out of the water. The ice was thicker there. He began punching it with his fist and formed a path. Gary was shouting out in pain each time he smashed it. There were bright smears of blood on the ice. When he pulled me onto the bank, I saw his hand was cut and bloody. The skin was ripped off his knuckles. I could see how white the bone was." Looking up at the moving stream of water, Terry opened and closed his fist.

"I don't know how he did it. When he took off his jacket and put it over me, he could hardly stand up. I was ice cold and too frozen to talk. He was shaking really bad in his T-shirt, but he didn't care about the cold. He ran me and sometimes carried me up the hill to the house. We really gave Mom a scare."

"Gary talked about everything," Drew said. "But he never told that story."

"I asked him not to," Terry said. "I thought it made me look stupid. But Gary was great about it. He said he would always be here for us, for Mom and me. Then he went to the war. Mom told me he would be back in a year, and everything would be the same as before. But he was killed over there in Nam. Then I was all alone. Dad was gone. Gary was gone. Mom was gone, too. I didn't know what to do. I didn't know how to feel." Terry lifted his head and looked at Drew. His face was glistening wet and clear in the light.

"You must know the answer, Mr. Benson. Your parents were killed in the park. You lost everything, too. You tell me. Tell me how it felt."

"I've never talked about the accident," Drew said. Subconsciously, he lifted his hand to his face and touched the scar. "People asked me. Maybe they wanted to help, but they couldn't. If they had gone through it, they would know not to ask. Only Shane understood. He never asked me anything. He knew there were no words that could do that, that could tell about the hurt."

"No words at all?"

"No words," Drew said. "There was just an emptiness inside."

"I felt dead inside," Terry said. "I guess it's the same thing." Terry became quiet, his facial features set tight and hard in the light. The buzzing noise grew louder, and Terry stared at the tree and the fish bodies stuck there. Then he turned his attention back to Drew.

"You seem all right now, Mr. Benson. Is it a simple time thing like everyone says? Just wait and everything will work out."

"No, it's not simple at all, Terry. I couldn't work it out myself. I needed help. I had good friends."

"I don't," Terry said. He got up and reached for his jacket. Drew stood up next to him.

"Maybe you need new friends," Drew said. "I was wrong what I said at the park. I think we should start over. I think . . ."

"Don't worry about me," Terry said, interrupting him. "I don't need new friends. Maybe it's easier being around people who don't mean anything to you. Then when they go away or die or something like that, maybe it won't hurt so much." Terry put on his jacket. "I have to tell Mom about the scholarship." He started to walk away. After a few steps, he turned and looked at Drew.

"Yesterday in the classroom when you pushed my face underwater," Terry began, "I don't know how. It was the craziest thing, but I thought I saw my brother. I thought I saw Gary."

"You were in shock," Drew said.

"No," Terry said. "I didn't panic or anything. I closed my eyes and was sinking in darkness. Bubbles were exploding in my ears like in the creek, and when I opened my eyes, I saw Gary's face. It was so clear. He was right in front of me. I was waiting. No, I was hoping he would swing out and punch me again." Terry laughed. He shook his head. "Figure that out."

"I think I can," Drew said. He started to speak but hesitated for a moment. When he did speak, the words came slowly, carefully.

"Sometimes I see my parents like you saw Gary. Not at first. It was months after the accident. I began to imagine they weren't that far away. I mean like they were just in another place. When I learned to shut out the accident and remember the times we were together, the really good times, I could see them more clearly. I think they were with me all the time."

"Maybe that explains it. Maybe that's how I saw him," Terry said. He looked at Drew and smiled.

"Gary liked you, Mr. Benson. I remember when you gave him those cymbals and planned your kite experiment. He came down here for two nights and clanged away. The noise got louder and louder, and Mom was getting worried. She thought he was practicing for the marching band or something. Then when he told her how he made the loudest thunder on the football field, we all laughed. Gary had some great times." Terry started walking up the hill and then turned and paused.

"Mr. Benson?"

"What is it, Terry?"

"I didn't mean what I said about being better than Gary. I don't know why I talk like that. I miss Gary so much. I play every game for him. It's why I try so hard to win. It's all I can do for my brother now. If you can, come watch us against the Eagles Friday night. Please sit close to Mom. She would like that. See you, Mr. Benson." Terry waved his hand, turned, and began walking up the hill.

Drew didn't say anything. He watched Terry's every step, the slant of his shoulders, the invisible weight there. He watched the car lights go on and heard the door slam. Terry started the engine, and the car made a rumbling noise going through the covered bridge.

Darting past Drew's head, a bat flew over the pool of water and circled back. More flies had found the dead fish and swarmed around the tree. The buzzing sound in the night air became louder and monotonous. Starting up the hill, Drew looked at the two car lights moving toward the house. Then they clicked off into darkness, and there was only the solitary porch light and the dim glow from the burning candles.

Halfway up the hill, Drew saw lights down the road, and he heard the dull sound of music. The yellow Jaguar was racing fast, and when it reached the covered bridge, it accelerated, hit the wooden foundation, and lifted in the air. It landed with a loud crunching sound. The engine noise and the loud *Bad, Bad Leroy Brown* music sent the pigeons flapping out the other end of the bridge. There were three figures bouncing in the car when it raced up the lane. The Jaguar reached the house, and Drew heard the blare of the horn through the darkness.

CHAPTER 14

The covered bridge was a dark shadow when Drew started the car. He drove down the country road and after a few minutes pulled into the line of cars on Route 23. Drew was about to made a right turn at Washington Crossing to get to his house, but at the last minute, he hesitated and then drove through the intersection.

At the Kimberton Mall, he pulled into the parking lot and stopped opposite the antique shop. He saw Mrs. Thompson alone at the desk. Drew got out of the car and walked to the door. Mrs. Thompson looked up when he entered and walked to the counter. She forced a smile on her face.

"Drew," she said. They shook hands. Her hands felt cold. "We heard you were back."

"Is Joyce here?" Drew asked.

"She took some things to storage," Mrs. Thompson said. She glanced at the open door in the corner of the room.

"Can I talk to her?"

"She's kind of busy," Mrs. Thompson said. She was nervous and held her hands together. "And later she's seeing someone, Drew. I think she has a date tonight."

"I'll just be a few minutes," Drew said. He walked across the room and stepped through the open door. He stopped when he saw her. Joyce took a glass figurine out of a box and put it on the top shelf. When she lowered her hand, Drew noticed the star sapphire wasn't on her finger. Joyce turned at the sound of footsteps and looked at him. She was about to say something, but her lips closed. She had a confused, hurt look on her face.

"I didn't mean to surprise you," Drew said. He walked closer and took her hands. "I should have come here sooner." He leaned forward to kiss her. She turned away.

"No, Drew," she said. "Please don't."

238

"I've waited so long to see you," Drew said. "To talk to you. To hold you again. I never thought it would be like this."

"Things are different now."

"We've been together since high school."

"You were gone."

"I wrote letters telling you how I felt," Drew said. "I would mail one and start on the next one. I told you in every letter how much I missed you. How much I loved you. I told you everything."

"Not everything," Joyce said. She stepped back and pulled her hands away. "You didn't tell me about your wife and child."

"It's not what it looks like," Drew said.

"I was waiting for you," Joyce said. "The war news was horrible. I prayed that you would be safe. I prayed that we would be together again."

"So did I," Drew said. "It's all I ever wanted."

"Then I heard you were married and had a baby," Joyce said. Her voice was soft, tears welled in her eyes. "I couldn't work. I couldn't do anything. I was miserable for days."

"I'm sorry," Drew said.

"And here you are. Like it never happened." Joyce rubbed the tears from her eyes.

"I can explain what happened," Drew said. "We need some time. There's so much I have to tell you."

"There's nothing to talk about," Joyce said. Her breathing was heavier. She wiped her eyes again. "Please leave. Go home to your family."

"Joyce," Mrs. Thompson called from the door. "Is everything all right?"

"Yes," Joyce said. "Drew's leaving." She walked to the door, and Drew followed. When they got to the entrance, Joyce waited for Drew to step out. Then she turned the sign to CLOSED and locked the door.

Drew walked to his car. As he pulled out, another car moved into the empty space. Looking through the rearview mirror, Drew watched Frank Jr. get out of the car and walk to the antique shop. The door opened, and he went inside.

Feeling hurt, confused, a fierce anger shaking through his body, Drew drove out of the parking lot. At the next intersection, he didn't see the stop sign and had to brake quickly to avoid hitting a white truck. His window was down, and the blaring noise of the truck horn echoed through the car. Watching the angry, contorted face of the driver, Drew sat back, his hands still tight on the steering wheel. He hesitated, and when another horn blew behind him, he went through the intersection. Drew drove slowly, and reaching the house, he saw Whin was standing on the porch. She came down the steps to the car.

"NuWhin is sleeping," she said. "I have to buy things at the store."

"I'll watch her," Drew said. He got out of the car and gave her the keys.

"I'll be back soon," she said, getting in the car and starting the engine. Drew waited as she backed the car out of the driveway. After she turned the corner, he went inside the house.

Drew sat down on the sofa. Looking into the blank screen of the television, he saw the dim outline of his reflected image. He strained to see his face, but nothing was clear. He was home and he was safe. He had a wife and family, but he had no sense of his future. Drew sat there and studied the image.

After a few minutes, there was a knock on the door. Drew got up from the sofa, opened the door, and saw Mrs. Collier. She was balancing a large covered dish in one hand and carrying a bag in her other hand.

"Mrs. Collier," Drew said. He took the large dish.

"I brought you some hot food," she said. She stepped inside, and they went to the kitchen. Drew put the dish on the table.

"Thank you," Drew said. A warm aroma rose from the plate. "It smells great. It smells almost like Thanksgiving."

"Turkey and stuffing," she said. "I decided it was time to meet your family."

"Whin went to the store," Drew said. "She won't be long. Do you want to see NuWhin? She's sleeping upstairs."

Mrs. Collier followed Drew to the hall and up the steps to the second floor. They walked past a large storage room, the bathroom, and into the bedroom. The curtains were yellow and decorated with small flowers. Against the wall, the dresser had a yellow covering that dropped orange tassels over the side. The rounded mirror behind it reflected the light. The bed was king size, and the smaller bed was next to it. Mrs. Collier looked at the fluffed pillows and the level flatness of the bedspread.

"The room's immaculate," she said.

"The whole house is," Drew said. "Whin works all day. She takes care of NuWhin and spends the rest of the time cleaning up after me."

"This is your new family," Mrs. Collier said. She walked to the bed and leaned forward. "This is NuWhin."

A blanket covered everything except the girl's face and small hands. Staring at the face, Mrs. Collier caught her breath. Breathing slowly now, she studied the facial features, the rounded chin and puffy cheeks, the soft curved lips, the high nose, and then the clear lines of the eyes.

"She's beautiful," Mrs. Collier whispered. She was smiling, a look of extreme happiness on her face. She reached down and gently traced her fingers over NuWhin's forehead, nose, and chin. Without taking her eyes of the girl, she straightened slowly. "This may sound strange to you, Drew. But I've seen this face before."

"This is your first visit. When could you have seen her?"

"When Shane was a baby, I memorized those facial features, and then I always dreamed what his baby would look like. The baby would look like NuWhin does now."

"Then you know?"

"I knew as soon as I saw her." She touched NuWhin's forehead, and the eyelids flicked open. "Look at the beautiful green color, almost identical to Shane's," she said in wonder. Mrs. Collier lowered her hand, and NuWhin reached up and curled her fingers around her thumb.

"I think she likes you."

"She's so precious," Mrs. Collier said. "I don't understand, Drew."

"What?" He stepped next to her.

"The baby," Mrs. Collier said. "You should have told us as soon as you got home."

"I know," Drew said. "I waited. I guess I was worried about May. I knew she would be hurt. I was even afraid to talk to Joyce."

"Of course," Mrs. Collier said. "May would be devastated. She's been waiting for Shane all these years. You were right to worry."

"It's no excuse," Drew said. "You and Mr. Collier had the right to know. I'm sorry."

"Oh, Drew, don't be sorry. Seeing Shane's baby, I can't explain how it feels. I just know it's something I've always dreamed of. And here she is. I can't believe it." Mrs. Collier smiled and gently placed NuWhin's hand on the blanket. "But how could this happen?"

"It's an impossible story," Drew said. "I don't know where to begin."

"Not now," Mrs. Collier said. She put both her hands over his. "When you first came to live with us, it was hard. You were so quiet. You had those nightmares. Wayne and I didn't know what to do. Then gradually you and Shane became like brothers. We took all those trips, and you began to laugh and talk. We began to see who you really were. Next to Shane, you were the best thing that ever happened to our family. That's what I want you to know." She squeezed her hands tighter over his. "In time, you can tell Wayne and me this impossible story."

"I will tell you," Drew said. "I want to tell you."

"When Shane is better, you both can tell us." Mrs. Collier walked to the bed. NuWhin was sleeping again. Shaking her head slowly, Mrs. Collier looked with amazement at the girl.

"I so much want to pick her up and hold her," she said. "But there will be time for that. I can't believe I'm not crying."

They walked out of the bedroom and down the steps. On the porch, Drew kissed Mrs. Collier on the cheek, and she walked to the car. Drew went back in the house. He sat on the sofa again and stared at the blank television screen.

When Whin returned home, they went to the kitchen, and Whin prepared some of the turkey. Whin occasionally looked at Drew while they were eating, but his head was down. He ate quietly, barely tasting the food. When they were finished, Whin cleaned up the plates and went upstairs.

Drew took the Sony recorder from his pocket and walked to the living room. Finding some cables in the cabinet, he connected the Sony to the full-sized cassette player/recorder on the shelf next to the TV. He put in a blank tape, pressed the record button, and began listening to the Sony tape.

Halfway through the copying, Whin came downstairs. She sat next to Drew on the sofa and looked for the picture on the TV. Then she saw the sound was coming from the Sony and laughed.

When there was some loud shouting on the tape, Whin stopped smiling and became very serious. The angry words became louder and changed to profanity. Whin shrugged her shoulders, not understanding what the shouting was about. Drew smiled at her confusion and told her not to worry. Whin lost interest in the loud noise and went back upstairs.

It was after seven o'clock when Drew finished copying the tape. He disconnected the cables and put the copied tape and Sony recorder in his pocket. Whin came down stairs and met him in the hall.

"I'm going to the hospital," he said.

"To see Shane?"

"Yes," Drew said.

"I would see him soon," she said. "I would see him with NuWhin."

"Maybe tomorrow," Drew said. "He's not awake yet." Drew tried to explain about the long sleep, but Whin didn't understand.

"I want to go," she said.

"OK," Drew said. "We'll go soon." He kissed her on the cheek and walked to the door.

Drew drove across town with the windows down. Clouds filled the sky, and there were dark shadows around Valley Forge High School and the buildings of the veterans hospital next to it. Caught in the wind and the bright glow of the spotlight, the large American flag at the hospital fluttered boldly in the night sky. Drew turned into the entrance of the veteran's hospital and parked in an empty space near the emergency exit. He saw Jackson waiting there. There was another man standing behind him in the doorway. Drew got out of the car and walked toward Jackson.

"How are you, Jackson?" Drew asked.

"I'm fine," Jackson said.

"How's Shane?"

"No different," Jackson said. "There are some people with him now. A big black man and a beautiful woman. I think she's Shane's girlfriend. I've seen her here before."

"The black man's a good friend," Drew said. "The woman is May. She and Shane have been together a long time."

The man stepped out of the doorway. He was tall, middle-aged, maybe six foot four inches, and had a muscular body. His hair was military short, and he was clean shaven. Drew saw a broken line of scars on the side of his face and forehead. There was a cold hardness in his face, his clear eyes staring into Drew. He reached out his hand.

"I'm Jake," he said. His grip was strong. Drew could feel the scar tissue on his hand. "I'm Jackson's friend. I was shot up pretty bad, and they sent me here."

"That was in 1950," Jackson said. "Jake was my roommate for two weeks. Those were two weeks I'll never forget."

"You look fully recovered," Drew said. "What happened?"

"It was like your friend Shane," Jackson said. "Jake was out of it. He didn't talk, didn't move, didn't do nothing."

"You were in a coma?" Drew asked.

"Yes," Jake said. "One moment I was on a snow-covered hill in Korea. I know it was night and freezing cold. There was a group of us on the perimeter. Then we heard the booming sounds in the distance, and shells began exploding around us."

Jake was quiet for a moment. His eyes looked beyond Drew at the large Sherman tank at the entrance to the hospital. The wind had subsided, and everything was quiet. The flags, furled against the silver poles, drooped motionless in the night air.

"One of the shells hit next to me. Right where my buddies were. That's all I remember."

"They brought Jake here to Valley Forge," Jackson said. "Like I said, we were in the same room. His hands and face were bandaged. They fed him through a tube."

"I don't remember any of that," Jake said.

"One morning the nurses came and took the bandages off," Jackson said. "In a few days, the redness left his face, and I could see the scars. Different doctors came in and studied him. They asked each other questions, and one of them would write notes on his clipboard. I don't know why, but then they stopped coming. Only the nurses came in. They took Jake to some kind of physical therapy two times a day. They fed Jake and cleaned him."

The front door to the building opened, and Drew watched May walk to her car. She started the engine and pulled slowly out of the parking lot. When she was gone, Jackson nudged Drew in the shoulder.

"That last week Jake was dead to the world," Jackson said. "Then everything suddenly changed. I remember that day like it was right now. I had Swiss steak and mashed potatoes for lunch. I was enjoying the steak and listening to the World Series on the radio. I love baseball. The Phillies and the Yankees were playing at Connie Mack Stadium. I hate the Yankees."

"I love the Yankees," Jake said.

"Well, I hate 'em," Jackson said. "I was rooting for the Phillies, the Whiz Kids. Robin Roberts was pitching a great game for the Phillies. It was all tied 1-1 in the ninth. In the tenth when Joe DiMaggio came up to the plate and hit a leadoff home run, I went ballistic. Maybe I did overreact to all the loud cheering on the radio when Joe was running the bases. The volume was turned up high, and the noise filled the room. I just couldn't take it." Jackson was quiet. He put his head down and looked at his feet.

"What'd you do?" Drew asked.

"I picked up the radio and threw it across the room," Jackson said. "The noise and cheering got louder when it flew over Jake's head. It sounded like a big jet plane was crashing in the room." Jackson looked at the puzzled expression on Drew's face. "Let me explain why that was," Jackson said. "The radio had a long extension cord so I could take it in the bathroom."

"I understand," Drew said. "But what about Jake's coma?"

"That's what I'm getting to," Jackson said. "The radio hit the wall and exploded with a loud bang, like a bomb or something, and pieces of plastic and radio flew all over Jake. Of course, the cheering and noise stopped, and everything in the room became really still. Out of the corner of my eye, I saw Jake sit up. He scraped away the plastic and radio parts and stared at me for a second.

"Who the hell are you?" he asked me. Then he removed those tubes from his arm like he knew what he was doing and got out of bed. He walked, well he couldn't really walk. He kind of stumbled to the window and stood there, legs still shaking, looking at the bright sunshine outside. The flap of his dressing gown was open, and there were these brown stains everywhere. It was the ugliest thing I ever saw. I panicked and began shouting for the nurse. She came running in; then some doctors came in with all kinds of instruments."

"And you don't remember anything?" Drew asked.

"The only thing I remember was the loud crash from the radio. I sat up right away and opened my eyes. I saw Jackson. That's when I got scared, and that's when I shit myself. It felt good."

"Smelt bad," Jackson said. He was laughing.

"The doctors gave me all these tests," Jake said. "Then we had a big meeting in the director's office, and they told me I was perfectly healthy. I was discharged in a week."

"And everything's all right now?" Drew asked.

"Except for the scars on my face and hands, I'm fine. My wife and I live in Collegeville. We have three kids, one already married."

"That's great," Drew said.

"See," Jackson said, "Shane will be fine. It takes time for the body to work things out."

"I was just up there," Jake said. "Shane looks better than I did when I was here." Jake nodded to Jackson. "I should be going home. The grandkids are coming tonight." He reached out and shook Drew's hand. "I hope your friend gets better soon."

"Thanks," Drew said. He watched Jackson follow Jake around the corner of the building. Then Drew stepped through the doorway and started climbing the steps to the fourth floor. The corridor was empty when Drew approached Shane's room.

Homer had his back to the door, looking out the window. The glow of lights from Valley Forge High School outlined his large frame. The only other light was from the front of the bed. Under it, Shane was motionless, straight as a board, staring at the ceiling.

"Homer," Drew said. He walked in the room. Homer met him by the bed, and they shook hands.

"I've been waiting for you," Homer said. "Boy, do we have some problems. Here, make yourself comfortable." They sat down in the two chairs facing the bed. Drew could smell the perfume.

"I saw May leave."

"She sat here since school was out," Homer said. "There hasn't been any change in Shane. The doctors don't know anything."

There was a vase with red roses on the bed table. Some pictures were arranged around the vase. The large one was Shane's senior football picture. There was the family picture and the group boardwalk picture at Wildwood.

"The Colliers were here," Homer said. "They brought the pictures. Mr. Collier was very serious, sad-looking the whole time, but Mrs. Collier was more relaxed. She was sure that everything would be all right. May went out of the room for a few minutes. When she returned, Mrs. Collier seemed to get quiet. I don't know what was going on."

Drew glanced at the picture again. Shane's face was pressed close to May's. They were laughing, their tanned faces handsome in the bright light. Shane's green eyes sparkled with youth and life.

"I just talked to a veteran who was here in 1950. He was wounded in the Korean War. He was in a coma like Shane. He walked out of here perfectly healthy after two months."

"That's good to hear," Homer said. He opened his briefcase and took out some papers. "But let's talk about some other problems. There's an emergency board meeting tomorrow afternoon."

"About me," Drew said.

"All about you and how you tried to kill those students in Valley Forge today," Homer said. He sat back in his chair. "You locked two boys, both football stars, and two girls, one the school attorney's daughter, in a log cabin for three hours?"

"More like three and a half hours," Drew said. "They went in right around lunch time. It was close to three thirty when the park police broke the lock and saved them."

"Drew Benson is guilty of severe negligence that put our young students in a life-threatening situation," Homer said, reading from the paper. "The outside temperature was eighty-seven degrees and over one hundred in the cabin. The students were exhausted, dehydrated, and barely alive when they got out."

"All true," Drew said. "I hope they also got some of that mucus-eye disease."

"You're taking this very calmly," Homer said. "I know some substitute teachers who would be really worried. I mean scared about losing everything."

"You forget, Homer. A short time ago I was being shot at. This is nothing like it was in Nam."

"I guess not," Homer said. "But this is happening now. Do you have any kind of insurance?"

"No," Drew said. "I didn't have time to get any applications. I'm not even in the teacher's union."

"I hear the parents plan to sue you and the school. The school is covered by insurance. Do you have any resources at all?"

"I have most of my parent's insurance money," Drew said. "I used some of it in Vietnam, but most of it is in the bank."

"They can go after it," Homer said. "They have a strong case."

"It's not as strong as they think."

"It looks pretty strong to me," Homer said. He put the papers back in the briefcase. "They have their witnesses all lined up and ready to go. The board will listen to the students, the park police, the doctors."

"And the board members can also listen to this," Drew said. He took the tape and the Sony recorder from his pocket. "The students weren't exhausted because of the heat. They created their own heat. They were doing drugs and had one big orgy in that log cabin. And I have it all on this tape."

"How did you manage that?" Homer asked, sitting back in the chair.

"I've been taping things for Shane," Drew said. "I wanted him to hear everything that we did together. Maybe if he remembered things from the past, he could recover from the coma more quickly. That's why I had the recorder with me in the park. After I locked the students in the cabin, I left it in one of those cracks in the logs. It recorded everything the students said."

"Have you listened to it?" Homer asked.

"Yes," Drew said. "These kids are crazy. I'll put in the tape. You and I . . ." Drew hesitated and looked over at the bed. "You and I and Shane can listen to it."

Drew put the Sony on the table next to the pictures and plugged it in the wall outlet. He put the tape into the recorder. He turned up the volume, and the Sony made a humming noise.

"The recorder's that small?" Homer asked.

Drew nodded his head. The humming noise stopped, and there was a static sound. Then Leroy's voice broke the static with a loud expletive. Laughter echoed from the speaker and filled the hospital room. The loud music of *Bad, Bad Leroy Brown* drowned out the laughter.

Drew walked over and shut the door. Then he sat down on the chair. It was after nine o'clock when the Sony clicked to a stop. Drew reached over and hit the rewind button. Shaking his head, Homer sat back and rested his chin in the palm of his hand.

"These kids are rotten," he said. "I never would have believed it."

"Speaking in their own unique Valley Forge vocabulary," Drew said. "I'm a fuckin' killer."

"Yes, but Principal West is a stupid face-fuck, whatever that is."

"I think they meant it as a compliment," Drew said.

"I came out pretty good," Homer said. "I'm only a black-faced nigger."

"The best kind," Drew laughed. "But what about Sally's father? According to her, he's a moronic asswipe. She takes his money, his whiskey, his dope, and he's nothing but an asswipe."

"When he hears this, he might just wake up and give her a big kick in the ass," Homer said. "I need the tape, Drew. I want to play it at the board meeting. And that stuff they talk about on the turnpike will be very interesting to Sheriff Hess."

"Here's a copy I made," Drew said. "It's on a standard cassette."

"The board members, especially Mr. Wentworth, are going to be shocked." Homer took the cassette and put it in his briefcase.

"How about the choice words they had for the principal's son. Frank Jr. was a superficial bastard of a principal. I think they got that one right. At the park today, I couldn't believe my eyes. Frank Jr. was there teaching the kids about patriotism. Frank is a perfect model for patriotism. He took off for Canada and completely dodged the war."

"Don't worry, Drew," Homer said. "It's only temporary. Frank's taking courses in administration at West Chester so he can be the next principal." The phone on the table rang.

"I got it," Drew said. He picked it up, listened for a second, and handed it to Homer. "It's for you. I think it's your wife."

"Probably is," Homer said, reaching for the phone. "I told her I would be here." After a few minutes of listening to his wife, he replaced the phone on the table.

"Brandy took some food over to your family. She wants me over there right away."

"Go ahead," Drew said. "Whin will be happy to meet you. I'll be right over." Drew watched Homer walk to the door. "And Homer . . ."

"Yes." Homer turned and faced him

"There's something else," Drew said. "When you see NuWhin, I don't want you to be surprised or anything. Mrs. Collier was really surprised."

"Why?" Homer asked. "What's wrong?"

"Nothing's wrong with NuWhin. She's beautiful. Mrs. Collier saw that. She knew right away that NuWhin isn't my daughter. NuWhin is Shane's daughter."

"Say that again," Homer said.

"Just go over to the house and look into NuWhin's eyes. You'll understand everything."

"OK," Homer said. He gave Drew a long, hard stare. "Everything's really getting complicated. You'll be over soon?"

"In a few minutes," Drew said.

"OK," Homer said. "I'll see you at the house." He lifted his hand in a good-bye gesture and walked into the hall.

Drew waited a few seconds and sat down in the chair. A horn sounded from the street, and then everything was quiet. Drew reached for the remote, turned on the TV, and scanned through the channels. The characters of *M*A*S*H* appeared on the screen, and Drew began watching the team of doctors in the operating tent. There was much talking and joking and even laughter during the surgery, and soon the sheet over the wounded soldier was spotted with blood.

Drew kept turning his head from the TV to Shane's bed. He studied Shane's face. It reflected the light and shadows from the TV. When Hawkeye and Pierce were finished with the surgery, they walked out of the tent still laughing and joking. A helicopter lifted off the landing pad, and the line of credits appeared on the screen. Drew shut off the TV. He went to the bed, and lifting Shane's hands from the folds of the sheet, Drew lowered them carefully across his chest.

"The whole time I wasn't sure," Drew said, looking deep into the green eyes. "I knew I was going to Vietnam like we planned, but I wasn't sure why. At one time, I wanted to quit college and come over, but Joyce talked me into waiting until after graduation. She had all these plans for us." Drew sat down next to the bed.

"Then when I graduated from college, Joyce said we were losing the war. She said it would be over soon, and there was no reason to go. Of course, she was right. And I guess I didn't see any purpose in it." Drew was quiet for a moment. "But I went anyway. I promised you I would. It really hurt Joyce that I left her. But now, at least, I know why I had to go to Vietnam."

Drew heard the light whirring sound of the elevator. It stopped, and the doors opened. There was the sound of footsteps, and the hall lights dimmed. Drew listened as the elevator doors opened again, and the elevator descended. A man coughed from the room across the hall, and everything became perfectly still. The moon was full and filled the hospital room with a soft light. Staring into Shane's face, looking for any sign of recognition in the green eyes, Drew spoke quietly, a slight quiver in his lips.

"Today the purpose became very clear, Shane. It was at the house when your mother saw NuWhin. It was the happiest I've ever seen her, and everything began to make perfect sense to me. In her face, I could finally see the picture I was searching for. It's a beautiful picture, Shane."

Drew stood up slowly. There was a tightness in his back and legs. He waited by the bed for a few moments and then walked to the door. At the side exit, Jackson was sitting next to an open cooler. He was holding a bottle of Sam Adams in his hand.

"It's all I drink now," Jackson said. He was red-faced, and his eyes were glazed over. "You know, since that night." Jackson pointed to the cooler. "You look like you could use a drink."

"You're drunk, Jackson."

"Kind of drunk," Jackson said. "I'm like this three, four, sometimes five times a week. This Sam Adams is special to me. And it's all your fault, Drew Benson. You know that, don't you?"

"I know," Drew said. "I introduced you to Sam."

"You sure did." Jackson smiled and pointed to the cooler. "There are a few cold ones left. You look like you could use one."

"No thanks," Drew said. "It's late. I have to get to the house. I'll see you tomorrow." Drew shook Jackson's hand. He walked to the car and got inside. Drew drove across the empty parking lot, past the row of motionless flags at the entrance, and turning onto Charlestown Road, he lowered the window and let the cold night air fill his lungs.

CHAPTER 15

D rew saw a group of people on the porch when he parked the car in the driveway. Homer's wife, Brandy, sat with Whin on the swing. Brandy was holding NuWhin in her lap, and Drew could see the girl's bright face in the light. NuWhin jumped off Brandy's lap and came running to him. Drew scooped her in his arms. Homer was sitting in the chair next to Mrs. Jablonski. She got up, and using a wooden cane, she met Drew at the top of the steps.

"It's late," she said, kissing Drew on the side of his face. Then she kissed NuWhin. "I'm so happy for you. She's a beautiful girl."

Mrs. Jablonski walked down the steps and slowly made her way across the yard to her house. Carrying NuWhin, Drew walked to the swing and sat next to Brandy. There was silence for a moment. Then Brandy smiled at Drew.

"As soon as I saw NuWhin, I knew," Brandy said. "It was those sparkling green eyes. I'm surprised Mrs. Jablonski didn't notice them."

"I think she's color-blind," Drew said.

"She was so excited about your family," Brandy said. "She plans to take you all to church on Sunday."

"We could do that," Drew said. "Church would be good for all of us." Drew lowered NuWhin to the floor, and she walked over to her mother. Whin was listening to the conversation on Mrs. Jablonski and seemed confused

"What does this color-blind mean? Is it very bad to have?"

"It's not bad," Brandy said. "People can't see some colors."

"Oh," Whin said. "No color. Maybe that's good." She got up from the swing. "I should get NuWhin ready for bed."

"I'll help," Brandy said. She took NuWhin's hand, and they walked inside the house. Watching the door close, Drew stretched and cupped both hands behind his head.

"Soon everyone will know about the baby, Homer." Drew swung back and forth slowly on the swing. "Mrs. Collier seems perfectly fine with NuWhin. In fact, she's excited, but the news would destroy May. When Shane recovers, I don't know what will happen to their wedding plans. I think it was the only time he cheated on May. And Joyce, Joyce won't even look at me now."

"I have a feeling it'll work out," Homer said. "You're dealing with good people."

"They are good people," Drew said. "I don't know how we got to this point. At first, Shane didn't know anything about the baby. He was writing letters daily to May, and when I found out that Whin was pregnant, I tried to talk to him. But whenever we were together, Shane was making all these plans. He and May would be married at the Washington Memorial Chapel in the park. I would be best man, and you would be whatever the second man in line is called. Shane had it all worked out."

"That can still happen," Homer said. He laughed. "A fall wedding would be great, and I can certainly do whatever the second man in line does."

"They've waited so long," Drew said. "Shane and May deserve to have a happy life."

"You said Shane had no idea about NuWhin?"

"The circumstances were so strange even I didn't know," Drew said. "But when I met Whin that first time, she and the baby became very important to me. I decided to take care of them myself."

"I can't imagine how you did it," Homer said. "You should feel proud, fighting a war, taking care of a mother and baby, and getting them safely out of Saigon."

"It was a crazy time," Drew said. "Actually it was poor timing. I arrived in Saigon in July 1972. The airport was busy with departing soldiers. The army was leaving. The last American combat troops were scheduled to be out of Vietnam by August."

"You said you were transferred and worked at the American Embassy."

"They gave us embassy identification cards, and that's where we got our orders," Drew said. "We stayed three more years, pretty hopeless years."

"When did you meet Whin?"

"That was my second night in Saigon. I was settled in the barracks and was just wasting time. Shane called and told me to meet him at the base checkpoint. When I got there, Shane was waiting with a jeep. It was great seeing him after so long."

"Did he look OK? I mean did he look better than now?"

"He looked stronger," Drew said. "His face was more hardened, and when we drove into Saigon, his eyes were alert to everything around us. He said Saigon was like a free-fire zone. Other than that, the way he talked and laughed, even his expressions were the same as when he was here. Whatever the war could do to people, it didn't change Shane. At first I was kind of scared, but Shane drove through Saigon like it was Valley Forge."

As Drew thought about Saigon, he saw himself back in the jeep racing away from the checkpoint. There were paddy fields on both sides of the road, and the hot tropical air swirled around them. Drew was excited and had hundreds of questions, but Shane was busy weaving the jeep around farmers, water buffaloes, and children everywhere.

The rice paddies disappeared, and braking suddenly, Shane steered the jeep into a series of narrow, congested streets that didn't seem to have any laws governing the mass of traffic. Cars, busses, motorcycles, taxi tricycles, and standard two-wheel bicycles all maneuvered in and out of the pedestrian traffic. The sound of horns; the dark exhaust from the stalled vehicles in front of the jeep; the uniformed policemen, guns in clear view, standing on every corner; the sudden blare of rock music from a bar; the loud shouts from the people; and the dark stares on some of their faces combined to create a scene that was completely foreign to Drew. Casual and relaxed, Shane took the role of a tourist guide and pointed out some important landmarks.

After the twenty-minute drive through Saigon, Shane parked the jeep in front of a large six-story restaurant. It was crowded and noisy inside, and clouds of smoke rose above the tables packed with both foreigners and Vietnamese. A Chinese waiter took them to a back area that was separated from the main room by an elaborate folding wall screen. Painted the length of the screen, a large green dragon with flaming eyes and gaping mouth and rows of pearly teeth hovered in the sky above a green forest of bamboo and a blue lake.

Three of Shane's friends were already in the room. Mr. Abrams, Shane said he was from Coatesville, Pennsylvania, was a senior officer at the American Embassy, and the other two men were high-ranking officers in the South Vietnamese Army. Shane introduced Drew to Colonel Minh and Lieutenant Fhon, and they sat down at a round table that nearly filled the area.

On the table, there were crispy chips, dried thin noodles, and small dishes filled with red and brown sauces. There were also two bottles of Johnnie Walker Red spaced between the sauce dishes. Shane took a bottle and filled the shot glasses.

"To Drew," he said, standing up and raising his glass. "Welcome to Saigon."

"Bien venue, Saigon," Colonel Minh said.

They all stood up and drank the toast. The whiskey tasted bitter and harsh. Drew made a twisted face as it burned his throat. They drank another toast and then another to strange-sounding Vietnamese names. With the bad taste of the whiskey still in his throat and his face reddening, Drew blurted out the last toast.

"To Valley Forge," he shouted.

Everyone drank the toast and sat down. Drew dipped some of the chips in the red sauce, and as he ate them, the warmth in his mouth and throat turned to a burn, and he made a loud gagging noise. Shane and his friends began to laugh. Drew drank some more Johnnie Walker, and the burn intensified, moving in a lava flow into his stomach. Trying to release the heat, Drew patted his shirt up and down. Watching his discomfort through an opening in the screen, the waiter hurried in with some kind of paste and seltzer water, and it brought a soothing sensation to his mouth and throat.

Then two new waiters came to the table and placed a dish in front of everyone. The dish had an ornate silver cup on it, and in the cup was what looked like a hard-boiled egg. Shane gave Drew a little knife and told him to crack the shell. Everyone was watching Drew. He smiled and hit the shell. A slight crack appeared. Drew hit the shell harder, enlarging the crack, and something white and feathery burst through the crack.

"What's under there?" Drew asked.

"Don't worry," Shane said. "Hit it like you mean it."

"Fine," Drew said. On his next attempt, Drew smashed into the egg, and the top half of the shell cracked open and fell in splinters to the table. Drew stared in amazement as the small head and yellow beak appeared. Resting on top of the tangled mass of wet, silky feathers, the chicken embryo was whole and intact.

"It's grotesque," Drew said, barely moving his lips.

Shane leaned over and told him quietly that it was important to eat the local food, or the hosts would be insulted. Drew looked at the Vietnamese officers who were digging into the egg. Shane also advised Drew to eat the embryo in one gulp. He said it actually felt good when the feathers tickled the throat on the way down.

"Watch me," Shane said. He lifted the embryo by the neck, little feet dangling out of the shell. He put it in his mouth and swallowed it whole.

"OK," Drew said. Closing his eyes, he lifted the silver cup to his lips and sucked the chicken embryo into his mouth. To his surprise, there was a tickling sensation in his throat, and he burped. Drew quickly drank some Johnnie Walker, and the burning liquid washed the tickles from his throat.

"The chicken thief soldier," Drew said.

"What are you mumbling about?" Shane asked.

"I ate the baby chicken, so that makes me the chicken thief soldier." Drew laughed. His head was spinning now, and he took another drink. When he slammed the empty glass on the table, the Vietnamese officers gave him a satisfied look of approval.

"The small shell of the chicken is like our country," Colonel Minh said. "First the French, now you Americans and Chinese devour us for your own purpose." The colonel was serious for a moment, staring at the faces around the table, and then he laughed and lifted his glass in the air. The others filled their glasses, and holding them up, they waited.

"To the new Vietnam!" he shouted.

"To the new Vietnam!" they all repeated and drank the whiskey. Drew coughed again as the whiskey gagged in his throat. He leaned over and whispered to Shane.

"This whiskey tastes like shit."

"It's not real Johnnie Walker," Shane said. "It's local brewed rice whiskey. They put it in the fancy bottles to impress us."

"Great," Drew said.

"Don't worry," Shane said. "It's safe. No organism of any kind could survive in that mix."

"I feel much better," Drew said.

The waiter brought more appetizers to the table. As they ate, Mr. Abrams talked about the last American soldiers being pulled out of Vietnam after fifteen years of war. Shane sounded bitter and talked about the American actress going to Hanoi last month and posing in a NVA military uniform. In the government building just blocks away from the Hanoi Hilton, she praised the defenders of North Vietnam.

Colonel Minh talked about how the North Vietnamese Prime Minister congratulated the actress and all the American demonstrators for their help in bringing peace. The colonel signaled to the Americans at the table, and he lifted his glass again.

"Nixon promised us peace with honor." Colonel Minh and the lieutenant gulped down the whiskey. His face was flushed when he spoke again. "But we have lost the war. There is no honor in Vietnam." Holding his empty glass, he looked directly at Drew and Shane and spoke in a loud voice.

"I am convinced you Americans will never win another war because you don't fight to win. You are the strongest country in the world, but your people and politicians back home give up and quit when things get tough." Placing the glass on the table, the colonel hesitated and began talking again in a low voice.

"You drank a toast to Valley Forge, Mr. Benson. I know Valley Forge. I visited there when I attended St. Joseph University. You Americans fought hard to be free, and now you are two hundred years a country. But you have changed and got weaker. You don't fight like that any more."

"The colonel is right," Lieutenant Fhon said. "Your political people are worthless. The stupid donkey and fat elephant. They are so weak and self serving. And they fight each other and can't see the real enemy. The Chinese dragon is expanding out of control, and it is ravenous. I am sure it will devour both the donkey and the elephant."

Mr. Abrams was about to say something in response, but instead of speaking, he sat back quietly in his chair. After a moment, Mr. Abrams leaned forward and mentioned about the break-in at the Watergate offices in Washington last month. He seemed to think the Nixon White House was in trouble. Abrams said that Vietnam and probably all of Southeast Asia would soon be forgotten by the press.

"We are already forgotten," Colonel Minh said. He filled the glasses and spoke in a sincere voice. "Except for you, our true friends. You stay with us until the end." He offered a toast to Abrams, Shane, and Drew.

When the toasts and appetizers were finished, the waiters brought a large plate and placed it on a revolving center platform. There was a gleaming silver cover over the plate. Drew could clearly see his face reflected on the silver surface. The waiter lifted the cover, and Drew's face disappeared in a thick explosion of steam.

When the cloud of steam dissolved, Drew saw the massive body of a duck on the plate. There were two glassy eyes in the duck's head, and the elongated orange beak was punctured by two deep, black nostrils. At the posterior end of the duck, a row of yellow and red feathers shaped in the form of a fan camouflaged the plucked skin of the duck's ass.

"Peking Duck," Colonel Minh said. "This is good. We should all start eating Chinese food."

There was a pause, and they all laughed at the remark. Drew hesitated, slowly beginning to understand, and he laughed, too. The waiters placed dishes, utensils, and clean napkins in front of them. They also placed chopsticks next to the dishes. They were ivory and beautifully carved with delicate pink-colored roses. Drew picked up the chopsticks and fumbled them in his fingers. Shane reached across, knocked them out of his hands, and gave Drew a fork.

"Thank you," Drew said, holding the fork in a ready position.

Mr. Abrams rotated the centerpiece, and Drew was glad to see the nostrils and beady eyes spin away from his face. When the centerpiece stopped, Abrams and the Vietnamese officers slid their chopsticks into the duck and adroitly lifted out steaming pieces of meat. Drew watched Shane clumsily stab his fork into the duck's side. It came back empty.

"Damn, I am drunk," Shane said and tried again. It was still empty. Shaking his head, Shane grabbed the duck's leg, ripped it off, and placed it on his plate.

"Good idea," Drew said. He reached out and grabbed the other leg. Lifting it to his mouth, he took a big bite out of the side. The steam rising in the air was strong and sweet. Chewing on the meat, Drew looked at Shane, who tried to smile with his mouth stuffed with a whole leg of duck. A line of juice dripped over his lower lip.

Drew finished his leg, and as the centerpiece of duck was rotated in front of him, he managed to fork out thick pieces of white meat from the ribcage. Everyone worked hard at removing the remaining meat around and inside the stomach cavity.

After thirty minutes, all the eatable portions of the duck were gone. The duck's arched skeleton, the orange, curved beak, and the five drooping feathers on the tail rotated slowly around the table. Feeling bloated and almost sober, Drew leaned forward and burped loudly into the empty ribcage.

Waiters appeared from two different directions and began removing the dishes and utensils. Shane talked briefly to the headwaiter who immediately left the room. When another waiter reached for the plate holding the duck remains, Shane told him to leave it there. The waiter looked at the orange beak and feathers and the empty rib cavity. He shrugged his shoulders and left the room. The headwaiter returned and put two unopened bottles of Johnnie Walker Red on the table next to Shane. Shane thanked him, opened one of the bottles, and filled everyone's glass.

"We will play a game before we go," Shane said, putting the bottle down

"What is it?" Abrams asked.

"It's similar to Russian Roulette," Shane said.

"Like in the *Deer Hunter*?' Drew asked.

"What are you talking about?"

"The movie, the *Deer Hunter*," Drew repeated. "Robert DeNiro played Russian Roulette with the Vietnamese. It was a fun game if you won. But the loser got his head blown off."

"Don't worry, Drew," Shane said. "There's no danger to this game. It's called Duck Roulette."

Colonel Minh had a confused expression on his face and said something in Vietnamese. Lieutenant Fhon also looked confused. Sitting back in his chair, Shane had a smile on his face.

"Duck Roulette is to honor my friend, Drew. I want him to always remember his first night in Saigon."

"Thanks, Shane, but I'm fine. I've drunk all this fake Johnnie Walker. I ate a baby chicken and a big Chinese duck. I think I'm done."

"You're almost done," Shane said. "The meal was the first part of your night. Duck Roulette is the second part."

"How many parts are there?" Drew asked.

"Only three parts," Shane said. "The best part is last. We'll get to that later. Now, let me explain the rules of Duck Roulette."

Shane reached his hand across the table and straightened the drooping duck's head so that the orange beak and deep-set eyes looked right over the edge of the plate. Licking the juice off his fingers, Shane smiled and leaned back in his chair.

"Now," Shane said. "Listen carefully. I will spin the plate, and where it stops is the most important thing." Shane spoke more slowly and clearly annunciated each word. "If the duck's beak is pointed to you, you have to make a toast and drink your glass. If the duck's ass is pointed to you, you have to drink two glasses. It's that simple."

"That simple?" Drew asked

"Yes," Shane said. "Just remember the rule. No one can drink until the duck's head or ass points at him." Before anyone could respond, Shane reached over and grabbed the side of the platform. With a twist of his hand, he sent the plate revolving in a tight circle.

Drew watched the spinning duck, a blur of orange beak and flying feathers, go by again and again. The plate slowed, the head slid past him, and stopped directly opposite him in front of Colonel Minh. The feathers of the duck's ass spread perfectly fan-shaped in front of Drew.

"To my American friends. May you have long and healthy lives," the officer stated and lifted his glass. They all clapped hands when he drank the whiskey. Their faces turned to Drew.

"Do I make a toast?" Drew asked, lifting his glass.

"No, just drink two shots," Shane said. He readied the bottle, and when Drew had drained the first glass, he filled it again. Drew gulped the whiskey down. Only on his second drink did he notice that the aroma was stronger, and the whiskey was smooth and velvety in his throat.

"It's different," Drew said. "It's much better. Is this what happens after you drink a bottle? Everything begins to taste great."

"No," Shane said. "This is real Johnnie Walker, only the best for your arrival." Shane spun the plate again. When it stopped, the orange beak pointed to the wall, but it was closest to Shane.

"To my best friend. Welcome to Saigon," Shane said, lifting his glass to Drew. Everyone stood up and clapped this time. Lieutenant Fhon shouted something in French. Drew thought it sounded like salute.

After they had taken turns giving toasts to each other, they began naming famous figures and events. The colonel toasted President Diem, who was the first president of the Republic of Vietnam and was assassinated. Abrams toasted President Kennedy, who was the thirty-fifth president of the United States and was also assassinated, and Drew toasted Baron von Steuben who died at an old age in the Mohawk Valley.

They toasted the battles of Khe Sanh, and more soberly, the horrific battle of La Drang Valley. On one controversial duck spin, the head stopped evenly between Drew and Shane. Drew leaned away from the pointed beak and fell off his chair. Trying to get up, he cracked his head on the edge of the table. Finally climbing back in his chair, he looked at Shane for help. Taking his glass, Shane got slowly to his feet and toasted the POWs.

When Abrams was hit by the duck, he toasted the big Tet offensive as a victory for the United States and the South and said more than ten thousand North Vietnamese Regulars and Vietcong were killed.

"That's more soldiers than we had left at Valley Forge," Drew said, wandering why he was talking.

"What?' Abrams asked.

"Nothing."

Abrams added that Tet was the worst defeat of the war for the North Vietnamese. There was a side discussion how the American press focused most of their coverage on the few Vietcong soldiers killed at the American Embassy. Colonel Minh said the reporters were blind behind their TV cameras and didn't know what victory was.

"And Eddie didn't help much at all," Mr. Abrams said. "His picture was on the front page of every newspaper."

"Who's Eddie?" Drew asked.

"AP photographer," Mr. Abrams said. "I met him a few times. He took the picture of the Saigon police chief putting a bullet in the head of a Vietcong murderer."

"I remember it," Drew said. "The man was standing there, a prisoner. He was unarmed."

"He was a VC," Shane said. "You didn't see any pictures in the Hanoi press of their unarmed executions. South Vietnamese government officials, their families, teachers, and priests were all murdered by the VC before Tet even began."

"The Police chief was a good man," Colonel Minh said, "He was just doing his job. Enough of that Tet talk. Let's get back to roulette. I like this game." Reaching out, he spun the duck with a strong twist of his hand.

Drew had a difficult time finding the duck on the table. The hollow black eyes and orange beak were rotating too fast for him to focus, and twisting his head with each circular rotation, he became dizzy. He was sure the Peking duck had flown off.

Drew blinked both eyes shut, and looking upward he found the duck spinning even faster on the blades of the ceiling fan. The duck wings sliced through the air and seemed to be descending closer to his head. Drew shuddered and looked quickly back at the table. When the duck finally landed and slowed to a stop, the beak was pointing directly at Shane. Shane raised his glass and toasted Dien Bien Phu. Then he shouted, "Dien Bien Phuey" and everyone laughed.

The Duck Roulette continued without a pause, and the shouting and laughter at the table became louder. By the time the two bottles were empty, Drew had taken seven shots. Somehow, one of the duck's red feathers was stuck behind his ear. Perspiration streaming down his face, he was warm all over, and his arms hung loosely at his side. Only with great effort and concentration could he place his empty glass on the table. Shane had taken more drinks, and he was in worse shape. Colonel Minh's left eye was shut tightly, and he had a grim smile on his face.

Holding the table for support, Shane stood up, balanced himself, and clapped his hands loudly. When nothing happened, he shouted something and clapped his hands again. Music started up from somewhere, and the middle of the folding screen pulled open, splitting the green dragon into two sections.

Blinking his eyes and wiping the perspiration from his face, Drew leaned forward and tried to understand what had happened. Then his mouth dropped open as he saw the most beautiful girls in the world dance through what looked like the gaping hole of the dragon's stomach.

There were five of them, and their feet seemed to float on the floor as they walked in a line of bright color and soft music. Circling the table slowly, each girl moved out of the line and stood next to her client. The girl who stopped next to Drew was dressed in pink and smelled of honey and was perfectly formed from head to foot. She slid her hand along the side of Drew's head and adjusted the feather so it stood straight in the air.

Drew heard a soft voice singing a French song and looked up. Through the haze of rising smoke and misty stupor, he saw Whin for the first time. She was at the end of the line. Dressed in a glistening yellow silk dress, she was regal in her movements. Her facial features were part Asian and part European, and she was a strikingly beautiful woman.

Drew watched her stop next to Shane and take his hand. Oblivious to the attention, Shane lifted his head and smiled. The manager came into the room and half ushered, half pushed the couples to a side staircase.

When he was stumbling up the staircase to the top floor, Drew began to realize the restaurant served more than food. It also served beautiful women to the patrons. Drew laughed at his discovery and playfully pinched his girl in the pink, silky buttocks. Removing his hand and shaking her finger at him, she ushered Drew into a room that was filled with elegant furniture. The tables held sweet-smelling burning candles and bowls filled with tropical flowers and fruit. One table had a bottle of champagne protruding from an ice bucket. The bed was the centerpiece of the room. It was huge, and the silk sheets were neatly folded open.

Drew's head was spinning when he fell back and his body sank into the mattress. Trying to lift his head, he became aware of the feather sliding over his right eye. Picking it up carefully, he placed it in the center of the pillow. There was a mirror on the ceiling, and Drew laughed when he recognized his clothes and the pale features of his face.

Struggling to sit up, Drew saw a large poster of a monument on the opposite wall. The stone walls and rectangular shape resembled the Memorial Arch at Valley Forge. Then he saw the words Arc de Triomphe written down the side of the poster. There was something strange on the top of the monument, and looking closer, Drew saw a huge white phallic symbol that pierced the blue sky.

"Bien Venue, Saigon," Drew read the words on the bottom.

The girl began pulling off his pants. Because of his clumsy movements, she had some difficulty in helping him undress. But after she unrolled his last sock, she dropped her pink dress to the floor and led him to the washroom. There Drew could only balance himself against the wall while she poured bowls of rainwater over his head. Pulling a towel from the rack, she began to gently rub the wetness from his body, putting soft pressure on his groin area and testicles. Even through his drunken stupor, Drew could sense the strong growing arousal.

The girl was expert and meticulous in the bathing and grooming. She was opening a condom wrapper when she led Drew back to the bedroom. Drew sat down on the edge of the bed, and she handed him a glass of champagne. He tasted it, the bubbles breaking on his nose, and as she touched and massaged his body, inducing a tremendous pressure of heat and pleasure, Drew drank the champagne quickly, too quickly.

Inexplicably, the room spun away from him, and he knew he was falling backward. He struggled, but he couldn't stop the fall. His eyes momentarily opened, and he saw two nude figures in the mirror above the bed. Bouncing off the mattress, he reached out his hand for the smaller figure with perfectly formed breasts. His hand closed harmlessly in midair. Drew became incredibly dizzy, and then there was complete darkness and quiet.

Drew woke up the next day at noon, not remembering anything that had happened. He searched for his escort, but the room was empty. Getting dressed, he saw the red feather on the pillow and laughed. As he walked to the door, he looked at the poster on the wall.

"Bien Venue, Saigon." Drew read the words.

Gliding back and forth on the swing, Drew watched the words disappear in the glow of the porch light. It was late, and there was no traffic on the street.

"That's how Shane and Whin met," Drew said. He looked at Homer. "Shane planned this great night for my benefit, and he got really drunk. We both got really drunk."

"A wild night," Homer said.

"A really wild night," Drew said. "It was a great time, except Whin got pregnant. I didn't know until months later. Lieutenant Fhon showed up one night and gave me a note from the manager of the restaurant. The manager wanted to talk to Shane and me. Shane was in Thailand for a few days so I went over there with the lieutenant. We found the manager in his office. He was friendly and easy to talk to. He just said there would be expenses if we wanted to keep the baby."

"Even though the father wasn't present, you decided for him."

"Yes," Drew said. "I said we wanted the baby. I gave the manager all the money I had and promised him more. I talked with Whin a lot that month, and she began to trust me. After, I don't know how many conversations, I convinced her to get out of the restaurant business. I gave the manager an additional three-month's salary so she could leave. Whin moved in with a relative."

"What about Shane?"

"Shane didn't know anything. He was too busy. We were losing the war, and he hated the thought of leaving his Vietnamese friends. I found out that he was getting the officers transferred to Udorn, this huge American base in Northeast Thailand. Then Shane began helping fly the families over. He got identity papers and passports from the black market. It was dangerous, and when I asked him about it, he said he didn't want me involved."

"Sounds illegal to me," Homer said.

"It was illegal," Drew said. "It was probably more illegal than shooting monster buck in Valley Forge Park."

"I knew I was teaching you boys the right things," Homer laughed. "I don't know about breaking laws, but Shane always did what he could to help. He thought so much about the people around him." There was noise in the kitchen, and Homer paused for a moment. Then he began talking in a serious voice.

"I saw some of the news coverage. Some of the scenes were really bloody. It's amazing you got out at all."

"There were a couple really bad times when I was stuck in the jungle with the rain and heat and bugs and jungle rot, and do you know what I thought about, Homer?"

"No idea at all."

"That night you took us to Valley Forge," Drew said. "I thought about the ice and the cold. I hated the mosquitoes the most and I pictured them freezing and their wings turning brittle and breaking off. I felt better then."

"I knew there would be some benefit from that trip," Homer said. There was some laughter inside the house, and listening to Brandy and Whin, Homer was silent for a moment. Then he looked up at Drew. "I still can't get over the baby."

"I don't know how Shane found out he had a daughter, but one day I saw an envelope with Whin's name on it in my locker. The envelope was filled with money. There was one in my locker every month after that."

"You never talked to him about her?"

"Only once," Drew said. "He said something one night in the jungle. After that, Shane never talked about it again." A car passed the house, and Drew followed the lights until they disappeared around the corner.

"It'll all work out," Homer said. "And tomorrow at the school, we'll deal with Principal West, his attorney, and the board. That audio tape should get their attention." Homer was quiet for a moment and then looked at Drew.

"There's something else you should know."

"What?"

"Do you remember the night in the park when you beat up the poacher?"

"Sure," Drew said. "I'll never forget that."

"We know who the poacher is," Homer said. "He's been seen roaming around Valley Forge, and he carries a rifle all the time. Mr. Wentworth warned all the school personnel to be alert. Tony says if he ever sees him on school property, he'll fix it so he'll never come near the school again. But no one can catch the guy. He just disappears."

"What's the poacher want?"

"Mr. Wentworth thinks he's looking for the kid who beat him up," Homer said. "He's looking for you."

"That happened so long ago."

"I know," Homer said. "But with that rifle, he's dangerous. So be on the lookout for him." The screen door opened, and Brandy and Whin came out.

"Let's go home," Brandy said, motioning for Homer to get out of the chair. "You have to work tomorrow."

"She's right," Homer said. "It's going to be a busy day."

"Good night," Brandy said. She kissed Whin on the cheek. Then she kissed Drew, and she and Homer walked down the steps. Drew waved to them as they got in the car. He watched the taillights turn the corner, and then he turned to Whin.

"I'm going out for a while," he said. "I won't be long."

"Be careful," she said. She always said that at night. Drew held her hand for a moment, and then he went into the kitchen. Opening the refrigerator, he took out a six-pack of Sam Adams. On the way out of the house, he waved the six-pack at Whin standing on the porch.

Drew walked to the car and put the cold bottles on the front seat. He drove into town and got a bucket of crispy chicken at the KFC drive-thru. The bucket was hot, and Drew placed it on the floor. Then he drove toward the park.

CHAPTER 16

D rew reached Valley Forge National Park in a few minutes. He drove past Washington Headquarters, past the log cabins on the top of the hill, and turned into the parking lot next to General Varnum's Headquarters. The moon was a bright circle in the cloudless sky, and it was cold.

Drew grabbed the six-pack and bucket of chicken, and as he walked toward General von Steuben, the cold air filled his lungs and chilled his body. Stopping under the towering black statue, Drew opened a Sam Adams, took a drink, and bottle in hand, he saluted the baron like Homer used to do.

Drew finished the drink and sat on the wooden bench behind the general. Following the unbroken gaze of the baron, Drew looked at the wide expanse of the parade ground in front of him. There was the shadowy movement of the deer, and far in the distance, Drew saw the curved outline of the Memorial Arch.

Opening another Sam Adams, Drew took a long drink. Then placing the KFC bucket in his lap, he peeled open the cover and pulled out a chicken leg. Drew took a bite. He took another bite and tried to swallow the meat, but it caught in his throat and he coughed loudly.

Drew drank more of the Sam Adams. Even though the air was cold and crisp, Drew began to feel the oppression of the tropical heat. His chest heaved as the thick, moist air filled his lungs. Thinking about the last mission and the village in the jungle, Drew sat back against the hard contours of the bench.

Drew remembered everything that happened during those three days. There was the thick jungle mist, the incessant rain, and the hunger that paralyzed his body, but it was the searing pain in his stomach that brought everything into sharp focus. Through the mist, he saw the village as if it were there in front of him on the parade ground. And standing alone in the village yard was the lost, forlorn figure of the chicken thief soldier.

It was the monsoon season. All air traffic had been grounded for two days by bad storms. The communications people at the embassy had lost contact with the mountain camp at Site 21, a remote outpost near the Cambodian border. When headquarters got the message that there was a break in the weather, the colonel ordered two helicopters to evacuate the reconnaissance team.

Drew and Shane were in the first helicopter. A fog developed, and it began raining when they approached the camp. There was a white line of smoke rising through the fog on the side of the mountain. Looking past the fog and smoke, Drew could see the outline of the camp and the perimeter of barbed wire and cut trees. A flare shot up from the trees and flashed red then orange in the darkening sky. The helicopter circled down and dropped to the ground in the middle of a small clearing next to the camp. The second helicopter was swirling high overhead.

Shane jumped into the mud, and Drew followed him. They raced to the edge of the clearing when Shane suddenly threw himself into the tall grass. He pulled Drew next to him, and mud and water splashed over Drew's face. Shane pointed to the row of sand bags and strands of barbed wire. Drew saw a body half covered by palm branches, twisted in the barbed wire. Further down, he saw more palm branches hanging from the wire.

"It's all wrong," Shane said. He searched the camp for any signal, any sign of life. Everything was completely still. "It's a trap. They're waiting for the second chopper."

Shane rolled over on his back, and taking the flare gun from his belt, he pointed it at the sky and fired. The signal flare was just moving upward when gunfire sounded from the camp. Bullets splattered into the mud and grass around him and Shane. Drew buried himself in the mud. There was a loud explosion from the tree line to his right, and Drew turned to see the thick smoke trail as the rocket propelled toward their helicopter still hovering on the ground.

The rocket hit with a horrific blast of fire, and a wave of heat radiated across the clearing. Covering his face from the heat, Drew could see the dark Vietcong figures jump up and begin shooting volleys at the second helicopter, which began turning away from the clearing.

The helicopter was a black shadow, whirling blades cutting through the falling rain. The flare was curving downward now and ignited a glow of light in the misty air. Drew could see Williams at the door firing lines of tracer bullets into the tree line. Then there was a bright burst of red fire on the side of the chopper, and the helicopter disintegrated into large sections of metal and twisted blades.

Loud cheering and shrill whistles erupted from the tree line. Shane grabbed Drew by the shoulder, and they began running away from the noise. The steady rain trapped the smoke in the clearing, and Drew and Shane disappeared in the thick cover. Drew couldn't see anything in front of him, tripped over a large chunk of hot metal, and fell in a pool of water.

Shane pulled Drew to his feet, and staying low to the ground, they both began running faster. The shooting became sporadic, but there was some shouting behind them. Drew's eyes watered, and smoke and heat filled his lungs. He could only see spotty images of Shane's green uniform in front of him. The smoke cleared slightly when they reached the edge of the clearing. Shane headed to a narrow trail, and they ran into the cover of the jungle.

They ran at a fast pace, and soon the lingering traces of smoke dissipated in the falling rain and oppressive heat. The trail became narrow, clogged with hanging vines and thick ground vegetation. The light rain and jungle mist hampered Drew's vision. He was breathing hard, and his body struggled against the jungle growth, but at the same time, he found his legs getting stronger. Running was something he understood, and as he slowly began to relax into his natural rhythm, Drew settled deep into his comfort zone.

There were muffled shouts that seemed to be getting closer, and Drew and Shane ran even faster. When Shane slowed in front of him, Drew ran past him and took the lead. He wove through the maze of trees and broke clear of the clinging thorn vines that cut deep into his flak jacket and fatigues. After a short time, there was only the sound of thunder and falling rain, and as they ran, panting and gulping for air, the jungle closed behind them.

It was only the diminishing light that slowed their progress. The rain became heavier and crashed in torrents through the canopy of trees. Exhausted and drenched to the skin, Drew stopped running and slumped down on a broken trunk. Wiping the water from his eyes, he saw his fingers were stained with blood. He looked at Shane next to him, and in the dark light, he could see the cuts and thin lines of blood across his face. Shane lifted his head, and his voice was clear.

"I know where we are, Drew," Shane said. When he talked, the rivulets of rain and blood mixed together and rolled off his chin. "I'll get us out of here."

Still breathing deeply, water spitting from his mouth, Drew was quiet. His legs hung heavy and lifeless against the tree. He and Shane slid under a thicket of vines and roots that covered the trunk of the tree. For a long time, the only sound Drew heard was their erratic breathing mixed with the steady sound of the rain.

At the first hint of darkness, the mosquitoes and myriad of other night insects began to swarm around the tree. Listening as the buzzing noises grew louder and feeling the stings on his face and neck, Drew was too tired to lift his hand and swing at them. His eyes closing, he thought briefly about a cold, icy Valley Forge wind that froze his body and dulled his senses. It was hours before his head collapsed into the vines and he drifted into a restless sleep, a sleep punctuated between burning stings and sudden flashes of heat.

In the morning, the rain had slowed to a drizzle, and there was a dim light filtering through the trees. Drew opened his eyes, and feeling the numbing pain that seemed to hurt every part of his body, he sat motionless. An ugly, bloated mosquito rose from his arm and began buzzing slowly in front of his face. When the mosquito reached eye level, Drew brought both hands up and smashed it with a loud crack. Opening his hands slowly, he saw the broken wings and smear of blood on his palm. The loud noise alerted Shane, and he sat up looking at Drew.

"What the hell are you doing?" Shane asked, a strange expression on his face

"Nothing," Drew said, studying the bite marks and puffy circles all over Shane's face. Recessed in the bruises and cuts of his forehead, the green eyes were clear and bright. "I remember you said something last night." Using his finger, Drew flicked the mosquito body parts off his palm.

"I don't remember saying anything."

"I think you said you knew where we are."

"Oh, that," Shane said. "I do know where we are." When he talked, his eyes focused on Drew, and he hesitated for a moment. "You look terrible. What happened to your face?"

"The same thing that happened to yours," Drew said. "It was kind of a feast for whatever bugs came by. You must be better tasting. I think they ate more of you."

"It feels that way."

"Well," Drew said. "Are you going to tell me? I'm dying to know. Where are we?"

"Right here," Shane said, pointing to the mash of roots and decaying leaves and mud. "Right in the middle of this fuckin' jungle."

"That's it?" Drew said. "That's all you know?" He stood up slowly, bracing his back against the tree. Shane stood up next to him. Drew saw the rip and stain of blood on the side of Shane's shirt. There was a black thorn sticking in it. Drew reached over and pulled out the thorn.

"Ouch!" Shane said and began rubbing the wound.

"It's nothing," Drew said. "At first I thought you were hit."

"The bastards got everyone," Shane said. "We were lucky."

"Nothing's lucky with you, Shane. Site 21 was overrun, and you knew right away it was a trap. You led us into the smoke cover. I don't know how, but you found the trail. We're the only survivors. You got us out, Shane. You have some kind of instinct."

"It's not an instinct, Drew. I did what you should have done." There was movement in the bushes, and a small black animal scurried from the cover and up a tree. "I'm beginning to feel you haven't learned anything."

"I don't know what you're talking about," Drew said. He caught a glimpse of the animal in the tree. It had a long tail like a possum but moved like a squirrel. "I did everything I could."

"You did everything you could at Site 21," Shane said. "But at the base, you wasted all that time bullshitting with Williams and James."

"I was nervous."

"You should have been in the communications hut with me," Shane said. "I know we were in a hurry, but I took the time to read the map on Site 21. I saw how the perimeter was set up. I saw the trails leading into it. Even before the helicopter left the base, I knew where we had to go if anything went wrong."

"You're right," Drew said, instantly understanding. "I should have studied the maps in the hut."

"You can't depend on me all the time," Shane said. "The longer I'm here, the closer it gets."

"What gets closer?" Drew asked. "What the hell are you talking about?"

"Remember the soldier in *Western Front*, that book we read in English Class?"

"Paul," Drew said. "His name was Paul Bäumer. You said you never read that book. I had to tell you everything about it."

"I read the last page," Shane said. "And I never forgot it. Paul managed to survive all those battles, but on a day when there was no fighting, he was killed. He stood up on a quiet day and was killed by a sniper. He was shot right here." Shane pointed to his forehead. "Right here between the eyes."

"Bullshit," Drew said. "Remarque never said where Paul was shot. He just said he died peacefully."

"He didn't have to say it, Drew. That's right where a good sniper would have shot him."

"So what," Drew said. "That was World War I. This is Vietnam."

"Wars are all the same, Drew. There's some Vietcong out there now. He could be sleeping, eating, making love. Or he could be cleaning his gun. Then in the next battle, he sees me, aims his gun, and it's all over. That's just how Paul got killed. I could be next."

"Bullshit," Drew said again. "On our first mission together that VC had four shots at me." Drew stood up straight and positioned himself chest to chest in front of Shane. "Look at me now. I'm still here."

"Wake up, Drew. That was a rice farmer pretending to be a soldier. A real sniper would have killed you."

"Maybe," Drew said. "Maybe not."

It began to rain lightly. Drew slid his boots back and forth in the mud. Looking at Shane, he forced a smile on his face.

"You were right about me at the base. I did waste time when I should have been getting ready. I'm sorry, OK. But I did manage to do one thing right."

"What was that?"

"I picked these up," Drew said. He reached into his top pocket and took out two bags of M&M's. "Here. Catch." He threw a brown bag to Shane.

When Drew ripped the corner off his bag and the strong aroma of chocolate filled his senses, he realized how hungry he was. The chocolate pieces were melted together. He lifted the open end of the bag to his lips and squeezed the lump of chocolate into his mouth. It was smooth and creamy and tasted delicious. He held it in his mouth as long as he could. Then sheltering the bag from the rain, he licked the inside of the wrapper.

"You did great," Shane said, chewing on the chocolate. A brown drop appeared on his bloodied lip, and he caught it with his tongue. "We really needed this. It's better than a cup of that Vietnamese coffee."

"Shane," Drew said, the sweet taste of chocolate lingering in his mouth and throat. "When you studied the map of Site 21, did you see anything else? I mean are we close to anything?"

"There's a village," Shane said. "I saw it on the map, and I saw patches of it from the helicopter. I think it's a safe village. We can get help there."

"How long will it take?"

"The village is two mountains away," Shane said. "It'll take a few days to get over them."

"We can't call in a helicopter?"

"They'd never find us in this weather," Shane said. "And we're too close to Site 21. We have to get some distance from here. We'll be fine." He folded the wrapper and put it in his pocket. "Do you have any more M&M's?"

"No."

"What the hell were you thinking, just getting two packages?"

"I don't know," Drew said.

"One bag was better than nothing," Shane said. "We'd better get started." He straightened slowly, stretching his legs, and moved away from the tree. "I think we'll make it if we don't starve to death or get eaten by a tiger."

"At lease we won't be dehydrated," Drew said. He held his head up to the falling rain, and the fresh water rinsed his mouth. Drew took two big gulps and followed Shane into the jungle.

Shane couldn't find a trail on the first mountain. Grabbing onto roots and tree trunks, they scratched and pulled their way toward the top. It was exhausting and slow, and by noon, Drew knew he wasn't going to make it. His stomach hurt, and then his whole body ached. At times, he swore he couldn't move another step.

During the descent down the side of the mountain, Drew lost his footing and slid and rolled for a long distance. When his body crashed into a tree, he didn't think he could stand up. Shane grabbed him by the shoulders and lifted him in the air. He supported him for a short distance, and then he pushed him forward when they reached a stretch of level ground.

There was a hard, steady rain when they stopped that night. Shane cleared away an opening in a thicket of bamboo and pulled Drew inside. They broke off some of the smaller, leafy branches and spread them on the ground. Removing his belt and holster, Shane sat down on the mat of leaves and broken vines. Drew sat next to him.

"You look terrible," Shane said, wrapping the belt around the gun and setting it on the ground. "You gong to be all right?"

"Don't worry about me," Drew said. He tried to smile, but he couldn't. "I'm fine."

Water dripped from the bamboo and trickled down his face. He turned his head upward so he could catch some of it in his mouth. He swallowed as much as he could. Some sharp object caught in his throat, and he coughed and spit it out. A small bug with black spiny legs was propelled through the air, smashed into a leaf on the ground, and stuck there

"Damn it," Drew said, watching the legs twist upward. "I'm starving. I should have just swallowed the fucker."

Drew lay down on his side and crossed his arm under his head as a pillow. When he slid his knees forward, his stomach cramped, and the muscles deep inside began to spasm. Fighting the pain, Drew closed his eyes and thought about the cold and ice of Valley Forge

"Damn it," he mumbled again when his mind didn't cooperate and went totally blank. Drew then concentrated his thoughts on the light tapping, dripping sound of the rain. The tranquil sound was soon disrupted by the loud buzzing of mosquitoes. They came at him in swarms. Then some crawling ants found his hands and face and ankles. In the darkness, Drew grabbed handfuls of leaves and mud and rubbed them into his exposed face and neck. The buzzing noise became angry and louder.

Drew made more of the mud-leaf-twig mixture and stuffed it in his ears. When he removed his fingers, he heard only a steady, dull, humming noise. Drew lay there still, breathing slowly into the wet, leafy camouflage, his body tense and alert to the next sting, the next needle bite that would pierce his skin. Some of the bites through his wet clothing were barely detectable; others hit with a deep, burning pain, and he had to catch his breath so he wouldn't cry out.

Just when the pain in his body was constant and almost bearable, he heard a loud rumble, and monsoon rain began pouring through the bamboo cover. Deep puddles formed in the leaves around Drew's face. He felt the liquid rising up the side of his cheek, and cracking open his eyes, he saw how his breathing created little bubbles that broke on the surface of the water.

Drew turned his head slightly and lifted his nose out of the puddle. He breathed deeply and closed his eyes. The darkness in his slumber was punctuated by sudden flashes of red followed by a burning pain. It was that way all night. There was nothing he could do. The seconds and minutes were lasting and forever. Drew didn't remember falling asleep. Then he heard his name being called from a great distance away.

"Drew."

"What?" Drew asked. "Speak louder. I can hardly hear you." He shook his head and began to pick the debris from his ears.

"Don't move, Drew," Shane said. He spoke carefully and with some urgency.

"What?" Drew asked. As he tried to sit up, he felt Shane's hand on his knee. It clamped down on something. There was a scratching sensation on his leg, and then the pressure was removed. Drew straightened and looked at the thing in Shane's grip. It was a long bug, dozens of spiny gyrating legs on the side of its body. The black oval head had two pinchers opening and closing in deadly unison.

"I got it," Shane said.

"What the hell is it?" Drew asked. Wiping his eyes, he looked at the black, sharpened pinchers and the row of thick scales that folded the length of the body.

"It's just a bug," Shane said, holding the twisting body in the air. "Some kind of mutant centipede. I saw one in camp last year. If those iron pinchers clamp down on your leg, you're done. The leg would be swollen double sized for a month. I hear it hurts like hell."

"Kill the fucker," Drew said.

"Watch," Shane said. He dropped the centipede to the ground, and lifting his foot, he crushed his boot into the body. Shane shifted all his weight onto the one leg and continued to twist his boot into the body of the centipede, making a deep hole in the mud. After a few moments when he lifted his boot, the centipede uncurled its body, and with legs scratching in military precision, it crawled out of the hole and disappeared under some leaves.

"Let's get the hell out of here," Drew said, pushing through the bamboo. Shane belted on his gun and followed him outside the thicket.

"You can learn something from that, Drew." Shane turned, unzipped his pants, and began pissing into the bamboo. Standing next to him, Drew tried to piss, but he couldn't.

"I'm too scared to piss," he said. "You trying to drown that thing? Is that what I can learn, piss kills mutant bugs?"

"No," Shane said. He finished relieving himself, and brushing the leaves and mud off his pants, he looked at Drew. "There are tigers and wild elephants out here, Drew. There are also monster snakes. But it's the little critters that'll drive you crazy. It's the bugs that'll kill you."

"I already know that," Drew said. The rain began falling harder, and he finally was able to piss into the bamboo.

"Still feeling bad?"

"How can you tell?"

"You look bad," Shane said. "You look like shit."

"If I could smell some fresh shit right now, I'd be so happy," Drew said. "It would mean I had eaten something and my body was working again. I hurt everywhere, but I think the hunger's the worst. I never thought it could be so bad."

"Hunger's good for you," Shane said. "When you stop feeling hunger, you know you're in bad shape. You know it's over."

"That sounds stupid," Drew said. "Where did you hear that bullshit?"

"I read it in some survival journal," Shane said. "It's the truth."

"Was that information on the last page?" Drew asked.

"I think so," Shane said. The stubble of beard on his blood-streaked face opened, and he showed a slight smile. "I think I read the last two pages."

"That's great," Drew said. He laughed and shook his head. "Did you ever read anything about what was safe to eat in the jungle?"

"We had some lectures on jungle food," Shane said. "But I never paid any attention." He cupped his hands to the falling rain and then took a drink. Drew did the same. They both drank for a long time. Drew began to feel bloated.

"Just pretend it's an ice cold bottle of Sam Adams," Shane said. "Or maybe a can of A&W."

"I'll try," Drew said. He felt a bubbling, convulsing sensation in his stomach, and then he felt explosive pressure building in his throat. Falling to his knees, Drew gagged and vomited a clear liquid onto the ground. There were some streaks of red mixed with the liquid. It splattered over the leaves and mud and was washed away in the rain. Drew felt weak and dizzy.

"Don't worry about that," Shane said. "We'll be out of here in a few days."

Shane helped Drew to his feet, and they walked into the jungle. The rain stopped, and a thick, moist fog rose out of the ground or descended from the sky. Drew wasn't sure. Grabbing onto Shane's sleeve as he stumbled forward, he could only see a few feet in front of him. Shane found a trail, and soon, they were moving upward at a sharp angle.

The fog lifted, and there was a hint of light in the sky. Drew didn't have the strength to look up. He focused his eye on the ground and Shane's boots in front of him. The dirt and mud of the trail turned into stone boulders and sharp cliffs of rock. The rain made the rocks slippery, and Drew had to strain to keep his balance. His feet became dead and heavy, and the muscles of his legs ached. Unexpectedly, even though there was a light drizzle, Drew began to experience a tremendous thirst, and his mouth felt dry and parched.

It was afternoon when they reached the top of the mountain. They rested a short time, and it was on the way down that Drew heard the animal noise above them in the trees. Straining his eyes, Drew saw the speck of black color in the green branches, and looking closer, he saw the monkey sitting there. It was a big black monkey with a red nose and a long tail that curled upward, and it was chewing on something. He reached for his gun, but Shane shook his head no.

"No way," he whispered.

All Drew could think about was food, and with a burst of energy sweeping through his body, he raced to the tree. Grunting like an animal, pulling at the branches and climbing as fast as he could, Drew was halfway up the tree when he heard the loud noise again.

Wiping the water from his eyes and looking up through the branches, Drew watched as the monkey tensed its body and then sprang high in the air. It drifted slowly with the light, falling drops of rain and landed with a crash into the leaves of a nearby tree.

The monkey collected itself and sat there on a large branch. It turned its head slowly and seemed to be staring at Drew. Drew was crushed. He slid awkwardly down the tree and fell heavily to the ground where Shane was waiting. Without saying anything, Shane handed Drew a green, mangled piece of fruit.

"What is it?"

"I don't know," Shane said. "Good job. You made the monkey drop his lunch."

Drew took the fruit. Half of it was missing. He looked at the green skin, the row of jagged teeth marks, and the yellow pulp inside. Scraping away some ants, Drew shoved it in his mouth and chewed ravenously. Seconds later, he bit hard on the large nut that was left and spit it out. Something stung his lower lip, and raising his hand, Drew picked off a small red ant and squeezed it between his fingers. He saw Shane watching him.

"I'm sorry, Shane," Drew said, looking up guiltily. "I should have given you some."

"I tasted it," Shane said. "I didn't like it." He reached down and pulled Drew to his feet.

As they descended the mountain, the trail widened slightly, and the trees became less dense. When they reached some level ground, Drew sensed something in the air. They were trekking through another downpour, but there was something different in the rain. There was a slight hint of smoke. In front of him, Shane was moving faster, and Drew made a great effort to keep up.

Drew was almost running when he and Shane broke into a pile of thick brush. The brush thinned suddenly, and they both stopped at the edge of a huge, empty clearing. Looking into the mist and drizzle, Drew saw the rows of tree stumps and thick, decaying, brown vegetation. Deep mudslides dissected the dead space that stretched across the valley and halfway up the side of the adjacent mountain. Shane stood in front of Drew and stopped him from stepping out of the brush. Everything was dead quiet. Drew studied the clearing and couldn't see any signs of insects or animals.

"We don't want to go near that," Shane said.

"What is it?"

"Agent Orange," Shane said. "It looks like the special ops people had some left over, and they discarded it here."

"What'll we do?"

"Walk around it," Shane said. He back stepped his way out of the brush. Soon, they were under the trees again, and they made a wide circle around the clearing.

It was evening when Shane raised his hand and stopped suddenly. Drew tripped forward, and Shane held him by the shoulders and steadied him. The rain was a light, steady drizzle now, and when Drew looked up, he saw the clearing through the trees. It was filled with grass, a few scattered banana trees, and it looked civilized and beautiful.

There was a broken fence and a row of four houses at the far end. All the houses were lifted off the ground by thick wooden pillars. Under the first house, Drew could see a hammock, some wooden chairs, and a long table. The black barrel of a gun stuck out over the edge of the table. Drew looked at the high front sights and the long curved magazine and recognized the AK47 immediately.

"Damn it," he said in an angry voice.

There was a slight break in the clouds, and the dim rays of the setting sun filtered into the clearing. Drew heard some noise coming from under the middle house, and then he saw the chickens began to move cautiously from the shelter. The chickens stood and chuckled noisily in the dim light. Drew became excited and pointed them out to Shane.

"Dinner," he mouthed the words. Soaked to the skin, his uniform ripped and tattered, his face and arms bloodied with deep scratches, Drew was transfixed. A big smile forming on his face, he couldn't take his eyes off the chickens.

"Stay here, Drew," Shane said. He removed his gun from the holster. "I'm going around the side to check the houses." Shane nodded to Drew to see that he understood, and then he walked backward into the cover of the trees.

Drew waited patiently. The rays of sunlight grew dimmer. Straining to see through the evening mist, Drew felt the muscles in his legs and back harden. He couldn't stand there any longer. Moving quietly around the trees, he watched the chickens scratch and peck their way into the open mud of the enclosure. There were five of them. Drew searched the shadows of the houses and couldn't see any sign of Shane. His head hurt, and his whole body felt weak. The strong pain in his stomach was debilitating, and it brought tears to his eyes and clouded his vision.

Dropping to his hands and knees, Drew crouched low to the ground and began a slow crawl into the clearing. His whole focus was on the lead chicken, a fat white-feathered hen. But as he got almost within reach, the sky darkened, black clouds moved over the clearing, and a sudden wind rippled through the leaves of the banana trees. On his hands and knees, Drew moved closer and saw the lead chicken pick a beetle out of a pool of water.

Then the sky went completely dark, and large raindrops began to pelt the enclosure. The big white-feathered chicken stretched high in the air and flapped beads of water from its wings. Seeing his chance, Drew jumped out of his crouch and lunged for the chicken. The other chickens scurried noisily away, but sliding across the mud, Drew grabbed onto the big chicken's leg. Its free leg clawing at Drew's wrist, the chicken tried to scratch itself loose.

As Drew got to his feet, he grabbed the chicken tightly by the head. He was about to break its neck when he heard his name. Drew looked at the house and saw Shane walk slowly into the open. He had his gun out and leveled. Drew turned and looked at the middle house where Shane was aiming. In the shadows, under the house, there was a thin Vietnamese man balanced on crutches.

There was lightning over the house, and in the bright flash, Drew saw clearly the AK47 in the man's hand. He wiped the rain from his eyes and saw the gun was pointed at him. Thunder rolled across the clearing. Drew was frozen in the mud. The chicken struggled in his grip, the wings beating furiously against his forearm.

"No!" he shouted in disbelief as he watched Shane lower his gun to his side. Still holding the AK47, the man seemed to study Drew. Even in the torrent of rain, Drew could see the front sights and the barrel of the gun. Making a terrifying volume of noise, the chicken twisted and clamped its beak into Drew's wrist. As Drew tightened his grip on the chicken's neck, he saw the red flash of gunfire from the shadows of the house.

Feeling an icy cold sensation, Drew felt himself falling backward. He hit the ground with a splash of water and mud. The violent fluttering of feathers at his side stopped. Prone on the ground, Drew fought against the cold that permeated his body.

The rain splashing off his face, Drew struggled to a sitting position and immediately saw that the chicken head was completely severed from its body. In his grasp, the beak twisted toward him dripping blood, and the lifeless eyes stared luminously in the evening light.

There was rapid movement in the mud at his feet, and Drew watched in amazement as the headless chicken jumped high, white wings flapping blood and water in all directions, and then the yellow legs began carrying the body toward the house. The chicken only traveled a short distance when there was a great gush of blood from its neck, and then the body somersaulted into a puddle and lay still.

Wiping his face, Drew pushed himself deeper into the mud. His eyes were open wide, and he shivered at the cold feeling that numbed his arms and legs. Overhead, thin lines of lightning crisscrossed through the evening sky, and thunder rumbled in the distance.

When the thunder subsided, Drew heard the splat of footsteps racing toward him. Mixed with the falling rain and wind and distant thunder, he heard loud voices and the inexplicable sound of laughter. As the footsteps got closer and stopped, the laughter drowned out the noise of the rain and the storm. A shadow bent over him, and Drew saw Shane, the green eyes glowing, the grin on his face widening.

"You're OK," Shane said. He reached out his hand and pulled Drew from the mud.

"What the hell just happened?" Drew asked. Adrenalin was still racing through his body, and his brain was overloaded with images. The rain slowly began to clean the mud and blood from his face and shirt.

"The chicken's dead," Shane said. He released his hold on Drew. "Colonel Vohn killed it. We'll have a big chicken dinner tonight."

"Dinner," Drew said. Trying to steady himself, he felt the dead weight in his hand. The clammy feathers and neck and jagged top of the chicken's crown protruded from his clamped fingers. He raised his hand and opened his fist slowly. Scrutinizing the chicken head, he was amazed at the perfect shot that had cut through its neck. Directly beyond the head, Drew saw the man on crutches. The AK 47 was gone, and the man had a pleasant smile on his face. Drew began to feel more relaxed and incredibly hungry.

"Give me that," Shane said, taking the chicken head. "I want you to meet Colonel Vohn. He's an old friend of mine." His hand still clammy and streaked with chicken blood, Drew shook hands with the colonel.

"Don't worry about anything. We'll take care of you," the colonel said. He was friendly and didn't seem to notice the sticky remains on his hand. "Then we'll eat your chicken. You must be hungry."

"I think I'm past the hungry stage. I'm at the point of starvation now."

The colonel smiled again, and walking easily with his crutches, he led them across the clearing. Heads appeared in the open windows of the houses, and Drew saw some young girls and a small boy. They were laughing as they talked excitedly to each other. A woman came down the steps of the first house, and Colonel Vohn introduced Drew and Shane to his wife.

The girls and the small boy came down from the house and formed a noisy circle around them. The boy had big oval eyes. He grabbed the chicken head from Shane's hand and began shaking it in the air. The girls began laughing when he jumped in the air and rolled around on the ground.

He made dying, cawking sounds, and the chicken beak danced grotesquely in his hand.

"The kid's imitating you, Drew," Shane said. "He's really good."

"I see that," Drew said. "The Drew headless-chicken comedy act. I'm probably the best entertainment they've had in a long time."

After the excitement, Vohn said something to his wife in Vietnamese, and she went back up the steps into the house. When she returned, she had a pile of folded clothes, towels, and a purple-colored bottle. Vohn led Drew and Shane to the corner of the house where there was a washroom.

The sides of the room, open at the top and bottom, were large sheets of corrugated metal. The wooden floorboards inside the room had gaps where the water ran out into a ditch that led to the trees. Four large brown-colored jars lined the one wall. They were waist-high and filled with clear rainwater. A silver bowl floated on the water in each of the jars. Drew and Shane began to unlace their boots.

"You can wash here," Vohn said. He spoke English slowly and precisely. "And there are dry clothes for you." He gave the purple bottle to Shane. "And put this on your cuts, even the small ones."

"Thank you," Shane said.

Shane took the bottle and pile of clothes, and he and Drew went through the hinged door into the washroom. They undressed and threw their wet, muddied clothes over the sides of the metal wall. Taking the silver bowls and dipping them into the jars, they poured scoops of water over their heads. There was a bar of soap in the holder, and when Drew began washing the blood off his face and arms, the soap burned into his skin.

"You know the colonel?" Drew asked. He grimaced in pain as he rubbed the soap into a deep cut on his neck.

"Years ago I flew with him," Shane said. "When his leg was mangled by a grenade, I stayed with him and helped him back to the chopper. The leg was bad, but that night when I went to visit him at the hospital, I couldn't believe they had amputated it. We drank into the morning hours, and then he asked me to leave. I went back the next day. He was gone. I never saw him again until just now."

"You recognized him?"

"Not right away," Shane said. "I was just about to kill him, and then I saw the crutches and got a good look at his face."

"Cool," Drew smiled. He poured more water over his neck and back and took a deep breath at the burning pain. "The colonel is a great shot."

"One of the best," Shane said.

They finished washing. Drew patted the cuts dry and then applied the ointment. The initial pain was like touching a hot coal, but after that, he experienced a soothing, numbing sensation.

"It's great stuff," he said, pouring some in his hand and offering the bottle to Shane. "I'm beginning to feel like a human being again."

Wispy clouds of smoke began to drift into the washroom. Drew finished smearing on the ointment and pulled on brown baggy pants and a shirt that had laces on the front. He tied the laces together and stepped outside. There were flip-flops on the ground, and he slipped into them. Coming out the door, Shane finished tying the laces on his shirt.

"Something smells good," he said. There was a thick glob of ointment on Shane's nose. Drew laughed and pointed at it, and Shane rubbed it away with his hand.

"Probably my chicken," Drew said, feeling clean and fresh and free of pain for the first time in days. "I know I didn't kill it, but it's still my chicken." He had a smile on his face, and his body was restless and animated.

"What?" Shane asked, studying him closely.

"I don't know," Drew said. "I'm starving. I mean really starving. Also, I was shot at, and I'm still lost somewhere in the jungle, and yet I feet great."

"And you'll feel even better after you eat," Shane said. He pulled Drew off the steps, and they walked under the house. Colonel Vohn was waiting for them at the porch, and he introduced them to his two daughters and son.

There was a square pit dug in the ground under the house, and clouds of smoke rose from the burning charcoal layered at the bottom and sides of the pit. Drew watched the colonel's wife sprinkle black, green, and then red herbs onto four cleaned, meaty, chickens.

After the herbs and seasonings were rubbed into the skin, the girls wrapped the chickens in banana leaves and placed them in the pit. Then they flattened out larger banana leaves and covered everything with hot coals. Soon the aroma of the chicken permeated the air, and Drew took a deep breath.

"I'm so hungry," Drew said. "I can't stop my body from shaking."

Drew and Shane stood next to a large mat placed on the ground. One of the older girls came down the steps from the porch and put plates and utensils on the mat. In the space directly opposite him, the daughter put two intricately curved marble chopsticks next to the dish. Drew watched closely as she placed a silk napkin over the dish.

There was some light popping sounds from the pit, and the sweet, heavy smell of the cooking chicken and emanating juices was almost unbearable to Drew. The muscles in his stomach began to convulse and tighten. The younger daughter set glasses next to the plates. Holding the crutches and balancing a bottle of Johnnie Walker Red in each hand, Colonel Vohn came down the steps. He opened one bottle and filled the glasses.

Drew saw a figure on the porch of the second house. He was an old man, and he descended the steps slowly. Reaching the bottom step, he walked toward them in a stiff, upright posture. When he got closer, Drew saw that he was simply but regally dressed in a North Vietnamese officer's uniform. Three rows of gold and silver medals crossed the front left side of the uniform.

"This is General Nugent," Colonel Vohn. The general shook hands with Shane and Drew. "General Nugent is from the North. He is my uncle."

"A real general," Shane whispered to Drew.

The general walked to the other side of the mat. Colonel Vohn gave his uncle a glass and waited while Shane and Drew took their glasses. Looking at them, the colonel lifted his glass slowly. Then he gave the first toast of the evening.

"To old soldiers," he said. "May they live long and prosper."

They drank the toast, and Drew felt the whiskey roar down his throat and send a blast of heat into his empty stomach. His face blushing red, he coughed and steadied himself.

After the toast, everyone sat down at the large mat. Drew struggled with his legs, and when he was able to cross his feet in front of him, he was pleased to feel the leg muscles stretch into place. General Nugent looked closely at Shane.

"Colonel Vohn is my favorite nephew," the general said. "His father was killed in Laos. Vohn told me you saved his life. I want to thank you."

"He's a good friend," Shane said. "When I went to the hospital the next day, I was sorry he had gone. I looked for him, but no one knew anything."

"He came home to his village," the General said. "Like it was for me, the war was over for him."

"There's been continuous fighting in these mountains," Shane said. "How is it your village can survive?"

"When the government troops come, I wear my colonel's uniform," Vohn said. He pointed to the tied-up cuff on his amputated leg. "They see my loss and show me respect. When the Vietcong come in, the general wears his uniform. My uncle was with General Giap at Dien Bien Phu. The Vietcong know this and treat him as a hero. They bring him food and gifts. We're all proud of him."

"And yet you fought for the government," Shane said. "You worked with the Americans. We were friends."

"Yes," Colonel Vohn said. "It's what I believed at the time. But I never stopped loving my village. I never stopped loving my uncle." He looked at the general and nodded his head approvingly.

"I have changed in my political views. I understand now my uncle was right."

The night darkness had settled around the house. There was a light drizzle, and the sky was black. The only light was from a few lanterns and the glowing coals of the pit. There were burning incense sticks on the porch railing and stuck in the ground below the house. Drew noticed for the first time the absence of the loud buzzing sound of mosquitoes.

Drew watched the activity at the cooking pit. Walking in a straight line, the colonel's wife and daughters brought steaming pots and filled the small bowls next to their plates with chicken soup. Although it was still hot, Drew drank the broth quickly and was amazed at the sweet taste of chicken and onion. He chewed on a lump of chicken meat, and his bowl was filled again.

"I can't believe this," Drew said.

"What?" Colonel Vohn asked.

"That I feel so alive," Drew said. "And I'm eating dinner with a legendary general from the North."

"You are my guest," the general said. "We should eat and drink and enjoy ourselves. It is the way it would be without the war."

The girls brought long loaves of French bread and placed them on the mat. Breaking off a piece, which was warm to the touch, Drew dunked the crusted bread into the hot soup. He brought it out soft and dripping, and when he put it in his mouth, he sat back, feeling weak and inebriated, and closed his eyes.

"Drew," Shane said. "Don't fall asleep now."

"I'm not sleeping," Drew said. "I just died and went to heaven." The smooth, delicate taste still lingering in his mouth, Drew opened his eyes. "Maybe it's because I'm out in the jungle and starving and didn't expect this. I don't know. Except for May's special sandwich, I've never eaten anything that tasted this good." He finished his loaf of bread and was reaching for a leftover crust in front of Shane when the servers brought the dishes of chicken from the pit.

The colonel's wife knelt next to the general, but before she could put the plate in front of him, he gently touched her arm and pointed to Shane. She stood up slowly and walked around the edge of the mat. Stopping next to Shane, she bowed her head slightly, knelt down, and placed the largest plate in front of him. Then she placed another large plate in front of Drew.

She untied the banana leaves, and when they opened flat on the mat, Drew saw the golden-brown chicken sitting upright and thick and juicy on the plate. Shane's chicken had a long neck that curved the beak and head onto the mat while Drew saw that his chicken was headless.

My chicken, he thought to himself.

The rising steam and aroma were already invading his senses, and Drew began rocking his body side to side in anticipation. He watched the colonel's daughters set the remaining plates on the mat before they collected themselves and sat down. Everyone was quiet, and then the general casually picked up his marble chopsticks and slid them into the side of the chicken. This was the signal to begin, and there was an excited burst of movement around the mat.

Surprised at his patience, Drew watched Shane stab his fork into the side of the chicken and deliver a large hunk of white meat into his mouth. The rapid chewing motion contorted Shane's facial muscles and bulged his cheeks outward. Without taking a breath, he swallowed the chicken and began his second helping.

Remembering his feast at the Chinese restaurant, Drew ignored the fork on the mat and ripped the right leg from his chicken. Lifting it in the air, a hunk of dark meat slid off, and Drew caught it in the air and shoved it in his mouth.

Biting into the dark meat and tasting the thick, sweet juice, Drew wasn't sure what he was eating. He tasted pepper and onion and salt and what he sensed might be garlic. But he wasn't sure of that either. He was only sure that his body craved more of the chicken, a whole flock of chickens.

Drew didn't notice the conversation around the mat, nor did he notice the passage of time. Without any regard for etiquette, he ate passionately, greedily, and with too much haste. Lowering his hand toward the plate again, he was surprised to see that it was empty but for a thick grease stain.

Oblivious to everything, he wiped his hand over the stain and began licking his fingers. Comfortable and feeling satiated, he sat up and looked at the people around the mat. It was then he noticed everyone was staring at him.

"What?" he asked Shane.

"The colonel's wife asked you how you liked the chicken."

"I'm sorry. I didn't hear her. It was delicious." Drew nodded to her in appreciation. "I can't believe how delicious it was. It was so delicious I swear I'll never eat chicken again."

"What do you mean?" Shane asked. "You'll never eat chicken again? What about when we get home and you see the KFC drive-thru?"

"No," Drew said. "Not even Kentucky Fried." He looked seriously at Colonel Vohn sitting across the mat. "Tell your wife I will never eat chicken again because no chicken in the world will be as good as this."

Drew watched as Colonel Vohn translated the statement to his wife. He used some French words. When he was done, his wife laughed and thanked Drew for the compliment. The daughters cleared away the empty plates and returned from the pit with smaller dessert dishes. One of the daughters placed a dish in front of Drew.

Looking closely, Drew saw two small fried bananas covered with a thick, syrupy liquid in the center of the dish. He forked one, and even though there was steam rising in the air, he slid it carefully between his lips. The warm, sweet taste of the syrup spread from his lips to his tongue, and then to the extremities of his mouth. Biting into the banana, he found the center to be extremely hot, and he opened his mouth and let the moist air and syrup flow over and cool it. Then he closed his mouth, chewed slowly, and swallowed the banana.

Without any hesitation, Drew ate the second banana quickly. He sat back, and with the sweet taste of syrup in his mouth and throat, he felt a steady flow of energy spread through his body. There was a slight tightening of his muscles, and he uncrossed his legs. Pulling his knees up to his chest and stretching and holding them in place with his hands, Drew felt totally relaxed. He looked at Shane and saw the swelling and redness was gone from his face.

The glow from the lanterns was getting dim, and the charcoal pit, except for a few red cinders, was dark. Drew noticed the incense stick on the nearest pillar flicker and burn out, and immediately, a mosquito buzzed by his ear. It landed on his wrist, the veins now pumped with blood. Drew watched the sting descending, and just as it punctured his skin, Drew crushed the mosquito with his hand.

The colonel's wife stood up, and in a few minutes, she and the girls had cleared the mat. Only the glasses and bottle of whiskey remained. The general got slowly to his feet and walked to the latrine at the corner of the house. At the end of the porch, there was a large basin filled with rainwater, and the daughters were busy washing the dishes. The men took turns visiting the latrine, and when Drew came back to the mat, he saw the glasses were filled. There was a light rain falling, and fresh incense sticks had been placed in the ground.

"My uncle, the general, had many American friends," Colonel Vohn said. "He fought with them against the Japanese in the big war."

"I was a young soldier then," the general said. He raised his glass saluting the past, and they all drank. Colonel Vohn carefully refilled the glasses and quietly addressed Shane and Drew.

"When the first American soldiers came and brought us guns and supplies, I knew we would win against the Japanese, and we did. Some of the Americans I met were killed in the fighting. They were very brave. I think they were brave like you." He raised his glass to Shane and Drew, and they drank a toast to the dead Americans and the two live ones. The bottle was passed around, and after the glasses were filled, the general continued his lecture.

"I thought the fighting would stop after the American president dropped the big bomb and the Japanese were defeated," the general said. "I thought we would be free. But I was wrong."

"The French wanted to come back and form another French Indochina, but it was too late," Colonel Vohn said.

"Yes," the general said. "Way too late. The French were done here, but they didn't know it. The French politicals were so stupid. When Japan surrendered, the French wanted to return like nothing had happened. And yes, the American politicals were stupid, too. The United States won the big war, and the United States could decide what was right. But the United States gave Vietnam back to the French." Raising his head, speaking in a low voice, the general looked across the mat at Shane and Drew.

"It was a terrible thing what the Americans did. I know your history. I know the French were with you in Valley Forge when you won your freedom. And I know the French gave you the great Statue of Liberty. That's why it was so terrible. You should not try to take from us what you live by. You should not take away our freedom." The general paused for a moment.

Wiping some perspiration from his forehead, Drew looked past him at the two girls in the back of the house. They lifted the large basin and threw the water into the yard. The clean dishes were stacked neatly on the table. Replacing the basin, the daughters walked quietly up the steps to the porch and disappeared inside the house. When the door closed with a scraping noise, the general lifted his head and began speaking again.

"And so we fight the French for another ten years," the general said. "Yes, we got some help from China. Yes, we are communists now. But we win for ourselves. At the great battle of Dien Bien Phu, the French lost most of their army, and we have our country again."

"We had great celebrations," the colonel said. "But the fighting wasn't over."

"Because of us," Shane said.

"Yes, because of the United States," the General said. "You continued the war. That's why I think maybe the American politicals are more stupid than the French. They could have studied and learned from the French, but they were blind from their victory over the Japanese. They were blind with their great power. So they thought they would win a war that the French couldn't."

The general lifted his glass and only tasted the whiskey this time. When Drew picked up his glass, he saw a small beetle with wide, black wings swimming in circles on the surface of the whiskey. It swam one wide circle, and then one wing closed and the beetle sank to the bottom of the glass. Drew made a face and drank the whiskey quickly. Placing the glass on the mat, Drew felt the slow burn of the whiskey in his throat.

"We had to fight the Americans another fifteen years," the general said. "Now we have finally won."

A bright flash of lightning lit up the distant mountain, and the low roar of thunder rolled across the valley into the clearing. Then except for the sound of the drops of rain falling from the trees and splashing into the puddles along the side of the house, it was eerily quiet.

"I have known nothing but war. It has been with me all my life." The general lowered his head and was silent for a moment. "Sometimes old people talk too much. It's late, and we should go to sleep. Tomorrow, my nephew will show you the trail to the river. The storm has past, and your people will get a clear signal. They can pick you up there."

General Nugent stood up, and slowly raising his hand to his forehead, he saluted the two Americans. Shane and then Drew returned the salute. Turning, the general walked toward his house. The lantern on each corner of the porch flickered brightly.

Colonel Vohn picked up his crutches and motioned them to follow. He led Drew and Shane up the steps to the porch of his house. Two mosquito nets were tied to the wall. Drew saw a pillow and mat under each netting. Colonel Vohn shook their hands and went inside the house.

"What a night," Drew said. He sat down on the top porch step, and Shane sat next to him. "Do you think we'll get out of here tomorrow?"

"I guarantee it, Drew. I know exactly where we are."

"I never doubted you for a second," Drew said, staring into the shadows of the empty yard. In the dim light from the lanterns, he saw a few scattered chicken feathers.

"Shane, do you believe in reincarnation?"

"You die and are born again in another life, another time," Shane said. "No, I don't believe any of that."

"I never did," Drew said. "But Kim talked about it, and I think I believe it now."

"You're a Christian, Drew."

"I know, but when I was about to be shot right out there," Drew said, pointing his finger at the chicken feathers and the mud and stalks of grass in the middle of the yard. "My mind went blank, and I was in another place. I was starving."

"You were starving, Drew. We both were starving."

"I know, but there was something white. It was snow and it got so cold I was freezing. I was holding the same chicken, and there was a man pointing a gun at me."

"That was Colonel Vohn."

"No, this man never fired his gun."

"So everything was fine just like tonight," Shane said. "You sat down and ate the chicken."

"No, everything wasn't fine. I was trying to steal this farmer's chicken, and somehow I was killed. It was so quick. I didn't feel pain or anything. But I was starving so bad I didn't really care." Drew looked at the dark sky, and shaking his head slowly, he was quiet for a moment.

"It's hard to explain, but it's what Professor JJ told me at Valley Forge."

"What did JJ tell you?"

"I would become a chicken thief."

"I worry about you, Drew. Sometimes I really worry about you."

"Don't," Drew said. "I feel great after that feast." There was a popping sound from the remaining coals in the pit under the house, and Drew watched a thin cloud of smoke rise through the air.

"You should feel great," Shane said. "They treated you well. It had to be difficult for them since they have so little here."

"What do you mean?"

"There are only young children left in the village. The men are all dead or still fighting. I thought I would hear dogs when we first arrived. All Vietnamese houses have dogs. There were none here."

"So?"

"So they ate them or traded them," Shane said. "The banana trees were all stunted and too small to give much fruit. And yet they did their best for us. They gave us their biggest chickens. That was a real compliment."

"I didn't know," Drew said. "I feel bad now. I really feel bad."

"You shouldn't feel bad, Drew. They were honored to do it."

"Because you saved the colonel's life?"

"Because they're good people," Shane said. A light drizzle began to fall, and Shane stood up. He put his hand on Drew's shoulder and pulled him to his feet. "It's late like the general said. Let's go to sleep."

"How the hell do you know all this stuff?" Drew asked, following Shane down the porch.

"I read a lot," Shane said.

"Yeah, the last page," Drew said. "Everything important is on that last page."

Shane laughed, and reaching the mosquito net, he slid inside. Opposite him, Drew got inside his netting and unrolled the straw mat. There was a small pillow, and Drew put it under his head and lay down.

The floor was hard, and a warped board of wood cut into his ribs. Sliding carefully on the mat, he found a straighter, smoother board. The air inside the mosquito net was hot and moist. His farmer's shirt soon became soaked with perspiration, and Drew untied the front laces.

There was a light drizzle, and low dark clouds moved over the village. It was pitch black in the jungle. Some animal jumped onto the branches hanging over the roof of the house, and large drops of rain spattered against the railing.

Drew looked up at the noise, and squinting into the darkness, he saw nothing. There was only the drizzle of the rain and the low buzzing noise of the mosquitoes as they flew into the webbing. Feeling weary and incredibly tired, Drew closed his eyes. The sound of the falling rain became softer, and even the insect noise was soothing and melodious.

"Drew," Shane said. His voice sounded strange.

"What?" Drew asked, his eyelids still heavy and closed.

"I wanted to thank you. I should have done it sooner," Shane said. There was lightning in the sky, and the dull sound of thunder echoed into the clearing. "It's about Whin. I made a mess of things. I know how you're helping her and the baby. I really appreciate that."

Drowsy and not alert enough to think clearly, Drew didn't say anything. He half opened his eyes and glimpsed the dark canopy of the mosquito net. But the heaviness was still there, and he drifted back into a restful slumber. A frog sounded from somewhere under the house. Drew thought he heard the frog again, and then, there was a slight splashing sound followed by complete silence.

The next morning, a light fog covered the clearing. It was thickened by spirals of dark smoke from the charcoal fire under the house. The daughters brought two plates of fried eggs and noodles and cups of steaming black coffee. Drew drank the coffee and felt a jolt of energy loosen the cramped muscles in his neck and back.

Drew and Shane ate breakfast quietly, and when they were finished, they walked down the steps of the house where Colonel Vohn was waiting. Balanced casually on the crutch, the colonel gave Shane a shoulder bag that Shane slid over his neck. He shook hands with Shane and Drew and directed them to the trail.

As Drew walked across the clearing, rays of sunlight began to scatter the fog. One scrawny chicken, naked neck blistered and red where the feathers had been ripped away, was scratching in the mud and wet grass. They reached the trail, and turning and looking back at the house, Drew saw the general and his family on the porch. He waved at them and turned to Shane.

"We ate their food," Drew said. "They have so little left. I hate to leave them like this."

"Try opening your eyes, Drew," Shane said.

"They are open."

"I mean open them wide so you can see what's in front of you."

"I can see," Drew said. He studied the lines on Shane's face. "What are you getting angry about?"

"Look at this place, Drew." Shane turned Drew by the shoulders so they both could see the line of houses. "You have a war victim on crutches. You have an old man who has fought so long he'll never be able to enjoy life. You have an empty village except for the girls and one boy, and you have a mountain of Agent Orange a few miles away. And you hate to leave them! This village is a fact, Drew. We're leaving it on the edge of an ugly, slow death, and that's the way we're leaving the whole fuckin' country."

"Don't be angry at me," Drew said. "You've been here so long. It's hard to see things like you do."

"I not angry at you," Shane said. "I'm angry about how we lost a war we didn't have to. We came here to win. We came here to give these people something better than communism."

Shane removed the bottle of Johnnie Walker Red from the shoulder bag and took a drink. He gave the bottle to Drew. Taking a gulp of the whiskey, Drew looked at the row of houses, the lone chicken in the yard, the row of banana trees, and Colonel Vohn's children laughing and waving at them from the porch. Drew gave the bottle back to Shane. Shane stuck it in the shoulder bag and spoke in a steady, softer voice.

"I don't understand it, Drew. Those damn politicians, reporters, movie stars and baby doctors, maybe they thought they knew something. Maybe they thought they were helping, but they should have left fighting the war to the generals. Instead of talking and protesting, we should have hit them with everything we had. But we didn't do anything like that, and we lost the war. Now, it's going to get real ugly over here. Communist China will supply that psycho, nutcase Pol Pot with the guns he needs to destroy Cambodia. Maybe the Vietnam War is over, Drew, but the real killing is just beginning. It's just like Homer said at Valley Forge."

"What?"

"The only bad war is the one you lose."

Shane straightened the pack on his shoulder and walked into the jungle. Taking a quick glance at the clearing, waving his hand at the children, Drew turned and followed him.

Five hours later, when they walked out of the dark shadows of the jungle growth, it was noon and the sky was clear. Drew could see the waters of the river through the branches of the trees. Removing the small transmitter from his pocket, Shane stopped next to a big tree. He was about to send the priority alert when he saw the look on Drew's face.

"What's wrong?"

"My stomach," Drew said, holding his side. "Something's happening in my stomach."

"It'll only take a minute to send out our location," Shane said.

"I can't wait," Drew said. "It really hurts. I haven't shit for three days. That fuckin' chicken did this."

"I can send the signal without you," Shane said. "Go sit in the river."

"Yes," Drew said. "Shit in the river!"

Holding his side, Drew took off racing down the trail. When he got to the bank, he unlaced and threw his shirt on the rocks. He bent over quickly, untied his boots, and kicked them in the air. When Drew straightened his body, the contractions in his stomach became critically painful. Struggling with the zipper on his pants and splashing through the water, he finally slid off his pants and placed them over his head.

Drew splashed forward frantically and sat down in the waist-deep water. Drew took a deep breath and twisted his body to face upstream. Then his stomach made a tremendous noise, and Drew shouted as the sudden violent explosion of gas and excrement lifted him out of the water and knocked him sideways into the current. Splashing his hands in the river, he fought awkwardly to regain his balance, steadied his feet in the mud, and then a second geyser of gas and liquid shit propelled his body forward a few feet.

"Fuckin' rocket fuel," he said quietly.

Holding himself in the current, staring at the curve in the river and the line of green trees hanging over the bank, Drew flexed his stomach muscles and waited. Nothing happened. He tightened his stomach muscles harder, and still nothing happened. But for the sharp stinging sensation in his ass, Drew felt good.

Standing up carefully in the current, he saw some movement on the opposite bank. The branches parted, and two men walked out of the cover. They wore the circular, coned hats and the green tattered uniforms of the VC, and each man was holding an AK47.

"Christ!" Drew said. He turned and began running toward the bank. Water splashing high in the air, he lunged forward, tripped, and fell on his face in the river. Getting up quickly and panting loudly, he reached the bank. Running faster now, Drew turned to look back at the VC when strong arms grabbed him and stopped him in midair.

"Where are you going?" Shane asked.

"VC," Drew gasped. "VC on the bank."

"I saw them," Shane said. "I think they're with the general. He probably sent them to make sure we got out safely."

"I didn't know," Drew said. "They scared the hell out of me. I didn't know."

"Here," Shane said. He took the pants from around Drew's head and handed them to him. "Get dressed and try to relax." Shane waved to the men on the opposite bank, and they lifted their guns in the air.

"I didn't know," Drew whispered. Putting on his pants and shirt, he looked at the two soldiers across the river. One pointed his AK47 towards Drew, and they began laughing.

"Sneaky bastards," Drew said loudly. He tied the laces on his shirt, and looking across the river again, Drew couldn't see anyone.

"Real sneaky bastards!" Drew shouted even louder, his words echoing into the trees.

Drew saw Shane sitting on a sandy section of the riverbank, his feet buried in the water. He walked over and sat next to him. Stretching his legs into the water, he watched the current swirl around his feet.

"That was a pretty nasty shit you took out there," Shane said. "You probably created a major pollution problem down river. Agent Brown. It's probably worse than Agent Orange. We could've won the war with that."

"Go to hell," Drew said.

"Relax, Drew. I know just what you need." Shane took the bag from his shoulder, opened it, and pulled out a bottle of Johnnie Walker Red. He took a drink and gave the bottle to Drew. Drew took a long drink and made a face.

"Do you still know where we are?

"Yes."

"Are you sure?"

"I'm sure," Shane said, kicking water in the air. "This is the Saigon River."

"This is the same river that goes through Saigon?" Drew asked.

"The same one," Shane said. "It starts in Cambodia and ends in Saigon. The capital's only one hundred and fifty miles from here." He took a drink and gave the bottle to Drew. "We'll be home in no time." He reached in the bag and pulled out a loaf of French bread. He broke it apart and gave half to Drew. "Eat some of this."

"Thanks," Drew said. "I'll try."

Drew tasted a small piece, and still feeling queasy in the stomach, he broke off a piece and threw it in the river. As it floated away, there was a boil of water, and a school of small fish swirled around the bread. Drew threw another piece of bread in the river, and the feeding frenzy intensified for a moment. Then spraying water in all directions, the small fishes scattered when a dark shadow moved to the surface. A huge mouth opened and swallowed the bread.

"What the hell was that?" Shane asked, lifting his feet out of the water.

"The Loch Ness monster," Drew said. He took a drink of the whiskey and began laughing. "How the hell should I know? I don't live here."

"That thing would kill you," Shane said. He took the bottle from Drew and lifted it to his mouth. When he finished drinking, he shook the bottle and saw that it was empty. Raising it over is head, he tossed it far into the river. After it bobbed up and down and then sank, he turned and saw Drew staring at him.

"What?"

"I've been thinking about this for a long time, Shane, but I never asked you."

"You thinking about something, Mr. College Graduate, why doesn't that surprise me?" Shane said. "What were you thinking about, Drew?"

"It happened way back in high school."

"What happened way back in high school?"

"What you did on Senior Night, our last football game. You could have scored the winning touchdown and been the hero, but instead, you threw the damn ball back to me. I didn't have to do anything. After you hit that safety and destroyed the kicker, there was no one in the way. I just walked across the goal line. I never understood that."

"You wouldn't understand it."

"Why?"

"It's hard to explain."

"Try me."

"It's just the way things were, Drew. Let's just say you earned it."

"I didn't earn anything. I couldn't play football. I couldn't even make a tackle by myself," Drew said. "I was completely hopeless. Like I said, I didn't earn anything."

"You're wrong," Shane said. "Consider my situation. I had everything. I had the best parents and the best girl. Football was so easy for me. Everything was easy. And . . . ," Shane began but hesitated. He slid his feet back into the river.

"And what?"

"And you had it pretty tough, Drew. You lost your parents. You had to live through that. I don't know how you did it. If it had been me, I wouldn't have made it. Losing your whole life like that. It would be like starting all over. Starting with nothing. A big zero."

"I had you."

"Like I said, a big zero."

'You were never a zero, Shane."

"Thanks."

"And I had your parents, too."

"I know," Shane said. "They're the greatest. But yet, it could never be the same. After the accident in the park, I mean when I saw you in the hospital bed, I thought what if it had been me. What if my parents were dead? I couldn't stop myself. I cried, Drew. For the first time ever, I cried."

"For yourself?"

"Mostly," Shane said. "Sure, I worried about you. But after the way you walked out of the emergency room with only that cut on your face and then all those crazy nights you were fighting some beast, I began to realize how strong you were. I really admired that because I don't think I could have done it. And then somehow you were past it. You punched Frank Jr. in the face; you went after that buck; you pounded the shit out of that poacher."

"That was nothing," Drew said. "He was old. He was a senior citizen."

"You didn't know that in the dark," Shane said He looked closely at Drew, and a big smile formed on his face. "And most important of all."

"What?"

"Somehow you managed to score at the shore."

"My first home run," Drew laughed, remembering the sand, the sun, the icy splash of cola.

"I mean like you started out so sad and you came out so strong. You were awesome."

"I didn't do that much."

"But you did, Drew. You saved Jackson from hanging himself at the arch. And Homer told me you outran him in the park. No way did he expect you to do that. Then you showed him that silver band you put on the cannon. He said you had more strength in you than anyone he knew. He called it a quiet, inner strength. He said you reminded him so much of Mr. Benson. Homer said your dad would have been so proud. I know he was proud of you when you scored that winning touchdown."

"Then that's why you did it," Drew said. "That's why you gave me the ball."

"Maybe it was, Drew. I don't know. I don't like to think too much about things like that."

"Thanks for telling me," Drew said. Glancing across the river, he thought he saw movement in the shadows and recognized the diminutive body of the Vietcong soldier. Dropping his head and looking into the flashing glare of sunlight on the Saigon River, Drew wiped at his eyes.

"I never heard you talk so much. Why didn't you ever say anything?"

Shane was quiet for a moment. When he spoke, his voice was barely audible above the lapping sound of the waves.

"Maybe some things don't need saying. Maybe they're just understood."

"Maybe you're right," Drew said, staring at the river, at the waves splashing at his feet and down the length of the sandy beach.

There was a low humming vibration beyond the bend in the river. The noise grew louder, and the helicopter roared into view. It descended low over the river, spraying water high in the air. Shane stood up and waved his hands in the air, and the helicopter turned toward the bank. Drew moved to get up, but the quick motion was too much. Numbed by the cheap whiskey and the cramps in his stomach, Drew was weak, and his legs buckled under him. Shane helped him up, and they walked, and then began to run toward the landing chopper.

Drew leaned back on the bench. All the bottles were empty, and the KFC container was filled with white bones. The moonlight was bright, and looking across the parade ground, Drew saw a large herd of deer grazing in the open field. He picked up the container and walked to the flat memorial.

"Chicken Thief Soldier," Drew said. He studied the lines that crisscrossed the stone face of the memorial. After a long pause, he knelt down beside the piece of stone.

"It's hard to explain," Drew said. "I feel so bad for you, the way you died. Because I understand. I felt your hunger. I felt your pain."

Drew flipped open the container and began placing the chicken bones carefully around the sides of the memorial. A wing here, a leg bone there, he took his time and emptied the container. Then he got up slowly and looked at the rectangle of bones jutting out from the ground.

Drew saw how the white bones, some slanted high in the air, were majestic like ivory in the moonlight. He was proud and smiled at what he had done.

He walked around the rectangle of bones that bordered the Chicken Thief Memorial, and then swinging the empty container in his hand, he went back to the stone bench.

There was no traffic this late at night. The park was quiet and peaceful. High in the cloudless sky, the moon was bright, and the towering statue next to the bench extended a long black shadow across the parade ground. Drew looked up at the darkened features of the baron's face.

"You may be impressive, General Baron von Steuben," Drew said. He turned and looked at the thin, jagged shadows from the line of bones, "but your statue will never be as fine and noble as the memorial to the chicken thief soldier."

There was a glow from across the parade ground, and Drew watched two headlights crest Mount Joy and flash a bright light on the granite façade of the Memorial Arch. After a few seconds the car moved into the grove of dogwood trees, leaving the arch and Mount Joy in total darkness.

"And someday," Drew said, turning his gaze back to the small rectangle in the ground, "someday, the people will know, and they'll come to the park to see you, Chicken Thief Soldier. They'll come to honor you for what you did."

Drew nodded his head at the flattened piece of stone and twisted bones. Then he gathered up the empty bottles of Sam Adams from the bench and returned to the car.

CHAPTER 17

E arly Wednesday morning, Drew's sleep was punctuated by gunfire and shouts from the Vietcong. The nightmare was vivid and real but totally incomprehensible because he and Shane weren't fighting the Vietcong in the jungles of Vietnam. They were on the hills of Mount Joy in Valley Forge. A squad of VC soldiers were in a screaming, maniacal charge up the hill, and as they got closer, Drew recognized the twisted faces of Coach Chuck, Frank Jr., and Leroy.

Drew woke up in a sweat. Lying there with his eyes tightly closed, he thought about the anger and hate he saw in the faces, and after a few minutes, he was wide awake. Being careful not to disturb Whin, he went quietly to the bathroom and threw water on his face. Returning to the bedroom, he kissed NuWhin on the cheek and put on his sweat pants and running shoes. Drew found his old George Washington High School sweatshirt, put the Sony recorder in the front pocket, and slid the sweatshirt over his head. When he opened the door and walked on the porch, the cold air chilled his face. Except for the dim glare of a porch light across the street, it was completely dark and quiet.

There was a heavy fog over the city, and Drew drove very slowly. He got behind an orange-and-black Frito Lay truck and followed it all the way to the park. At the red light at Washington's Headquarters, Drew watched the driver, a young man with sunglasses, a moustache, and black Red Sox baseball cap with PETE written across the front, open a large bag of chips. The driver was still eating the chips when the light turned green. After a few seconds, Drew rolled down his window and shouted.

"Hurry up, Pete!"

The driver turned and waved and moved the truck across the intersection. He continued on Route 23 toward King of Prussia, but Drew drove straight up the road and stopped on Mount Joy at the same spot in his dream where the

Vietcong were attacking. Glancing down the slope of the hill, he saw only some tree shadows in the thick fog.

Drew looked for the familiar deer shapes, but there weren't any. After a few minutes, he drove slowly forward and parked the car in the small lot next to the Memorial Arch. The arch itself was a dark silhouette looming out of the fog.

Beginning his stretching routine at the corner of the lot, Drew breathed the freshness of the air. He felt the cold deep in his lungs. Drew lifted his knee to his chest and was beginning to feel the stretch in his calf muscle when there was the slightest scraping sound a short distance down the jogging path.

Drew looked up and saw only the thick covering of fog. Everything was completely quiet and eerily still. Lowering his leg slowly, Drew became quietly alert. He studied the field and the clumps of trees, and as on Mount Joy, he couldn't see any sign of the deer population. The breeze shifted, and he instantly recognized the faint odor of burnt weed.

Drew finished his stretching and walked to the jogging path. The rising sun was a white orb with a dim halo of light on the horizon. As the light filtered downward over the park, Drew could see branches protruding out of the fog. Beyond the trees bordering the path, there was a line of three cannons. The large circular wheels were barely visible, and slanting upward from the ground, the barrels seemed to disintegrate in the fog. There was a black form perched on the end of the nearest cannon.

Moving closer, Drew concentrated his gaze on the form and saw black wings lift in the air. The crow began a series of shrill, piercing caws and flew down the jogging path. Following the diminishing cries of the bird, Drew started his run. He ran past the cannons and was approaching a clump of bushes when two large figures stepped out of the cover of the heavy, drooping branches. They wore dark pants and blue Valley Forge varsity jackets.

"Mr. Asshole," Leroy slurred. He smiled and clenched his fists. Standing next to him in the fog, Chester had a wide, toothy smile that glimmered a dull gold glow through the fog. The smile widening, Chester crouched down in a low, linebacker stance. Drew slowed and stopped directly in front of them. There was noise from behind, and as he began to turn, he saw another varsity jacket materialize out of the fog.

"Get him, Rusty," Leroy said, and the large, amazingly quick tackle lifted Drew's body in the air and slammed him down onto the cement of the jogging path. Then Drew was kicked in the stomach and chest, the air exploding from his mouth. The Sony recorder dropped out of his pocket onto the cement.

"What the hell is this?" Leroy asked. He smashed the heel of his foot into the recorder, and then he kicked the broken pieces of plastic and brown ribbon into the grass.

"Help me pick up the fucker," Chester said. He and Rusty pulled Drew to his feet and held him in front of Leroy.

"Locking us in a log cabin," Leroy said. "You dumb bastard." He swung fiercely and punched Drew in the eye.

Drew saw a sharp flash of red and sudden darkness. Falling back in the darkness, his arms still held strongly by the two football players, Drew muttered the words "junkyard dog" and kicked his foot upward fast and hard into Leroy's groin. Drew heard a loud shriek and then shouts of profanity as Leroy collapsed, his body twisting downward, his head hitting the gravel in front of Drew.

Blood began swelling in Drew's left eye. He was struggling to pull his arms loose when he heard a bellow followed by a loud thumping sound. The pressure was instantly released from his arm, and Rusty's huge body dropped at his feet. With his arm free and using Kim Lee's powerful attack technique, Drew swung his open palm into Chester's mouth, smashing through his lip and busting off two gold crowns. Blood spraying in the air, Chester hit the ground and lay still.

Drew straightened and wiped the blood from his eye. He turned around and saw Jackson standing there. He held a Louisville Slugger in his hand.

"Got the bastard," Jackson said, pointing the end of the Louisville Slugger at Rusty. Then he looked at Drew and the blood dripping onto the George Washington sweatshirt. "They hurt you?"

"It's nothing," Drew said, listening to the groans around him. "Lucky you were here."

"I'm here every morning," Jackson said. Rusty rolled on the ground and tried to get up. "Should I take another swing?"

"No, Mr. Whiz Kid, he's had enough." Drew picked up the smashed recorder and slid it in his pocket.

"I used my best form," Jackson said, lifting the bat behind his shoulder and taking a giant swing through the moist, clinging fog. "My home-run swing." He looked again at the blood on Drew's face. "We should get that eye fixed."

"I'll wash it at the house."

"It needs stitches," Jackson said. "I'll take you back to the hospital. I know the nurse there. She'll close it up for you. No problem at all."

Drew removed his hand from his eye and saw the blood. More blood was dripping down the side of his face.

"Maybe I should see the nurse," he said. Leaving the three football players moaning on the ground, he and Jackson walked to the car.

"Want me to drive?" Jackson asked.

"I'm fine," Drew said, getting in the car.

Jackson went to the passenger side. He slid in and rested the Slugger across his knees. Driving past the arch now visible through the morning fog, Drew looked at the clumsy movements of the three football players on the jogging path. They struggled to stand up, holding onto each other for support. The body of one of them began to sway and dropped back on the path.

As Drew turned the car onto Outer Lane Drive, the log cabins and artillery pieces in the park began to take shape in the morning light. Looking through his one good eye, Drew saw the massive statue of Mad Anthony Wayne.

"Mr. Benson," Jackson said, his eyes searching the fog.

"What?"

"I'm in the park before dawn almost every day. Sometimes I get this creepy feeling like I'm not alone. Like there's someone watching me. Do you ever feel that way when you're running?"

"Sometimes," Drew said. "I don't know how to explain it. It's just some kind of presence. Why do you ask?"

"I had that feeling this morning."

"You mean the football players?"

"No, there was someone else. He was real close, but I couldn't find him."

Drew approached the traffic light on Valley Creek Road. Seeing the light was green, Drew drove on without slowing down. The light turned yellow, suddenly red, and Drew braked. The car skidded forward and stopped. Jackson reached for the Slugger, but it rolled off his knees and hit the floor. Drew looked at the old Louisville logo and grained wood on the bat.

"Jackson," he said. "You love baseball, don't you?"

"Ever since I was a kid," Jackson said.

"Did you ever see Jackie Robinson play?"

"Are you kidding me?" Jackson asked. "I seen him lots of times. He was the magic man. He was unbelievable."

"He was that good?" Drew asked. The light turned green, and Drew turned the car onto Route 23.

"Hell, when Jackie was in the game, I wouldn't dare leave my seat. I mean, I couldn't take a piss, go for beer, or nothing. Because at one game, I was just buying a hot dog from a vender right there in the aisle. I was counting my change when this loud roar went up and the people around me began jumping. I looked back to the field. There was this crowd at the plate, the umpire, the catcher, and Jackie getting up, brushing off his pants. He had just stolen home."

"I heard Jackie was fast," Drew said.

"He was explosive. Nothing but energy," Jackson said. He gripped the Slugger in his hands. "He didn't hit for power, only had a home run now and then. But when he got on base, it was like a triple or home run because he stole bases whenever he wanted to. And do you know what? Jackie was loyal to the Dodgers that first got him into major league baseball. He didn't do this jumping from team to team like now. He stayed with the Brooklyn Dodgers the whole time. And when they went to trade him, he quit baseball. Rather then play for another team, he just quit."

"Yeah, I heard about that, too," Drew said. He drove past the flags and Sherman Tank at the entrance to the Veterans Hospital. Except for a few cars, the parking lot was empty. "You never mentioned that Jackie was black."

"Don't need to. Color had nothing to do with his game," Jackson said. "Jackie was a player. That's all that counted. Like when I was fighting in Korea, I wanted soldiers next to me, not fools or assholes or cowards. Those kinds could get you killed. If you wanted to stay alive, you hung out with real soldiers, black or white. They were your only friends."

"It was the same in Nam," Drew said, feeling the throbbing above his eye increase. "You always stayed close to your friends."

Drew parked the car at the front entrance of the main building. The blood was dry on his face, and looking in the rearview mirror, he saw the lump beginning to form above his eye. He got out of the car and followed Jackson into the building and down the hall to the nurse station. Seeing Jackson swinging the Louisville Slugger and Drew with his bloody face, the nurse showed immediate concern.

"Why'd you hit this man, Jackson?"

"I didn't hit him, Nurse Ann," Jackson said, lowering the bat to his side. "He got ambushed in the park while jogging."

"Since when did the park get so dangerous?" she asked.

"Sometimes," Drew said, "I think it's more dangerous than Vietnam."

"Don't talk crazy," Nurse Ann said. She cleaned Drew's face, closed the cut over his eye with three clamps, and covered everything with a clean bandage. When she was finished, she smiled, gave him a small zip-lock bag of ice, and said he would be fine in a few days. Drew thanked her, and he and Jackson went back to the car.

"I'll watch out for your friend," Jackson said.

"I know," Drew said. "Thank you." Holding the ice over his eye, he started the car and backed out of the parking space. A large truck and a line of cars began pulling into the Veterans Hospital. Drew waited for the end of the line to pass. Then he pulled onto Charlestown Road and drove past the high school into Phoenixville. The fog had lifted, and the sky was bright and clear when he reached the house.

That morning when the boy walked by the bush, Jeb Wood was close enough to touch him. He had seen the three football players arrive earlier and knew they were planning something. They looked around and then took positions by the jogging path.

They're setting to ambush someone, Jeb thought. One of them lit a match, and Jeb saw the glow of light.

"Stupid fucker," Jeb said. He aimed his M1903 Springfield at the tiny light and was tempted to extinguish it and teach the smoker a good lesson. But he heard the car engine coming up Mount Joy, and he lowered his rifle. When the car stopped and the door opened, Jeb knew right away it was the boy who took his eye.

Jeb watched the light go out, but he could still smell a slight trace of the smoke. The boy would know, too. But the boy wouldn't know that there were three of them waiting. Jeb decided to wait also, and after a few minutes, the boy walked right past him. He could have hurt him bad right there, but he wanted to see what would happen with the ambush.

The Blue Jackets did good at first. Even though the fog distorted everything, Jeb enjoyed watching and hearing the tackle and hard punches. The boy was on his way down, but Jeb wasn't sure what happened after that. He jumped up from behind the bush and left in a hurry.

You dumb bastard, he said, feeling uncontrollable anger at himself. The other man came to help the boy, and Jeb never knew he was there.

"You blind, dumb bastard!" he spoke the words this time.

Jeb walked at a fast pace along the tree line. After fifteen minutes, he pushed some branches aside and stepped onto a narrow path that only he knew about. It took him another twenty minutes to reach his property. He heard the barking sound of a dog in the distance. Then there was another, closer bark.

"Fuck," Jeb said. Moving quickly through the underbrush, weaving his way around the bear traps, Jeb approached the clearing of the ninth hole of the Lafayette Country Club. Bright on the horizon, the sun was burning off the last layers of fog over the golf course. The dog barked again, and Jeb saw it clearly in the middle of the driving range two hundred yards away.

It was a big German shepherd. Head lifted high, nose sniffing the air, the dog was motionless. Then it barked again and took off running down the perfectly-trimmed field of grass.

Jeb casually lifted the Springfield, and scoping the dog, he saw the black body and powerful back and shoulder muscles bouncing in a smooth rhythm of motion. When the German shepherd was ninety yards away, Jeb fired the Springfield and blew off the right side of the dog's head. The German shepherd was dead instantly. Its body lifted sideways in the air, hit the ground, and rolled five yards before it stopped.

Jeb picked up the cartridge, and grabbing a heavy chain, he pulled a bear trap over the spot that he was standing on. Shouldering the Springfield, Jeb walked into the woods to the trapdoor, cleared some sod to find the handle, and then lifted the door in the air. Before he descended down the steps, he looked through the trees at the blue sky and saw a vulture circling overhead.

"He's all yours," Jeb said, lowering the door. After shaking it back and forth to settle the dirt on top, Jeb locked it and began to walk down the dark passage.

It was cool, and the damp earth smelled good to Jeb. Reaching the cellar, he opened the door, stepped inside, and closed the door behind him.

Jeb leaned the Springfield against the bear-skin wall, lit the lantern, and going to the cabinet, he picked out a bottle of champagne from the box. Jeb uncorked it and laughed at the bubbles splashing down his hand. Jeb took a long drink, laughed again, and sat down on the bed.

Jeb always drank a bottle of champagne when he killed one of their dogs. The light, bubbly drink for rich people helped Jeb forget his anger. He was happy now, smiling at the picture stuck in the clay wall.

"Just got the third one," Jeb said to Joshua. "This was the biggest one so far." Jeb took another drink, and studying the picture, he felt good to see the bright look on his brother's face.

"And the boy's back. I thought I saw him on Monday, but I wasn't sure. But he's back in the park." Jeb put the half-empty bottle of champagne on the floor. Leaning back on the pillow, he crossed his hands behind his head.

"I got to get serious now," Jeb said, not looking at his brother any more. He stared at the bear skin and the Springfield propped against it. "I got me some real plannin' to do."

Jeb reached his hand under the bed and picked up the only book in the house. He didn't have no reading skills, but he took his time and he could make out some of the meaning. And this book had a lot of pictures to help. Jeb looked at the cover.

United States Army Sniper Manual, Jeb read the title slowly.

Jeb knew from years of opening the book and looking at the pictures that expert snipers went for the chest when the target was over 330 yards away or more. But for closer targets, Jeb knew you shot for the head.

Just like the dogs, Jeb thought. *Just like the dogs.* Jeb opened the book to the marked page and began studying the words he had looked at a thousand times.

At the house, Drew showered, put on his dark blue suit, and opening a stained, gift box, he pulled out a red tie with blue elephants on the front. The elephants formed circles down the length of the tie. Looking in the mirror, Drew saw one elephant, balanced on his hind feet, standing majestically high in the air.

Drew finished the knot on the tie and hurried downstairs. While he was eating breakfast, Whin asked him about the bandage over his eye, and he said it was nothing. Sitting on his lap, NuWhin kept stretching up trying to kiss his face. When she couldn't reach it, she played with the elephant tie.

Drew drove to the school, found an empty parking space, and entered the building quickly. As he climbed the steps to the second floor, some of the students said good morning and looked at the bandage over his eye. Drew took a drink of water at the fountain and went to his classroom. Walking into the room, Drew saw a thick red Magic Marker line drawn across his desk. He also saw an envelope with the school's Patriot mascot stamped in the corner. Drew opened the envelope and read the administrative directive.

TO:	Mr. Drew Benson,
FROM:	Mr. West, Principal
SUBJECT:	Your removal from the Valley Forge School District and the subsequent criminal and civil charges that will be filed against you.

Drew crushed the memo in his hand without reading the rest of it. Dropping the paper in the wastebasket, he saw the bright red line on his desk was actually an arrow. The end of the arrow pointed to the corner drawer. Sliding open the drawer, Drew immediately noticed a paper plate covered with a napkin. When Drew removed the napkin, he saw the peanut butter sandwich.

"Cool," Drew laughed. He picked up the sandwich and took a bite. Then he took another bite and finished it. Tasting the honey in his mouth, Drew wrote the morning's assignment on the board. Then he sat down and began picking the crumbs from the plate. The first students began moving down the hall, forming groups around the lockers. A few minutes before the morning bell, May walked in.

"Thanks," Drew said, getting up.

"Was it good?"

"Delicious," Drew said. "Just like I remembered."

"I wish everything could be like it used to be," May said. "I saw Shane last night. He still doesn't recognize me. The doctors keep working with him, but he isn't getting any better."

"He will," Drew said. He saw May looking at his face.

"What happened to your eye?" she asked, coming closer. "Here I am talking about Shane."

"It's only a small cut," Drew said.

"Please don't let anything happen to you, Drew. It would be too much right now."

"I'm fine," Drew said.

"Good," she said and pointed to the tie. "I like those elephants."

"Thanks."

"Oh, before I forget," May said. The bell rang and May backed away from the desk. "I wanted to wish you good luck at the emergency school board meeting. There are some wild stories going around."

"They're all true," Drew said. Some students began entering the room. May was at the door when Drew called to her.

"Wait, May." Drew walked around the desk and joined her in the hall. Taking her hand, he ushered her off to the side.

"What?" May asked.

"Did you see Betty Collier?"

"She was at the hospital last night," May said. "We took care of Shane together."

"There's something important we've got to talk about," Drew said. The last rush of students began filing into the room.

"Homeroom's starting," May said. "Can we talk later?"

"Sure," Drew said. "Thanks again for the sandwich." He raised his hand and waved as May walked across the hall to her room. The speaker above the blackboard cracked on, and there was the noisy shuffling of chairs as the students stood up for the National Anthem.

After the National Anthem and the Pledge of Allegiance, the student council president read through a long list of announcements. The last announcements consisted of testimonials from senior players about what the football team would do to the Eagles on Friday night.

One player shouted in a tough voice and boasted that no team, not even the Philadelphia Eagles could beat them, and then he guaranteed an easy victory and an undefeated season. After the announcements were over, noise erupted in the hall, and cheerleaders ran by shouting slogans and waving banners.

Clapping their hands and screaming, some of the students pushed away their desks and rushed to the door. One of the boys, Melvin Brown, a thin boy in jeans and Valley Forge T-shirt, shouted something and raced down the hall after the cheerleaders. The students in the doorway cheered him, returned noisily to their seats, and eventually began working on the assignment. Melvin never did come back to the classroom. Drew circled his name on the seating chart. The class went well, and at the end of the period, Drew erased the circle.

The second and third classes went without incident. During the fourth period, a cute brunette, Stacy, sitting in the front seat, had a worried look on her face when she saw the cut over Drew's eye, and she asked him if it hurt. Drew said it didn't hurt. Shining her bright eyes at him and smiling sweetly, Stacy added that he already had one scar and it made him look handsome in a tough kind of way. She wanted him to be careful because she didn't know what two scars would do to his face. They might make him look like Rocky.

"I've always wanted to look like Rocky," Drew laughed. He reached down, opened her book, and pointed his finger to the assignment. When he straightened, Stacy had a mischievous smile on her face.

"Oh," she said, the smile growing wider. "I really like your tie."

"Thank you," Drew said and returned to his desk. At the end of the class, the students left for lunch. Drew was on his way to the door when a loud voice boomed from the speaker.

"Mr. Benson, report to the office now!" There was a pause, and Drew could hear heavy breath hitting the microphone. The principal shouted into the microphone again. "Mr. Benson, are you there?" There was a longer pause. As the microphone clicked off, Drew looked up and saw Anthony Bartoli at the door. The janitor had a big grin on his face.

"The hell with the principal," he said. "Come on. It's time for lunch like the old days."

Drew followed Tony down the back steps. In the corridor at the bottom of the steps, a group of cheerleaders and students were talking and eating pizza. Brushes and small paint cups were scattered around the edges of a long banner that nearly covered the whole floor. The outline of a fire pit and log cabin was in the center of the banner. The fire was burning in the pit, and on the spit above the flames, Drew saw what looked like a large plucked chicken.

Roast the Eagles was written in red letters across the bottom of the banner. Melvin Brown, T-shirt now spattered with paint, was outlining the bottom letters on the banner. He stood up quickly when he saw Drew.

"You never made it back to the room, Mel."

"I'm sorry, Mr. Benson," Mel said. "I should have asked permission."

"You missed the whole lesson."

"I'll get it done, Mr. Benson. I promise. I'll do it tonight." Mel put his head down and fingered the brush in his hand. He lifted his head slowly. "Did you turn me in?"

"No," Drew said. He pointed at the fire pit and the bruised Eagle on the spit. Twisted feathers stuck out of the bloated body, and the burnt wings were painted in black and red colors. The mutilated beak was open and screaming ***HELP ME!*** and ***SAVE ME FROM THE PATRIOTS!***

"Did you have anything to do with that?" Drew asked.

"I painted it."

"That's our national emblem."

"It's an Eagle. We're going to kick Eagle ass Friday night."

"That's what I like to hear," Drew said. "Listen carefully, Mel. I have something important to tell you."

"What?" Mel asked.

"First, I don't know what you're doing wasting your time at Valley Forge," Drew said seriously. "***SAVE ME FROM THE PATRIOTS***, that's the best art work I've ever seen. I'm going to recommend you for a scholarship to the Philadelphia School of Arts."

"Wow, Mr. Benson, that's great." Mel laughed. "You're the first one to notice my talent."

"It was the same with Picasso," Drew said. "I want to buy your first masterpiece." He waved his hand at Mel and walked down the hall.

"You can have it for free for not reporting me," Mel said, and then he shouted. "That's a great tie, Mr. Benson. I never saw one like that before."

Drew caught up to Tony and followed him to the side exit. It was chilly outside, and the sun was hidden by dark moving clouds. A blue-and-gold golf cart was at the door, and they got inside. Turning the key, Tony jumped the cart into motion, and soon they were racing across the parking lot. The rush of air whipped Drew's tie across his face, and Drew grabbed for it. As he tucked the tie in his shirt, he saw the yellow Jaguar turn sharply and skid to a stop in a No Parking area. The doors swung open, and Chester and Sally stepped out. Moving slowly and struggling to stand up straight, Leroy was the last one to leave the Jaguar.

Tony drove the golf cart to the football stadium, went through the open gate, and around the track that bordered the field. He turned the golf cart behind the bleachers and raced the length of the chain-link fence to the far end of the stadium. There he braked and maneuvered the cart though a side exit onto a narrow dirt road lined with trees and brush.

"I don't golf," Tony said, steering the cart over the high grass and ruts in the road. "But I love this machine. It gets me away from that building. They can call all they want, but they can't find me. It's my lunch, and I want to enjoy eating it."

The dirt road led to the entrance of an old storage garage. Tony bounced the cart through the sliding double doors and stopped next to a large table, set of chairs, and sofa. He and Tony stepped down from the cart, and Tony removed the big basket from the back. Placing it in the center of the table, he opened the cover. Drew could immediately smell the fragrance of the garlic and spaghetti sauce, and the aroma of fresh bread.

"A special treat for you," Tony said. "It's good to have you back."

Tony spread the plates and silverware on the table, and taking two glasses, he filled them with a dark wine. He took one glass and gave the other to Drew.

"I know about your new family," Tony said. "To a happy future for you and your wife and your daughter." He clinked the side of his glass against Drew's, and they drank the wine. Tony put his glass down and began to study the tie on Drew's shirt. With a smile on his face, he reached over and lifted the front of the tie in the air.

"I thought so," he said.

"What?"

"This elephant there dancing in the middle of the circle is doing a bad thing."

"What?" Drew asked, twisting the tie around so he could see it.

"He's humping the smaller elephant," Tony said. "His dick is harder than his tusk!"

"Damn," Drew said. "No wonder I was so popular this morning." He laughed when he looked at the elephant. "I've been distracted all day. I never paid any attention to it."

"The students will appreciate the elephants," Tony said. "But Principal West doesn't have a sense of humor."

"I know," Drew said. "A fornicating elephant could get me in a lot of trouble. Shane gave me the tie last year when I turned twenty-four."

"Shane should be here like before," Tony said, shaking his head. "I visited the Veteran's Hospital twice, but he didn't move or say anything. My wife and I just sat there at his side. It was difficult to see him like that. You and Shane were my best friends."

"You taught us everything about the school," Drew said. He tasted the wine again. "You know more about how the school works than anyone."

"I know some things," Tony said. "Tell me about your face. What did you run into?"

"Some students in the park this morning," Drew said.

"You mean the football players," Tony said. "They are real bastards." Tony drank some wine and spoke in a low voice. "I have some friends, Drew. They can fix this right now. Just let me know what you want."

"Thanks," Drew said. "But everything's fine. It was fixed this morning at the park."

"OK then," Tony said. "Just remember I know some important people who you can trust."

"I'll remember," Drew said.

"Then let's eat," Tony said. He filled the dishes with spaghetti, grated fresh cheese over it, and put the toasted garlic bread on the side. Talking about the old times and the old school, they ate and drank. The wine relaxed Drew, and the time passed quickly. When they finished and Tony packed everything in the basket, he motioned Drew to the back door of the garage.

"I want to show you something," he said.

Drew followed Tony through the door and down a trail overgrown with tall grass and brush. There were only a few white clouds high in the sky, and the afternoon sun was warm. Loosening the elephant tie and opening the top button on his shirt, Drew stepped over the body of a dead possum. The trail ended at a huge sinkhole. The rounded crater was filled with broken desks and chairs, a refrigerator, some half-buried shop tables, dented file cabinets, and an overturned tractor, its red color fading to orange.

"Debris from the old school," Tony said. "The contractors were in a hurry and didn't want to haul everything away to the dump. Principal West saved a lot of money by leaving it here." Tony grinned and gave Drew an all-knowing look. "Who knows where all that money went?"

"Maybe a scholarship for Frank Jr.," Drew said.

"Or maybe for the expensive golf clubs he keeps in the back seat of his car," Tony said. He pointed across the sinkhole to the massive, half-buried blocks of granite. "Look here, Drew. This is what I wanted you to see."

The blocks of granite were part of the old school façade. They rose out of the rubble and broken pieces of stone of the sinkhole. Drew looked at them carefully and could only make out a few words.

"**GEORGE . . . HIGH . . .** , " he read slowly.

"That's all that's left of the school," Tony said. "They'll bulldoze this soon, and George Washington High School will be gone forever."

A bell rang in the distance, its tone a dim echo when it reached the secluded area around the sinkhole. Looking at the large, meaningless letters on the cracked blocks of stone, Drew remembered the grand features of the old school and shook his head.

"We had the best times there," he said.

"And we'll always have them," Tony said. "It's good that they can't bulldoze our memories."

The long ring of the bell sounded again. Tony turned at the sound, and he and Drew walked back to the garage. They got in the golf cart, and Tony gunned it up the road to the football field. Drew saw someone standing at the exit gate, and when they got closer, he recognized the overweight figure of Coach Chuck. Chuck stood in the middle of the road. Tony skidded the golf cart to a stop, and he and Drew stepped out.

"Benson, you're a real bastard!" Coach Chuck shouted, his face red with anger. "You're getting thrown out of here today!" Chuck began shouting louder, and little bubbles of spittle formed on the corners of his mouth.

"Leroy and Chester called in late. They're both hurt bad. Rusty has a big gash on the side of his head. They said you ambushed them this morning. What is it with you, Benson? Being a loser all your life, you can't stand it, can you? You can't stand to be near winners."

"Wait a minute, Mr. Coach," Tony said. "You and I should talk privately. Let's go over here." Tony took Coach Chuck's arm, and they walked to the side of the gate. Standing next to the massive bulk of Chuck, talking quietly right in his face, Tony looked small and insignificant.

But as Tony talked, Chuck's body seemed to slump, and the patches of red anger left his face. His mouth dropped open, and Chuck stood motionless. When Tony finished talking with a long, hard stare into Chuck's face, and Chuck quiet and studying the white lines and grass on the football field, Tony walked back to the golf cart and motioned Drew to get inside. Without looking at Coach Chuck, Tony drove the cart through the gate.

"What happened?" Drew asked.

"Many years ago my family moved here from Jersey," Tony said. "They did things and became very rich. I could have joined them, but I decided to do my own work as a janitor. It keeps me busy, and it's quiet work. My family, they are busy in their own way, and I still love them."

"That's what you told Chuck?"

"No," Tony said. "I just told Chuck that if anything happens to you, I would introduce him to my family members. When they finished communicating with him, maybe he would have to learn how to coach football from a wheelchair."

"Cool," Drew said, shaking his head. "I wish I had known your family members when I was a senior."

"There was nothing to worry about. I was always watching out for you and Shane," Tony said. "But Vietnam was too far away. I feel bad that Shane's hurt like he is. I won't let anything happen to you, Drew. It's how I feel about family."

Tony drove the cart to the front entrance. Drew thanked him for the great lunch and went inside. Cheerleaders and pep club members were still putting up posters and painting slogans on the lockers. A sports reporter from Philadelphia was interviewing Terry, who stood next to the Patriot soldier. The large crowd of students in front of the log cabin chanted and shouted loudly when he finished. The TV cameraman turned and videotaped their excitement.

The Patriots against the redcoats, Drew thought. *It's like the Revolutionary War all over again.*

A red-clad dummy dressed as an Eagles football player was thrown high in the air at the Patriot soldier. On the second throw, the player's armpit was speared by the bayonet at the end of the musket, and the dummy hung there motionless. Loud cheers and clapping erupted from the lobby and balcony. Watching from the top of the steps, Drew could barely hear the bell to begin afternoon classes.

In the school conference room on the first floor, dressed in an expensive dark blue suit, white shirt, heavy gold cuff links, and flashy red tie, Attorney Sam Grimes sat behind a polished oak desk. His daughter, Sally, and Leroy and Chester sat opposite him. They had just finished reviewing a joint statement on the Valley Forge log cabin incident, and Sam was reading it back to them.

Looking over the top of the paper, Attorney Grimes noticed that both football players were experiencing some kind of pain. Leroy didn't smile, and he had a hurt look on his face whenever he moved in his chair, and Chester held onto his side with both hands. Attributing it to football injuries, the school attorney continued reading.

The statement was only two paragraphs long. It clearly stated how the students participated on a field trip to Valley Forge National Park. In the morning, they helped clean the area around George Washington's Headquarters.

Then at noon, when the lunches arrived, they went into one of the log cabins to get out of the sun. They were eating quietly when the substitute teacher, Mr. Benson, came running in and began shouting at them about trespassing.

Leroy tried to explain they would finish lunch in a few minutes and go back to work, but Mr. Benson threatened him. He was real angry and started using profanity. When the students got up to leave, he slammed the door and locked them inside. They were stuck in there all afternoon. It got really hot, and some of them became sick. Sally testified that she was weak and hurt by the confinement and would be under a doctor's care for a few days.

All three students agreed that they didn't understand why the substitute got so angry. Leroy said he acted like one of those "crazies" from Vietnam. Attorney Grimes finished reading the statement and looked at them.

"Is that how it happened?"

"Yes," Sally said. The two football players nodded their heads.

"Sign it on the line above your name," Attorney Grimes said. He slid the statement and a pen across the table. Leroy signed it and looked up.

"Will my dad get the money like you said?"

"Your dad should get a lawyer. He has every right to sue Mr. Benson for what he did. It was careless and negligent."

"Then Benson's done here at the school?" Leroy asked.

"Mr. Benson will be dismissed this afternoon."

"That's good," Chester said. "I was sick and could hardly breathe. My mom and dad want to sue, too. They're talking thousands of dollars."

"He should be put in jail for what he did," Leroy said. Turning in his seat, he grimaced at the sharp pain in his groin.

"Sheriff Hess will listen to your stories," Mr. Grimes said. He checked the signatures, and folding the statement, he stood up. He walked around the table and opened the door.

"Thank you for helping us," Chester said. He and Leroy shook hands with the attorney and stepped into the hall.

"Thanks, Dad," Sally said, kissing him on the cheek. "Leroy and Chester think you're great. Mr. Benson is a wacko."

"He didn't do anything else, did he?" Mr. Grimes reached down and took her hand in his.

"Like what?"

"He didn't touch you or anything like that?"

"No," Sally said. "In the biology room, he grabbed my arm for a moment, but I shook loose. Leroy and Chester and Terry were there so nothing would have happened."

"And nothing will happen again," Mr. Grimes said. "We'll take care of Mr. Benson this afternoon." He let go of Sally's hand. "Will we see you for dinner?"

"There's a big pre-game party tonight. All the football players will be there. I'll probably be a little late coming home."

"Please be careful," he said. Mr. Grimes watched his daughter turn away and join Chester and Leroy in the hall. The class bell rang, and students began to empty into the hall. Mr. Grimes saw Terry Evans walking with a girl he didn't recognize.

"Terry," he called. Terry and the girl came over. "We haven't seen you at the house lately. Is everything all right?"

"Everything's fine," Terry said. "Just getting ready for the big game."

"If you need anything, let me know. And good luck Friday night." He shook hands with Terry. Then Terry put his arm around the girl's waist, and they walked down the hall.

Mr. Grimes watched them. The girl was cute but very ordinary looking. Her face had no makeup, and she wore a plain, colorless dress. Mr. Grimes had never seen her at the house with the other football players.

The phone on the conference table rang, and Mr. Grimes walked quickly into the room. After a second ring, he picked up the phone and heard the voice of Mr. West at the other end. The principal said he had contacted the board members, and a majority of them were coming in for the emergency board meeting. They agreed with him that Mr. Benson was negligent and his actions had put the students in danger. They would vote on this in closed session, and then the board would meet with Mr. Benson and formally dismiss him. The local newspaper reporter would be there, but not the parents. He would call them personally and tell them of the board's decision. Mr. West then said that Homer Matthews who had started all the trouble would not be present. He had sent him to a meeting in Philadelphia.

"Then everything's in order. This should go very smoothly," Mr. Grimes said. "I have the student depositions. I'll bring them up to your office."

With a smile on his face, Mr. Grimes put the phone down. After dropping off the folder at the principal's office, he went outside to the reserved area of the parking lot. Mr. Grimes got in his car and exited school grounds. A short distance down the road he pulled into Walt's Bar and Restaurant. Inside the light was dim, and there were no customers in the darkened room. The one TV on the wall was tuned to a soap channel. Mr. Grimes walked around the pool table to the bar and ordered an Old Fashioned and a BLT sandwich. He watched the figures on the TV while waiting for his drink.

Drew was sitting at the desk when the bell rang to begin the last class of the day. The aspirin he had taken that morning had worn off, and his head began to throb. A group of students entered the room and sat down. Then Terry walked to the corner of the room and took a chair next to the aquarium. Just as the late bell sounded, a student came in, handed Drew a note, and sat down.

Unfolding the note, he read that Leroy, Chester, and Rusty were excused from class. It was signed by Coach Chuck.

The students worked on their reading assignment the whole period. There were no questions, no talking. Except for the bubbling noise from the lifeless fish aquarium, the room was completely quiet. When the dismissal bell rang, the students put the completed papers on his desk and left quietly. Terry was the last one to come to the desk. He looked at the stitch bandage on Drew's head, and then putting his paper with the others, he left the room.

Drew was checking the papers when there was a quiet knock on his door. He looked up as Mrs. Henderson walked in. She was older, very frail looking, and she moved slowly. Drew stood up, and when he took her hand and greeted her, she had a friendly smile on her face.

"Drew, it's good to see you again," she said. "It's been a long time, twelve years since seventh grade."

"Please sit down," Drew said. He pulled a chair next to the desk. "You haven't aged at all."

"Thank you, Drew, but I feel old, and I don't like it." Mrs. Henderson coughed slightly and sat down. "The Old Man in Hemingway's book was right, Drew, and you were wrong. Young people have problems, but September is the most difficult time."

"You're not teaching any more?"

"I was tired, but I thought I was doing fine. Then the principal gave my room to a new teacher, and I was assigned a storage room. It had space for ten desks. The office placed marginal students in the new class. All of them were discipline problems. I tried teaching them for three weeks, but it was too strenuous for me and I retired. Mr. West was glad to get rid of me."

"He was doing his job," Drew said. "Saving the taxpayers' money."

"Quite a lot of money," Mrs. Henderson said. "I was at the top of the salary scale." Mrs. Henderson coughed again and smiled at Drew. "But he didn't get rid of me. I ran for school board and won. I've been at every meeting for the last five years, and I know the right questions to ask. Mr. West can't do anything now. He just sits there like a wounded dog."

"You're here for today's meeting?"

"Nasty business," Mrs. Henderson said. "Mr. West called me this morning and advised me how to vote. He said you're a very dangerous person, Drew."

"I know."

"That bandage on your head," she said, looking at him closely. "Are you all right?"

"It's nothing," Drew said. "I'm fine."

"Good," she said. "I know you, Drew. I know your family. And I know all about those students that were in the log cabin. I don't believe anything Mr. West said."

"Mr. West and I never got along."

"How could you? How could anyone get along with him?" Mrs. Henderson said. "To get along with that man, you have to kiss his ass every day. Excuse my language, Drew."

"I've heard worse," Drew laughed.

"The school board members have no clue. They have their own agenda for being on the board. Do you remember Janice Turner?"

"She graduated before I did," Drew said. "I remember hearing that she broke some rules and was kicked off the cheerleading team."

"That's Janice," Mrs. Henderson said. "She stayed late after a home wrestling match, and when the wrestling coach returned to his office, he found her on the mat being pinned by the team heavyweight." Mrs. Henderson put her hand to her mouth and started to laugh. "That was his only pin all year."

"I never heard that story," Drew said, laughing with her.

"Unfortunately, that pin was the end of Janice's cheerleading career. She blamed it all on the teachers, and she hates this school now. She's against everything and everyone in this school."

"Then she'll vote against me?"

"You can bet on it," Mrs. Henderson said. "And Pastor Sanders, the only reason he's on the board is to get a Bible study class in the curriculum. He'll vote against you, too." She looked at Drew and smiled. "Unless you were reading the Bible to the kids in the log cabin."

"I wasn't," Drew said. "I believe like Ben Franklin that everyone should have religious freedom and there should be complete separation of church and state."

"The pastor wouldn't understand that."

"That's unfortunate," Drew said. "When Franklin died, every minister of every faith attended the funeral. They appreciated what he had accomplished."

"Pastor Sanders sees things differently," Mrs. Henderson said. "He'll vote against you. Three other board members go golfing with Mr. West every Friday afternoon, and they always vote his way no matter what it is. In fact, they just returned from a golf fact-finding conference in Myrtle Beach."

"Will I get any support at all?"

"The Board President Mr. Wentworth will want to find out what happened in his park. He'll ask the right questions. And of course, you'll have my vote."

"I appreciate it," Drew said.

"I wish I could do more."

"You've always been a big help," Drew said. "And I have some other evidence to give to the board. It may not show I was right in locking the log cabin, but it will show that the students were lying."

"I'll look forward to hearing that. I'd better go to the conference room now," Mrs. Henderson said. She got up and shook Drew's hand.

"I'll see you at the meeting," Drew said. He got up and ushered her to the door. When she left, Drew walked to the aquarium in the back of the room.

Bubbles from the two buried air stones rose in the crystal clear water and broke noisily on the surface. Drew looked at the sunken ship and the undulating motion of the long plants for a few moments, and then he turned off the light and returned to his desk.

It was four thirty when the secretary entered Drew's room and summoned him to the meeting. Going down the spiral staircase into the main lobby, Drew saw a group of cheerleaders putting the final banners around the log cabin. The crowded lobby was decorated with blue-and-gold Patriots colors, and large, life-size posters of the football players looked down from the wall. Drew recognized the smirk on Leroy's face, the wide, open-mouthed golden smile of Chester, and the more serious look on Terry's face.

The secretary walked with Drew to the conference room, and Drew went inside. Looking at the upturned faces that lined one side of the table, Drew saw the empty chairs on the other side and sat down in the middle one. Mr. Wall, the superintendent of schools, who he had never met, and Mr. Wentworth, school board president, sat at the end of the table. Attorney Grimes and Principal West sat next to them.

There were open folders lying in front of the board members. Pastor Sanders and Janice Turner sat next to each other. Drew saw the darkly-tanned faces of the three board members, and sitting next to one of them was a lady holding onto a note pad. Drew recognized her immediately as the reporter from the *Evening Phoenix*. Visibly out of place, Mrs. Henderson was the only board member with a smile.

Pastor Sanders read a short prayer, and the superintendent welcomed everyone. Principal West stated the business of the meeting, and then Attorney Grimes read the statement from the students regarding the Valley Forge field trip. With heads bowed, the board members were looking at their handouts and reading along with him. In the middle of the statement, Pastor Sanders shook his head and looked sternly at Drew. The reporter was writing in her notepad. Everything was very quiet and civil.

Separated from the board members by the width of empty table, Drew was expressionless. The top button of his shirt was open, and the elephant tie hung loosely from his neck. Leaning forward and staring at Drew, the pastor seemed to be studying the tie.

When Attorney Grimes finished reading the statement, the board members looked up from their folders. With complacent expressions, they stared directly at Drew. Everything had been decided in closed session. They waited for the final formality of the board's pronouncement.

"By majority vote of the board, Mr. Benson has been removed from the substitute list of the Valley Forge School District," Mr. Wentworth began.

"Can you please state each board member's position on the vote?" Mrs. Henderson asked, without waiting to be recognized. Mr. Wentworth was not bothered by the interruption.

"The vote was five to two," he said. He read the names of the five yes votes. Lowering the paper, he looked at the faces of the board members.

"Mrs. Henderson and Mr. Wentworth are the two dissenting votes," he said. The reporter wrote the names quickly on her paper.

Speaking with a slight irritation in his voice, Principal West gave a strong statement of how the administration strived to protect the students in its care. He pronounced that as long as he was the principal of Valley Forge High School, the students' safety would always be the first priority.

Then Attorney Grimes mentioned the legal consequences of Mr. Benson's actions. He expected lawsuits against the school and against Mr. Benson himself. Most of the burden would fall on Mr. Benson since the administration had followed school policy on the field trip, and there was more than adequate teacher supervision. It was only because of the substitute's willful and negligent actions that the students were in danger.

Attorney Sam Grimes talked about his family's personal involvement in the case. His daughter was emotionally upset and under the care of a physician. But it could have been much worse. The heat and trauma could have damaged her permanently. Mr. Grimes said this should never happen to any student, and he had recommended three provisions for the board to consider, and the board had passed each of the provisions. Staring at Drew, Mr. Grimes began to read from the paper.

"The first provision is that Mr. Benson be removed from the substitute list. The second provision is that Mr. Benson would not be permitted on school grounds." Attorney Grimes was about to read the third provision when the door to the conference room opened, and holding onto a briefcase, Homer Matthews stepped inside.

"I'm sorry I'm late," he said. He pulled out the chair next to Mrs. Henderson, put the briefcase on the table, and sat down.

"We're about done here, Homer," Principal West said. "Since you missed the closed session, let me explain the board's action. Mr. Benson, who you called against my wishes, has been removed from our substitute list and can never teach here again. I'll give you all the details after the meeting."

"Mr. Wentworth," Homer said, not looking at the principal. "I have some firsthand information on the park incident that is relevant to this case. I request the board listen to it now."

"This is out of order," Attorney Grimes said. "The vote has been made. The decision is final."

"If there is important information, we should listen to it," Mrs. Henderson said.

"I agree," Mr. Wentworth said. "We can go back into closed session at any time." He looked down the table at Homer. "You say the information is important?"

"Yes," Homer said. "It will show exactly what happened in the park."

"Then, let's see it." He nodded for Homer to begin.

"Hear it," Homer said. "It's an audiocassette." Homer opened his briefcase and pulled out a battery-operated cassette player. He slid it to the middle of the table and turned it to face the board members. Homer flipped open the cover and put the tape cassette inside.

"This is a recording of what happened inside the log cabin after Mr. Benson left. The voices are the students who were inside the log cabin. You will easily recognize them since they address each other by their first names."

"Wait," Attorney Grimes said. "If this concerns our students, it should be done in closed session."

"I agree," Principal West said. "We should clear the conference room." Getting up and shoving his chair out of the way, he walked to the door and waited patiently while the reporter collected her papers. After she and Drew left the room, Mr. West closed the door and returned to his seat. In the hall the reporter stopped and looked at Drew.

"I know you from somewhere," she said, looking at his face closely. "You're the kid from the Memorial Arch."

"That's right," Drew said. "And you're the reporter who took the pictures."

"My first big story," she smiled. "I remember your name. It's Drew. I'm Gwen."

"I'm happy to see you again," Drew said. They shook hands. "It's way off the subject, and I'm sorry for mentioning it. But the best thing I remember that night, next to Jackson's survival, were your legs. They were beautiful."

"Thank you," Gwen said. "That's probably why you were smiling at me the whole time I was taking notes. Do you want to know what I remember about you?"

"Sure."

"You were in some kind of shock and you smelled like beer," Gwen said and smiled. "So I can't take any of your observations about my legs seriously."

"I was in shock and, I think, a little scared," Drew said. "I don't think I was that drunk."

"You're not scared now?" Gwen asked. "I wouldn't want to be in your shoes. This log cabin story looks pretty bad."

"I've been through worse," Drew said.

"If you want," Gwen said, "I'll show you the copy before I print it. You can add whatever you like."

"Thanks," Drew said. "But go ahead and write what you think. I'll be fine with it." He shook Gwen's hand again and walked down the hall to the front exit.

Later that evening Drew sat on the front porch of his house. The top buttons of his shirt were open, and the elephant tie dropped loosely from the open folds of the collar. With no car traffic going by and the one corner light giving off a dim glow, the neighborhood was very peaceful. Drew watched two headlights enter the darkened street, and a car turned up his driveway. Homer got out and walked up the steps to the porch.

"The meeting went on forever," Homer said.

"Am I still a criminal?"

"Of course," Homer said. "What do we have to drink?"

"The good stuff," Drew said. He went inside the house and returned with two bottles of Sam Adams. He handed one to Homer and sat down. Homer took a long drink.

"What's the school board going to do?" Drew asked.

"Let me explain it this way," Homer said. "Did Professor JJ teach you much about electricity?"

"Sure," Drew said. "It's simple. Electricity travels in a straight line from circuit to circuit."

"Straight line, Drew," Homer said. "That's exactly how a school board works. Like electricity, the board always takes the path of least resistance. They turn on a switch, get things done quickly and smoothly, and get the hell home before something or someone breaks the circuit"

"Someone like me?"

"Exactly like you, Drew. You interrupted the circuit and set off all these sparks. Professor JJ would have been proud."

"Big sparks?"

"Big enough," Homer said. "But Attorney Grimes set off bigger ones."

"What do you mean?"

"At first the attorney was fine. He was under control. He argued that the audio tapes could not be used against the students. They were inadmissible because they were obtained illegally."

"The students have rights to privacy," Drew said. "Even when they smoke weed, swear, threaten, and screw each other on school time."

"Their privacy is protected at all times," Homer said. "In the classroom, in the hallway, in a log cabin. They and their parents have to be informed of any surveillance."

"Then I'll be fired, maybe arrested?"

"No," Homer said. He finished the Sam Adams. "Do you have any more of this?"

"Sure," Drew said. He went back to the kitchen and returned with two more bottles. Homer reached out his hand and took the bottle, holding the cold side briefly against his forehead.

"This feels so good," Homer said and took a drink. After he lowered the bottle, he had a large smile on his face. "Like I said, Attorney Grimes set off the bigger spark. I started the tape, and everyone began listening. For a small room like that, the sound quality was excellent, and you could hear everything."

"I wish I could have been there."

"You would've loved it," Homer said. "We were only into a few minutes of the tape when daughter Sally bragged to everyone in the cabin how she had taken the bottle of expensive scotch out of her dad's locked booze cabinet."

"How did she do that?"

"Way back in junior high, she had her own key made. Bragged about it right there on the tape. She mentioned that Leroy had a key, too, in case she lost hers."

"The junkyard dog knew what he wanted," Drew said.

"The log cabin party really got going, all that laughing and music and their own colorful profanity. Sally blurted out that her dad was the 'dumbest mother-fucker' she knew. That's when our school attorney jumped out of his chair. He shouted something incoherently and grabbed the cassette player right off the table. Attorney Grimes threw it on the floor and began stomping on it. He couldn't stop. The board members just sat there watching him go crazy. When he was too exhausted to jump around any more, there were pieces of plastic, some batteries, and ripped tape everywhere."

"Cool," Drew said, fingering his tie. "I didn't think he would like any of those names his daughter called him."

"He didn't like any part of it. When he regained his composure, Mr. Grimes picked up his briefcase, papers flying everywhere, and stormed out of the room."

"That was it?" Drew asked. "That's how the meeting ended?"

"No," Homer said. "It only got better. The superintendent talked briefly. He was composed the whole time. But our board president was angry. Mr. Wentworth said he agreed with the school attorney that our students had certain rights. But Valley Forge is sacred to him, to the whole country, and he hated the thought of students desecrating the log cabin with their drugs and drinking and sex. He criticized the students' actions, and then he went after Attorney Grimes. Wentworth said that when Mr. Grimes destroyed the tape, he was negligent in his duties as school solicitor. In fact, he prevented the board members from hearing the truth, and for that blatant obstruction, the board president put forth a motion that Grimes be fired. Mrs. Henderson seconded the motion. Then the board voted and fired Grimes. They may even bring a lawsuit against him."

"I don't believe it," Drew said, staring at Homer. "Where does that leave me?"

"You're still removed from the substitute list," Homer said. "By locking the students in the log cabin, you resorted to a form of discipline that the school doesn't condone. The students could have been injured."

"But they weren't."

"The board discussed that," Homer said. "Mrs. Henderson brought it up. She asked the question why only one of the injured students, the solicitor's daughter, had seen a doctor. When all the board members were quiet, she answered her own question. She said the only reason Sally saw a doctor much later in the day was because her father was a lawyer and all lawyers like documentation. None of the other students went to a doctor immediately after they got home because any qualified doctor would know they were messed up with drugs and alcohol."

"They were messed up," Drew said. "But so was I. I was wrong the way I dealt with everything." He took a drink and sat quietly for a moment.

"It was a mistake coming back, Homer. How can I teach here when I don't understand any of the kids? I've misjudged them all. Even the good ones. I was stupid. I even hurt Terry. I'm not right for this kind of work."

"Don't think like that, Drew. You're perfect for this kind of work. There are problems now, but that's only because you did your job. You did a good job."

"Then why do I feel so miserable?" Drew asked.

"You need some rest," Homer said. He put the empty bottle of Sam Adams on the table and stood up. "We both do. Sleep in tomorrow. Relax and spend some time with the family. That always works. And make sure to come to the game Friday night. It'll be exciting. Bring the family. I bet they would enjoy American football."

"I can do that," Drew said. "Thanks, Homer." He stood up and shook hands. Homer walked down the porch steps and turned to face Drew.

"Remember, Drew, get some rest."

"I will," Drew said. He waited on the porch until the red taillights on Homer's car disappeared down the street. Then he went inside the house, the door shutting quietly behind him.

CHAPTER 18

The next morning Drew woke up with a headache. He dressed in jeans and sweatshirt, took two aspirin, and went downstairs. The kitchen had a warm aroma of bacon and coffee. Greeting him with a smile, Whin filled his cup with coffee and handed it to him. Drew sat at the table and admired the full dish of bacon and fried eggs. The yolks were thick and orange and perfectly round. Already finished with breakfast, NuWhin was in the living room watching cartoons on television. Drew listened to her laughter as he ate. The coffee was strong with a bitter taste

"It's just what I needed," he told Whin, holding the cup in the air. He took another drink, and after a few minutes, the pain in his head was barely noticeable. Standing near the window in a glow of bright sunlight, Whin took the pot from the stove and filled his cup.

"No school today?" she asked.

"No," Drew said. He finished eating the egg and the last piece of toast. "I think we'll take a trip today. Do you want to see our ocean?"

"Ocean, now?" Whin asked. "But it's cold outside."

"We won't go swimming," Drew said. "We'll just go for the ride. I'd like you and NuWhin to see it. And it's a beautiful day."

"OK," Whin said. She started to clear off the kitchen table. After washing the dishes and putting everything away, she found a hat and jacket for NuWhin. When everyone was dressed warmly, they walked out to the car. The temperature was in the low 50s, and the sky was overcast.

Drew drove the Schuylkill Expressway into Philadelphia. In the downtown area, the traffic was bumper to bumper for a while. Whin pointed to the tall buildings and the lines of cars and trucks. Drew made a sharp turn off the parkway, and soon, the car crossed under a brightly colored dragon arch.

"What is this?" Whin asked, straining to look at the arch.

"Chinatown," Drew said. "We'll come here and spend a day sometime."

"Yes," Whin said. She pointed to a Vietnamese restaurant. "Yes, we should come back soon."

Drew turned onto Race Street, and the traffic came to a stop. As he moved slowly past a small park, he saw the towering stainless steel sculpture fracture the blue sky. Sunlight flashed bright sparks the length of the steel surface, and looking at the large, vertical key at the base, Drew had a smile on his face. Whin pointed through the open window.

"What is it?" she asked.

"Lightning," Drew said. "A bolt of lightning and a kite and a key."

"What do you mean?"

"Lightning from the sky," Drew said. "It was built to honor Ben Franklin, a great American inventor."

"I don't know what you mean," Whin said, staring up at the memorial. She placed her hand over her eyes to protect them from the bright glare.

"When there is a storm and much bad weather," Drew said. "Lightning comes down from the clouds." He lifted one hand from the wheel, and making a loud thunder noise, he traced a lightning bolt in the air. "It's very dangerous."

NuWhin laughed at him, and Whin looked at him closely as he made the thunder noise again and traced another lightning bolt. A loud car horn sounded behind him, and Drew drove forward.

Whin said something in Vietnamese, and when Drew didn't respond, she said "fulgurer" in French. Drew didn't understand French either and shook his head. The traffic gradually cleared as they made the long, circular approach to the Ben Franklin Bridge. Both Whin and NuWhin were excited as the car entered the wide expanse of the bridge and drove under the giant granite portals. When they crossed into New Jersey, the traffic moved faster. Drew was able to maintain a steady sixty mph and reached Wildwood by eleven thirty.

Drew was surprised that the streets were so empty. The lots only had a few cars, and there was very light pedestrian traffic. Drew parked next to the boardwalk, and locking the car, he paid the attendant and led Whin and NuWhin across the lot to the sidewalk. At the end of the sidewalk, the sound of the ocean surf and seagulls getting louder, they jumped on the wooden ramp and began walking faster.

Whin and NuWhin reached the boardwalk and ran to the railing. They stopped at the wooden barrier, and with NuWhin clapping her hands, they looked at the expanse of sand and breaking waves. The ocean air was cool and refreshing, and there was a light blue sky that stretched to the horizon. One ship, a large oil tanker, seemed motionless in the hazy glare of sun and ocean.

Seagulls flew over their heads, some of them landing on the railing next to NuWhin. She laughed and chased them squawking into the air. Then she and

Whin were down the steps onto the beach. Drew followed them to the edge of the ocean. In the glistening sand of the receding tide, NuWhin collected some white shells and small oval stones. She was excited and laughing. More seagulls flew overhead, and some landed at a safe distance.

Along the entire stretch of beach there were only two people walking in the sand. Drew turned, looking back at the boardwalk, and saw one man riding a bicycle. Shaking his head at the emptiness, Drew thought about the summer vacation and the hot afternoon when the beach was a crowded patchwork of flat, brightly colored towels and umbrellas and tanned bodies.

He remembered the incessant noise of people laughing and talking and the blare of the loud music in the background. He remembered Shane and May darting under the boardwalk and the circle in the sand and the shifting patterns of light and shadow that danced around them.

Drew remembered the fragrance of Joyce, and when they touched and came together, he remembered the soft contour of her body. It was a magical time, and Drew thought it would be like that summer after summer.

There was loud laughter on the beach, and Drew saw NuWhin reach down and bury her hand in the sand. She picked something up, scraped the sand away, and ran excitedly to him. When she opened her palm, Drew saw a red stone, the rays of sunlight glistening brightly off the smooth surface. Drew folded her fingers over the stone and took her hand.

They walked back to the boardwalk. At a small restaurant there, they had pizza and drinks. Then they shopped in a few stores before returning to the car. Drew reached Philadelphia by two o'clock. The surge of the afternoon traffic rush had not yet begun, and he was able to reach the house by late afternoon.

That evening, Drew took Whin and NuWhin to the Valley Forge Veterans Hospital. Cleaning up after dinner, the orderlies were moving carts and trays down the halls. When Drew went into Shane's room, he saw there were more flowers, and a few blue-and-white **GET WELL SOON** balloons floated high in the air. He picked up NuWhin and walked to the bed. Whin followed and stood next to him.

Shane's chest was rising and lowering slightly under the white sheet. His head was turned to the side, and with his eyes open and bright, he was staring directly at them. His face was clear and shaven. Moving closer to the bed, Drew put his arm around Whin's shoulder.

NuWhin was very quiet. Drew put her down on the edge of the bed and then placed Shane's hand in her lap. She held Shane's finger, lifted it gently, pulled on it, and when there was no response, she looked up at Drew and Whin. Her face was calm, but Drew could see the slightest expression of confusion, of fear. Her eyes opened wide and glistened green and bright. Drops of moisture formed on her forehead, and when she began to cry, Drew picked her up and sat down in the chair next to Whin.

Whin didn't say anything. Staring at Shane, she was oblivious to both NuWhin and Drew. The profile of her face was sharp and stunning, frozen in the soft glow of light from the window.

Drew untied one of the balloons and waved it in front of NuWhin. She stopped crying and laughed. Drew put her down, and she walked to the window swinging the balloon.

There was a knock on the door, and Mr. and Mrs. Collier came in the room. They exchanged greetings, and Mr. Collier pulled the extra chairs next to the bed. Mrs. Collier picked up NuWhin and held her. They talked quietly for an hour. When the Colliers got up to leave, Drew walked with them to the hall and said he wanted to stay for a while. He asked if they could take Whin and NuWhin home. They agreed, and Drew watched them walk down the hall together. NuWhin was still swinging the balloon in her hand when she stepped into the elevator.

The doors of the elevator closed, and Drew went back in the room and sat in the chair. The fragrance of flowers was strong. One of the balloons began a slow descent from the ceiling. Drew watched it sway back and forth and fall lightly onto the sheet. It moved gently with the rhythm of Shane's breathing and then rolled down the side of the bed.

Drew heard footsteps in the hall and turned to see two people walk in the room. The woman was short and was dressed in a fashionable pink dress with a white collar. Drew thought she would have been pretty but for the tight lips and the hard expression on her face.

The man was in military uniform. He was slightly taller than the woman, and his left arm was in a sling. He held the woman's hand, and walking with a limp, he stopped at the bed and stared at Shane. There was no sound in the room. The man continued to stare at Shane, and then he turned and faced Drew.

"Shane looks a lot better now," the man said, shaking Drew's hand. "I'm Bill Davis. This is my wife, Linda."

"I'm Drew Benson. I'm glad to meet you Mrs. Davis and," Drew hesitated, "Lieutenant Davis."

"You know who I am?"

"I talked to Shane when he was in the hospital in Tokyo. He told me a little about the mission, that there were only two survivors. He mentioned your name."

A loud ringing noise echoed through the room. Drew walked over to the table and picked up the phone. It was Tony from the school. He asked Drew to stop over that evening. Drew said he would after he was done at the hospital. Replacing the phone, he pushed another chair next to the bed.

Mr. and Mrs. Davis had pushed their chairs closer together and were talking quietly. Drew sat next to them. Mrs. Davis broke off her conversation with her husband and straightened in her chair.

"Shane saved my husband's life," Mrs. Davis said. "That's why we came to see him. We had to thank him."

"It wasn't that long ago," Davis said. "Before we flew out, I remember Shane talking about you. He said you would be there soon." Lieutenant Davis leaned back on the cushion and looked at Drew. "We waited for you as long as we could."

"I didn't make it. That night has been haunting me ever since. It really bothers me."

"Then forget it," Davis said. "Just consider yourself fortunate. There was nothing you could've done. It was a suicide mission."

"Shane said you were in Cambodia."

"Yes," Davis said. "There were six of us. We thought we had a chance to get Brother Number One."

"Pol Pot?"

"The butcher himself," Davis said. "It was the last thing we wanted to do before getting out of the country. Brother Number One controlled the Khmer Rouge Army. If we could get him, we thought we could cripple the Khmer Rouge."

"I heard Shane talking about him. He hated Pol Pot."

"He had reason to," Davis said. "Pol Pot and the Khmer Rouge got the latest weapons from Communist China, and they were getting stronger. They took the old capitol Odongk and destroyed it. The town officials and teachers were murdered, and twenty thousand people were scattered in the countryside. His program for Cambodia was to destroy it, destroy everything foreign and start over."

"And you went after him?"

"Our Cambodian intelligence told us he had a camp in the mountains across the border from Tay Ninh," Davis said. "We were to confirm the exact location and send the coordinates to the bombers. The B-52s from Thailand were already on route."

"What happened?"

"We got in Cambodia without any trouble," Davis said. "The chopper dropped us in the landing zone and took off immediately. Shane knew the area and stayed with the chopper. He was to wait in an abandoned outpost on the Vietnamese side and then pick us up after the strike. We thought we would be there a few hours, but it was over in minutes."

Lieutenant Davis was silent, and turning his head, he looked at the bed. His wife put her hand on his shoulder.

"We had some hill people with us," Davis said. "They were guides. We only advanced a short distance from the drop zone. They were killed first. They were machine-gunned along with our front three men."

"Ambush?" Drew asked. Beginning to feel nervous and restless, he kicked at the blue balloon at his feet. It lifted slightly in the air and floated back to the floor.

"The Khmer Rouge soldiers were waiting," Davis said. "Two more of our men were killed by grenades. I radioed the bombers to drop on the mountain, and I called Shane and the chopper back. Then the bombs started falling. It was great. The B-52s were right on target. I only heard this whirring noise, and then the whole side of the mountain began exploding into rocks and trees. I saw some green Khmer Rouge uniforms and pieces of bodies twisting in the air. Like I said, it was great."

"We never talked about this," Mrs. Davis said, sliding her hand off his shoulder. She had a worried look on her face. "I'm going to get something to drink downstairs."

"Sure, Honey," Davis said.

She leaned down and kissed him on the cheek. Then she left the room. Lieutenant Davis was quiet for a moment. He was staring at the bed.

"It's amazing how peaceful Shane looks," Davis said. "When I last saw him, he was covered with blood. I thought for sure he was dead."

"Was it from the bombing?"

"No," Davis said. "The bombs smashed that mountain and jungle but left the landing zone intact. It was so weird. After the bombing, everything became deadly quiet. I thought we might have done it. I got excited when I heard the whirling noise, and the chopper came into view." Davis took a deep breath and looked at the bed, the flowers on the table, the suspended **GET WELL SOON** balloons.

"I was with Tom Majors. He's the one who took your place. We were the only two alive now. I saw the chopper land and Shane jumped running from the door. He was still running when he lifted his rifle and fired right at us. I didn't have time to move or do anything. I swear I could feel the heat of the bullets go by my face. I turned and saw the chest of the Khmer Rouge soldier open up, blood spraying everywhere, and he fell back in the grass. I didn't know where he came from. It all happened so fast."

Lieutenant Davis took a deep breath of air. Lines of sweat streaked down the side of his face. He wiped the moisture away with his hand.

"Then mortars began going off from the jungle. Two hit around the helicopter, and I saw a body fall out of the door. The last mortar exploded next to Shane. It sent his body spinning through the air like a toy soldier. I thought he was dead for sure. I thought we all were dead."

The lieutenant heard footsteps in the hall and turned his head. A nurse holding a tray with a pitcher of water and some glasses walked to the door. Looking at Lieutenant Davis, she studied the dark expression on his face for an awkward moment.

"Excuse me," she said weakly. "I brought some water." The nurse walked to the small table next to the bed, put the tray down, and quickly left the room. The lieutenant slid forward in his chair and spoke in a quiet voice.

"More Khmer Rouge soldiers came out of nowhere and began firing. Tom was hit in both legs. I was lucky. I was just hit here in the arm." Lieutenant Davis pointed to the sling.

"I should have been there," Drew whispered, his heart racing fast. "Shane and I were in an ambush last year. Everyone was killed but us. We got out together." Drew began to sweat, and a salt mixture burned into his eyes.

"Like I said before, forget that. You wouldn't have survived this one. It was a miracle we got out."

"How did you?"

"I was holding my arm and trying to stop the bleeding. I didn't see Shane get up. He should never have survived that mortar, but there he was right in front of us. He pushed me forward and grabbed Tom around the chest and began dragging him back to the helicopter." Oblivious to Drew sitting next to him, Lieutenant Davis looked nervously around the room, his gaze returning to Shane in the bed.

"We were still in this high elephant grass when two Khmer Rouge soldiers jumped right out of that shit. They were so close you could touch them."

Lieutenant Davis jerked suddenly away from Drew. His eyes were open wide, and there was a tense expression on his face. Looking at the table, he took the pitcher and poured water in one of the glasses. After taking a drink, he held the glass in his hand. His hand was shaking, and water flowed down the side of the glass.

"It happened so fast," Davis said. "It was over in a second, not even a second. Shane was holding onto Tom with one arm, and with his other arm, he slid his rifle under Tom's armpit. I heard this loud screaming and saw the look on Tom's face. He was terrified and struggling to get out of the way. The bastard had his rifle pointed right at Tom's head, but because of his busted legs, Tom couldn't move or do anything. He was suspended there helpless. Shane fired at the Khmer soldier, and Tom stopped screaming. I fired right after Shane did. His bullets went through the soldier's chest. My round hit him in the forehead. That was our big fuckin' stupid mistake."

"Why?" Drew asked.

"We both shot the same guy. The other Khmer Rouge blasted a quick round point-blank into Tom's face and neck. The bastard was so close when he fired. I can still hear the roar. The bullets hit with such force, they smashed Tom's head back into Shane's face. He and Tom both hit the ground like they were glued together."

"But Shane was never hit?"

"No," Lieutenant Davis said. He took another drink and put the glass on the table. "He wasn't hit. Somehow, I managed to shoot the Khmer Rouge soldier. Then I saw Shane and Tom." Lieutenant Davis stared directly at Drew, his fingers nervously rubbing into the sling on his arm.

"At first, I couldn't figure it out. I saw them both, but I had no idea."

"What?" Drew asked.

"It's the way they fell. Tom's body completely covered Shane's. That's what confused me. Tom was lying on top of Shane, and I could see his shirt covered with blood, but it was Shane's face that was looking up at me."

"I don't understand."

"When I pulled Tom's body away, I saw his head had been severed and was tilting to the side. Somehow, his heart was still pumping, and there was blood everywhere. I rolled his body off Shane into the high grass. I hated to leave him like that."

Lieutenant Davis was silent for a moment. He looked at Drew, the face drained of color, the erratic breathing, the eyes closed tightly.

"Are you OK?"

"Yes," Drew said, feeling a tight pressure in his lungs. As he listened to the lieutenant's story, Drew had formed a series of pictures. There at the end, the pictures became more and more terrifying, and Drew found he had trouble breathing.

"Please tell me everything just the way it happened," Drew said, opening his eyes.

"The pilot was the only one alive at the chopper. He came running over and helped me lift Shane up. I could hardly look at Shane. His face was covered with blood and pieces of hair and scalp. Some of it was in his mouth. Little bubbles were forming in the blood around his nose so I figured he was breathing and still alive. And when we were carrying him to the chopper, I felt movement in his chest."

Lieutenant Davis fell back heavily against the cushion. He twisted his body around, trying to get comfortable. Carefully lifting his arm, he pulled the sling closer to his chest. All the time his eyes were focused on Shane.

"The chopper lifted, and we were out of there. When we were way above that shit hole of a mountain, I looked to see how Shane was. The side of his face was still covered with blood and dark tissue. There were pieces of brain in his hair. Worse of all, Shane's eye hung loosely from his right eye socket. I was worried about that the most. Later at the hospital, I learned from the medic that it wasn't Shane's eye. It was Tom's. It was stuck there when Tom was hit."

Lieutenant Davis lowered his head and sat deeper in his chair. The room was quiet. Drew tried to stand, but his legs were weak. All his thoughts ran together. Nausea and the vivid pictures in his mind overwhelmed him.

Drew's thoughts raced from the headless figure of Tom Majors to the drunken figure on the floor of the Bamboo Bar. The two figures fused together and became one person. Drew was sick and tasted the whiskey and bile in his throat.

Drew got clumsily to his feet and stumbled across the floor to the bathroom. He went in, closed the door, and dropped on his knees in front of the toilet. Drew stared obliquely at the blue toilet water, his stomach retching, but nothing happened. The pressure in his throat mounted, and Drew went through a series of dry heaves. Falling back against the wall, he sat there for a few minutes. When he stood up, there was only a dull, throbbing pain in the back of his neck.

Drew walked back in the room just as Mrs. Davis entered from the hallway. His mouth was dry, and he found it difficult to talk. Drew managed to mumble a "thank you" to Mr. and Mrs. Davis for coming to see Shane. They shook hands, and Lieutenant Davis and his wife left the hospital room.

Drew remained motionless next to the bed. Looking at Shane, focusing his gaze, Drew watched the last pictures of Cambodia and the Khmer Rouge sink and disappear in the unfathomable depth of the green eyes. Breathing more evenly, the pain in his head lessening, Drew realized it had never been about him. It had never been about Tom Majors.

Drew knew with a clear certainty that it was about Shane. Shane had fought the enemy to the end. Shane had helped bring another soldier home safely from the war, home safely to his wife. Shane was a hero. He had always been the hero. And Drew, he was just who he was. He knew he was more than the drunken soldier in the bar.

But not much more, Drew thought.

Everything was so quiet. Listening to Shane's delicate, rhythmic breathing, Drew heard footsteps in the hall. He turned and saw the nurse walk in the room. Another nurse was waiting at the door with a chart.

"We're here to check on Shane," the first nurse said. She walked toward the bed, and her foot kicked the GET WELL SOON balloon to the corner. When she began straightening the sheets on the bed, Drew said good night to her. Then he said good night to Shane.

Drew stopped at the fountain and took a drink. After splashing a handful of cold water on his face, he went down the back steps, pushed through the door, and walked to the car. The lights from Valley Forge High School glowed in the darkness. Drew started the engine, and remembering Tony's phone call, Drew drove down Charlestown Road and turned into the school entrance.

There were three vehicles, two cars and a red truck, in the Valley Forge High School parking lot. Ignoring the No Parking signs, Drew drove up to the bus unloading zone at the front entrance of the school and stopped at the curb. Getting out of his car, he saw Tony at the door. Tony held the door open, and Drew walked inside.

"Why'd you call me?" Drew asked.

"It was a favor," Tony said. "One of the students asked me to help. He can explain better himself. He's waiting in your room."

There were only a few recessed ceiling lights on in the lobby, and the corridors leading out of it were totally dark. The glow of light reflected off the blue-and-gold uniforms of the football players in the life-size posters pasted the length of the circular wall.

Drew and Tony walked past the log cabin reception area and up the steps to the second floor. Reaching the top of the steps, Drew looked down the hall and saw all the rooms were dark except the one at the end. The door to the biology class was open, and light streamed from the room.

"I'm going to check the exits," Tony said. "Then I'm going home. When you're finished, just turn off the lights and close the door. I'll see you tomorrow."

"Not tomorrow," Drew said.

"Then when this mess is finished and you come back." Tony smiled and walked down the steps.

Drew looked down the darkened corridor. As he walked down the hall, he heard voices and saw shadows move in the light. Drew recognized one of the voices, and when he reached the door, he saw Terry standing at the front counter. There were two students with him. Drew had never seen the girl before, but the boy's face had been on the sports page of the newspaper. He was on the football team.

"Mr. Benson, I'm glad you could make it," Terry said. "I want you to meet my friends. This is Sarah Allen."

Drew stepped forward and shook hands with the girl. She was tall, just a few inches shorter than Terry, and when she smiled, her face was pleasant. There was a lively sparkle in her eyes, and she seemed relaxed and friendly. Sarah wore Terry's varsity jacket, and it fit loosely on her trim body.

"And this is her brother, Randy Allen. He's the wide receiver on the team.

Although Randy's face was tanned and lined from the sun and Sarah's was soft and clear, Drew could see the similarity in their eyes and in the profile of their chins. He shook Randy's hand. Unlike his sister's, it was hard and calloused. Randy was about six foot four inches, and there was no heaviness to his body

"I met you years ago, Mr. Benson. I was just a boy. It was after that football game when you scored the touchdown. You were in the mall with a pretty girl."

"The Kimberton Mall?" Drew asked. Trying to remember, he searched the boy's face.

"Yes," Randy said. "I asked you about football. I asked you what I had to do to make the team. I was only in fourth grade, but when I saw that game, I knew I had to play."

"What did I tell you?"

"You told me I should run. I should run every day."

"I remember," Drew said, thinking back to that night. "You wore blue jeans, and your shoes were caked with mud and hay. You were a skinny farmer kid then."

"I still am a farmer," Randy said. "After you talked to me, I made trails on the hill behind the barn. I was able to run when I finished the farm work. I made the junior high team, and I've been playing ever since. I love football."

"Better than farming?" Drew asked.

"Way better," Randy said. "I can't imagine doing anything else."

"Randy's got three scholarship offers," Terry said. "He's the best receiver in the Colonial League. He set the record for touchdown receptions last year."

"You threw the passes," Randy said. "It's your record. Terry's the greatest quarterback in the state, Mr. Benson."

"That's what I read in the paper," Drew said.

"He'll prove it tomorrow," Randy said. He turned to his sister. "We should get home. I don't know. With all the excitement, I don't think I can sleep. I'm glad I met you again, Mr. Benson." Randy reached over and shook Drew's hand. Sarah said something to Terry and kissed him on the cheek. Then she and her brother left the room.

"Is this a good time to talk, Mr. Benson?" Terry asked. There was a note of concern in his voice as he studied the cut above his eye and the pale features of Drew's face. "You don't look so good."

"I'm fine," Drew said. "You have two scholarship players on the team?"

"Four," Terry said. "Riley's going to Bucknell, but that's for track; and the kicker, Wesley Foote, is phenomenal. He can do anything with the football. He's going to Delaware."

"I met them both," Drew said. "What about Leroy and Chester?"

"They had some offers, but their grades are bad," Terry said. "I don't know if they'll make it to the next level." Terry turned and looked out the window. There was one yellow security light in the corner of the football field. On the hill behind the stadium, the buildings of the Veterans Hospital were dotted with light.

"I'm sorry about what happened in the park," Terry said. "Leroy and Chester visited me that night. They wanted me to go with them. I would have gone, but Mom made me stay at home."

"They're your friends," Drew said. "Did you know what they planned to do?"

"No," Terry said. "Leroy just said they wanted to have some fun. But you never know about Leroy."

"He's bad news," Drew said.

"Yeah," Terry said. "Bad Leroy. You should meet his dad. He's a nutcase."

"That's no excuse for Leroy."

"I know," Terry said. He turned and looked at Drew. His eyes were bright, and there was a look of anticipation on his face. "But enough talk about that jerk. I want to show you something."

Terry went to the door and turned the switch, dimming the room lights. Then he started walking to the back of the room. Drew followed him. When they reached the aquarium, Terry reached over and hit the switch on the hood light. The long fluorescent tube hummed and flickered and then flickered again. Then bright light flooded the water in the aquarium, and Drew could see the bodies of brightly colored fish.

"What's all this?" Drew asked. He recognized orange fish with black swordtails, striped angelfish, one dark blue Siamese fighting fish, fins stretched out in stunning color, and four pearl-white kissing gouramis among the myriad of swimming bodies.

"Is it OK?"

"It's fantastic," Drew said. He looked closer at the fish and assortment of plants. The water was crystal clear, and the schools of fish swam through and around the bubbling air stones. "It's better than it was before."

"I'm sorry about that day, Mr. Benson. It was really stupid what I did," Terry said. The outline of his face reflected off the glass side of the aquarium. "We just finished putting the fish in. Sarah works at the Fins and Paws Pet Store. She selected most of the fish, but I insisted on the blue fighting fish. Do you know why, Mr. Benson?"

"School colors," Drew said. "It's a good choice."

"There was a lot of excitement before you came," Terry said. "I put two fighting fish in the tank."

"Let me guess," Drew said. "One of them was red."

"That's right, Mr. Benson. And the blue fish kicked all kinds of red ass."

"Not ass," Drew said. "Fighting fish don't kick ass. They just grab on tightly and rip off fins."

"That's what my blue fighter did," Terry said. "I felt so good. We were all cheering."

"That's what you'll do Friday night against the Eagles?" Drew asked.

"Sure thing," Terry said. "Just like the blue fighter did tonight. When we put this aquarium back together, Sarah taught me a lot about fish, Mr. Benson. Of course, I knew about the fighting fish. But I didn't know there were so many other fish that you couldn't mix together."

"Some can't live well with community fish," Drew said. "They're too aggressive."

"Like Leroy and Chester," Terry said. "They beat up on people for no reason. They just want to fight. I was like that. I was with them in everything."

"Why?" Drew asked.

"I don't know," Terry said. "We had all this attention during the football games. Then when we got back to school, we were just normal students. Leroy and Chester, and then I joined them, we began to act up, and soon everyone began to notice us. We were popular all the time. We didn't care what we did, who we hurt."

"You're over that now?"

"I'm spending more time with Sarah and Randy," Drew said. "Leroy made fun of them because of the farm work. But I like them both. I guess they're the only real friends I have now."

"Did you ever read Ben Franklin's *Poor Richard's Almanac*?" Drew asked.

"Gary talked about how you always went around quoting Ben Franklin."

"The first quote I memorized was the most important. Do you want to hear it?"

"Sure."

"A true friend is the best possession," Drew said. "I really believe that."

"You and Shane."

"And Gary," Drew said. He was still staring at the fish. "You did a fantastic job here. I don't think Mrs. Deal will notice the difference."

"Great," Terry said. He reached his hand toward the light switch on the hood.

"No," Drew said. "Leave the light on tonight. It'll be easier for the fish to acclimate to their new home."

"I hope they like it," Terry said. He and Drew walked toward the door. "Mr. Benson."

"What?"

"In the park yesterday. I guess it wasn't much of a fight."

"I had some help," Drew said. "My friend hit the big lineman with a bat."

"You know about this fighting stuff," Terry said, stopping in the doorway. "What you did to me, I was helpless. I mean I couldn't move. Is it difficult to learn how to do that?"

"Very difficult," Drew said. "Especially if you're born clumsy."

"Can you teach me?" Terry asked. "I don't want to be a tough guy like Leroy. I just want to be able to protect myself. And Sarah, too."

"Sure," Drew said. "I can teach you. We can begin when football season's over. I'll come out to the farm. We can practice at the creek by the covered bridge. There's that level ground next to the tree. It's where we used to jump."

"Where I nearly drowned," Terry said.

"And, Terry," Drew said. He looked back at the glow of light surrounding the aquarium. "I really appreciate what you did."

"It was easy," Terry said. "Except I didn't know how expensive tropical fish were. Even with the Sarah discount, I had to borrow money from Mom." He shook hands with Drew. "And one other thing, Mr. Benson. I haven't been up to see Shane yet. I feel bad about that. Is it all right if we take him the game ball Friday night?"

"That's an excellent idea," Drew said. "Absolutely excellent. Shane, all the Colliers, would appreciate that. It would bring back memories of our game. It would kind of connect the two teams."

"I'll never forget your game. Going home, Mom could hardly keep the car on the road. She was crying the whole time. She was so happy, so proud of Gary."

"You can make her feel that way again," Drew said.

"I want to," Terry said. "Mom would love it, and so would I. I never thought one game would be so important. We'd be undefeated, the best team in the state. Just like when you beat the Eagles, it was the greatest thing that happened at the school. People still talk about it."

"The more I think about the game, the more you remind me of a player on the team."

"Gary?"

"Sure, you're a lot like your brother," Drew said. "But you remind me more of Shane. You and Shane were the best athletes in the school. And you have another quality he has, something more important than natural ability."

"What's that?"

"Compassion for others. You worry about your mom, about Sarah, even about Shane. What you did with the fish tonight, it shows you care. You're considerate, Terry. You're not a selfish bastard any more." Drew had a smile on his face. "Pardon my vocabulary."

"But I was a bastard, wasn't I?" Terry said. He laughed at the language. "I thought I was having fun. What a joke! You never know how things are going to work out, do you, Mr. Benson?"

"No," Drew said. "You don't."

"Good night, Mr. Benson, and thanks. Thanks for everything. I feel better now. All we have to do is beat the Eagles tomorrow night."

"You will."

"Yeah, we will," Terry said. They shook hands, and Terry walked down the darkened hall.

Drew listened to his steps descending the stairs. When the exit door scraped shut below, Drew turned and looked at the shimmering glow of light in the corner of the room. Drew walked down the aisle, and as he approached the aquarium, he could see the blue fins of the Siamese fighting fish spread wide against the front glass. The fins closed, and the fish disappeared.

Drew noticed a red form curled up in the corner of the tank. Looking closer, he recognized the injured fighting fish. Its lips were white and swollen, and its fins were thin barbs stripped of color. Grabbing the net off the bottom shelf, Drew slid it down the side of the aquarium and scooped the fish out of the sand. It flopped once and fell motionless in the bottom of the net. Drew walked to the front counter and dropped the red fighting fish in the sink.

"HELP ME," Drew said in a squeaky voice. "SAVE ME FROM THE PATRIOTS." Drew laughed, and reaching for the faucet, he turned it on full force and a burst of water erupted into the sink.

"Too late," Drew said, watching the swirl of water spin the fish down the drain.

Drew turned off the faucet, and replacing the net, he walked to the hall. Valley Forge High School was empty and quiet. Drew pulled the door shut, and it locked behind him.

Drew walked down the hall, and when he reached the circular stairway, he stopped and looked down at the main lobby. A line of blue lights lit up the roof and corners of the log cabin, and standing in front of the cabin, defiant to all red coats and red-and-white Eagles, surrounded by the circle of football players, the Patriot soldier, his musket raised high in the air, stood solitary and tall in the deserted lobby.

Even driving without lights, Jeb Wood saw the narrow tire track when he turned the truck into his lane. He pulled off to the side, and getting out he walked to the back of the truck. It took him a few minutes to take the two deer carcasses, tied and wrapped in burlap, from the bed of the truck. Jeb dragged them deep into the underbrush and walked back to the truck.

Sheriff Hess and Henry Wentworth sat in the front seat of the park van. Henry had backed it behind some trees, and it was hidden from the Jeb's cabin and the dirt road. It was a little past midnight, and it was cold in the van. The sheriff began to tap his fingers on the dash.

"He's not going to show," the sheriff said.

"We'll wait a little longer," Henry said. "I appreciate you coming with me."

"I'm happy to help," the sheriff said. "I have some time now. We just cracked the turnpike case."

"All those robberies," Henry said. "That's been going on a long time."

"Four years," the sheriff said. "But it's over. We gave one of the suspects a pretty good deal. She talked her head off."

"Her head," Henry said. "One of the robbers was a woman?"

"You'd be surprised, Henry. But that's all I can say now. You'll hear all about it tomorrow." The sheriff looked at the porch light, the broken banister, the sloping roof of the cabin. "You think Jeb's really dangerous?"

"He knows guns," Henry said. "He knows how to kill."

"Where'd he learn that, in the war?"

"No," Henry said. "The army wouldn't take Jeb. Said he was too psycho. He learned guns from his older brother Joshua."

"What war was Joshua in?"

"World War II," Henry said. "But he never really fought in any battles."

"Why not?"

"He was more unstable than Jeb. Wouldn't listen to anyone. But they needed men, so they kept him on the base. He was an instructor for three years. And I heard he was a good one."

"Who the hell did he teach?"

"Snipers," Henry said. "Joshua gave Jeb his Springfield sniper rifle, and it's in good condition. It looks like it's never been fired."

There was noise outside, and the sheriff rolled down the window. The noise got louder, and the sound of the truck drifted closer to the cabin.

"He's coming," Henry said. "Jeb knows me. Let me do the talking."

"Sure," the sheriff said.

With his lights off, Jeb looked into the shadows as he drove the truck down the lane. Feeling pleased with the night's hunt, he was whistling *Yankee Doodle*. He kept repeating the same lines of the song because they were all he knew. Keeping his eye on the dim porch light, Jeb turned the truck around in front of the cabin and backed up slowly to the steps. He opened the door, and when the van lights flashed on and blinded him, he stopped whistling.

"Jeb," Henry said, his body a black shadow in the bright light. "It's me, Henry."

"Get out here, Henry. Where I can see ya'." Picking up the Springfield on the front seat, Jeb stepped down from the truck and closed the door.

"Put the gun back!" Sheriff Hess shouted. He was completely hidden behind the bright lights of the van. "Put it back now!"

"So," Jeb said. "There's a bunch of ya'." He took the Springfield and slid it through the open window onto the front seat. "What'd ya' all want?"

"Just to talk a little," Henry said.

"Then shut those damn lights off," Jeb said. "I need to see who I'm talking to."

"OK," Henry said. He signaled to the sheriff, and the lights went off. The clearing was momentarily black, and Henry couldn't see anything.

"That's better," Jeb said.

The porch light flickered and went off, and the darkness was complete. Then it came on again. In the dim light, Henry could see Jeb and the truck. The sky was clear, and there were dark shadows in the trees.

"Who's back there?" Jeb asked.

"The sheriff."

"What's he doing on my land? I ain't done nothin' wrong."

"I didn't say you did," Henry said. He walked closer to Jeb. "It's late, and I want to get this over with, Jeb."

"Get what over with?"

"This trouble with the golf people," Henry said. "Someone's shooting their dogs. And some are just plain missing."

"And when did this happen?"

"The last six months."

"I ain't been here," Jeb said. "No one can say I been here."

"I know," Henry said. "The sheriff's been watching the cabin. There's been no sign of you, no sign of anyone."

"So why you here then?" Jeb asked. He walked around the front of the truck to the steps. A large moth began pinging off the bulb, and the porch light flicked off, leaving Jeb in shadow.

"We want this trouble with the golf club to stop," Henry said.

"Trouble," Jeb said, his voice coming out of the shadows. "We owned all that land. Then the bankers took it, and you see what they done with it. They made it into a game for rich people."

"It was all legal," Henry said. "They didn't break any laws. But killing guard dogs is breaking the law."

"I wouldn't know nothin' about that," Jeb said. "I get by with what I got. There's no law 'gainst that, is there?"

"No."

"Laws don't mean much anyway," Jeb said. "The golf people got half my land. The park got the other half. I just got this shack left. And I ain't gonna lose it to no one."

"Enough of this bullshit," Sheriff Hess said, walking out from the van. He looked at the shadow on the porch. The bulb flicked on suddenly, and in the bright light, the sheriff saw the scarlet patch over Jeb's eye. "What the fuck!"

"Don't come near my porch," Jeb said, shielding his eye. "I know stuff. I got rights."

"You got no rights when you break the law," Sheriff Hess said. "You're going to lose your rights. You're going to lose this shack. The next time there's a dog hurt over on that golf course, we're going to come and get you. You're going to lose everything."

"The sheriff's right," Henry said. The moth circled again, its wings hitting the bulb, and the light blinked off. Clearing his voice, Henry spoke into the black darkness of the porch. "This is the last warning we're giving you, Jeb. Keep away from the park and keep away from the golf course. Stay on your own land."

There was nothing but silence. The light flicked on again, and the porch was empty. Henry shook his head, and he and the Sheriff walked back to the van. Henry got inside, started the engine, and turned on the lights. The clearing was well lit now, and Henry could see the truck and the cabin surrounded by the dark circle of trees.

"Where'd the hell he go?" Sheriff Hess asked.

"I don't know," Henry said. "Let's get out of here." He drove around the truck and down the lane. When he got to the turnoff, there was a loud crashing bang against the side of the van.

"Shut the engine!" Sheriff Hess shouted. He took his gun from the holster and looked out the window. Except for Henry's rough breathing, there was nothing but silence. The sheriff opened the door and stepped outside. Grabbing a flashlight from the glove compartment, Henry followed him.

"Over here," Sheriff Hess said. He put his gun back in the holster and pointed to the side of the van. Henry flashed the light on the deep indentation on the smooth surface.

"Hell of a dent," Henry said. He moved the light slowly down to the ground into the underbrush. There was a dull reflection of color in the leaves. Sheriff Hess walked over and looked at it closely before reaching down.

"Son of a bitch," he said, lifting something in the air.

"What is it?" Henry asked.

"Fuckin' champagne bottle," Sheriff Hess said.

"Look," Henry said. He pointed right past the spot where the bottle was. Jutting a few inches out of the ground, the silver, newly-polished, grinning teeth of a bear trap shone ominously in the bright glare of light. A grunting, muffled chortle emanated from deep in the shadows of the trees.

"One crazy bastard," Sheriff Hess said. Dropping the bottle, he jumped back in the truck and slammed the door. Almost as fast, Henry was in his seat. He started the engine and gunned the van out of the lane onto the main road. When Henry turned onto Route 23, he slowed the van.

"What do you plan to do?"

"Get a warrant," Sheriff Hess said. "I'll come back in daylight and get his guns. Check them with the slugs from the dogs. If they match, Jeb won't be drinking any more champagne."

"I guess not," Henry said.

"Fuck you and your laws," Jeb said after the van pulled away. He was holding the M1903 Springfield in his left hand. In his other hand he held a full bottle of champagne.

Jeb drank some champagne and took off walking along the tree line. There was some noise in the clearing, and Jeb saw some nice-sized buck, but he wasn't interested in stopping. He took another sip of champagne and began humming *Yankee Doodle*.

> Yankee Doodle went to town
> Riding on a pony
> Yankee Doodle went to town
> To buy some macaroni

Jeb liked macaroni and repeated the line again. Humming and whistling *Yankee Doodle* in the night air, he walked all the way to Mount Joy. There he went to his secret hiding place in a dense clump of trees and sat down.

Jeb got comfortable. He lowered the Springfield in the two notched supports that were stuck firmly in the ground. The barrel of the Springfield pointed across the Grand Parade ground toward the big general's statue.

"Von Steuben," Jeb muttered, slurring the 's' sound in Steuben. "Just you, me, and the boy."

Jeb lay down and looked through the scope. The full moon flooded the area with light. He calibrated the focus on the scope and had a clear shot right in the middle of the general's forehead. Then he lowered the Springfield and moved it to the right.

"There it be," he said, focusing clearly on the rectangular piece of stone in the ground. He could see the grooved lines on the surface, and there was something else that wasn't there before.

"What the hell!" he muttered, looking at the pieces of white bone.

Jeb shook his head. He took a drink of champagne, and when he saw the bottle was empty, he placed it next to the other one. In the bright moonlight, Jeb could see the parade ground and the general's statue and next to the statue was the open area where the flat stone was buried.

I don't know why you come here to visit the chicken stone like you do, but one of those times, I'll be waitin', Jeb thought. *I got all the time in the world to wait.* Wishing he had another bottle of drink, Jeb sat back against the tree and closed his eyes.

CHAPTER 19

It was six o'clock when Drew pulled up to Collier's house and parked the car in the driveway. He knocked on the door, and Mrs. Collier let him inside. They walked into the living room, and Drew went to the mantle. Lifting the top of the plastic trophy case, he removed the blue football helmet. The gold-stenciled number 17 was clear and bright on the side of the helmet.

"I'll take it to Shane," he said. "Maybe if he sees it and holds it he'll remember something."

"We were there this afternoon," Mrs. Collier said. "They were giving him physical therapy, but he didn't respond." Mrs. Collier reached over and slid her hand across the helmet. She traced her fingers over the number 17.

"Tonight was the night of the big game. We'll never forget it. Shane made all those tackles. You got the touchdown to beat the Eagles. Tonight's game will never be that good."

"I'm surprised you and Wayne are going," Drew said.

"It's the only game we go to," Mrs. Collier said. "We look forward to it."

"Thanks for picking up Whin and NuWhin," Drew said. "It'll be their first football game. I'll look for you at halftime."

"You remember the old seats?" Mrs. Collier asked.

"Yes," Drew said. Holding the helmet in his hand, he walked to the door. "I'll bring this back in a few days."

Drew left the Collier's house and drove to the hospital. He had to maneuver his way around the double lanes of traffic backed up at the entrance to the high school. Drew slowed the car and saw groups of tailgaters in the parking lot. Spiraling lines of smoke rose up from the barbecue grills. But for a few clouds in the sky, it was a clear October evening.

The stadium lights blinked on, and Drew could hear the sound of band instruments from the back of the school. He drove through the gate of the hospital and parked the car. There was a small set of binoculars on the seat, and he picked them up and put the strap around his neck.

When Drew entered Shane's room, he saw that the long table behind the bed was now covered with bouquets and elaborate floral arrangements. The aroma from the roses was sweet and fresh. Framed by the shades of red and yellow and white blossoms, Shane was perfectly still in bed, his hands resting outside the sheets. It seemed like there was more color to Shane's face, but Drew wasn't sure.

Drew reached for the handle at the side of the bed and cranked it slowly until Shane was in a sitting position. Taking the blue-and-gold helmet, he placed it on the bed right next to Shane. Then lifting Shane's hand, he laid it on top of the helmet. Drew reached down and opened Shane's fingers over the number 17.

"It's your old helmet," Drew said. "It's Senior Night."

Drew stepped behind the bed and began pushing it slowly across the room. When he reached the front of the window, he stopped. He checked the angles and the view in front of him and slid the bed slightly to the right. Then looking over the pillow and the top of Shane's head, he saw the rows of stadium lights, the bleachers, and the white lines of the football field. The large glass window framed the entire football stadium.

"It's your own special TV," Drew said. "You can watch the whole game."

Drew walked around the bed and opened the window. Cool air and noise from the bleachers began to flow into the room. Drew brought the chair next to the bed and sat down. He watched the growing activity on the field and in the bleachers, and at the same time he glanced at Shane and the helmet under his hand.

There were shouts and some occasional loud horn blowing as fans drove around looking for any empty space. The night air filled the room, and Drew could smell the faintest odor of cooking food.

Looking through the binoculars, Drew saw the long line of people waiting at the ticket booth. Then someone stuck a sign, SOLD OUT, on the booth, and the ticket window closed. Shouting at each other and pushing and shoving, the people ran to get open spaces along the fence. Behind them, the music from the band suddenly kicked into high volume and began to move toward the football field.

Drew listened to the band's progress, and focusing the binoculars on the parking lot, he saw the whirling red lights of two police cars. The gate for emergency vehicles swung open, and the cars drove to the side of the bleachers. Drew watched three dark-suited officers leave the vehicles and walk to the squared cement building that was the Patriots dressing room.

A crowd began to form at the entrance to the building. After ten minutes when the officers returned, the crowd was six-lines deep and very noisy. The officers led two football players in blue-and-gold uniforms out the door and through the crowd. The first player was taller and bigger than anyone in the crowd, and Drew easily recognized Leroy Schaffer. Trying to hide his face, the other player was Chester Greenwood.

As the noise and shouting became louder, the people in the bleachers stood up and joined in the clamor. An officer opened the door of the first police cruiser, and Leroy bent low to get in the back seat, but his shoulder pads wouldn't fit through the opening. It was when Leroy straightened and raised his hands over his head that Drew first saw the handcuffs.

The crowd doubled in size, and there were thunderous roars from the Eagle fans when two officers began pushing and shoving Leroy and his equipment into the back seat. After they finally squeezed Leroy inside, the same two officers inserted Chester in the back seat of the second cruiser.

The sirens blasted on, and with red lights spinning, the two police cruisers headed for the gate. One officer stayed behind. Drew recognized Sheriff Hess right before the sheriff was surrounded by a large crowd of shouting fans.

After the police cruisers left the stadium, the Patriots band lined up on the football field, and when the bleacher noise quieted, they started to play the National Anthem. Drew stood up next to the bed. Placing his hand over Shane's, he listened to the clear strains of the anthem. Then he listened to the "Patriot Alma Mater." Loud cheering followed the song, and when the football teams lined up and charged through the huge colored banners, the noise exploded upward into the room.

Drew squeezed Shane's hand and looked into his face. In the dim of noise and blaring horns, he saw the eyes move slowly toward him and stop. Then the eyes rotated back and stared through the window. Shane's face was serene and expressionless. The stadium noise lowered in intensity and then quieted for the senior recognition ceremony.

Drew lowered Shane's hand on the helmet and watched the seniors and parents walk across the field. He recognized Terry and Mrs. Evans immediately. Terry walked straight and strong in the blue uniform, but instead of holding his mother's hand as the other players did, Terry had his arm draped over her shoulder.

"Gary's younger brother," Drew said loud enough for Shane to hear. "Gary would be so proud." Drew watched Terry and his mother step into the line of senior players and parents. Mrs. Evans stretched upward and hugged Terry.

It took a few minutes for the family members to exit, and then the officials and team captains walked to the center of the field for the coin toss. When the official spun the coin in the air, Drew heard someone in the hall. He turned and saw Jackson walk into the room.

"Good to see you, Jackson," Drew said.

"I came here to watch the big game. It's better than sitting on the fifty-yard line," Jackson said. Sliding a chair in front of the window, he looked at the helmet on the bed.

"Number 17," Jackson said. "Is that Shane's old number?"

"Yes, I wanted Shane to have it. I wanted him to be ready."

"Ready for what?"

"Ready to remember Senior Night," Drew said. "The game's sold out. It's crazy down there. The game hasn't even started, and the noise is the loudest I've ever heard. Maybe Shane can hear it. Maybe it will help him wake up."

"Sure," Jackson said, beginning to understand, a big smile forming on his face. "Just like what happened to my friend Jake."

The whistle sounded from the field, and looking through the window, Drew saw that the Eagles had won the coin toss and were already in their positions to receive the kick. The sideline official lowered his arm, and Wesley ran up to the ball and blasted a low line drive way out of the end zone. There was instant mayhem, and the Patriots fans cheered loudly.

The cheering stopped on the first play from scrimmage. The Eagles quarterback handed off to his halfback, Burton, a five-foot-eleven-inch speedster already accepted at Boston College, and Burton ran fifty-eight yards through the middle part of the Patriots defense before he was knocked out of bounds by Riley, the safety. On the next play he ran right up the middle again for a touchdown. It was the first touchdown allowed by Valley Forge all season. The Patriots fans sat paralyzed while the opposite bleachers were stomping with noise. Jackson turned away from the window and faced Drew.

"That was too easy," he said. "What's wrong with the Patriots?"

"The two best defensive players were arrested," Drew said. "I think they're in jail now."

When the Eagles kicked off, the receiver mishandled the catch and was tackled immediately on the fifteen-yard line. On the first offensive play, the Patriots center was cracked hard by the tackle and spun around to the right. Then the Eagles linebacker hit him harder and twisted the upper part of his body to the left. All three players hit the ground together, but the Eagles players jumped up quickly slapping hands. The Patriots center didn't move after the double hit and was carried off the field with a dislocated knee.

On second down, the replacement center fumbled the snap, and the Eagles recovered. They scored immediately. When the Eagles scored their third touchdown late in the second quarter, loud noise and cheering echoed across the field. The Eagles band boomed out the fight song, and the thousands of their fans started celebrating and rocking the bleachers.

"This is real bad," Drew said to Jackson. "We have no defense, and our starting center's out."

The noise intensified, and the crowd of people along the fence began jumping and pushing into each other. The sudden pressure caused a section of fence to break loose from the post. The crowd, made up mostly of red-and-white jackets and sweatshirts, rushed through the opening, flattened the fence on the ground, and stampeded down the hill to the field.

"I'm going to see the family," Drew said, shaking his head at the confusion and noise. "I'll come back after the game."

"I'll be sitting here," Jackson said.

The strong glow from the stadium flooded in through the window and framed Shane's bed in a bright radiance of light. Drew looked at Shane and saw his hand had fallen off the helmet.

"I thought this would be a great game for you to see," Drew said. "I was wrong. I'm sorry, Shane. I'm really sorry."

Bending over the bed, his shadow covering Shane, Drew picked up Shane's hand and replaced it on the helmet. Deep in shadow, Shane's eyes moved slightly to the right. Walking away from the bed, Drew didn't see the eyes follow him to the door. Drew walked into the hall as the microphone clicked on below and the announcer shouted through the speakers about another Eagles touchdown.

Drew walked across the parking lot to the fence. Finding the hole, he slid through it and started down the old path on the hill. Trees had been planted, and at times Drew had to detour around broken trunks that were in the middle of the path. It was halftime when he reached the bottom of the hill and walked out from the side of the bleachers. He looked at the scoreboard and saw the Eagles were winning 28-0.

"Mr. Benson!" a loud voice shouted at him. He turned and watched Sheriff Hess break away from a group of people. "I hope you're enjoying the game because I know I am." He walked closer to Drew and stopped there. "I could have arrested those two Patriot bastards yesterday, but I thought to myself. Why not wait one more day? Why not be sure we have enough evidence?"

"So you waited until the beginning of the game?"

"I sure did," Sheriff Hess said. "I read Leroy and Chester their rights in front of the team, put on the handcuffs, and I took them right out of there."

"You should feel proud of yourself."

"I've waited a long time for this," Sheriff Hess said. "Payback does make a person feel good." He smiled and looked at the bandage above Drew's eye. "I heard they beat you up a little this morning. I'm sorry I missed that. I bet you could have used some help with that gang."

"I had enough help," Drew said. "I didn't need you."

Leaving the sheriff standing there, Drew turned and walked into the crowd of people on the track. As he reached the last set of bleachers and saw Mrs. Collier wave to him. He climbed to the top of the steps and sat next to Whin.

It was the only empty seat left in the bleachers. NuWhin saw him and laughed. Drew picked her up, and NuWhin wrapped her hands around his neck. Sitting in front of them, Mrs. Evans turned around and motioned Drew closer.

"We'll do better in the second half," she said. She pointed to Terry on the sideline. Not going into the locker room with the rest of the team, Terry was taking practice snaps from the new center. "I'm selling the house and farm. I'm moving closer to where Terry goes to school."

"That's great," Drew said. Lifting the binoculars, he looked at the packed bleachers across the field where the center section of Patriots students was mostly quiet and inattentive. Behind the bleachers, the hill, the broken path between the trees, and the fence were clear in the stadium lights. The towering squared structures of the Valley Forge Veterans Hospital on the other side of the fence were in shadows. Drew could see the nearest building and the open window on the fourth floor. A figure stood up and leaned his head out the window. It was Jackson.

The teams ran back on the field with three minutes left in halftime. Drew saw Coach Chuck stop and have an animated, arm-swinging exchange with Terry. Ignoring him, Terry took a few more long snaps and joined the team huddle.

Valley Forge received the kickoff to begin the third quarter. The kicker was laughing and pointing to the scoreboard. When the whistle blew, he ran at the ball and muffed the kick. The ball sailed out of bounds, and the kicker quickly ran to the end of the bench away from the shouting coaches.

The Patriots center was sharper and more accurate now, and from the shotgun, Terry completed his first five passes, the last one being a touchdown to Randy. With Wesley's extra point, the score changed to 28-7, and the Patriots were finally on the scoreboard.

Terry completed eight more passes to Randy, and then late in the quarter, on their own twenty-three-yard line, he called for the bomb. When Terry got the ball from the center, he waited and waited, counting the timing pattern in his head. Then he saw pressure coming from the side and ran out of the pocket. In full sprint and being sure of his count, he fired the ball in the air.

Drew and everyone around him stood up when the ball left Terry's hand. It was a hard, strong spiral, and Drew watched in amazement at the length of the throw and its high-arching, missile-straight path toward the two figures racing down the far sideline.

Randy was running stride for stride with the corner. Then listening to that silent number in his head, he nudged the corner slightly in the shoulder and raced faster. Grunting loudly, the corner fell a step behind. To a tremendous roar from the stands, Randy caught the pass and ran twenty yards for the touchdown.

Drew was shouting and jumping and holding on to NuWhin, and the binoculars swung around and hit him on the side of the head. The volume of noise was overwhelming. Calming down slightly, Drew put his hands over NuWhin's ears. At the veterans hospital on the hill, lights began turning on in many of the rooms, and Drew could see patients swinging their arms through the open windows. After Wesley kicked the extra point, the numbers on the scoreboard glowed bright and showed 28-14.

In the fourth quarter, the Eagles quarterback used long counts and called nothing but running plays. Seconds and then minutes burned off the clock. Drew became worried, then extremely nervous. After each long count and three and four yards gained by the Eagles, he could sense the tension building in the stands around him. With under a minute left in the game, the Eagles had the ball fourth and three on the Patriots' forty-five-yard line and were forced to punt.

Coach Chuck called timeout, and when the team reached the sideline, the assistant coach from Penn State took Riley aside and talked to him face to face for a long moment. Then the coach took out the slower defensive linemen and replaced them with wide receivers and running backs. With forty-seven seconds left on the clock, the whistle sounded, and the Patriots team sprinted to their positions on the field.

"Watch Riley!" Homer shouted back to Drew.

"Who?" Drew asked.

"Riley!" Homer shouted. "The state record holder in the high jump!"

Standing fifteen yards behind the line of scrimmage, and with the thunder of noise building, Riley knew he wouldn't be able to hear the snap count. He watched the Eagles center and the defensive linemen get down in their stance, and at the exact moment the center's helmet descended ever so slightly, Riley took off running. Listening to the crashing sound of bodies against helmets and pads in front of him, Riley saw the football spiral back toward the punter.

Riley jumped high over the line, his shoe scraping against the center's helmet. The punter grabbed onto the football just as Riley hit the ground and bounded toward him. The punter hurried into his motion and was bringing his foot upward for the kick when the two bodies collided.

The football hit hard off Riley's shoulder pad, and a second later the spiked shoe slammed into his ribs. Riley's body absorbed the kick, his momentum knocked the punter backward, and they both crashed down on the ground.

Terry saw the ball catapult high in the air behind the two bodies. Avoiding the blocker and accelerating quickly into full stride, he watched the football spin obliquely through the blazing glare of stadium lights and then disappear into the infinite darkness of the night sky.

Swinging her arms and jumping to her feet, Mrs. Evans watched her son run toward the football. It was descending near the Eagles bench, and there was complete pandemonium when Terry caught the ball only yards from the Eagles players and coaches and ran in a blur of blue-and-gold color down the sideline. Terry crossed the goal line and tossed the football into the crowd, and the noise was a thundering wave that shook through the bleachers and echoed up the hill to the veterans hospital.

All the players and the whole bench made a mad rush to the end zone and mobbed Terry. Some helmets were tossed in the air, and blue-and-gold bodies crashed into each other and rolled on the ground.

His chest hurting and trying to breathe normally, Riley was the last player to the end zone. Terry reached his arm around Riley's shoulder pads and walked with him back to the sideline. Wesley kicked the extra point, and the crescendo of noise grew louder and buried both teams.

Blanketed by the noise, the stunned Eagles walked to the sideline with drooping shoulders and bowed heads. A line of furious coaches met them there and began shouting in their faces.

Hearing the roar of noise and cheers from the stadium, Jackson jumped up from his chair and looked out the window. He saw the Valley Forge team surround a player and help him back to the sideline. He also saw the numbers on the scoreboard change to 28-21. Jackson turned at the sound of footsteps at the door. Walking briskly into the room, Nurse Ann shook her head at Jackson when she saw the bed near the window.

"What are you doing moving the patient over there?" she asked. There was a loud roar and shrill cheering from the football field. "And why don't you shut that window with all that racket? A hospital room should be quiet."

"Not this room," Jackson said. "The Patriots are fighting back. We need the window open to hear all the celebrations."

"What do you mean 'we'?"

"Shane and I," Jackson said. "I'm sure he can hear this noise, and believe me, it's going to make him better."

"Don't let Supervisor Wilma see this," she said. The nurse walked to the bed and began straightening the sheet. Then she reached for the helmet. When she tried to take it, she felt resistance. She tried again to lift it, but the helmet was tight in Shane's grip.

"Well, I'll be," she whispered.

"What?" Jackson asked.

"Shane's holding onto the helmet," Nurse Ann said. She put her hand over Shane's forehead. "He's never done anything like that."

"Is that a good sign?"

"Yes," the nurse said. Shane's forehead was warm, and there was a thin film of moisture on the nurse's hand. "I'll check back later. Be sure to put the bed back where it belongs." Wiping her hand on her skirt, the nurse walked to the door. Jackson stepped to the bed and reached slowly for the helmet. He pushed it on the side with his fingers, but it wouldn't move.

"Good for you," he said, a smile forming on his face. "Good for you, Shane. Just keep fighting. Just like down there. Just like the Patriots are doing on the field."

Jackson was smiling when he walked back to the window. The band was playing, and the whole Patriots side was stomping and clapping to the music. Jackson looked at the scoreboard clock and saw there were thirty-four seconds left in the game.

Sitting quietly on the bench, ignoring the mayhem of noise and celebration, Wesley Foote also watched the changing numbers on the scoreboard. The special teams coach was shouting for him, and Wesley stood up slowly. He was in no hurry. He had been waiting for this moment all his life. Fastening the snap on his helmet, Wesley began walking in a casual, confident manner to the circle of players.

"It's his time," Homer shouted. He turned around and shouted to Drew. "It's his time!"

"I know," Drew said. "Wesley, the killer kicker."

On the sidelines, Coach Chuck was excited and shouted for the unbalanced formation and the high kick. Not hearing a word the coach said, Wesley waited patiently with his hands swinging loosely at his side. Riley came up behind him, and grabbing the swinging arm, he pressed it tightly.

"You gonna do it?" he asked Wesley.

"You bet," Wesley said. As the Patriots team ran onto the field, Wesley looked across the field and focused his eyes on a tall Eagles player on the frontline. When Wesley reached the huddle, he looked at the circle of faces.

"Number 22," Wesley said, holding the football in his hands. "The tall, goofy looking kid third from the sideline." Some of the players turned to look. "He won't know it's coming, and he won't know what hit him. And make sure you take out the whole frontline so they can't recover the ball." He clapped his hands, and the team roared "Patriots!" and broke the huddle. Wesley caught up to Riley and spoke to him in a clear, steady voice.

"You all right?"

"I'm fine."

"Don't go running up there out of control," Wesley said. "Hang back and look for the ball. I don't know where it'll go after it hits him." Riley nodded, and Wesley went to place the ball on the tee.

On the sidelines, Coach Chuck was angry and swearing profanities when he saw the Patriots players leave the huddle and run to their regular positions. He was still shouting for the unbalanced formation when the official dropped his hand and blew his whistle. At the first decibel of sound, the line of Patriots exploded forward in a fierce charge.

Wesley ran at the ball, and focusing all his strength on the leather ties, he kicked it as hard as he could, harder than he ever had before. The tall lanky Eagles player had just put on his tough face and was settling into position when he saw a brown blur of movement coming right at him. He had time to blink, and then the ball cracked into his face guard with such force it broke the snap, spinning the helmet off his head.

The thundering noise was loud and spontaneous, and the people jumping to their feet tried to find the ball in the collision of bodies. The more alert fans saw the ball bounce back toward the Patriots line. Others saw the red Eagles helmet fly in the air, and they began cheering when players from both teams tried to recover it.

Even though the ball hit Number 22 so hard and fast, Riley saw everything clearly, and he timed his run perfectly. He raced to the spinning ball, got excited, and tried to scoop it up with one hand. The ball felt wet and slippery, and when Riley took a quick first step, he fumbled it. He watched it hit the grass and roll away.

Riley dove through the air and covered it, and then his body was hit by a mass of players. The ball was buried somewhere in his stomach. The umpire blew the whistle to stop the clock and began to pull the bodies off Riley. When they were all cleared away and the umpire put the ball down, Valley Forge had possession on the forty-seven-yard line.

Two rows down from Drew and the Colliers, Homer Matthews was jumping high in the air. He was swinging his fist over the heads of the people in front of him, and his shouts were louder than the volume of noise that exploded from the Patriots bleachers. His wife was tugging on his shirt, but he kept jumping higher. Homer turned and waved his fist to Drew, who was also on his feet. Standing next to him, Whin was confused by all the excitement, and NuWhin began crying again. Drew held her tightly against his chest.

Jackson stood stationary at the window. Even during the Phillies Whiz Kids games, he had never heard such a racket. He noticed windows were now open on all sides, and patients and some late visitors were shouting and whistling.

Wearing a blue Patriot cap, the navy lieutenant on crutches in the next room leaned his body through the window and waved a crutch at Jackson. Jackson waved back and turned to look at Shane. There was a sheen of moisture on his face, and his green eyes were clear and bright in the light.

"I hope you're seeing this," Jackson said. "I hope you're seeing this!"

Jackson turned his attention back to the field. Although no one had sat down on either side of the bleachers, the noise in the stadium was subsiding. Then the people began stirring, and the noise built up again as the Valley Forge offense walked back on the field.

The Eagles defense was still in their huddle on the sidelines. Coach Fielding was red-faced and shouting profanities. He reminded the players of the Eagles-Patriots rivalry and how the bastard Patriots stole their chances for an undefeated season eight years ago.

"Eight years!" he shouted, holding both hands up and shoving eight fingers into their faces. "Eight years we've waited for this!" Coach Fielding then pointed to the clock on the scoreboard. "Hold the Patriot bastards for twenty-eight seconds!"

Standing there listening to the tirade, the team captain, Scooter Lewis, a six feet five inch, 230-pound defensive end, a player who preferred to punish the ball carrier rather than tackle him, echoed the coach's words about payback and revenge. The Eagles listened to his every profanity and were fired up with fresh energy. Some of them felt a kind of primitive hatred as they jogged onto the field.

The Patriots players broke the huddle and ran to the line of scrimmage. Terry took the snap, and dropping back, he watched Randy and the end do a simple cross pattern. Waiting for Randy to make his turn to the sideline, Terry avoided one tackler and another, and then he threw the pass. Randy caught the football at the Eagles thirty-six-yard line and ran out of bounds with nineteen seconds on the clock.

The Patriots players ran to midfield and got down on a knee in the huddle. The dim of noise settled around them, and talking loudly but clearly, Terry outlined the next two pass plays to Randy. The first play was a screen pass which they had done before. The second play was a quarterback screen which they had never practiced. Terry spent extra time explaining it, and then the head official ran over and shouted to him to get the Patriots on the line.

Scooter was watching everything closely, and when the ball was centered, he flattened a blocker and charged at the quarterback. Terry saw him coming, planted his feet firmly in the ground, and raised his arm back to pass. Scooter threw out his hands and dove at Terry.

The dark form grew larger, partially blocking out the stadium lights, and Terry pulled the ball into his chest. The impact was brutal in its quickness. In a blur of motion Scooter smashed into Terry, and then the full weight of his body fell on him, twisting him solidly, painfully into the ground.

"You dumb fucker," Scooter shouted, slamming his fist against the side of Terry's helmet. He looked for the football and was surprised to see it in Terry's grip. The whistle blew, and raising both fists in the air, Scooter stood up to a roar of noise and loud cheers.

Standing at the hospital window, Jackson shook his head. The Patriots were forty-six yards away from a score, and time was running out. He watched the Patriots quarterback get off the ground slowly and call timeout. The Eagles were jumping in the air celebrating the sack. Directly across the line from the celebration, the Valley Forge team had their heads up and were listening quietly to Terry in the huddle.

"This is it, Shane!" Jackson said, turning to the bed, shouting above the loud volume of noise. "Six seconds to go!" Jackson was about to turn back to the window when he saw the slightest movement on the bed.

"What the hell!" Jackson exclaimed. Shane's eyes were open and alert, and he cradled the helmet in both hands now.

Waiting on defense, Scooter was maxed out. All the helmet butting and loud congratulations after his sack made him feel unbeatable. As he focused on Terry walking up to the line, every nerve, every muscle in his body was ready to destroy. There was no question in his mind when it would happen. It would happen in the next six seconds.

Terry was slow and deliberate as he set up the offensive formation. He saw how the whole defensive secondary shifted to Randy's side of the field. Because of the noise, the ball was centered on a silent one count, and the line exploded forward. Dropping back with the ball raised high over his shoulder pads, Terry kept his eyes on Randy and Scooter.

"Another fuckin' screen," Scooter shouted, recognizing the formation instantly. He barreled through the one guard in front of him, and without slowing down, he crashed into Terry just as Terry rifled the pass to Randy. Terry and Scooter both rolled to the ground, but Scooter instantly released his grip on Terry's pads.

"Shit!" Scooter blurted the words out, sensing everything was too easy. He jumped to his feet in a panic and ran toward Randy.

Time ran out on the scoreboard, and the horn sounded.

Listening to the blare of the horn, Terry got to his feet quickly and jumped over two fallen players. Arms pumping forward, he circled wide around the end and began sprinting fast and hard down the fifty, the forty, the thirty-yard line. Except for a lone official on the ten-yard line, the field in front of him was empty.

Holding the ball, trying to stay calm, Randy spun clear of a charging lineman. Seeing Terry and the empty end zone, Randy reversed himself and ran toward the charging Scooter. Just as Scooter, panting loudly and cursing, leaped at him, Randy threw the ball in a twisting spiral toward the goal line.

Randy saw Scooter's eyes open wide. The ball flew over his head, and Scooter swore and crashed violently into Randy.

"Fuck you!" Scooter swore again as they both hit the ground together.

"No, fuck you," Randy said. He pushed Scooter away. Getting quickly to his feet, Randy was stunned by the mounting intensity of the noise that exploded from the track and bleachers. Jumping in the air, he looked downfield for Terry and the football.

The deepest Eagles defenders were on the twenty-yard line. They turned and watched the ball fly over their heads. Sprinting at full stride, Terry was amazed how everything shifted into slow motion. He saw the stunned Eagles defenders drop their hands to their sides, the solitary official standing there with eyes open wide, black whistle squeezed between his lips, and he saw the football turning awkwardly through the night sky.

Running smoothly, Terry caught the ball, crushing it tightly against his chest, and crossed the goal line. With the stadium imploding around him, he stopped a few feet into the end zone and turned in time to see the whole team of Patriot blue-and-gold bodies racing down the field. As the players closed around him and began bouncing him all over the end zone, Terry began thinking about the extra point. The score was 28-27, and time had run out.

The top row of the bleachers was shaking violently. Drew held onto NuWhin with both hands. Somehow, she had adjusted to the noise and was laughing. Drew saw Homer jumping with the rows of gyrating bodies. In front of Drew, Mrs. Evans stopped screaming and wiped at the tears streaming down her face.

"This is like Gary's game," she shouted to Drew. "No, this is better than Gary's game!"

Drew put his hand on Mrs. Evans' shoulder. In the blinding daze of noise and light, he lifted the binoculars and looked up at the dark silhouette of the hospital buildings. There on the fourth floor, Drew saw movement, and Jackson appeared at the window.

And there was something else at the window. There was something behind Jackson. Shutting out the noise and taking a deep breath, the binoculars pressed tightly into the circles of his eyes, Drew could clearly identify the blue-and-gold colors of the Patriot football helmet. Jackson stepped back from the window, and the helmet followed him.

"Shane," Drew whispered. He quickly handed NuWhin to her mother. "I'll meet you later at the house."

"Is everything OK?" Whin asked.

"Yes, everything's fine," Drew said. He waved to the Colliers and Homer and began squeezing past the mass of bodies packed into the bleachers. Excited and feeling clumsy, he made slow progress. It was even slower on the track where the noisy crowd of people rushed past him on their way to the end zone.

"Extra point team!" Coach Chuck shouted. "Extra point!" he shouted again, forgetting to say the word team.

Coach Chuck was overly agitated. The special teams coach stepped in front of him and finished giving the line assignments. Then Coach Chuck shouted something incomprehensible, and the players broke the huddle and ran onto the field.

At the fifteen-yard line, Terry called them together. He didn't know how many of the players agreed with Coach Chuck's decision to go for the tie. He didn't know how many players felt like he did. He didn't care either way. When they gathered around him, he studied their faces.

"Hell with a tie," he said. "Let's go for the win."

"Let's do it!" Wes shouted excitedly. He hadn't missed an extra point in three years.

"Let's win this for the seniors," Riley said.

"We want to do it," Randy said. "We want to end our senior year with a win."

"OK," Terry said. "We'll go with our fake extra point. You linemen hold your blocks. I'll take the snap. Wes, you do the fake kick routine. Warren . . ."

"You'll get it," Warren interrupted. "You'll get my best snap."

"Good," Terry said. "They won't expect this. Randy, give me a few seconds on the roll-out, release your block, and run like hell to any empty spot in the end zone. I'll find you, Randy. I will. That's it! We win the game! OK?"

"Patriots!" the team shouted in unison. They shouted so loud the whole Eagles team looked up. The Patriots clapped their hands and walked toward the line.

At the back of the end zone, the Patriots band director was waving his arms wildly and shouting directions to his band members. A young freshmen drummer stood on the right side of the line. Awestruck by the tremendous emotion of the crowd and the great volume of noise it generated, the drummer was excited and had his arm poised to strike on the director's signal.

Measuring the distance behind the center, Terry bent down on one knee in front of Wes and extended his hands for the snap. Looking past the offensive line, he saw the white circular bar of the goal post suspended in the pitch black sky. Beyond the bar standing in the back of the end zone, the Patriots band members were restless, and one began beating a fast cadence on his drum.

Coach Chuck was frantic on the sideline. Shouting to everyone that Terry was out of position and the whole extra point formation was wrong, he began jumping up and down and trying to call timeout. No one heard him. The roar of the noise from the thousands of people on the bleachers and on the track was stifling.

There was mass hysteria on the track as the fans charged closer to the field to see the extra point attempt. Drew barreled his way past some people and tripped. The strap around his neck was torn away, and the binoculars fell in the dirt and were trampled. Reaching out, Drew grabbed onto a red jacket for support. The man turned and shouted something and pushed Drew away. Drew stumbled forward and regained his balance. When the crowd thinned on the outer edge of the track, Drew broke free and made his way to the bleachers.

Leaning against the railing, Drew rested for a moment. After catching his breath, he ran to the hill. Everything was in the dark shadow of the bleachers, but above the shadows the top half of the hill was ablaze in the stadium lights. Shielding his eyes, Drew saw the outline of the path. He followed it carefully through the growth of trees and underbrush, and at the top where the fence was, he saw Jackson. Drew straightened, and his body tensed. There at Jackson's side, the blue-and-gold helmet was clearly visible in the light. Shouting loudly with excitement, Drew sprang forward and began to sprint up the hill.

Then suddenly, the noise from the field became a thundering roar of chants and screams and piercing whistles. Drew lost his footing on the loose gravel and tripped. Catching himself with both hands, he sat there and listened as the entire row of bleachers vibrated and quaked to the wild rhythmic cheering from the Patriots student section.

Blocking out the noise, Terry shouted the count, and Warren rifled the ball into his hands. Grabbing the ball and jumping up in the same motion, Terry saw the defensive tackle charge past Warren. Wes followed through with his fake kick and buried his spikes in the tackle's stomach. The tackle fell moaning on the ground, but behind him, Scooter charged like a crazed animal through a gap in the offensive line.

When Warren centered the ball, Randy threw his forearm out hard and fast and hit the defensive end solidly, knocking him to the ground. That left only the defensive corner in front of him. Randy charged right at him, and the corner tripped backwards, swore loudly, spitting through his face guard, and fell awkwardly on the goal line. Randy bolted past him and raced across the back of the end zone. Both the defensive end and corner scrambled to their feet and chased wildly after him.

Along the back line of the end zone, the front members of the Patriots band formed a screaming human fence. Some of the band members tried to move back when they saw Randy, but they were held into position by the crush of bodies behind them. Randy sprinted faster and put his arm in the air.

Racing in the direction of the quarterback, the Eagles safety somehow saw the blur of blue-and-gold motion in the end zone. The Eagles safety was a four-year starter. His older brother, standing and shouting in the bleachers behind the bench, had played on the losing Eagles team eight years ago. Both the safety and his older brother knew instantly what was happening. The safety was strong and fast and experienced, and he reacted to the pass play with lightning quickness.

Terry was retreating from Scooter and two big linemen. Each step took him closer to the sideline, and he was running out of space. Pivoting away from the charge and turning his head, Terry looked for any movement in the back of the end zone. He saw the line of blue-and-gold band uniforms, and in front of the line, he saw Randy's hand go up.

Terry stopped back-pedaling and set both feet. Scooter closed with incredible speed and lunged. Judging the distance accurately, Terry quickly adjusted his throwing angle and managed to loft the ball over Scooter's outstretched hands. But his whole body was open and exposed when Scooter smashed into him. Terry felt the impact and experienced complete darkness before he hit the ground.

Turning and moving in the direction of the pass, the Eagles safety saw Randy alone in the end zone, and he felt a surge of anger and energy. It took only seconds for him to reach full speed.

Breathing hard now and focusing on the flight of the ball, Randy lost all sight of the band members. He sensed the frantic movement of the charging defensive end and corner behind him.

The denseness of the noise seemed to hold the ball suspended in the air. Randy sprinted hard his last two steps and jumped upward, hands outstretched, and then he felt the leather and fabric of the football. It was barely in his hands when he saw the large red shape descending.

Making contact in full stride, the Eagles safety hit Randy with a loud crack of pads and helmet. In the same strong motion, he swung his fist down on the protruding end of the football. It was a powerful swing that snapped two of Randy's fingers back, breaking them instantly.

The ball was knocked loose and disappeared somewhere in the line of band members. Randy felt himself falling downward, his helmet cracking against the ground first. Then his body hit the ground and stuck there in a crunched position. There were bright flashes of red and white, and Randy found that he couldn't move.

Arriving seconds late but wanting to get in on the tackle, the corner and defensive end hurled onto Randy's prone body and stuffed the blue-and-gold colors into the ground. Watching everything closely, the umpire reached for the yellow penalty flag in his pocket, and then struck in the face by the volume and intensity of noise, he changed his mind and ran for the exit.

Getting to his feet slowly, Drew was amazed at the pandemonium from the field below. As he climbed up the path, the noise pounded against his eardrums. Then there was a loud moaning gasp from the Patriots bleachers, and everything became deadly quiet. Drew stopped for a moment. The only sound he heard was the booming echo of loud cheers from the end zone.

"Mr. Benson," someone called from the hill.

Looking through the shadow of trees that clogged the path, Drew saw Jackson move in and out of the light, and directly behind him, he saw the blue-and-gold helmet bobbing up and down.

Jackson burst from behind a tree, and the helmet he was swinging in his hand fell to the ground. It hit a rock, bounced in the air, and rolled to a stop at Drew's feet. Drew reached down and picked it up by the iron face guard. Kicking stones and dirt, Jackson slid awkwardly down the path and grabbed onto a tree to slow his descent. He straightened up slowly and stared at Drew.

"I'm sorry, Mr. Benson," Jackson said, his lips moving, his words barely audible. "Shane's dead."

Holding the helmet against his chest, Drew felt himself sliding backward. Unable to catch himself, he hit the ground hard. There was a moment of total silence. Then Drew heard an ocean of noise rolling in waves over the stadium, and he had the strong sensation that he was drowning. Staring into the stadium lights, he fought to remain conscious.

The pain was unbearable, and it was difficult for Randy to breathe. He pushed himself slowly to his knees. Feeling nauseated, Randy heard loud, incomprehensible noise as fans and parents and cheerleaders swarmed past him to join the celebration of Eagles players and coaches. A heavy-set, bearded man bumped roughly into his shoulder pad, and Randy fought against the spasms of pain that knifed through his body.

Looking through his face guard, tears blurring his vision, Randy saw the two blood-soaked fingers bent upward and sticking grotesquely in the air. One fingernail, dripping blood, was twisted off to the side. Standing next to him, the drummer stared horrified at the mutilation, and then spewing a dark liquid from his nose and mouth, he began pushing his way through the crush of band people and spectators.

Randy unsnapped his helmet with his good hand and let it drop to the ground. In disbelief, he studied the two broken fingers that had touched the football, that had touched the championship. Feeling the great agony of the loss, Randy inexplicably grabbed the loose hanging fingernail and ripped it off.

Randy screamed out. The shock of the pain overwhelmed his senses, and left a numbing, empty feeling in his body. Between the intermittent red flashes that clouded his vision, he saw the wild jumping celebrations of the Eagles. Tears began flowing freely down his face, and Randy lowered his head.

Jackson's body was a dark shadow against the bright lights. He reached down and helped Drew sit up. Drew managed to balance himself, and when

Jackson spoke through the blinding shafts of light and noise, Drew concentrated on his words.

"I was at the window watching the game," Jackson said. "Then we got the touchdown, and the noise was crazy. It filled the room. It was coming in from everywhere, even the hallway. When it was the loudest, I heard coughing and looked at Shane. He coughed again and tried to say something. I don't know what it was."

There was a sudden outburst of whistling and cheering from the field. Jackson hesitated, waiting for the noise to subside, and then he looked at Drew.

"I saw Shane move forward, and he lifted his head. I think he was trying to sit up. There was so much noise and all that excitement from the game. And Shane knew. He had this expression on his face. I can't explain it. He was so calm and peaceful."

"He wasn't in any pain?" Shane asked.

"No," Jackson said. "There was nothing like that. He was leaning forward, his elbows propping him up, and then he fell back. The helmet rolled off the bed. It rattled there on the floor. I was scared then. When I was pressing the emergency button, I was watching him all the time. He closed his eyes and lay perfectly still. Nurse Ann came running in the room. And then two attendants came. They tried everything."

Drew slowly got to his feet. It was still difficult to breath, and his head hurt. Jackson held him by the arm. Drew's feet seemed thick and heavy, and grasping the helmet at his side, he trudged up the hill. At the fence, he was exhausted and sat down, his back resting against the chain links. Jackson sat next to him.

Drew sat there looking at the field below. There were so many people that it was difficult to see the grass and the white lines. The noise was not as loud as before, and one of the bands was playing.

Through the music and noise and lights, Drew remembered Shane on the field. He saw the blue-and-gold figure turn and toss the football toward him. Drew caught the football, and watching Shane crush the kicker, he crossed the goal line.

"We won," Drew said. He held the helmet in his hands and felt the smoothness of the surface.

"What did you say?" Jackson asked.

"We won for the first time," Drew said. "That's when we knew we were somebody. We knew we were important."

"You were always important," Jackson said. "Both of you." Jackson put his hand on the broken lines of scar tissue on his neck.

Drew shook his head. He looked at the stadium and saw the jumping mayhem of people in the end zone. When he tried to focus his thoughts back to the present, the mass of players and fans became distorted and began to blur together. The cacophony of noise grew louder and then was suddenly shattered by a piercing blast from an ambulance. Listening to the lingering echo of the siren, Drew turned and followed Jackson through the hole in the fence.

Terry slowly got to his feet. His chest hurt, and his eyes were glazed over. He was dizzy for a moment and struggled with his balance. Looking past the crowd of fans and players, he saw Randy in the end zone. Terry began pushing his way through the crowd. He slowed when he saw Randy holding his wrist and how the broken fingers protruded in the air. Terry knelt down next to him

"I'm sorry," Randy said, wiping his face. "I dropped the ball."

"No, it was my fault," Terry said. "It was a bad pass. It was a floater."

"But I had it. I had it in my hands."

Terry put his arm around Randy's shoulder pads and lifted him up. Balancing their bodies against each other, they made their way out of the end zone. As they approached the circle of jumping and cheering Eagles, Terry hesitated. He stopped when a loud voice boomed out in front of him.

"Get out of the way!" Scooter shouted. Making hard contact with his hands and forearms, Scooter muscled his way into the crowd and began clearing a path for Terry and Randy. When Scooter picked up a stubborn, wild-eyed student by the shoulders and threw him into a group of screaming cheerleaders, all the frantic movement and yelling stopped. Everyone stepped back quickly, forming a broken path through the circle of fans and red uniforms.

Scooter motioned to them, and Terry and Randy began walking down the path. The Eagles safety, who was perched on his brother's shoulders, jumped down and roughly pushed a bearded man out of the way to give them more space.

The other Eagles players, their eyes moving from the blood on Terry's jersey to Randy's smashed hand and the twisted fingers that bent upward, stood at quiet attention. Coach Fielding was at the end of the line.

"Great game, boys," he said, removing his red Eagles cap.

Coach Chuck was still on the sidelines when he saw Terry and Randy. His face flushed dark with anger, he ran onto the field. The assistant coach reached for his arm, but Coach Chuck broke loose.

"You son of a bitch," Coach Chuck shouted. "You lost the game. You . . ." Chuck was still shouting when the assistant coach and manager pulled him back toward the sidelines.

Red lights spinning, the ambulance made its way down the track through the crowd of people. It stopped in front of Terry and Randy, and the back doors flew open. Randy was helped inside, and Terry climbed in after him.

"I'm coming with you."

"I'm fine, Terry," Randy said, lifting his hand toward Terry. "You don't have to go to the hospital."

"I want to go," Terry said. "I'm your friend, and that's what friends do." He looked closely at the dried blood on Randy's hand. "Just don't point those fingers at me again."

"OK," Randy said. "But I don't know what to do with them."

The ambulance bounced across the track, up the hill past the broken fence, and pulled onto the parking lot. Cars moved to the side of the road as the ambulance went by. One of the drivers began to blow his horn, and that started a flurry of horn blowing that followed the ambulance down Charlestown Road. People leaned out their windows and waved hands at the ambulance. Coming to an intersection, the driver slowed down and stopped at a red light. He slid open the back window.

"Are you guys all right?" he asked.

"Fine," Terry said.

"That was a great game you played."

"But we lost," Randy said.

"You forget that kind of thinking," the driver said gruffly. "I've been parking this ambulance at Patriots games for twenty-one years now. And this was about the best game I've ever seen. It was like magic on the field tonight."

"I don't understand," Terry said.

"You showed us what it's all about. You didn't settle for the easy thing. You went for the win. That's what true Patriots do. They go for the win!" The driver looked at them and smiled. "What the hell else is there?"

Horns were blowing loudly, and traffic was backed up in all four lanes of the intersection. Turning his head, the driver stared at the traffic and the line of bright lights, and laughing, he hit the siren. The blast echoed through the ambulance, and when the whirring noise stopped, the driver looked back at the two passengers.

"And I'll tell you something else, Terry. You're not the first Evans I've had in this ambulance. Your brother took this ride with me."

"His senior year?" Terry said. "His last game."

"Yep," the driver said. "Gary wouldn't come out of the game. He played the fourth quarter with those cracked ribs. You're a lot like him. You got guts. Both you and Randy got guts. I don't like you being hurt like that, but I'm proud having you two players riding in my ambulance." The light turned green again, and the intersection was empty. Car horns were blowing from all directions. "I'd better go," the driver said and slid the window shut.

He cranked up the siren and raced down the road, scattering cars in all directions. The car and truck horns competed with the siren, and the loud parade of vehicles doubled in length and snaked through the town. As they neared the hospital, Terry shook his head when they raced by the entrance. The intercom squawked on, and the driver's voice filled the ambulance.

"You guys are OK," he said. "I didn't want this ride to stop. We're going to loop the town one more time. It's the victory parade you both deserve."

The line grew longer and backed up traffic on the side streets. As the driver raced through the town's main intersection, a police car slowed and stopped in front of the ambulance. Sheriff Hess got out and spoke to the driver. After a short exchange, the sheriff returned to his car, turned all his lights on, and moved out, siren blaring on full volume. The ambulance pulled behind him, and the intercom squawked on again.

"The sheriff asked me what we were doing," the driver said. "When I explained everything to him, he said he would make sure the roads were clear for us."

Terry looked at Randy and laughed. He was still trying to hold the wrist steady. The fingers were swollen black and blue. There was exposed tissue on the one finger, and fresh blood trickled onto Terry's hand.

"It looks real ugly," Terry said. "Does it still hurt?"

"I'm used to it," Randy said. The ambulance hit a bump, bouncing them both in the air. Terry tightened his grip on the wrist, and seeing the grimace of pain on Randy's face, Terry began to feel weak and nauseous.

"Mom told me once that if you touch someone's pain, you can share it and maybe lessen the hurt."

"Thanks," Randy said. "But it still hurts."

"I think it's making me sick," Terry said, forcing a smile.

The victory ride lasted another six minutes. People were now standing on corners waving at the ambulance. Somehow, a fire truck broke into the middle of the line of cars, and its siren blasted louder than the sheriff's car. The makeshift parade only quieted when the ambulance turned into the hospital entrance. The driver slowed and pulled into the crowded emergency parking area.

Mrs. Evans, Sarah, the entire football team, the Patriot Marching Band, the cheerleaders, and crowds of students were waiting there. The band began playing the Patriot fight song when the ambulance doors swung open. Randy and Terry stepped out to cheers and whistles. Mr. and Mrs. Collier were standing next to Terry's mother, and they began clapping loudly.

At the Valley Forge Veterans Hospital, Drew and Jackson walked up the steps and down the corridor to Shane's room. When he saw the bed was empty, Drew thanked Jackson, and carrying the helmet in his hand, he went to his car. There were only a few vehicles in the parking lot. Drew turned onto Charlestown Road, and when he drove by the school, the stadium lights blinked off into darkness. Drew took one hand off the wheel and placed it on the blue-and-gold helmet.

The Collier house was dark and empty. Drew parked his car and walked to the porch. Sitting on the top step, listening to the blare of horns in the distance, he held the helmet in both hands and waited. Drained of all feeling, Drew fought against the emptiness that deadened his body. His mind was triggered with memories of Shane.

He remembered all the times they sat on this porch and carefully planned their lives. Drew remembered *Ring of Fire* and the burning kite in the sky. He remembered the trip to the shore and the time Shane pushed him headfirst into the buck's stomach and how they made the shit bond of friendship. He remembered the freezing night in the log cabin, the Chinese restaurant and the spinning duck's head. He remembered sitting on the bank of the Saigon River. And he remembered the glory of Senior Night.

Two cars and a fire truck drove down the street. There was laughter from the open window of the fire truck, and a sudden blast from the siren echoed the length of the street. The neighbor's dog started barking, and birds scattered noisily from the nearby trees. Then everything was quiet again. Drew sat motionless on the steps. The helmet felt cold in his hands.

It was late when the Colliers returned home. They were excited and still talking about the noisy caravan to the hospital. Holding the helmet tightly in his hand, Drew walked down the porch steps and met them in the middle of the sidewalk. He was quiet for a moment. Reaching out, his hand shaking slightly, he gave the helmet to Mr. Collier. Then, in the dark and desolate silence of the evening, he told them Shane was dead.

CHAPTER 20

At Shane's funeral service, the church was filled to capacity, and crowds of people lined the street. Shane's former classmates from George Washington High School arrived early and were seated together. There was a large group of teachers and school staff. The older men in the community were in suits and ties, and the women wore dark dresses. There was also a scattering of military uniforms in the crowd.

The entire Valley Forge football team filled three side pews. Wearing a cast smudged with signatures, Randy sat next to Terry and spoke to the Colliers when they came in.

Surrounded by flowers and a row of candles in the front of the church, the open casket was set under the elevated podium. After the formal ceremony, friends and relatives were invited to speak.

Shane's uncle from Boston, a World War II veteran, spoke about the soldier's sacrifice. Tony, who was sitting next to a man in a thick-padded suit, walked up and talked about the boy he had lunch with for five years, a boy who never said a bad thing about anyone. Jackson was dressed in full military uniform. At the end of his talk, he pointed to Drew and said, "I wouldn't be here now but for what he and Shane did."

May struggled the most when she talked about how much she loved Shane. With her pink handkerchief, wet and crushed in her hand, she broke down and couldn't finish. Joyce walked slowly from her seat, and putting her arm around May, she ushered her back to the pew. Homer talked about Shane's character and pure energy for everything he did, and how Shane made the people around him better people. He spoke about the athlete and the friend.

Then Homer spoke about the soldier. He spoke about the Valley Forge winter of 1777 and how the American soldiers who served and died at Valley Forge would understand who Shane was and would welcome him as an equal.

Homer sat down, and in the silence there was a pause, interrupted by a slight tapping sound from the back of the church. Drew turned to see an old figure with a cane moving slowly down the aisle. Professor JJ walked around the open casket, and his cane hit lightly on the steps leading up to the podium. The professor was attired formally in a black suit, black tie, and he still wore the same oval antique glasses he had in the classroom. He straightened and spoke clearly and strongly into the microphone.

"When I retired from teaching, Shane came to my house with a gift. He brought me a cake. It was the ugliest cake I have ever seen. It was red, white, and blue and very patriotic. In the white icing across the top, Shane had scratched something, but I couldn't tell what it was. Shane said he had planned to bring me a cake earlier in the hopes of getting a better grade, but he changed his mind because it wasn't right to do that. I'll never forget that cake. I'll never forget Shane.

"It was extremely difficult for me to find words that could make any sense of Shane's death. I could find only one acceptable truth, one old quote from Ben Franklin." Professor JJ paused for a second. He looked over the rows of people. When he spoke, his voice was low but carried to the people standing in the back of the church.

"'A long Life may not be good enough, but a Good Life is long enough.'

"That was Shane's life. It was strong and meaningful, and it was resplendent with duty and honor and service to our country. The first patriots, as Mr. Homer Matthews said, served us well here, and Shane bravely built on that tradition. The soldiers of the Colonial Army that wintered at Valley Forge, and the citizens and soldiers who live in Valley Forge now, we are all proud of this soldier, this Patriot." Professor JJ finished and reached for his cane. The church was quiet as he made his way back to his seat. When he sat down, there were loud steps in the back of the church.

Drew turned and saw the sheriff, dark sunglasses over his eyes, move out of the shadows. Impeccably dressed in full uniform, he walked slowly down the center aisle. His boots made a sharp clicking sound in the quiet church. When he reached the podium, he turned and removed his sunglasses.

"I didn't plan on saying anything today." The sheriff spoke in a brusque voice. "I came here for parking and traffic control, and to make sure the procession route wasn't blocked. It's the biggest crowd I've ever seen at a funeral. I was standing in the back and listening to everyone speak about Shane. Then I felt the need to speak, too.

"I didn't know Shane at all. I never talked to him. I only met him but the one time. It was on the football field, and I was the last one between him and the goal line. If I could have stopped Shane, the Eagles would be undefeated, and we would have the best record in school history. But it never happened because I didn't stop him. I couldn't stop him. No one could stop Shane."

The sheriff looked down at figure in the coffin. "He was the best, the strongest person I've ever met. That's all I have to say." Looking up from the coffin, the sheriff put on his sunglasses. Then he walked down the aisle and into the crowd of people in the vestibule.

Mr. and Mrs. Collier went to the podium next. They stood together, and he held her tightly around the waist. They talked about family stories, the senior football game, the summer vacations at the shore. They talked about Shane and Drew and how they took care of each other. Some of the stories were very funny, but most of the people had tears in their eyes when Mr. and Mrs. Collier finished speaking.

Drew was the last speaker. He wore his blue blazer and a white shirt, and he wore his blue-and-red elephant tie. At the podium, he was nervous, and his face glistened with moisture. The open casket below the podium seemed to fill the front of the church. Drew wiped his forehead with his hand and saw that his hand was trembling. Looking at Shane in his military uniform, Drew became confused and felt weak. He had a difficult time breathing. It was then that he knew it would be impossible to continue.

Drew began to lower his head when the memory flashed in front of him. It was so clear. He and Shane were in the room, and Shane seemed angry and stood directly in front of Drew.

"When things like this happen, you have to be strong," Shane said. "I'm tired of seeing you cry over anything. I want you to stop it."

"And if I don't?"

"I'll punch you into next week," Shane said, a big smile on his face.

Drew whispered the words slowly, his lips barely moving, and he began to breathe easily. He looked at the rows of mourners, faces frozen upward, and his gaze focused on the football players. They all wore their blue V-neck sweaters with gold letters, white shirts, and blue ties. Sitting in the front pew, Randy lifted his cast and slid it carefully, painfully, into the sling.

Sitting next to him, Terry had a strong, stoic expression on his face. He turned his gaze from the casket and stared directly at Drew. Seconds passed during the exchange, and then Drew suddenly realized that everyone in the church was watching him intently. He relaxed, looked at the entire congregation of people, and willed his voice to be steady.

"Shane and I grew up together. I never realized how much he taught me, how much we shared. It was the family vacations and crazy hunting trips. It was school stuff and football. In our senior game, he let me score the only touchdown of the game. He knocked down a tackler. Like the sheriff said, he hit him pretty hard. Shane was always clearing away every obstacle in front of me. I never knew why, except he was my friend.

"In high school, I thought I understood what friendship was. Shane and I hung out together, partied together, played sports, went to the Jersey Shore, went on double dates. That was what friendship was in high school. But in Vietnam, I found there was more to it. When I first got there, even after training, I didn't know anything. I did stupid things. I probably should have been shot, maybe killed.

"Shane pulled me out of danger more than once. He risked his life for me. He took three Purple Hearts, two of them standing next to me. Then I understood what friendship was. It was being there for your friend no matter what the danger.

"And Shane was my friend, my best friend. When my parents were killed in the accident, I could never talk to anyone about it. I hurt inside for a long time. Shane helped me get better, and I thought I would never hurt like that again. Now after fifteen years and older and having more understanding about these things, I feel I hurt even more. The only thing I know for sure is that Shane won't be here to help me.

"Shane has no wounds," Drew said. "He never did. Shane was always the strongest. I'll never understand his death."

Drew's gaze went briefly to Mr. and Mrs. Collier and the other family members. There was a row of candles in tall silver holders in front of the casket. Looking through the line of flames, Drew focused his eyes on the sharp outline of Shane's face.

There was no movement in the church. All noise, the quiet whispers, muffled sobbing, had stopped. Drew's voice was low, much softer now, but his words, amplified by the microphone, were perfectly clear.

"I'm sorry, Mr. and Mrs. Collier." Drew slowly lifted his head. "I should have been there to help him. I'll have to live with that for the rest of my life. And when I see Shane again, when I see those green eyes and that smile, I hope he'll understand. I hope he'll forgive me."

Drew stepped back from the podium. The tears were burning in his eyes, but he held them back. Still staring at Shane's face, Drew took a deep breath and lifted his shoulders.

Mrs. Collier stood up and walked towards the podium. As she moved by the casket, the flames flickered and then danced more brightly. She gently took Drew's hand, and they walked together back to the front pew.

At the end of the service, Drew approached the casket with the other pallbearers. He stood in the front, opposite Homer. He had asked Terry to help carry the casket. Tony was opposite Terry, followed by Shane's two uncles. As they moved down the aisle, *Ring of Fire* played over the sound system.

Mrs. Collier had asked Drew about the music, and Drew told her that it was Shane's all-time favorite song. Seeing May in the aisle, Drew paused for a second, reached for her with is free hand, and kissed her on the cheek. He immediately noticed the salty, bitter taste of the moisture and moved his lips to her ear.

"Shane loves you, May," he whispered. "He always will." As Drew released her hand and stepped back, the triumphant guitar and trumpet rhythm of the song filled the church.

Love Is A Burning Thing
And It Makes A Fiery Ring
Bound by Wild Desire
I Fell Into a Ring of Fire

I Fell Into A Burning Ring of Fire
I Went Down, Down, Down
And The Flames Went Higher

Listening to every word of the song and gripping the handle of the casket tightly, Drew formed the clearest picture he had ever seen. It was a picture of the kite gliding over the football field, but there was no fire or smoke, and the kite didn't burn and come crashing down. It just kept going higher. On the horizon there was a brief flash of lightning and an echo of thunder.

A gust of wind pulled the kite higher, and Drew felt the slightest tug on the line and the tension of the string between his fingers. Opening his hand, he let the string unwind, and the kite was free. The sky was Patriot blue, and the kite soared higher and higher. The silver key trailing the kite reflected a brilliant flash of sunlight, and Drew was momentarily blinded. Clearing his eyes, he watched the silver light grow dimmer and dimmer and disappear in the heavens.

Drew saw Professor JJ in the end pew and nodded to him. The professor straightened his oval spectacles and smiled. Carrying the casket, the pallbearers moved through the vestibule and onto the front steps of the church. When they reached the sidewalk, attendants from the funeral home took the supports and slid the casket smoothly into the hearse. Drew shook hands with the other pallbearers and went to the car where Whin and NuWhin were waiting.

The Memorial Cemetery was next to Valley Forge National Park. When Drew reached the top of the hill and stood at the burial plot, he could see the Memorial Arch in the distance. A brisk wind blew, and the sky was overcast. The narrow road through the cemetery was lined with cars, some double-parked, stopping all traffic. The sheriff's car was in front, and the whirling lights on the roof were still flashing bright colors.

A long procession of people walked up the hill and joined the widening circle around the burial plot. Drew saw Homer and Brandy. Terry was with his mother and Sarah, and they were talking quietly. Moving in a large group, Randy, Wesley, Riley, and the other members of the football team covered the hill in blue and gold. Mr. Wentworth and Mrs. Henderson followed behind them.

A large, brown station wagon came down the middle of the road and stopped. There was an American flag and a black MIA-POW flag attached to the front hood. Lieutenant Davis stepped out of the wagon and met his wife on the side of the road. Shielding his eyes with his hand, he looked at the crowd of people on the hill. He took a step forward and hesitated.

There was a low, dull sound high in the sky over the park. The sound became louder, and straining to see past the cloud cover, Lieutenant Davis saw the small, dark outline of an airplane. He watched it for a second. Then opening the door for his wife, he walked to the driver's side of the wagon. Getting in carefully with his bandaged arm, he started the engine and drove slowly down the road.

Jackson stood at the edge of the crowd of people around the grave. It was very still, and he could hear the whispers and quiet sobbing from the people in front of him. He was watching the priest when he sensed that that there was something wrong. There was another presence close by. Feeling uneasy, Jackson turned and looked at the hill across the road.

There was a large oak tree in the middle of the rows of tombstones. Jackson studied the tree, and after a few seconds, he saw the slightest movement in the darkness behind the tree. He didn't know what it was. He thought there was a figure there, but he wasn't sure. He saw a flash of red and the slight, momentary glow of light from what he thought looked like a solitary eye staring out of the shadows.

Holding NuWhin's hand, Drew stood next to Whin. The girl was bundled warmly against the cold October air. Under the brim of the dark hat, her face was blushing. She grasped Drew's finger tightly. Her green eyes were bright, and she smiled when Drew twitched his finger. Being attentive to both NuWhin and Whin, Drew listened to the priest say the final words. When the casket was slowly lowered, bright sunlight and dark shadows moving across the faces of the mourners, Drew held NuWhin tightly in his arms. Seeing a red rose on the ground, he picked it up and put it in his pocket. At the end of the ceremony, Mrs. Collier walked up to him and Whin.

"You are so special, Drew," Mrs. Collier said. She looked at the sparkle on the girl's face. "You kept Shane alive. You brought a part of him back to his family."

Mrs. Collier took NuWhin's hand, and putting her other hand around Whin's shoulder, they walked slowly down the hill. The sun broke through the dark, fast-moving clouds. Mrs. Collier looked up at Drew and squinted in the light.

"We love you, Drew. We love you very much."

People came up beside them and whispered condolences. Walking next to Mrs. Collier, Drew saw the happiness in NuWhin's face. Joyce caught up to them, and without saying a word, she took Drew's hands in hers. Joyce lifted her other hand in the air, and a bright star sparkled in the center of the sapphire ring.

They walked under a large tree, and a cold wind blew some dry leaves to the ground. The leaves were brittle and broke into pieces. NuWhin stepped on a large leaf that made a cracking noise, and she laughed.

Thinking quietly to herself, Whin fell a few steps behind Drew and the Colliers. Listening to NuWhin's laughter, she happened to glance up. Her gaze went over the spinning lights of the sheriff's car to a large tree on the opposite hill. She saw some movement in the shadows. A dirty, ragged figure with a red covering on his head stepped momentarily from behind the tree, stared intensely, menacingly at the funeral group, and then suddenly disappeared.

Whin experienced a strange feeling, a cold chill that made her body shiver. She almost screamed out, but caught her breath and was very quiet. She searched the shadows under the tree, but the specter was gone. The clouds moved away, and the sun shone brightly on the hill and the tree. Lowering her head, Whin hurried to join the group.

When they reached the car, Drew and Joyce and the Colliers waited outside, talking and waving to the people as they slowly drove by. A short distance down the road, Drew saw a large, black limousine. Homer, Tony, Mr. Wentworth, and the tall man in the dark suit were huddled next to it talking seriously to each other.

Drew called and waved, and they waved back and continued talking. Without taking his hands out of his suit pockets, the tall stranger stared at Drew. After ten minutes when most of the people had left the cemetery and the road was clear, Drew and the Colliers got in the car and drove to the house.

CHAPTER 21

It was late afternoon, and the young couple sat in the car a short distance from the Memorial Arch. Dennis and Beth Harris had done some shopping in King of Prussia and were on their way home when Dennis pulled the car off the road and drove behind a clump of Dogwood trees. Dennis had just lowered the seat and was sliding his hand up Beth's leg. Only fingers away from the warm, moist spot, he clamped down hard.

"What the hell!" he said, looking out the bottom of the window.

"That hurts," Beth said, reaching for his hand.

"I'm sorry, but don't move."

Dennis pushed her deeper in the seat, and leaning forward, he looked out the window again. The man had some kind of burlap covered with leaves over his jacket, and he was carrying a rifle. When the man turned toward the car, Dennis saw the bright red eye patch.

"We're out of here," Dennis said. Without putting up the seat, he started the engine, drove on the grass, and circled around the Dogwoods back to the road. When they were a safe distance away, he stopped the car and reset the seats.

"What was it?"

"This guy had a gun," Dennis said. "And he looked real crazy. He had this ugly, red patch over his eye and a thick beard." Dennis stopped talking when he saw a Valley Forge park van crest the hill. Jumping out of the car, he stood on the side of the road and waved it down. The van stopped, and Mr. Wentworth rolled down the window.

"What's the matter?" he asked.

Dennis began talking very quickly. He told Mr. Wentworth about the old man with the gun. He told him about the burlap camouflage and how dirty the man looked and about the eye patch. Dennis was able to describe the Dogwood trees where he had parked and the thick pine trees where the man had gone.

When he was finished, Mr. Wentworth thanked him. Dennis got back in the car, and the couple drove away.

Mr. Wentworth turned the van around and drove to the Valley Forge Tourist Center. It was closed. He unlocked the door, went inside, and used the phone on the information desk to call the sheriff's office. The sheriff picked up the phone on the first ring.

"Sheriff, it's Henry."

"We just were at the funeral together. What do you want?"

"Jeb's in the park, and he's got a gun."

"Bullshit," the sheriff said. "We got his guns this morning. We already sent them out to be tested."

"How many guns?"

"I got two."

"He has three," Mr. Wentworth said. "I don't know what he's up to. Are you coming to get him?"

"I guess I have to," the sheriff said.

"I'll meet you at the Memorial Arch. Come up the back way. I'll have that road blocked," Mr. Wentworth said. "And bring some help."

"Are two deputies and one meter maid enough?"

"Leave the meter maid in the office," Mr. Wentworth said, replacing the phone on the desk.

Mr. Wentworth hesitated a moment and picked up the phone again. He made two more calls, one to Homer Matthews and one to Anthony Bartoli. Both calls lasted only a few seconds.

After two hours of talking to friends and relatives at the Collier house, Drew was exhausted. He said good-bye to the Colliers, and he and Joyce drove to his house. Drew parked the car next to hers, and they stepped outside.

"It's been a tough day for everyone," Joyce said. "You handled everything great today, Drew. I don't know how you did it."

"I learned that from Mom and Dad," Drew said. "I see them all the time. I can talk to them whenever I want. I feel the same about Shane. I see him everywhere, especially when I look at NuWhin. The Colliers see it, too."

"She's a perfect child," Joyce said. "And her mother is a beautiful woman." They walked to her car, and Joyce took his hand. "I don't know how to ask it, Drew. Now that you're married and with Whin all the time." Joyce hesitated.

"What, Joyce?"

"It feels strange," Joyce said. "We're back together, even engaged again, but Whin is still your wife."

"It'll take a little time, but I'll fix that," Drew said. "Whin and I will get a divorce. Then she and NuWhin can move in with the Colliers. Mrs. Collier would be so happy."

"How is Whin going to feel?"

"Whin is all about her daughter," Drew said. "She's the perfect mother. She puts up with everything I do or don't do. And it's because our marriage was best for NuWhin. It got her safely out of Vietnam."

"Did she love Shane?"

"She never got to know Shane," Drew said. "It was just that one night. So how could she feel any love? But ..." Drew didn't finish the sentence. Instead, he put his arms around Joyce and kissed her. Then he looked deep into her eyes.

"What were you going to say, Drew?"

"I remembered my first time with you," Drew said. "I've loved you ever since that day at the shore."

"I felt the same," Joyce said. They reached the car. Drew opened the door, kissed Joyce again, and closed the door. Joyce looked at him through the window.

"Where are you going now?"

"To the park."

"You're not running, are you?'

"No," Drew laughed. "I'll just be there a short time."

"I'll see you tomorrow," Joyce said. "I'll come over and make breakfast."

"Then you'll run with me?"

"Sure," Joyce said. "Believe it or not, I missed running with you. I missed everything about you." Waving her hand through the window, Joyce drove down the street. She blew the horn and waved again when she reached the corner.

Drew went in the house and removed his coat and elephant tie. He changed quickly and was pulling on his George Washington sweatshirt when he heard talking on the porch. Drew went down the steps, and looking through the door, he saw the Colliers and Whin standing there. Mrs. Collier was holding NuWhin.

"Where are you going?" Whin asked, looking at the sweatshirt.

"To Valley Forge."

"Please don't go," she said, a worried look on her face. "Please stay here with us."

"Why?" Drew asked. "Is something wrong?"

"What is it?" Mrs. Collier asked.

"I don't know," Whin said. "But I feel afraid for Drew to leave now."

"It's been a difficult day," Drew said. "Everything's fine now." When he put his arms around Whin and hugged her, she began to cry. Seeing her mother crying, NuWhin also began to cry.

"Good-bye," she said, wiping away the tears.

"Don't be so sad," Drew smiled. He got in the car, and lowering the window, he called to Whin. "I'll be right back."

Jackson returned to the Veterans Hospital and changed into his work clothes. Walking past the nurse station, he was grasping the Louisville Slugger and talking to himself. Nurse Ann looked up from the counter.

"Jackson," she said. "What's wrong?"

"I don't know."

"Where you going in such a hurry?"

"To the park," Jackson said. "To the Memorial Arch."

"Why?"

"I don't know," Jackson said again. Uncertain about what to say, he looked nervously at Nurse Ann. "I have to go. It's where I saw the angel."

Jackson walked quickly down the corridor. Thinking about the angel, he felt a sudden dryness in his throat. He slowed his pace and touched the scar on his neck. The scar felt hot. It seemed swollen. Massaging the scar gently, Jackson began to experience an overwhelming thirst.

Jackson's small workroom was next to the exit. As he approached the exit, he turned suddenly and opened the door to his workroom. Jackson walked straight to his bed, cracked open the cooler there, and reached his hand into the pile of ice. The bottle of Sam Adams was cold in his hand. He opened it quickly, and lifting the bottle to his mouth, he drank greedily, gulping the beer without any pause. When the bottle was empty, he reached for another one. The Louisville Slugger slipped out of his hand and rolled across the floor.

Stretched out in the shade of the tree, Jeb sighted the M1903 Springfield on General von Steuben's nose. Feeling so angry, he was tempted to pull the trigger right then and shoot it off.

The bastards got my guns, he thought. *But I ain't done yet.*

Jeb heard the car engine coming from way down the road. Then when it got closer and pulled into the parking lot right next to the big statue, he knew it was the boy. The boy got out of the car and walked across the grass. Jeb scoped him up close, saw the scar on his lip. Jeb wondered how he got that.

Then a lone jogger came into view. Swinging her arms and running like she was born to do that, she moved right in front of the boy, turned her head, said something, and he answered. Jeb could see his lips move, and then she kept running.

Joshua always told me to be patient, Jeb remembered. *Don't waste your bullet on just anyone. You be patient. And you wait for the target. And here he was just like Joshua said.*

Adjusting the scope slightly, and seeing everything through a thin film of red color, Jeb didn't know if it was just his bad eye or the setting sun that did the color. Jeb watched the boy walk over to the flat stone in the ground. The boy took something out of his pocket. He bent down and placed it on the stone. Jeb moved the scope to the stone, and he saw a red rose there.

"Damn," he said. "You'll be gettin' a whole bunch of roses yourself."

Jeb maneuvered the Springfield, and calibrating the scope carefully, blinking away the red color, he focused it in the middle of Drew's forehead.

"Jeb Wood!" He heard his name being called from the outside. "Jeb!" He heard his name again, and his body froze motionless into the ground. Lying in the deep shadows, he knew no one could see him.

Jeb looked through the scope. He saw the boy pick something from the dirt, the piece of chicken bone, and put it next to the rose. The stone, the boy, the grove of trees, and the big general standing there and looking at him from way across the field, they were all covered in red now.

Jeb wondered if he was concentrating too much and making his eye bleed. That happened to him once before.

"Jeb, we know you're in there," the voice said, and there was the soft movement of feet to his right and behind him. But the one behind him and on the side couldn't do nothing. There were sharp thorns in those places.

You don't know nothin' if you don't hear nothin', Jeb thought. So he hardly breathed and he didn't say nothing. Jeb just looked at the face of the boy he hated all these years. He tightened his finger on the trigger just a little.

Standing at the corner of the Memorial Arch and looking through the most powerful binoculars he had ever used, Anthony Bartoli saw the shimmer of red heat deep in the middle of the shadows of the pine trees and thorn bushes. The heat rose flat off the ground from a figure that did not move. Anthony raised his hand and gave the signal.

Above him, standing precariously on the very same ledge that Jackson had used years ago, the man in the dark suit pulled the trigger. The silencer made a slight popping sound. He shot again with the same popping sound and climbed down from the ledge onto a folding ladder. Bagging the rifle quickly and grabbing hold of the ladder, he and Anthony Bartoli walked across the field and got into a black Chrysler limousine.

With engine already running, the chauffeur pulled onto the road and drove away, the engine barely audible above the noise of the crickets. He drove only a short distance and met a truck that was angled across the road blocking traffic.

Homer Matthews was sitting in the driver's seat of the truck. Clutching the wheel tightly with both hands, beads of perspiration streaming down his face, listening to a Willie Nelson song on the radio, Homer steered the truck out of the way. When the limousine passed, he looked at Anthony Bartoli, who simply nodded his head. Homer pulled in behind the limousine, and the two-vehicle procession moved slowly down the road.

I love you, Joshua, Jeb thought. *I love you for all the stuff you showed me.* Looking at the imaginary line in the middle of Drew's forehead, Jeb smiled, and the muscles in his forearm tightened slightly.

Jeb heard the softest sound of a leaf falling, and then there was nothing. The first bullet hit him in the cerebellum at the base of the skull. The second bullet went straight though his good eye and left a big empty hole. The hole slowly began to fill with blood.

"Jeb, we've waited long enough," Sheriff said. "We're coming in." But Sheriff Hess didn't move. Putting his hands on his knees, he leaned forward, studying the shadows under the trees.

"Well, Sheriff," Mr. Wentworth said. "What are you waiting for?"

"Do you think Jeb has those bear traps in there?" the sheriff asked.

"Hell no," Henry said.

"Let's wait a little longer anyway," Sheriff Hess said. "He'll be getting hungry or thirsty soon."

"Damn it," Henry said.

"What?"

"This will take all night," Park Superintendent Henry Wentworth said, shaking his head. "You should have brought the meter maid."

EPILOGUE

VALLEY FORGE 1975

D rew stood alone in the shadows of the large tree next to General Steuben's statue. The sun was setting and cast a faint red glow of light over Valley Forge National Park. Off to the right, Drew saw some movement in the tree line. When the deer appeared in the shadows, Drew stared in amazement. An albino doe stepped out slowly, cautiously onto the parade ground. Its head high in the air, the doe stood frozen there.

Another deer moved past it and lowered its head to the grass. Then two small deer and a buck with a majestic rack of antlers came onto the field. Moving at a slow pace, stopping to graze every few yards, the herd made its way quietly across the splendid radiance of the Grand Parade ground.

Drew heard footsteps and turned to see the jogger on her return run. She waved at him, and he waved back. He watched her momentarily, and then he stepped closer to the newly-adorned memorial. Kneeling, he brushed off some dirt and grass and moved the small white bone and red rose to the center of the flat stone.

"The Chicken Thief Soldier," Drew whispered.

Getting to his feet, Drew walked over to the bench next to General Steuben's statue and sat down. In the distance, he heard the long, staccato noise of an approaching ambulance. The buck straightened, its antlers lifting high over the herd of deer, and then swinging its head downward, it continued to graze.

Amazed at the tranquility of the scene, Drew leaned back on the wooden bench and relaxed. The red glow of light from the setting sun grew brighter and burned across the Grand Parade ground to the edge of Mount Joy. Rising from the shadows of the mountain and nestled in the outline of towering trees, the monumental stones of the Memorial Arch were etched in gold against the darkening night sky.

Printed in the United States
138042LV00006B/79/P